SHADOWLANDS

LEVIATHAN

SHADOWLANDS

ALAN KESSLER

LEVIATHAN

Interior format services by TotenCreative
Cover Design: Shaun J. Kessler

Editor: Fern J. Hill

Leviathon Press

1

PLAYING IN THE BACKYARD of his home, a small boy tumbled and spun. He laughed, reaching for summer light sparkling on a windblown leaf. Steve watched the leaf float away. At the base of an old tree, he sat in the grass and poked a stick into the rotted ground. One bee flew out, then three. Thinking cartoon thoughts of stretchers and sirens and ambulances for bees, he dug harder.

The hive swarmed over him. Crawling bodies wrapped his face. Blind and screaming, he stumbled toward the house where he knew his mother would stop the wings from beating inside his mouth and hold him.

Sarah hit him with a towel.

"Why, why, *why*, can't he play like other children," she asked the walls.

"They didn't sting," he wanted to say. "I am strong. Love me."

Twin baby sisters cried and his mother left. She no longer let him into her quiet bedroom where, after dressing him in a skirt, he'd sit silently on the bed waiting for her to bring him to her breast. He stood alone among dead bees that still buzzed inside him with the sound of his mother's words.

Six months later, on Halloween, Sarah took him by the hand down the hallway of their house to his grandmother.

"She's waiting. Go inside."

Steve pushed the door open.

The corpse sat stiff in its chair. Shiny eyes, black and unmoving, watched him slowly cross the room.

"Closer," his mother said. "Kiss her good-bye."

The fleshless mouth caked with bright red lipstick vented the smell of decay as he leaned closer. His lips almost touched the corpse's when its jaw snapped open.

"Nu, another time," he heard his grandmother say cheerfully as he jumped away and stumbled backward. "Maybe next Halloween or the one after that. I'm not going anywhere. I'll come quietly, at night, give you a little poke like I always do when no one is looking and again tell you stories about witches and murderers and no good men who run out on their wives. Haven't I always lived with you? Why should that change just because I'm dead?"

"No, touch me now," Steve said.

"What are you saying?" Sarah hit him across the ear. "Don't act crazy around me. I asked only one thing, that you show some respect. Instead, you're mumbling like a feeble-minded. Don't you have a heart? Didn't she do enough for you? What's the use talking? You're like your father—a stone. The girls are only babies, but they knew what to do. They gave her a hug. Go. Leave. Get out of my sight."

He turned and ran away, feeling his grandmother's eyes

crawl up his back in this hallway where shadows formed the faces of dead things. He now understood why the tree had stuck its long tongue of bees out from underground and covered his face with tiny legs and wings that didn't sting. Masks protected against ghosts. Children wore them on Halloween to hide from gray skinned grandmothers who, rising from the grave this one night of the year, searched for their grandchildren to haunt and eat. To protect himself, Steve wanted a different face or a friend like Fishmouth who never got hurt.

In the backyard where the night made him invisible, he breathed in slowly to taste the cold. A twig snapped, warning him.

"Grandmother."

He ran back to the house.

"They took her," his mother said, opening the door just wide enough so he could get in. "You had your chance. Go to bed." She locked the house tight.

Pulling the covers over his head, Steve Goldblatt, age six, listened to the wind shake the bee tree branches. The tree had saved him, its snapping branch warning that his grandmother was shuffling toward him in the night. Trees had knowledge. They were life. Steve closed his eyes and felt the rattling branches cradle his head to plant their seed inside him, the best place for a tree to grow. The bee tree's soft moans carried him gently into sleep.

Sarah found the last of the swarm from summer, a dead bee wedged into her floor. She swept it up and after putting the broom away, took out a box from under the sink. She had learned as a child that trees were death. Once they caught a heart they never gave it back. In the backyard, she again poured rat poison into the bee hole and talking to herself, filled the air with words that would soon buzz and begin to cover her son's face.

2

I STILL HAD TREASURES in my desk; an old green cigar, a birthday card and pen, one plastic bag, and a collection of keys.

"Call for you on line one, Mr. Goldblatt. Says he's an old friend."

I put the shot glass down.

"Friend?"

"Yes, sir."

"What's his name?"

"Tom."

I repeated it, the sound full of summer and shit. Why the fuck was he calling now?

"Hello…"

"Steve. How are you doing, buddy? Bet you thought I died."

I hadn't thought about him at all.

"How long has it been?" I asked.

"Exactly seventeen years. You sound the same. How's everything going?"

"I can't complain."

"I see you're a lawyer. Good for you. Probably making lots

of money."

"I do okay…"

"I'm sure of it. You were always the clever one. We've got to get together, catch up on old times. Remember how I always wanted a boat? Well, I just bought one. Why don't you and I try it out? Go fishing."

I laughed. "I've got a pretty busy schedule. I'm not sure I can squeeze in a fishing trip."

"Come on, Steve, it'll be an adventure. Plus, I need some legal advice. I'm thinking about expanding my company."

"You have a company?"

"Yep, we sell cemetery plots."

"Imagine that. Real estate. I would never have guessed you'd become a businessman."

"I'm not smart enough, right?"

"That's not what I meant," I said. It was.

"Yea, funny how things turn out. So, about the fishing. No excuses. I'll meet you tonight at seven, in Milford. Park by the old mill. Don't disappoint me, Steve. Otherwise, I'll have to come and get you."

This time, he laughed.

I hung up the phone and drank until again feeling independent, cold, in love with the dead.

After work, after turning the office's door handles three times making sure they were locked, I drove home to The Neighborhood where I lived in a home I'd built on Dane's old land. Down the street, in the field where Tom had caught white butterflies, and we once searched for a pirate chest top, my bulldozers groaned on, still expanding my housing development. The day's heat had continued into dusk, July radiating from the asphalt streets and driveways, and the shadowy rows of concrete apartment buildings I'd made fashionable by adding spiked and coiled façades. I had paved over the field's weeds and butterflies years ago.

It's six o'clock. Where is she? I looked around the house. She wasn't there. Esther would again have to sit outside and wait for me in the dark. I had never given her a key to our home and when leaving, I always locked the doors tight.

I took a beer from the refrigerator and drank while admiring my kitchen. The cabinets were perfect, worth all the effort. I'd searched abandoned houses until I found the right kind of old wood, and after building the cabinets with it, painted them the correct shade of green, blistered the finish, then added, again from memory, the booze stains. The rusted sink had been a lot easier to duplicate. There were plenty of them in junkyards just over the river in Milford. When building my home like Dane's, I tried to keep everything authentic. Chugging down the rest of the beer, I carefully positioned the can on top of the other empties I had stacked in the sink the same way Dane's father used to pile up his. Upstairs, I changed into fat-concealing baggy clothes and slapped my face hard so the broken veins blended.

Dane's black willow grew nicely in my front yard. Only the splinters I'd made hacking it down marked the place where Tom's dead tree had taken up good space. I drove the red convertible knowing it would impress him. When across the bridge into Milford, and after turning at the old mill, I found the river waiting motionless and silent. I liked that. My life was good, stable and powerful, and my home in The Neighborhood perfect, but I had always lived in my skull. Why not, before Tom arrived, use this quiet to go even deeper inside me to where consciousness ended and I could vacation in minutes of emptiness? Drinking always helped me taste oblivion. I parked and finished the bottle.

The sound of wheels on gravel pulled me back. A pitted truck with attached trailer and busted taillights pulled up, Tom smiling at me through a dirt smeared window. He backed the trailer down the ramp and got out. I went over.

"You're fat," he said, briefly shaking my hand.

"And you're fucking old. I can't believe you're still wearing that hat."

"Important things you keep. The rest is just shit. Help me with the boat."

"This is what you bought? Does it float?"

"It serves its purpose."

We pushed the rowboat out and climbed in. Heavy and warped, its wooden sides stained by fish blood, the boat settled low in the water. Its wobbling, made me lose my balance. Tom caught me but not before the unhinged edge of the metal bench cut my leg.

"Just a scratch," he said while paddling us through weeds and into the black water. "I wouldn't worry about infection."

After five tugs, Tom started the small motor and the rowboat sputtered toward the middle of the river.

"Nice car, Steve. Nice shoes."

"Do you really own a company?" I asked.

"No. Fishmouth's dead."

"Fishmouth…" I had known him.

"Interested in what happened?"

I waited.

"He threw himself on a grenade."

"I'm not surprised. The guy was always crazy."

"Yeah, imagine getting blown up just to save a few of your buddies. You and I aren't heroes, are we? Remember the bird's eggs you broke when we were kids?"

"Did I?"

"We're like that, aren't we, Steve. Broken and can't be fixed. Karla, too. I hope you haven't forgotten her." He stood up. "Ready, pardner? Trick or treat."

"Where's the fishing poles?" I asked.

"Guess I left them at the cemetery." Tom swooped down as if holding a butterfly net and pushed me over the side. I think I hit my head. He grinned at me through ripples in the Hog River.

That was a few seconds or hours ago…

Fuck it. Tom's an idiot, always was. I'm Barnabas. Perfect. In control. When I swim out of here, I'll sue his ass.

Except I can't swim. Never could…

For now, I'll just drift along, enjoying the ride. I don't often take the time to visit all the rooms in my head. Especially on Halloween.

ALAN KESSLER

3

I HAD MET FISHMOUTH first. He lived near us in The Neighborhood, the poor part of Cloverdale. I played in his boarding house rooms every day until, in first grade, we moved out of our small house with its dying bee tree and bought in the best section of town. For a while, I stayed friends with him. He was a firecracker, a ball bouncing off walls. It wasn't easy to fool grandmother at Halloween. Choose the wrong pirate or clown mask, and she'd see through it and try to kill me. If I made a mistake in Halloween costumes, I hoped Fishmouth, with his crazy energy, would protect me. Even when he became someone I called only when Tom wasn't around, I always got Fishmouth to invite me for a sleepover on Halloween. When I met Dane, I didn't need Fishmouth anymore to keep me safe from ghosts.

After Fishmouth, but before Dane grew inside me, I knew Tom. For a while, we were best friends. Even now, I hear them both.

I'm nine. It's summer. Lying in the grass in Tom's front yard, my eyes half-closed, I feel bright sunlight on my face and arms. Across the street from his old farmhouse, the last house in

Cloverdale, the rotted planks of a fence marked the beginning of a field tangled by weeds and brambles growing among bushes burned brown by the sun. Above the bushes, white butterflies filled the sky. The field, acres of pollution reaching the Hog River, was in Milford, a city of apartment buildings and factories. The factory owners, men like my father, lived in Cloverdale and never considered The Neighborhood a part of their town.

Tom's small yard bred insects inside cans. Hearing August speak to me through the steady beat of trapped bodies hitting rusted tin, I rolled toward this pleasant sound and smelled mother. The crushed lily under me had the same loving odor her fingers made when stroking her dog, the tiny rat thing she either carried or cradled on her lap. The trapped insects began to buzz just like mother's words.

What if I can't hear or smell? Or maybe I'll just go blind…

I stared at the sun, quickly closed my eyes and got up.

Everything was okay. I had Tom, and he believed in magic. To stay his friend, I needed only to pretend I did, too. I went to find a sword.

"It's important to have just the right kind," he had reminded me before heading off to his secret place. "There's Indians out there and pirates. We'll have to fight them off." He slashed the air with his arm.

As soon as he left, I stretched out on his grass. He had a secret, the hole, or box, or rotted stump where he hid his dad's fishing hat. I hated Tom for not taking me there. I was his best friend, the one person he should share everything with and keep close. To get back at him, I waited as long as I could before looking for a stick.

In a pile of sticks in front of the rotted trunk which had ended one of Tom's many blindfolded winter sled rides down the slope of his icy front yard, I picked up a stick the length of my arm. Good enough, I decided. Speckled with mildew and small toadstools, the stick had a heavy swinging weight that I used against the trunk that Tom pretended was still a tree, each hit making my arm tingle and feel more alive.

Blurred at the edges by sunlight, Tom ran toward me. Of course he wore that stupid hat. Even from a distance I could read the faded letters on front as though they were billboard size *Jacoby's Worms*; see the small plastic fish on top; smell the canvas stained with his dad's sweat. Tom had stuffed newspaper inside—so what? The large round cap still slipped over his forehead. I knew every detail and wanted to rip the lie apart. My father was alive. He walked and sat, read the paper, and although never speaking to me, proved his love by kicking me in the sides. My father was flesh and hands. He had red, lively eyes. Tom had no right pretending an old hat advertising worms and once worn by a dead man buried someplace in another state gave him a dad to touch.

"Not bad," he said, looking at my stick.

"Took a while to find it," I said.

"Let's go." He ran ahead, his arms and legs swinging in the shimmering heat. Father also left me behind, but running after him when he walked fast made little sense. Tom was different. He did things with me. I could use him to fill a whole summer afternoon. All I had to do was catch him.

At the edge of the field, Tom put his hand on the high end of the fence and hopped over. I stepped across the boards angled down. We crunched on dried weeds until he stopped and reached into a cluster of shriveled bushes.

"Have some." Tom held out a handful of berries.

Mother buzzed. She didn't want me to eat unwashed fruit.

"I'm not hungry."

"Pirates live off the land. Not everything's easy like this, just waiting to be picked. We were lucky. Before we get back to the ship we're gonna have to catch a few turtles and some snakes, skin and cook 'em." He threw me a berry—bright red, too perfect looking to be anything but poison. Tom gobbled down the rest. Using his stick like a machete to whack at the tallest bush in front of him, he charged the field.

I dropped the berry and after grinding it under my shoe, ran up behind him on the path he'd cleared.

"Eat it?" he asked, not looking back at me.

"Yep. Only thing better would be a snake. I'll keep an eye out for one."

Tom turned and pushed me.

"You almost stepped in quicksand. Guess I've got to teach you everything."

I stepped over the splotch of oily mud. Sweat burned my eyes. Scratching made the chigger bites on my arms hurt and bleed.

"Look at him. Playing in filth and garbage because he's with someone too poor to do anything else. Stevie and his friends," these last four words the shrillest part of mother's buzzing. And the pit wasn't any closer. I needed to be there—*now* to show her sometimes believing was enough. Sticks weren't swords. Tom's hat didn't love him. There wasn't anything magical in the world, but there was a treasure chest top left in Milford by pirates searching for the sea. Tom told me he had found it, and he never lied.

"Look mother, look at it. I'm rich. Tom needed *me* to drag the heavy wood out."

I had been to the pit once before with Fishmouth, finding only stinking black sludge oozing around the openings of sewage pipes. But we'd gone in fall and the few old trees near the pit had covered it in leaves, hiding anything valuable. Fishmouth had only one talent—he could thrash about not caring whether he got hurt, never did. He hadn't been smart enough to find the treasure chest top. Tom was different. He'd have discovered it in a foot of snow. Still, summer was his best season. The sunlight helped him make up games. He had things for us to do every day. We were pirates. We were Indians. We built a spaceship and made secret maps with disappearing, lemon juice ink. But sometimes he didn't think. Yesterday, when I stayed in bed, my two months of seven a.m. butterfly hunting giving me the right to sleep in once without him getting upset, he'd decided to find a treasure chest top.

"Should have been there," Tom said sitting balanced on the railing of his front porch, his long legs dangling.

"I was sick. Threw up all morning."

"Sorry about that but I could have used you. I kept after

the butterflies and when far into the field at the pit, I saw old wood poking up from the ground. I knew right away what it was."

"You're sure?"

"No one knows more about pirates than me. I've read books about them and studied all their secret ways. Bet you there's all kinds of bones and gold coins at the pit, too, but that's going to take some real exploring. First, we've got to bring the top out before anyone else finds it."

"Let's go now."

"Can't. I've some chores to do around here. Want to help?"

"Yeah, but I promised mother I'd cut the grass." I didn't feel like working. I planned to sneak over to the drug store, order some ice cream and talk to Mr. Petty. Tom would never know. "Should I come back later?"

"We'll go tomorrow. It'll be safe until then. I hid it really good." He jumped down and taught me a secret handshake. We were pals.

And so, that next day, I kept trudging toward the pit through chiggers and heat filled with mother's shrill laughter. I wanted to stop but knew each step brought me closer to filling my head with silent, cool air. Mother liked money almost as much as father did. She protected her nice things, covering carpets and sofas in plastic and locking her house up. When I showed her the treasure chest top, I knew she would drop the twin, sister things on the floor and rushing over, hug me.

"Did I ever buzz?"

"I don't remember," I'd answer, resting my emptied skull

against her breast.

"Over here. Right where I left it." Jumping up and down at the pit's edge, Tom waved his arms. My arms opened, too. I ran to mother....

The chiggers bit harder while the wind and withered bushes spoke inside waves of spinning, clacking heat. The loudest voice was hers. Stevie and his friends Stevie and his friends— I'll always hold your sisters tight. There'll never be any room for you. Nice treasure.

I stared down at four rotted boards held loosely together with string.

"Just like I said. See the initials? C. K.—Captain Kidd. I've found Captain Kidd's treasure chest."

Tom didn't notice I had melted away. Mother's face grinned up at me from the pit.

"Grab the end," he said. "This is a real antique, probably worth, ten, no, twenty thousand dollars. I'll give you half even though I found it. This is going to help my mom plenty."

I guess I had legs because I moved. I saw my hand. It held wood. Liar liar, Tom, but I knew, even while thinking this, he wasn't a liar, just a fool too weak to keep mother from buzzing inside me. Mother had warned me two days earlier while I stood in the field watching Tom run after butterflies...

"Again with the bugs. He has nothing better to play with. You have a whole room full of expensive toys. Go on, be a follower, see what good it does you. He'll never beat me."

Tom swung his net through the bushes. He chased butterflies around me. I couldn't leave the field until he'd filled his jar and holding it up made me listen to the last butterflies he caught tap their wings weakly against glass. The hunt over, I still wasn't free. Tom enjoyed trapping me in his room. I had to go there and sit with the dead.

After skipping across the road and jumping up his porch two steps at a time, Tom ran into his home, and although I couldn't see him, I knew he was hurrying upstairs to his small bedroom and quickly shutting the door. Earlier in the summer I had run with him. That day I walked. Once again, I used the secret knock and he let me inside to fringed cowboy lamps, bunk beds, and the smell of closed in decay. The odor always made me feel Halloween had a hot and sticky summer season that brought grandmother along into Tom's bedroom where she sat invisible and rocking, waiting for me. But I was smart. I always controlled my thoughts. I knew the smell wasn't hers but came from the sheets in Tom's drawers and closet filled with the pieces of summer he had caught and mummified. I sat against the wall. He took my space away by bringing his collection over along with pins, a few rusted tuna cans, and the jar of butterflies from the field. His sheets of paper displayed moldy bodies and crumpled wings; insect eyes stared at me; little mouths moved wanting me to help. Tom opened his killing jar. When he caught a butterfly, he pinched its body, crushing it. The cotton balls in the jar, soaked with rubbing alcohol, killed any butterfly still alive. Carefully taking out each body, he put it in his relaxing chambers, the tuna cans he had lined up in a row between us, a piece of damp cloth at the bottom of each. The dampness softened the bodies out of their death curls. I heard them breathe and ask, "where is the light? When will we again smell air and fly?" The water would evaporate in a few days and the butterflies stiffen. Then Tom would stick them—as he did that day to the butterflies he had caught earlier in the week; straight pins crunching into bodies, one after the other, pinning them onto a blank page; dry, tiny voices gurgling and choking.

Tom took a stubby pencil from behind his ear and recorded the date on the paper.

"Best yet." He smiled and proudly held the collection in front of me. Stupid nut. Because only white butterflies lived in the field, all his pages were the same. I would have arranged the butterflies beautifully, given them no reason to speak.

"Super," I said and saw in his eyes he loved me. I thought that important. I hadn't yet realized mother's power over him— if she wanted, she could buzz inside him, too. He didn't show his weakness until I learned in the field's chigger and bramble heat that his treasure chest top was nothing more than rot tied together by a fool's imagination...

I carried the boards from one end, Tom on the other, shuffled backward. The butterflies above us flying higher looked like specks of snot he had sneezed into the sky. I felt the sticker bushes rebuild my melted face by using pain. We crossed the field, fence, and Tom's front yard. His shiny, happy, dancing eyes burned me. Drop by drop, as if I were bleeding, my sweat slickened the boards and I almost dropped them.

"Careful." Tom said, backing up to where his mother stood hanging white sheets to dry. She took a clothes pin from her mouth and smiled at me.

"What you two got there?" Her eyes were as sparkling blue as Tom's.

"A treasure." Tom moved too quickly and I lost my grip. Splitting the string, the boards fell hard and landed in broken pieces on the ground. *There's* your pirate bones. I wanted to say when seeing his sad face.

Tom looked at his mother.

She walked over and studied the wood.

"Unusual, that's for sure. Don't see many boards like these nowadays. You called them a treasure?"

"A treasure chest top," Tom kicked a stone. "I thought we'd found something left by pirates…"

"You have. Knew it right away. The wood's old and was once good and strong, the special kind you'd use when making something to hold diamonds and gold. At one time, so I've been told, that field over there was just full of pirates who floated down here on the Hog River." Sunlight mixed into her long, brown hair. Tom hugged her, but she again smiled only at me. For the past year, I'd slept over on Friday nights. I would sit beside her in the kitchen and we'd paste trading stamps into books. Under my fingers, the worn, familiar places in the table's smoothness said, Hello, Steve. Welcome back. In the quiet space next to her, Tom someplace in the room, bread baking in the oven, I'd feel her arms hold me as she looked in the catalogues at stereos and TVs. I knew in the morning she would make me pancakes and later, for a snack, say "Here, Steve, have some of my warm, chocolate chip cookies. I baked them just for you." Tom always spoiled my Friday nights by doing something silly so she'd laugh. And instead of saving more stamps and getting something really neat, he redeemed the books for junk like his butterfly net. I felt sorry for his mom. Tom embarrassed her. I should have been her son.

"Anyone interested in some apple pie and milk?" she asked while hanging up the last sheet.

"Yeah." Tom shouted, heading for the front door.

"Let's put the treasure chest top in a safe place," I said. Tom was useless against mother, but I needed him. He was more fun than Fishmouth and less dangerous.

"Good thinking, Steve."

We dragged the boards under his front porch and covered them with burlap. When I bulldozed Tom's house, the boards were still there. I burned them.

"Beat you to the kitchen." He held my arm, then let go and ran.

"Cheater."

The screen door slammed again, this time behind me. I almost fell backwards as the throw rug in his living room slid out from under my feet, but I balanced myself and skidded into my chair just as Tom scooted up to the table in his.

Tom's mom served me first.

"After we're done here, let's tape flashlights to our heads and crawl through Mrs. Humphrey's garden," he whispered to me.

"The dog…"

"That's the fun of it." Tom took a big, smacking bite of pie.

"Okay, count me in." I was scared but had nothing else to do. Mr. Petty's drug store had a sewage problem. Mother had locked her doors.

"Tomorrow morning we'll hunt butterflies again. Don't get sick on me, Steve."

"I won't."

A milk mustache on his lip, still wearing his father's hat, Tom reached out and caught a fly.

Trapped, I heard its buzzing.

4

I REMEMBER CLOVERDALE AS a town of invisible people. Whenever adults were outside, they stooped as if pressed down by the unexpected weight of the outside air and fearful of having to nod hello to some chance passer-by—a mailman or delivery boy—never looked up while hurrying to get back inside their houses or cars. No child ever played in the large, uniformly green yards that remained untouched except on Saturdays when work crews, emerging from battered trucks, cut and sprayed, and in an hour were gone, returning the houses and residents to invisibility and silence.

The five streets of Tom's neighborhood were different. Prevented by busy Treemont Avenue from spreading east into the good part of town and bordered at its west end by the Milford field, The Neighborhood of small homes used clutter and noise as lawn decorations. Toys grew everywhere, on stairs and chairs, in narrow driveways and rutted yards. Children carrying fall leaves or snowballs in winter, rushed laughing into battle across unenforced property lines. Summer made inflatable pools playmates eager to splash and dunk. By crossing Treemont and entering The Neighborhood, I escaped into a place where mothers hugged their children and didn't cut down trees. Our neighbor the dentist, concerned about the leaves on his grass, once spoke to father.

"But it's the last one," I said to mother. In bed, at night, I had watched the oak's branches reach out, wanting to hold me.

"Roots damage the foundation," mother answered. "And who wants trouble with the neighbors. We're quiet people."

She ordered the tree cut down. Another call and yard men pulled out the stump I had been sitting on and replaced it with chemically treated sod. That wouldn't have happened in The Neighborhood. Trees were everywhere, even Tom's stupid dead one that reminded me of what mother wanted to do to the ones alive. The Neighborhood had life. Only where Fishmouth lived, in the boarding house next to Tom's home, did the gravel yard in front with its brown flowers and a tomato plant stay quiet and orderly. The landlady, Mrs. Humphrey, didn't like mess. I'd often see her standing at the kitchen window, looking out into the back yard while continuing to wash her hands in the sink. I didn't understand what that meant until years later.

The afternoon I met Dane, Tom and I were together first, reading comics and drinking lemonade on his front porch. I heard Tom's mom in the kitchen baking up something good. The summer sun warmed me, mother's buzzing hardly a sound. It was almost peaceful. I saw Fishmouth before Tom did.

"What's he want?" Keeping Tom close meant staying alert.

Tom jumped off the porch, so I did too.

"Met someone new." Fishmouth said, jerking and twitching by the dead tree. He could never stand still. "And you won't believe where—at the old Riley house."

"You're kidding," Tom said.

"Went right in."

Tom's expression changed from 'wish-I'd-been-there' to one much worse. His eyes widened and he stared at Fishmouth as if in the presence of someone holy—and all because of a ghost. Everyone in The Neighborhood knew old man Riley had hanged himself in his attic and that after dark his dangling shadow, swinging back and forth, haunted different rooms of the abandoned house where he'd once lived. One night, on a dare, Tom made it halfway up the walk and would have gone the whole way and knocked on the Riley front door if Fishmouth hadn't started shouting and banging a stick against the broken fence. Ghosts frightened me only when they were supposed to, on Halloween. I could have pounded on the door that night, but when Tom and Fishmouth raced out of there, I ran, too. What was the use doing something Tom wouldn't see? It should have been me going into the old Riley house and impressing Tom. Now, I'd lost the chance. Tom liked Fishmouth. I had to act quickly.

I stepped between them and called Fishmouth a liar. He pushed me, but not very hard.

"Leave Steve alone," Tom said. I liked that.

"Let's head over there right now. You'll see." Fishmouth shifted from one foot to the other. "Come on—unless you're chicken."

"Let him go," I said.

"And miss out on an adventure? Beat you, Fishmouth." They

ran together across Tom's backyard, Tom moving farther away from me. I hated Fishmouth. With all her talking, mother used so many words that sometimes, by accident, a few made sense. Fishmouth *was* a wild Indian. Reckless, unhurt in any game, he'd gouge and scratch, hit with his knees, not out of meanness but because he believed playground rules allowed using pain. He never complained if someone tried knocking him over. Few attempted it but those who did went home crying. To lessen the chance of getting hurt, when we picked teams I did my best to get on his. Fishmouth slammed and thrashed about trying to make good plays but never intentionally crippled a teammate. Except when I slept over on Halloween, I played with him only when I had no other choice. Now, he had tricked me. To keep Tom, my best friend, I had to go with Fishmouth to a stranger's house. What if Tom liked this new kid better than me? Something had happened to summer. There was danger all around.

I knew Tom and Fishmouth had taken a shortcut across Mrs. Humphrey's garden. Tom and I often played hide and seek and other games in there. It was a small patch, full of weeds. The landlady grew hard corn you couldn't eat and dark onions. Now I was alone among corn stalks swaying and making little clicking sounds. As I crawled between the rows, I wasn't afraid of Mrs. Humphrey catching me. It was her dog that killed. I had barely escaped Wolf once before…

A few weeks earlier, I had followed Tom on a spy mission through the garden. Staying close to the ground, I peeked over a rusted wheelbarrow while Tom, in the middle of the onions, threw a pebble at Fishmouth's window. I wanted to see Mrs. Humphrey. I liked the way she dressed—black stockings, short black skirt, her white blouse buttoned high around her neck. Even while washing her hands at the sink, she looked dressed for a date. When near her, I felt the same warm queasiness inside me I had the morning mother opened the bathroom door and saw me sitting on the toilet. Mrs. Humphrey was beautiful. I tried to get a closer look.

Yellow eyes across the wheelbarrow stared back at me. Two long fangs gleamed.

"Nice boy," I said, trying not to move. I called quietly for Tom. Wolf, smelling like rotted meat, put his mouth on my throat. The dog was mangy and grey, and except for its large, fleshy head, all bone. When owned by her boarder, Mr. Wolf from Cincinnati, the dog had been named Jake. Mr. Wolf and Mrs. Humphrey were friends, I could tell that by how close they stood to each other while talking. When Mr. Wolf moved out suddenly, at night, he left Jake tied to the boarding house's back porch. I figured Mr. Wolf gave Mrs. Humphrey his dog so she wouldn't be lonely. She named Jake, Wolf, and no matter what the weather, took him for long walks on a short chain. A year after Mr. Wolf left, Wolf died, all dried up. I was sure, at the time, Mrs. Humphrey had loved him, her sad eyes turning even darker as she stood at her kitchen window, the water running, and swung his leash back and forth over the sink. Wolf had just stopped eating. Old dogs did that. I didn't learn until later she had starved him to death.

Caught by Wolf on my spy mission, his teeth on me, the

dog still very much alive, I had again whispered for Tom—cursed him for not being there when I needed him.

"Good doggy," I said slowly. Wolf tightened his grip. I knew then how I was going to die: eaten by a skinny, balding dog in a vegetable patch.

"Hey, Wolf." Tom emerged from a row of corn. Wolf rolled backwards and thumped his tail on the ground. "Wish I had a dog like this." He rubbed Wolf's belly. "You weren't scared, were you, Steve?"

"Are you kidding? I've had lots of dogs at my house. Big ones. I just wanted you to come over and play with him." I got up and wiped the slobber from my neck.

"Yeah, Wolf's on our side." Tom said, "a member of the spy team. He was getting you used to torture in case you got caught. Good boy." He threw him a stick.

I don't remember if Fishmouth joined us or what we did the rest of that day, but I'm sure it was fun. I know when Tom was rubbing Wolf's stomach; the dog kept one yellow eye on me and growled. Now, again in the garden, alone and on the way to the old Riley house, I watched for Wolf. The corn shook its red and black kernels. Onions bumped against each other down the line in a chain of motion thudding toward me, but I was almost out. Just a few feet more—I saw the tattered ears first, then the huge head. Eyes and fangs flashing, Wolf leaped at me. *Tom.*

Fishmouth kicked Wolf in the side, sending the dog sprawling.

"Never show anyone you're afraid," he said, straightening

his thick glasses.

"Where's Tom?" I asked.

"Race you to the Riley house." Fishmouth sprinted off. He'd always wanted Tom for himself. Now he was using this new kid to take my best friend away from me. I would never let that happen.

Tail between its legs, Wolf had limped to the boarding house. While lying below Mrs. Humphrey's kitchen window, the dog stared at me as if measuring the distance between us. I backed out of the garden slowly, turned and ran, expecting at any moment to be attacked from behind and clawed to the ground. Dogs knew I hated them. With Wolf and mother's tiny, disgusting Munchkin, I actually had a reason.

"What took you?" All shaking and jittery, Fishmouth paced back and forth in front of the broken, backyard gate.

"This is stupid," I said to Tom who had just finished ducking and hiding while checking out the house from different angles.

"Will be for sure if we don't attack from the side. We'll scoot behind those bushes over there, jump the barrel and tires and rush the door. No one will see us coming. We need rifles. Any good sticks around?"

"What are you talking about?" Fishmouth's glasses fogged over and his big teeth stuck out even farther than usual. "I told you I went inside. I'm friends with this guy and he said I could come back anytime I want. You went up half-way, Tom. I fixed it so we never have to sneak around here again."

"Hit him," I whispered to Tom who just looked at me. Fishmouth jumped the fence and Tom did, too. I pushed the gate. It fell over. On a walkway of broken concrete slabs with weeds growing through the cracks, I heard Tom's sneakers ahead of me speak—

Sorry, Steve, he likes Fishmouth and soon, this new boy, too. Makes sense, doesn't it? You mother controls houses. She used this one so you'd lose your best friend. It's sad, Steve, but what can we do? We're only shoes. *Squeak, squeak.*

Sweat burned my eyes. Tom's sneakers were right. I saw the dark omens: the rust spotted squares of busted concrete looked like they'd been repeatedly smashed by a bloody hammer; worms and quicksand mud had replaced the sidewalk's missing blocks; paint didn't peel from the house's wall but had been slashed by a knife into hanging, twisted smiles. Tom and Fishmouth stood together at the back stoop. Mother had won. I was alone.

"Good thing you came with Fishmouth, otherwise I'd have shot you." The boy banged the torn, screen door open and stood in front of it, arms folded. "Trespassing's a crime. Everyone knows that. Who brought the little mutt?"

"That's Steve," Fishmouth said. "He's okay. Tom, this is Dane."

"You really got a gun?" Tom asked.

"Three of them. And a machete. Want to see them?"

"Yeah." Fishmouth's face lit up and he followed Dane inside.

"We should leave," Tom said.

"I can't."

Tom and Dane had blond hair but Tom wore his long and

chased butterflies. Dane had buzzed his short and played with guns. Tom used sticks; Dane had a real machete. Their faces were different, too—Tom's, soft and full of imagination that turned rotted boards into a treasure chest top for mother to laugh at; Dane's hard grey eyes had warmed me. He was tall and strong, and I could tell not someone easily digested by words. Mother had once smiled at Tom. I knew she'd hate Dane.

I went into the house, Tom probably behind me.

The beer cans stacked on food stained dishes in the kitchen sink showed me how much Dane's family enjoyed life. I looked into the small living room and saw more plates and a television with its coat hanger aerial twisted into a face. Old man Riley's? Except for this ghost, everything in Dane's home was normal—messy, lopsided, broken and dirty, the way rooms should look if there weren't any maids.

Dane grabbed my arm.

"You got nose trouble? Quit snooping around." He pushed me toward Jesus hanging above a jagged hole in the wall at the hallway's end. The black velvet painting absorbed light. Only the eyes gleamed, shiny and blue, almost gray. Was this Dane's secret? Could he, through his god, keep ghosts away? Old man Riley? My grandmother on Halloween? I carefully touched the mother-of-pearl frame. Through it I felt the smooth quietness of Dane's voice. When around him, when he spoke, my head felt clear and mother didn't buzz. He almost slammed his bedroom door on me, but I knew how to squeeze through the smallest space. Mother had trained me. When letting me into her house, she barely opened the door.

"Where's the guns?" Fishmouth asked, rocking back and forth. Tom stood in a corner.

"Under the bed with the knives," Dane answered. I sat down next to him. He pushed me away. "Hey, Fishmouth, your friend Stevie is a goddamn faggot. I'm not going to show you anything. I thought you were cool."

"You don't know anything about us," Tom said.

"I know fools. Anyone want a beer?"

Cocktails and highballs. I didn't have to hear mother buzz to play back in my mind the constant flow of words that began whenever we drove by a bar or saw someone drunk on the long rides we took in the station wagon with the doors locked, the sister things eating cupcakes or salami in the middle seat, father driving, silent, never turning his head, while I sat in the way-back, looking out the rear window at what we'd passed and unable, even back there, to escape the sound of mother's non-stop droning—

"Did you see that place. The lights. The drunks. That woman sprawled out in the alley. All because of alcohol. I read in the paper every drink kills millions of brain cells. What a shame to destroy such a beautiful thing like a brain   .   And for what? To escape life? Better these people should spend more time with their families, then they wouldn't have to become floozies and bums, rolling around in the gutter."

I thought mother was warning me that if I ever tasted one of the small bottles father hid in his desk downstairs I'd end up slobbering and blind. I learned later, when I was older and mother less polite, who she was really after.

"Remember this, Mr. Big Shot, all the cocktails you have with girlfriends before coming home and all the highballs you drink when you think I'm not looking, are going to rot your brain. You'll end up dead in the street."

Father did, but not the way she imagined.

During all those long, slow drives in the station wagon with us, he always stayed inside himself, actually never came out, even when in the house, unless to show love by kicking me in the sides.

Dane had offered me a beer, invited me into his jolly kitchen, and silent mother couldn't stop me.

"I'll have one," I said.

"You're quite the little man." Dane laughed in my face. He had beautiful teeth.

"Quit picking on him," Tom said.

"Sorry, Stevie, no booze left. My old man drank it all. But I've got something even better for you—smokes." Dane pulled an old cigar box from under his bed and opened it. "Which do you want?"

A fat, gray cigar leaked yellow oil. Small, hair-like fibers grew from the glistening green one.

"You'll get sick," Tom said.

"Dare you," Fishmouth said.

I picked up the gray cigar. It almost slipped through my fingers.

"Looks like your dick," Dane threw a matchbook over, hitting me in the eye. After four tries, my fingers sweating a little more with each failed strike, I had only one unbroken match left.

"What a goofball," Dane joked.

I knew he could light a match with the flick of his thumb. Praying to his Jesus in the hallway, I took a hard, wild swipe, tearing in half state bird of West Virginia on the cover. The match caught fire. I hadn't let Dane down.

"Light it," he said.

The heavy, damp tobacco didn't even smolder. Tom mumbled something unimportant. Was Fishmouth still in the room? I cared only about Dane.

"Take a big bite," he said, wanting to help me, so I did. Half the cigar dissolved in my mouth. When the match burned my finger, I swallowed. Not wanting to throw-up in his neat room, I held my stomach and made it outside to the tall weeds of his backyard.

Dane was the first one to run over and see if I was okay. Standing above me, his face became part of the sun.

"What a mess. You're a pig." And I was. I was still little Stevie. "I should make you lick it all up. I'll let you go if you eat this." He held out the other cigar. Tom knocked it from his hand.

"What are you? His mother?"

"That's a good one, Dane," I reached for the cigar. He stepped on my fingers.

"Hey, there's your sister." Fishmouth said. "Hi, Karla."

The girl stood at the yard's edge. As tall as Dane, she had his boney shape and blood but wasn't as pretty.

"He's not home," Dane told her. "Use my room."

Head down, she walked quickly past us.

"Your sister's cute," Fishmouth said. Dane punched him in the stomach.

"Don't ever look at her that way."

Amazing. I had never seen Fishmouth's eyes cloud over. Anything that might unsettle the rest of his strange, pale face by adding a new spasm or jerk, never affected the shiny black center of each eye. Magnified by his glasses, this visible part of his invulnera-bility—the dark holes, meant that confusion, even an accidental insight, might play at the edges of his warped field, but with the game on the line, he'd stop thinking and with black eyes glaring, go instinctively for the throat. By making Fishmouth almost cry, Dane had done the impossible.

After hiding the broken pieces of the green cigar in my pocket, I got up and ignoring Tom, ran into the front yard where Dane leaned against an old willow that immediately welcomed me into its shadows. Through the swish and rattle of the branches Tom once called Riley's bones, I felt Dane inside the bark. Of course mother hated him. She hated trees, especially a blond one of knowledge and life. She couldn't buzz when he was around. He had beaten my grandmother by using Jesus to kill ghosts—I was sure old man Riley no longer swung from the rafters in Dane's home. I didn't need Fishmouth anymore for sleepovers on Halloween, and I didn't need Tom. Dane's roots were inside me. He was now my best friend.

He hacked at the willow with his pocket knife.

"I know a girl. Let's visit her. She lives in a big, fat house."

"Sounds fun." Fishmouth said.

"Steve and I are going to play ball," Tom said. I thought he'd left.

"I'm staying with Dane," I said.

"Not unless Tom comes along, too." Dane threw a stone at my head and deliberately missed.

"How about it, Tom? Be a friend."

"Jeeez, Steve, a girl. Why go there? It's just a waste of time." But he did what I wanted. Tom was good at that. Dane and Fishmouth had already started ahead.

"I don't like this guy," Tom said, hurrying after me as I walked fast. Dane glanced back at us.

"Little Stevie, hot to trot. And I thought he was queer."

A homo. How funny. I only loved him. Light hearted, I skipped down the sidewalk.

The Neighborhood's five streets intersected narrow, potholed Cassidy Drive. Heading up Cassidy, we reached busy Treemont and crossed to where, on the other side, a mayor of Cloverdale had installed at the curb concrete pylons in an attempt to prevent truckers from turning off Treemont and taking a shortcut up wide, tree lined Cassidy Boulevard in the good part of town. Dane and I—and Tom—kept walking; Fishmouth stayed behind and playing with traffic, sticking his foot out from between the smashed barriers and yanking it back just before a car zoomed past.

"Fishmouth's nuts," Tom said.

"You're a pussy." Dane called out.

"Yeah? Well watch this," Fishmouth yelled over the sound of rushing cars and trucks. Dane had walked away. I wanted to catch up to him but the weight I felt when entering this zone of big houses and invisible people, pressed down harder. The Watchers were here, the women with lacquered hair and painted eyes who watched me from behind long, pleated drapes and reported back to mother. How else could she know everything I did? The cut lawn's sweating chemicals burned my skin. My legs bowed, each footstep slower than the last, I fell behind and saw Dane blur and out of reach, disappear.

Tom waited for me.

"We could be fishing."

"Where did Dane go?" I asked walking past him and immediately tripped over a foot cleverly hidden inside a row of trimmed bushes. Dane. When hitting the sidewalk and tasting blood in my mouth, I felt father.

Dane stepped out grinning.

"Why do you like being so mean," Tom butted in.

"Am I, Stevie?" He knew I understood. Love was painful.

"No, Dane, it was fun."

Tom offered me his hand. I got up myself. He turned and frowned.

"I didn't know we were coming *here*."

Molly Adam's house, where gardeners had squared the treetops and there were never any birds. She liked Tom and thought I was a toad.

"You told me you'd go inside," Dane said. "Where I'm from, only assholes go back on their word."

"I never promised that."

"You did. I heard it." Fishmouth said, running past us and

toward the front door.

"Be a friend, Tom. Remember, it's what you little pal wants. Right, Stevie?"

"Right, Dane." I nodded just to make sure he knew I would always be on his side.

Tom and I walked slowly up the driveway, the wings of the stone angel casting its shadow in front of us. Like other Cloverdale residents on this side of Treemont who wanted to add a little outside ornamentation to their houses while keeping the lawns open and useless, Molly's parents had built a marble fountain in the driveway and surrounded it with flowers so bright and melted together they hurt my eyes. The fountain waited until Tom passed, then the angel spat water in my face. The metal eyes of the lion door knocker made even the roots of my unblond hair hurt. Fishmouth kept banging.

Maybe no one's home…

"What's he doing here?" Molly asked, looking right at me.

"Tom wouldn't come without him," Dane said.

"Tom." Molly's face turned school bright. Her dimples moved her freckles higher and her smile could have cooked a small potato. She stepped toward him. Tom stepped back. Fishmouth and Dane shot inside.

"Don't be shy," Molly slipped her arm through Tom's, leading him into the house, she kicked the door. Once again, I managed to jump through a narrow opening just in time.

"Where's the table?" Dane asked.

"Downstairs," Molly answered. "Don't break anything."

"See ya," Fishmouth went with Dane.

"Want some cake?" Molly asked Tom who hadn't moved far from the door.

"Uh, no thank you." He pulled at his shirt collar. She still had his arm locked.

"Think I'll find Dane," I said.

"You're not going anywhere. I can't believe I even let you in here."

"You have a pool table, that's nice," Tom shuffled his feet and nervously looked around the hall. He wasn't Dane. I could tell he didn't know what to do.

"And a rec room. Want to see it?"

"Okay, if Steve comes."

Molly crinkled her nose but didn't stop me.

Mrs. Adams' living room, on display like mother's, only smaller, and decorated almost the same with crystals, metal tables, and a white fireplace tinged orange by electric logs, had grey rugs and seascapes while mother preferred in hers white carpeting covered in plastic and paintings of dark haired girls whose oversized eyes I wanted to poke out. Ahead, in the kitchen, a fat maid, her face broad and cheerful, paused at mixing batter and waved at Molly with a wooden spoon.

"How's my birthday girl doing? I'm fixin' you something special."

Our maids never remembered my birthday.

"You must pay her a lot," I said.

"You're a creep," Molly turned back toward Tom and smiled sweetly. "That's just LuLu. The rec room's down here, Tommy."

We descended into cool, damp air, the carpeted basement

finished in knotty pine. I stood behind Dane who chalked his cue at the pool table. Impatiently waiting his turn, Fishmouth tapped his foot against the wall. The large, mounted swordfish above him shook.

"Can't you see I'm getting ready to break? Quit looking at my ass, faggot, and get away from me.

Dane liked to tease me.

I chose the corner nearest to him and from there watched his hands, commanding space, create in the pool table a world of moving colors he let roll on or die. Zoom. Crack. The red ball disappeared, and by shooting it hard, he made the black one form lines of ebony across the table's green top. Before mother cut down the tree in our yard, its branches had called to me on windy nights. By hitting the purple and yellow balls together, Dane brought back the sound of the tree's song. His hand on the pool table's side added its own cream shaded motion to the swirling patterns in the dark wood. After he scratched his head, he scratched his leg, and I saw how graceful and strong the table's legs held the floor. The seventeen small, mother-of-pearl circles on the bumpers twinkled at me with warm Dane-light.

When he touched the felt, he touched me.

Dane farted.

"Stevie's stinking up the place," he said, and I laughed with Fishmouth. Tom sat on the front edge of a folding chair. Molly moved her chair closer to him.

"Watch this." Dane held the cue stick straight up and bringing it down quickly, skipped the white ball over the rack and into a pocket.

"I can do that." Fishmouth said.

"Let me show you how I learned my ABCs." At a small blackboard with a teddy bear border, Dane wrote A-asshole, in chalk. "B-balls. Can't wait 'til I get to F."

Tom blushed.

"You shouldn't do that," his stupid face all cookies and milk. Molly giggled thinking this would make Dane like her better than me.

"What's the problem, Tom? Don't people swear around here?"

"No, Dane, they don't."

"Stevie, say fuck."

"Fuck."

"Guess I was wrong," Tom said quietly.

"Probably not. Your pal's just a dick head."

We heard the sound of something ripping.

"Oh, no." Molly's mouth stayed open. Solemnly, as if gathered around a grave, we stood looking down at the pool table. A slash of white slate grinned up at us from where Fishmouth's shot had torn the felt apart.

"Maybe it's not so bad," Tom said. "We could try and tape it."

"Her daddy's rich. He'll just buy another one." Dane, a true leader, tried keeping everyone calm.

"Yeah, yeah—think so?" Fishmouth said, jerking and twitching more than usual.

"My parents are going to kill me." Molly whimpered.

I heard heavy, pounding feet coming down the stairs. The maid? Mrs. Adams thudded in front of us, her large body bulging out of its small tennis outfit.

"Lulu said you were here with boys. Why are you crying? Did they do something to you?"

Molly pointed a trembling finger at the table.

Mrs. Adam's pig-sized eyes became even smaller.

"Who is responsible for this?"

"Me," Dane said.

She whirled on him.

"You did it? On purpose?"

"I didn't want them here," Molly blubbered. "Dane forced his way in and brought this other boy they call Fishmouth and that midget over there everyone hates but don't get mad at Tom, he's the good looking one, he listens and didn't do anything wrong—and neither did I."

"Bullshit." Dane said. "Your little princess invited me over. All I had to do was make sure her lover boy came too."

"He's lying."

"Out of here. All of you. Destructive trash." Her face, turning purple, Mrs. Adams looked about to explode fat.

"Sure—bitch," Dane said and easily ducked away as she swung a cue wildly at his head. She hit the wall and fell spread-eagle on the pool table, the swordfish falling and sticking nose down between her elephant sized legs.

Tom went over and tried to apologize. What a fool. I brushed past him and jumping steps, headed toward Dane. Fishmouth had escaped first, of course.

"Goodness," Lulu said, the word expelled with a rush of air as I crashed into her stomach. Pushing off, I kept going. The hall had grown longer and twisted; playing tug-of-war, the heavy front door pulled me, but I yanked it open and outside spun inside the center of bright swirling white space that smelled summer new. Mrs. Adams couldn't catch me. I had beaten The Watchers. Charged by freedom, I knew I could outrun mother's car and the endless motion of words and wheels, but why do it? I didn't need her small breasts anymore. I had Dane.

Maybe he's hiding again, waiting to trip only me.

Tom called my name. I laughed and ran away from him. Probably he followed. In those days, I never looked back.

ALAN KESSLER

5

LATE ON A SUMMER afternoon that August, I saw the invisible come to life on Miracle Mile, Cloverdale's name for what in Milford's downtown was simply called Main Street. Gripping shopping bags and purses tight in one hand, heads jerking side to side, mothers afraid of missing something fashionable to buy marched from store to store while dragging small children by the arm. It was back to school time. Only a few more blocks, I told myself...

The waiting, plastic faces made me stop and look up at them.

It's not fair, I said. Summer isn't over.

The mannequins didn't care. They had a job to do. Mother's. She wanted me locked up for another nine months. Whether crowded in the windows of Taggert Clothing or Cavanaugh's Department Store, the mannequins of the Back-to-School sales smiled the same dead smiles and each August summoned me to them.

"Hi, Steve, remember us?" the ones in front of the department store greeted me. Their mouths didn't move. Motionless boys and girls of different shapes and sizes skipped together down a vomit green road lined on both sides with yellow cardboard bricks. A finger shaped sign pointed To School, while mothers, painted on paper houses with one dimensional flower boxes under the windows, cheerfully waved good-bye. Carrying lunchboxes and book bags, the mannequins followed a small boy who held above his head a large ruler illuminated by other-worldly light.

"You can like school," the mannequins said, "even bring a piece of summer along." The same pee color as the bricks, a cut-out sun with large eyes, dangling from a string, swung back and forth over the procession.

I waited until a gaggle of mother-shoppers who didn't see me bumped close to the store. When hidden by their bundles and arms, I took from its protected place deep in my pocket the rusted key I had found in an alley and scratched it deep and long across Mr. Cavanaugh's window.

"That's not very nice," the mannequins said.

"Fuck you," I answered like Dane. The mothers clucked on.

With hanging plants under their fashionable, striped awnings giving downtown shoppers all the nature they could handle, the brick and chrome boutiques squeezed between Cavanaugh's on one end of the block and Taggert's pressing in from the other, mysteriously hid by using obscure store names to advertise what they sold inside. Hanging Melons, Cornucopia of Delights, Zs, Poofies. During the occasional rides that weren't just purposeless motion with mother's constant talking attached, but actually had a destination—a trip to buy the sister things clothes at a specialty store for the large and fat and a family dinner at a hotdog drive-in—I learned, while sitting by myself in the last seat of the station wagon and looking out the back, that those in Milford wore white T-shirts and jeans like Dane's, and when shopping, didn't need to decode sissy words. (As a child I'd often wondered if Hanging Melons on the Miracle Mile sold fruit or underwear inside). In Milford, if you were hungry, you ate at Willie's Dogs, Tony's Pizza or the B&B Diner. The cracked and faded stores didn't pretend. People lived on numbered streets, not sectioned off into estates, manors, and villas. If you needed your car fixed, you went to a gas station. Father took his Cadillac convertible to Cloverdale's Import Service Centre where a certified Auto Technician speaking with a heavy, German accent, reluctantly scheduled an appointment. Judging from mother, Cloverdale parents stopped at a Milford toilet one bladder emergency out of five, and only after telling the offending child he should have gone at home and not to touch anything. In Cloverdale's powder rooms, white gloved attendants holding perfumes and sprays made sure the rich had shit that didn't stink. Milford bowled. The low, windowless building with its seven duck pin lanes, never changed; the neon sign outside flickered the same burned out letters year after year. The sports minded in Cloverdale dressed in plaid and rode around in little carts. They sipped wine at the Hollyhill Tavern of the Cloverdale Regency Inn where above the bowered entranceway the carved wooden sign of a chicken in knickers holding a golf club made sure no customer missed the chance of eating quiche beside the inn's putting green. Constantly renovating, the hotel advertised, with a poster in the window, the fall opening of its Jungle Lounge complete with waterfall, a mechanical gorilla, and live parrots. Milford bowlers sat on stools and drank beer.

Only one store in Milford had an un?ambiguous name—The Barn. It was where mother shopped for the sister things.

Cloverdale had exceptions, too. The Taggert and Cavanaugh stores were large, plain buildings with no mysteries inside. Although evil, the mannequins didn't pretend or lie. I actually agreed with mother that Mr. Taggert and Mr. Cavanaugh were nice men.

"Businessmen, but they have time for their families," she constantly reminded father. Competitors, but also friends, they strolled along the street together, smiled at children, and with a tip of the hat, said a cheerful hello to the adults who, during shopping seasons, actually left their houses and cars, and at Miracle Mile stayed outdoors long enough to hurry from one shop to another. Once, the old men even patted me on the head. Active in Cloverdale's small, Presbyterian Church, Mr. Taggert and Mr. Cavanaugh showed their tolerance by displaying in their store windows Hanukkah decorations next to Santa Claus. They participated in town politics and had their opinions printed in *The Beacon.* Best of all, the two store owners lived in Milford.

Shops on Miracle Mile came and went. Taggert and Cavanaugh's remained and are still there now, even bigger, with less competition, their prices always about the same. The old men were very helpful to me.

I crossed the street to a smaller area of stores where two large mothers, cut off from the main herd, and angry at my intrusion into their space, stared down hard at me. Wanting the best, most expensive school clothes and supplies they could find and having only a few weeks to buy them, Cloverdale mothers pushed, pulled, grabbed food on the run and even at secondary stores, bulled over anyone in their way while rushing about full of the Hanukkah and Christmas season meanness mannequins caused in summer. Mother was too smart for that. She shopped at The Barn for the sister things and ordered my clothes out of a catalogue sent from New York.

"He'll end up looking like a bum anyway, but it won't be because of me," she said when the packages of pleated pants with little buckles in the back and rugby-style shirts arrived. "You can't beat New York City for fashion." She had never left Ohio. Until meeting Dane, I wore what mother wanted. I thought it clever the way she shopped for me without leaving her house and avoided not only the August back-to-school frenzy but the December holiday one, too.

"These are yours," she'd say, giving me unwrapped toys while the giggling sister things ripped the blue and white Star of David paper off their presents, mother whispering so they couldn't hear, "you're too old to believe in the Hanukkah Fairy. Santa hates Jewish children. That rock tumbler came from Nebraska."

Outside the Regency, sunlight on parked limousines made me feel cold and more alone until I turned into the alleyway and saw Mr. Petty's drug store. The slightly rotted, squat building, softly veiled by a dirt filled haze, waited for me. I didn't need books or mother's house. My brain was already smart and a nice place to live. But the drug store tilting toward a large hole was my second home. In there, mother hardly buzzed.

I shut the door quickly before anyone else could get inside.

Surrounded by cartons and racks in musty, sweet smelling space, I felt the caring touch of shadows blurred into softness by the airless heat. I smiled on the inside when seeing Mr. Petty behind the counter, staring at his hands. Although a shy man, he liked listening to me.

"Hi, Steve." Tom called out, throwing a brick into the silence. A small, cherry phosphate in hand, he spun on his stool.

"Sorry," I said to Mr. Petty. Without looking at me, he moved stiffly away.

"You don't have to be so loud."

"Was I? I'm just happy to see you." Tom slapped me on the back.

"I didn't know you were going to be here." I sat on my special stool and, touching under the countertop, found the secret scratches and old gum only I knew about.

"Think school will be hard this year?" Tom asked.

"No. It never is."

"Will you help me," his eyes, unlike Dane's, watery and weak.

"Don't I always?"

"You're the best. A real buddy." Tom made dry sucking sounds through his straw. Mr. Petty took the glass away and placed a dish with three scoops of ice cream in front of me.

"Thank you." When I paid him our hands almost touched.

"Five dollars? For that? The ice cream's gray."

"Shhhh. Mr. Petty knows what I like." I bit down on something hard, probably a nut. "Seen Dane around?"

"No, and I'm glad. He's a troublemaker. We should keep away from him."

"Hey, you do a lot of crazy things, too. He's just showing off because he's new here and wants to be our friend." My stomach hurt a little. It always did when I ate Mr. Petty's ice cream.

"I don't like him," Tom said.

"You don't have to."

He flicked a few drops of phosphate at me from the end of his straw then lowered his voice as if someone had died.

"Butterball got left back."

"So?"

"That's the worse thing that can happen."

"No, what's worse is not having a best friend."

"Pardner." Tom gave me a big hug. I pushed him away. He smelled like sweat.

"Come on, Steve, time for our million dollar cigars."

On a bent metal shelf with rusted ones below it, between a large jar of brown pickled eggs and an artificial leg, pretzel rods in a plastic bucket sold two for a nickel. Reaching into his pocket, Tom took out a small ball of string, some shiny stones, half a stick of gum, three nails, a cat's eye marble, and finally, his plastic coin purse. I felt bad for Mr. Petty, a patient man waiting for Tom's money. Faded red, with a scattering of white across its center that I knew were the remains of a name—Penny Savers Bank, but Tom had called a secret code after finding the coin purse in the school yard, he squeezed the middle open and one by one counted out five pennies into Mr. Petty's trembling, twisted hand. Tom handed me the longer, saltier pretzel and held the other one like a cigar. He was rich. A big boss. I knew Tom had a better chance of becoming a pirate than someone important like my father. Still, I played along.

"When I'm grown-up I'm going to buy my mom a mansion, gold necklaces, a mink coat and fancy car." One leg crossed over the other, he leaned against the wall and flicked imaginary ash from the end of his pretzel. He went on, might have mentioned a few other things than he had in the past, the rocket ship factory and the cowboy ranch, added a couple more. The list changed and expanded whenever we played, even the expensive gifts he planned for his mom could transform. The mansion once became a fort in Tahiti, then a large tree house with secret passages and trap doors. The mink coat turned into leopard skin on the same summer afternoon he decided his mom should wear diamonds instead of gold. Often Tom traded the car in for a jet plane or time machine, but he never gave up his boat.

"It'll have masts and sails and with mom and you and me on it, we'll travel all over the world. Discover lost islands. Swim in the ocean. Become pirates."

It was my turn to play.

"I'll burn down Cloverdale elementary and plant trees in the space. Summer will be forever. We'll be free."

"Yeah, and we can pay an amusement park to set up on the

playground," Tom said. "We'll put on red noses and be clowns together."

I scraped my foot along the warped linoleum tiles. Tom closed his eyes and hummed. It had been a good summer—no, a great one. I saw Dane walking toward me.

"You're a Jew, ain't ya?"

Fishmouth stood behind him—Fishmouth, who before Tom moved to The Neighborhood in second grade had run between moving swings on my dare and even this summer filled an hour or two when Tom wasn't around. I'd slept over his house; he had protected me on Halloween. What was he doing now?

Mother buzzed her answer.

"You think the goys are your friends. Let another Hitler come and they'll gas us all."

Jew, Dane had said. Jew different, Jew exposed, a child of white fish and salami who Santa Claus hated. My face burned. I hid it by looking down.

"Don't drag you nose on the ground," Dane said. "It'll grow even more."

"Everyone's got their own religion," Tom said. "I'm a Methodist. So, what?"

"So, Stevie's had his dick cut down to the size of a peanut. That's what Jews do, right kosher boy?"

My face concrete, it pulled me closer to the floor.

"I need a comb."

Glancing up, I saw Dane reach over between stained boxes of Epsom salt and rip a package open. He put the comb in his back pocket.

"You'll have to pay for that," Mr. Petty said.

"Eat shit, old man. Mess with me, and I'll come back and break your windows." He and Fishmouth ran out of the store, Fishmouth turning once to look at me as he pedaled away with Dane riding on the bike's handlebars.

Mr. Petty curled his blue-veined hands into small fists. He knew the number of gumballs and penny candies in the vending machines and had, twenty years earlier, taught his young son a lesson about right and wrong when the boy took a ten cent bag of peanuts from the drug store without paying. Of course the lesson hurt. A father's love always did. I'd heard the story from mother who said Mr. Petty had tried to save his son and make him into a *mensch,* but a parent could only do so much and it wasn't his fault the boy grew up to become a thief the police had to shoot dead. A kind man with high morals, Mr. Petty guarded his candies, poisons, and combs. But I understood why he just stood there, watching Dane get away. Although Mr. Petty would play ball with me if I asked him; was as silent as father but listened to me; let me breathe in his head ointment and leaking Ben Gay, Dane was stronger.

"We should go. Mr. Petty has work to do."

"I hate that Dane," Tom said as we walked toward mother's house.

"Three more days…" I felt the wind hurl summer into twilight, then evaporate it in a sudden burst of night. Ahead, dark and looming, mother-sized houses drowned their lights in invisible yards. I couldn't see Tom's eyes. We stopped at the corner of Cassidy Boulevard and Treemont.

"Why don't you come over," he said.

"Can't. Mother made dinner. You leaving tomorrow?"

"Yeah. It's a long trip."

"Iowa, right? Where your dad's buried."

"Arkansas."

"That's what I meant. Well, have fun. I'll see you in school."

"I won't be LATE." Tom shouted, booming the last word as he crossed the street toward The Neighborhood.

"The old bag hates anyone who's TARDY." I called back also mimicking the 5th grade teacher's man voice.

When I couldn't hear Tom anymore, I ran in circles until they became tired and spun me out in the only direction left, mother's house.

ALAN KESSLER

6

HOPING FOR A MISTAKE and knowing she hadn't made one, I walked with heavy legs to the back door. Locked. I tried all the windows: basement, bedrooms, baths; then the laundry room entrance, and finally, the least likely place of error, the solid oak front doors. They didn't budge even when I kicked them. As I looked in the dining room window it grew a white eye. Even this approximation of life couldn't survive for long. The passing car kept going, the reflection of its headlight on glass ending in darkness that left mother's house again solid and dead. I knew someday I'd make her crystals and locked away rooms pay.

Night blew inside me. I didn't know how long I would have to wait outside. The duration of mother's rides depended on the number of words she wanted to use. At the laundry room, I shoved my hand through the mail slot cut into its door. Look mother, I'm in. My fingers dangled inside the cold emptiness. Pulling out slowly, I scraped my arm back up the metal channel.

Why can't I have a key? I asked her treeless space. The sister things do. Big shiny ones hanging around their fat necks.

Even when she wasn't around, on this subject mother never deviated or took a breath.

"Again with the key. Your sisters have one because they won't let anyone into the house who will break all the beautiful things it took me years to get. Why should I trust you with my property? Someone who doesn't lift a finger around here to help me." She, of the night shades, continued to buzz inside me as I inhaled her sound. Wondering what it would feel like to make a key by cutting notches into bone, I dug the old rusted one I'd found into my finger. No blood. No pain. I smiled imagining how mother's surprise at finding my severed finger sticking out of the laundry room door would turn to horror when she saw me standing inside her house.

I'll make my bone into a permanent key.

Go ahead, she said, I'll just change the lock.

The night air laughed.

I sat on concrete steps and watched the road. Another light, another car…it also kept going. I rubbed my arms and huddled in. With only three days of summer left, the night had answered mother's summons and turned hours of free time into ice.

No, I jumped up determined to keep warm and summer alive by playing. But play what? Tom wasn't there to help me get started. I had a wonderful brain, full of color and sound, but it wasn't good at foolishness. I picked up a stone and making sure I missed, threw it at a window. The explosion blasted me to the ground where, hands across my chest and surrounded by the sweet smell of chemicals, I rested face up on a slab of asphalt.

Closing my eyes, I listened to the whispers blowing in from mother's field of black grass.

"I knew he would get in trouble playing with that Tom and Dane," she said while standing over me. Mother opened her robe. Velvet Jesus smiled from between her white breasts.

Father had been in a car accident. Arms out and headless, he walked in circles.

"Sorry," Tom said, "sorry. If we hadn't broken Molly's pool table she wouldn't have killed you." He put a white rose from his dad's grave in my hand. We rode the Ferris wheel together.

With a yarmulke at a jaunty angle across his forehead and playing the kaddish on the black comb he'd stolen from Mr. Petty, Dane hovered above me in a halo of light. The light intensified into car beams prying my eyes open.

"Hurry up and get inside before we let in mice," mother said, Munchkin, the little fur ball, nestled against her chest. "What are you doing, sleeping in the driveway? What will the neighbors think? Couldn't you have at least waited in the back yard where they wouldn't see you?"

I saw plump sister thing legs and father's tall body squeeze into the house through the barely opened laundry room door. I got up and followed mother. She quickly locked the door behind me.

"I need a key," I said while walking into the large, metal kitchen. "They have one."

"Your sisters know how to behave," mother answered.

"Thank you, mommy," the things' high pitched squeaking slightly muffled by the refrigerator they had stuck their heads inside in order to graze.

"Tom's mom likes me."

"Isn't that interesting?" mother said, her face inches from the newspaper covering father's face. "Everyone's mother is better than his own. He treats her with respect while making a nothing out of me. I'll bet you this Tom of his doesn't talk to his mother the way your son talks to me. That boy has jobs to do. He helps around his house. Know where they live? Next to a field of trash. We have a beautiful home. He's always running after his friends, copying what they do. Why doesn't he also copy how hard they work? Your son never once thinks *I* might need some help around here."

"You have a maid," I said.

The newspaper rustled.

"We love you." the sister things said, their mouths full of spaghetti.

"Listen how he talks to me."

The newspaper fell and father's shadow covered the world. He pushed me down and kicked. His eyes were red. Mother pulled him away. Still eating, the sister things cried.

Upstairs in my room, I lay in bed with the alarm clock close to my face. It all made sense. Father showed his love by hurting me, Dane did the same thing calling me a Jew. Dane vanquished ghosts and mother never buzzed when he was around. My new, best friend was the creator, Tom was only good for a few laughs.

The next morning, the alarm clock's rhythmic ticking left the house when I did and amplified by the thump-thump of cars driving over man-hold covers on Treemont, followed me into The Neighborhood where it hovered behind my head making sure I heard its metallic breathing. I hid in the center of weeds growing below Dane's willow and drew his face on the soft, summer ground. The sound of him snapped back and forth in the drooping branches. He breathed through leaves. Of course, through the smiling, peeling paint on his home, he invited me in, but I didn't want to bother him. The ticking grew softer, the voice of it, mother's, drowned out by imagining Dane running with me across a field of sunlit butterflies. I left when the moonlight became too bright.

The three full days before school became minutes, seconds, until finally, the ticking cadence in every room of the house shook the last sands of summer out.

"Tomorrow's school," mother said while stroking Munchkin. "You can't be late. Go to bed."

I had learned, probably in school, the source of all terrible information, the effects of radiation. With the clock near me, the glowing hands casting green shadows over my face and arms, I still hoped what I had begun in early summer, a prolonged, close exposure to its radiation, would sicken me. Or maybe the alarm will just burn up. But I knew that couldn't happen. The clock was indestructible, a gift from mother, she used to tell me through its penetrating ticks the precise time for the death of summer.

I won't go to sleep.

The alarm woke me in the morning, the sound of it louder and shriller than ever before. I knocked the clock over and tried smothering it with a pillow. The monster fought back, thumping down and across the floor, jangling even after I kicked it against the wall. Its glowing green numbers, like twelve distorted eyes, glared defiantly at me. My feet turned colder on mother's plastic, the only real carpeting in her house. I hurried to the bathroom where the tile was warmer. Light through the window pried my eyes open after I'd fallen asleep brushing my teeth. I plastered my dark curls down with water. On an iron chair, its back in the shape of a heart, the maid had left my neatly folded, first day of school clothes: corduroy pants, a stiff, button down plaid shirt, bright new saddle shoes. The pants rubbed against the inside of my legs when I walked. Using one of the techniques I'd perfected with school books, I banged the shoes into the metal baluster and scuffed them slightly down the sides.

"What's the noise up there." mother yelled from downstairs. "We are quiet people. This is a quiet neighborhood." I knew father liked his silence. No one looked at me when I entered the kitchen.

"Good, French toast," the sister things said, dark syrup running down their cheeks. Afraid of getting too small a portion of the fried potatoes the maid brought to the table, they watched each other suspiciously while guarding with their faces the food already on their plates.

"What can I fix you," Mae asked me. "Pancakes? Eggs?" The sister things chewed with their mouths open. From experience, I knew the difference between their naturally ugly features and the twisted distortions they did on purpose. Syrup dripping from their teeth, they made faces at me. Even cold cereal would burn today.

"I'm not hungry," I said.

"If you don't eat it's your own fault," mother said. "It's not like there's no food in the house. I don't want you going to school and playing the poor boy."

"Wonder what the weight limit is on the bus this year," I said, looking at the twins.

"Mommy, Steve's making fun of us."

"I heard," mother said, talking into the newspaper. Father's eyes floated up.

"I'm leaving." I was almost at the door.

"Did you wash your hands?"

"Yes."

"Clean your eyes, ears, toes?"

"Yes."

"Comb your hair? It doesn't look it."

"Yes." *Yes.* The buzzing hurt so much…

"Lift those pants. I can't see your new shoes. God in heaven. What happened to them?"

"Nothing."

"No matter how hard I try, you're still going to school like a bum."

Compressed by mother's voice hammering down and my legs pushing up, trying to run, my stomach became a hard ball of pain. I kept turning the door handle.

"I'm going to be late."

"Then go already, but remember this. If I'm not home after

school, I don't want you waiting outside in the front yard like a feeble-minded. Listen to the teacher for once in your life. Make a few Jewish friends. Don't forget—"

She tried to rush another instruction at me, but I escaped and out the door, shot through clouds of breath swirling up into the morning chill. Free. Although not as bright as they had been a day earlier, the leaves still glimmered with enough summer dew to hurry me on. Shafts of sunlight supporting the blue sky reminded me of the sharp, jagged lines I painted in art class controlled by old women worried about what I drew. I jumped and laughed. My head was a book. Playing games with teachers by doing only what I had to to kept them from filling my report card with As. I didn't need someone else telling me I was smart. Then I saw the car and stopped. Still looking back at me, the school-bound children strapped inside widened their terrified eyes. Mother had almost tricked me into rushing toward the morning bell. I walked slowly, dragging each foot. I still had a half-mile left. I had outsmarted her, too.

Tom waited at the corner.

"I was beginning to think you'd left me. Come on, we don't want to be LATE." He swung around the lamp post and gave me a good-natured push. "Race ya."

Like hell. But I did. Summer could end…I'd let it die. Dane was the only constant. The faster I ran, the sooner I'd see him. We shot across streets toward Cloverdale Elementary. I almost won.

The building stared at me with black, icy windows draped in a welcome back to school banner printed with Frankensteinlooking letters. Flesh eating vines growing up the walls slowly drained the light out of a piece of the sun trapped among the thorns. Small, shadowy bodies with arms outstretched, rose from the pitted ground.

"They must have painted this place over the summer," Tom said. "Looks pretty good."

I followed him up the steps and into a hallway lined on both sides with rows of gray narrow lockers. In front of an open one, I stepped over torn notebooks and a leaking pen while Tom, almost reverently, avoided disturbing an oversized turquoise jacket lying on the floor with one arm twisted through the handle of a Bozo the Clown metal lunchbox. I was impressed. Lockers were never overstuffed and unable to close on the first day of school.

"Butterball," Tom said softly. I glanced back at the stairwell. Butterball was downstairs, next to the furnace in a room for slow learners.

In Miss Sheridan's class, Dane and Fishmouth sat by themselves in the last row. The ceiling's fluorescent light concentrated its glare on the only desks left, both in front of the room. Tom sat in one. I didn't have a choice, I took the other.

Miss Sheridan wrote her name on the blackboard. Even her chalk sounded loud.

"Together again," Tom whispered.

"Yeah, isn't it great." I wanted to turn and smile at Dane.

"No talking." Miss Sheridan stared right at me. "If any of you have something to say, raise your hand. I hate noise."

She snapped the piece of chalk in two. A large woman with a small head, she could move quickly. In a few strides she crossed the room and slammed the heavy metal door shut. Henry, the Booger Man, jumped in his seat. Peter Shapiro couldn't stop shaking. Even goody-two-shoes Molly looked a little sick. 7:15. Five minutes of free time left and Miss Sheridan had stolen it from the sun.

"Jeeez," Tom said under his breath.

Screw her, I thought and slumped down, my legs slightly out. I couldn't see Dane but I was sure I was sitting just like him, defiant and tough.

"Steve. Straighten up." Miss Sheridan ordered while walking over to Molly's desk. I figured Dane had already seen me act cool, so I did what she wanted, slowly, on my terms, I'm sure of that....

"Everyone is to put their name on my seating chart," Miss Sheridan said and handed a paper to Molly who immediately began writing. "Each morning, when you come to class, sit in the same place. Have your pencil ready and your work book out. All other books go neatly under your desk. Don't talk."

I barely heard the school bell ring.

"School is your job. You are here to work. I expect competence, and I don't tolerate troublemakers. I'm very good at weeding out those who don't belong in my class. Either you learn or you leave, it's that simple. Any questions? I didn't think so. Just one more thing. Don't be LATE."

The windows shook. I saw Tom wipe his palm on his pant leg.

Two uniform stacks of new books and one lumpy pile of used ones waited on Miss Sheridan's desk for our selection. It happened every year. Different teacher, same process, same rules. Called up alphabetically on the first day of school, we'd choose our books. Girls and those boys living in the good part of town took new ones; boys from The Neighborhood picked from the old. I was the only exception. I hated books. Inside them were other people's ideas of what the world meant. Except when mother's buzzing made it hard for me to think, I could figure out things for myself. Battered books served my plan. By starting with ones no one wanted and destroying them slowly during the school year, when I turned them in, the teachers never complained about the mangled covers and torn pages that looked caused by normal wear and tear. No one knew I'd thrown the books in mud puddles, snow banks, pits, gutters, sewers, and holes. I went to school and chose what rules to follow. Mother, trapped by Cloverdale society, assumed without anticipation or pride but as the natural order of things that I'd end up in college and hoped I would never do anything to embarrass her. Although having no need for friends, mother cared what people thought about her; she knew social rules were a sacred part of the religion of Cloverdale with shame being the terrifying punishment for those who sinned against the village code. Cloverdale women expected their sons to attend a university, preferably Ivy League, graduate as professionals, marry well and have polite, intelligent children who would keep out of the way when grandma visited. Mother wasn't a country club person. She had her house. But we were members of Cloverdale's Excelsior Club and sometimes we went there. While sitting by myself, I'd hear the Cabana women reinforce through nuggets of tasty gossip the rules of the social order while playing mahjong and eating finger sandwiches.

"The Shapiro boy. Did you hear? Dropped out of college and joined the Navy."

"I'm sure you know the Keatings. They live on Heritage— nice house, no pool. She wears all that flashy costume jewelry, the husband sells cars. Well, I was having lunch with Francis the other day, and she told me that Mrs. Keating just found out her oldest son is a homosexual. Can you imagine that? In a family that makes such a show of going to church every Sunday. She's putting him in counseling—a little too late, if you want my opinion."

I had my own ideas. I might go to college, but I would do it on my terms. Each year I not only chose used books but the worst ones. Most old books had legible pages but a rare few didn't. Those were the ones I liked best. If I carefully looked over the assortment and was lucky, I'd sometimes find books with whole paragraphs missing or covered in stains. Relying on the work of master saboteurs who had used these texts before me meant I could spend hours reconstructing a lesson instead of studying it. It was great fun fooling mother while at the same time keeping other brains from stabbing their thoughts into my own.

Molly smiled at Miss Sheridan and carried an armful of shiny books back to her desk.

"Dane Beneby," Miss Sheridan intoned while scanning

down her list.

At the back of the room, a chair scraped along the floor. Black, pointed shoes with metal tips clicked forward. Attached to the belt loop of battered old jeans, half a broken chain swung back and forth, almost touching my leg. Its sleeves rolled up tight, the pure white T-shirt passed in front of me. I saw proud eyes—*Dane* swaggered to the book desk.

"I'll take this, teach," he said flipping a coverless English book open. "And I like this one, too." He held the second book out by its covers. Without a spine, the insides sagged low in the middle.

"You're new to Cloverdale, aren't you, Dane?" Miss Sheridan asked, her voice so quiet it made me shiver.

"Yeah, that's right."

"Your family moved here from Virginia and rented a house. You have one sister. Your mother works part-time and your father's on disability. You stayed back in first grade."

The Booger Man snickered. I hated him for changing Dane's face.

"How do—"

"I know all this? I have files, Dane, on the students in my class. I study the information, then plan how best to use it. That way I can give each child exactly what he or she deserves." Miss Sheridan reached under the pile of old books. What she pulled out made me jealous. I tore and dunked my books; she held in her hand the work of someone who understood, in its purest form, the art of destruction. Rusted thumbtacks and nails formed spirals in the center of thin cardboard covers. Their edges purple and blood red, sections of the dried out pages crumbled off. Partially covering them with brown smears, the artist had even tried to erase the titles.

"These are yours." Miss Sheridan handed them to Dane. "There's no need to return them. This is my way of saying welcome to Cloverdale."

She let the class laugh. Dane didn't care. He'd lost something and looking down for it, walked back to his seat. Henry kept snickering. Assholes. I hated all of them. But I wasn't perfect either. I'd been disloyal, too, by wishing Dane's books were mine. It wasn't the last time I betrayed him…

"Nice having you in my class this year, Steve," Miss Sheridan said when it was my turn at the book table. "I'm sure you'll do well and won't be a bit of trouble." Her small, black eyes became even darker. All the used books looked great to me. A warped spelling book had a particularly interesting paint splash across the front. Miss Sheridan tapped her pencil. Her eyes wouldn't let me go.

I piled my new books high.

"Back to your desk now, like a good boy," Miss Sheridan said.

Sitting hunched over didn't help. I still felt Dane staring at my back. I hoped he would forgive me. Tom took all his old books and with each one making a smooth, sliding noise, carefully slipped them into covers I could have used to shield my eyes, desk, and the rest of the room from my new books' bright, radiating glare. I put my hands over them and nodding whenever Miss Sheridan looked at me, pretended to listen.

When I could, I glanced at the clock and willed its creeping minute hand toward recess. Finally, the bell rang. I was out of there—

She kept talking.

"No one moves until I tell you. You exit in an orderly manner and return the same way. Recess isn't an excuse to start acting like wild Indians. Now, I want the front row to line up. Good. Row two." Only when everyone was in place did she open the door. "Forward, march."

I walked looking at my legs, trying to hold them back. They wanted to run. Doors, walls, water fountain, hall flag, Butterball's locker. Finally, the outside. I bolted into the bright, sunlit haze full of the high-pitched screams and laughter of children suddenly set free. After cutting between two first graders taking turns trying to shoot a basketball into a net-less hoop, their two-handed shots barely getting the ball above their heads, I jumped over a faded four-square and, reaching the wide, playground grass, stretched my arms out to the side. Open space surrounded me. I brought it inside my head. Spinning, breathing in the blue sky, I flew turning circles into wind. Tom joined me.

"We're airplanes." he said.

"See Dane anywhere?" I asked. He chased me, I chased him. When I finally gave up, Tom somersaulted to a stop and flopped on the ground.

"Wonder how much time we have left?"

"All of it." I answered. Around me, the voice of play echoed unafraid of bells. Face to the sun, I let its heat close my eyes.

"Do you believe Miss Sheridan?" Tom got up and making an airplane sound, buzzed my head.

"Don't," I said.

"You were asking about him. There he is with Fishmouth. Dane's going to get it if he keeps messing with her."

"She's the one who'd better worry." I ran off, the grass becoming a kickball field too far from the school for anyone to use. Beyond the soft, yellow sway of dandelions in the infield, I jumped over the ruptured sand bag of third base and found Dane sitting beside Fishmouth on an old log.

"Nice books, Stevie," Dane said. "Afraid of the teacher?"

"He wants to learn, nothing wrong with that," Tom said. He'd tagged along.

"He doesn't want to get in trouble. Look at those shoes. Stevie's a mommy's boy."

"That's me, all right." I loved Dane's jokes.

"Who laughed at me?"

"That kid over there in the sweatshirt," I pointed toward the jungle gym. "His name is Henry. We call him the Booger Man."

"Thanks, Stevie. I like a snitch. Here, help me up."

He liked me. I touched his hand. Dane pulled me over the log. Tom pushed him, Dane pushed back, Fishmouth joined in.

"Let's play King of the Hill." Dane said, standing on the log.

"Not me," Tom said.

"Afraid?"

"I'm not." I jumped up beside him.

"Little Stevie thinks he can knock me off."

I was about to say something but didn't have the chance. Dane tripped me and I fell, hitting my head hard on the ground. The silence inside me filling with bright colors, sang. I couldn't even remember what mother's buzzing had felt like. Above on the log, in indistinct shadows, his arms swinging, Fishmouth charged and went spinning off as Dane shifted slightly to the side. Tom helped me up.

"Want to hear my plan?" Dane asked.

"No," Tom answered.

"I do," I said, the air and voices again so clear. Tom walked away.

"Guess it's just gonna be you and Fishmouth at the first meeting of the Bowie Knife Club. You want to join, right Stevie? Come over to my house after school?"

"You bet."

Last year, I helped Tom deliver his papers. Now I was in a club and had something much better to do. I couldn't wait. Making it even more exciting, Dane patted me on the head.

With Miss Sheridan watching, when the bell rang ending recess, we lined up outside the school and marched in like little soldiers. Tom glanced over at me and half-smiled. What did he want? Couldn't he see I was enjoying looking at the back of Dane's shiny, black hair?

Because I knew what every child did: time slows down as the school day approaches dismissal, it didn't surprise me when the afternoon dragged on under the weight of Miss Sheridan's lesson about George Washington. Why should I care about him? He was dead and couldn't do anything for me. The information was just noise—noise that grew arms and reaching out from inside Miss Sheridan's mouth, hung on to the minute hand of the white-faced clock preventing it from moving to 3:15. I had never seen this before. Although the minute hand finally managed to drop to the bottom of the 3's black belly, its shift downward was the result of gravity unconnected to time, this proven again when I watched the red second hand begin another leisurely drift toward 12 and still no bell.

Mother's doing this to me. I'll be trapped in here forever. Please, Dane, help me...

He must have heard. The bell rang—a small, distant sound reminding me of the ping of car locks mother reluctantly opened after one of our family rides to nowhere; a release only the finest ears could hear. I shot up, ready to go.

"Sit down." (Maybe I did), Miss Sheridan scanned the room, her hard, lifeless eyes withering back into their seats all those foolish enough to have made the slightest twitch upward. "I want you to leave school like ladies and gentlemen. On my count now, 1-2-3, everyone stand. Form your lines."

Unlike at recess, our feet stomping urgency, barely under control, would have trampled Miss Sheridan if she hadn't kept staring at us. Even so, I noticed how cleverly she had moved a few inches to the side of the classroom door.

"Don't lose your books." she ordered. "Study. Get your homework done. Hold it. I didn't say you could go."

We swayed in front of her. Arms folded, Miss Sheridan

tapped her foot, waited, and grimacing trying to hold it in, finally gave up and squeezed out "dismissed" through pressed lips.

"No running in the hall." she called after us, her mouth enlarging. "Bright and early tomorrow. DON'T BE TARDY." Her loud, pounding voice made my head feel like it had been slammed between two jagged rocks. I didn't care. I was almost free. As the line picked up speed and blew apart, I rushed ahead of everyone and once through the door, shouted "Yes" while jumping in the air.

"We made it. School's over." Tom spread his arms to the sun and laughed.

"And there's still summer left."

"Time to get the papers, pardner."

Last year, when delivering his route, we played Big League Pitcher by seeing who could throw a newspaper closest to the customer's door. I had gotten pretty good and knew after our summer off I'd come back with a side arm toss even better than Tom's. Now that wasn't going to happen. I didn't have time for children's games. I had joined the Bowie Knife Club. But where was Dane?

"I've cut the number of houses way down," Tom said. "You're coming with me, right?"

"Guess so." I saw a puddle my arithmetic book might enjoy but before I could drop it in, Dane ran up from behind and smacked me in the head. He felt just like father.

"If you don't stop picking on Steve, I'm going to bust you in the mouth," Tom said, his face red. He looked like a clown.

"Gee, I'm scared," Dane said. "Let me get this straight—you want to fight me over him?"

"I don't want to do anything with you," Tom answered. "Steve and me are leaving."

"He's coming with me, isn't that right, Stevie?"

"I already made plans," I told Tom. Dane put his arm on my shoulder. Sprinting toward us with long strides, Fishmouth slipped on the grass, got up and continued on as if nothing had happened.

"You should have seen it." he said when next to us, his face sweating and eyes wide. On his toes, bouncing and punching, Fishmouth twitched out more energy than usual. "Pow. Smack. He was walking, not even noticing us and Dane hit him right in the stomach."

"Who?" Tom asked.

"The Booger Man."

"He shouldn't have laughed at me," Dane said. "No one gets away with that."

"All that fast action," then suddenly, Fishmouth seemed calmer, as if trying to think. "The light and sound meant something. The hitting was more than hitting. It had a reason. I wanted to be part of it. To do something important..." His voice, so low it seemed as if he were talking to himself, trailed off. It wasn't Halloween but, once again, I felt safe because of Fishmouth. He could never take my place. Dane didn't want a crazy best friend.

"Think I need help beating up a Jew?" Dane punched Fishmouth hard in the arm. "okay, over to my house. I know you can't come, Tom. I've made you second in command anyways."

"Of what?"

"The Bowie Knife club."

"No, thanks." Tom left to get his papers. Dane and Fishmouth played tag crossing Treemont, and I was right behind them, running down Cassidy, Dane never out of my sight.

The snake waited, curled up on the top back step of Dane's home.

"Didn't think you'd be here," Dane said to it. And the snake spoke:

"You not thinking? Why that's a real surprise."

I looked up from the cobra tattoo on the man's arm. The snake drew me back. One of its eyes glared red, the other, a large mole, bulged hairy and black. Jaws open, three drops of milky white poison dripped from its shiny fangs. An erect hood of fire blazed above purple scales coiling the body down into a blade shaped tail of blood. Half-dressed, a girl with long blond hair rode the snake's back toward her destination, Hell, the faded blue letters of the word covering a jagged scar. I always remembered that tattoo and used a snake as the logo for my investment company. I kept the fangs and venom while getting rid of the girl and the silly idea of damnation.

"I should charge you admission," Dane's father said.

"I'm sorry—"

"No need to apologize, Curly, I take it as a compliment. So, boys, how are you doing?"

"We're leaving," Dane said.

"When I say you are," Mr. Beneby's snake arm shot out and grabbed one of Dane's books.

"Judging from the condition of this, the teacher doesn't think much of you, does she son?" Squinting, he read the cover page. "Arithmetic. That's useful for figuring out how much money a person's cheated you out of but that other piece of shit you're carrying is probably as worthless as it looks. Learning doesn't come from a book written by some hoity-toity professor who's never worked a day in his life with his hands and wouldn't know how to piss out a fire. Words aren't bricks. Paper doesn't build houses. All it's good for is to wipe your ass. What happened today, Dane? Did going to that fancy school make you think you can look down your nose at me? If I had my way, we'd all be back home where we belong, and you'd be pulling your weight and thanking me for teaching you what life's really about. But I wasn't raised to be wasteful. You can't turn away from a relative who's offering cheap rent."

"Yeah, especially when we don't have any other place to go," Dane said, letting me, but not Fishmouth, hear him. "Give me back my book."

"Sure," Mr. Beneby said, holding the old cardboard out. "Take it."

"They'll get on you again if I go to school hurt."

"Yep, that's how I spend my days, Dane, worrying about little scrawny necked teachers."

"I was talking about the cops."

"Think I really give a shit." Mr. Beneby had a round,

handsome face but it shriveled in like a rotted tomato, and he threw the book to Dane. He was smart. He knew books were crap. I felt the love flowing between him and Dane. I loved the snake.

"Can't get enough of it, can you, Curly?" Mr. Beneby rhythmically moved the cobra and girl up and down.

"No, sir," I said.

"I like you. You're polite. Dane could learn a lot from you. What's your name?"

"Steve."

"Jones? Smith?"

"Goldblatt," Fishmouth said, the word dumped into the clear, after school air of Dane's backyard where his father had sat relaxing until jarred by the sound of this word, more internal organ than name, landing with a splat in front of him.

"Goddamnit." Mr. Beneby slapped his knee. "I was wrong about you, Dane. You are better than me. I never had a Hebrew for a friend. Don't get me wrong, Curly. I've got nothing against Jews, there just weren't any of your kind where I come from. Why, many a night I'd lay in bed, praying Dane would someday have a nice Jewish friend and now, sure as hell, he does. Who would have thought it? Bet you're real good in school." Friendly and smiling, he leaned toward me, the few teeth he had straight and not very dark.

"Is your daddy rich?"

"They have a really big house," Fishmouth said.

"Shut up," Dane not wanting his dad to feel bad.

"I'd like to see that." Mr. Beneby said. "Maybe the

Goldblatts will invite us over for dinner. Wouldn't that be nice, Dane? See how the other half lives. What's your daddy do, Curly? Dentist? Lawyer?"

"He owns a factory."

"You don't say? Must have lots of people working for him. I've had some health problems but if the right opportunity came along I'd be willing to clock in again. Help some factory owner get rich. How would that be Dane, me working for your little friend's old man?"

Dane didn't say anything. Mr. Beneby kept looking at me.

"What does the factory make?"

The snake wouldn't let me lie.

"Underwear," I said quietly.

"Underwear? Panties and bras? My, isn't that interesting. A real essential industry if you ask me. Do you want to be like your daddy when you grow up?"

"No, sir. I want to be just like you."

The cracked veins in Mr. Beneby's slightly off-center nose turned purple and his eyes sucked back into the tomato face. He wobbled standing up, sending an empty beer can clinking down the steps.

"Be careful what you say to me, boy. I ain't no one to fool with." Mr. Beneby staggered toward me, whirled on Dane when near him. "I'm not forgetting you. I'm sick of your back talk. I want you inside the house, now."

Looking deep into each other's eyes, their faces close together, I could tell by the unafraid way Dane passed his dad that they were a father and son who played catch together and when shopping for ham and beer, walked side-by-side down the supermarket aisle. My father loved me, too, but I preferred Mr. Beneby's way of showing affection. He hadn't kicked Dane in the stomach. Even as a child, I knew closeness was better if it didn't involve too much touching.

With Fishmouth, I scooted past Mr. Beneby, the snake's wonderful, hairy eye winking only at me. In the kitchen, Dane pushed me against the sink, rattling the empty beer cans stacked inside.

"Make fun of my old man again and I'll kill you."

Of course. I'd deserve it. In the hallway, the black velvet Jesus welcomed me back.

For the first order of business of the Bowie Knife Club, Dane, sitting on his bed, taught us how to make the knives. He wrapped a small piece of masking tape around the bottom of a straight pin he took out of a box marked Cloverdale El.

"Simple, right? And when that bitch Sheridan isn't looking, you throw a Bowie Knife at her fat ass. If you get caught, Goldblatt, the club, the knives, everything was your idea. You stole the tape and pins."

"Sure, Dane," I said.

"This is really neat." Fishmouth said, his leg shaking.

"Get to work." Dane took one of my school books and began reading. I built up my pile of Bowie knives and kept it bigger than Fishmouth's. In the smooth, cool quiet without mother, the only sound Dane slowly turning pages, I watched twilight through the dusty window form a halo around his head. Too soon, the room went dark. At his desk made of an old board balanced over packing crates, he switched on a small metal lamp.

"I'm the president of the Bowie Knife Club. Everyone has to do what I say. Here's my homework, Stevie. Finish it."

I didn't get the chance. I heard singing.

"We shall gather at the river, the beautiful, beautiful ri-i-ver—." Outlined by the hallway light behind her, the thin shadow with electrified hair, shuffled forward, arms outstretched. But I knew this wasn't a ghost or my grandmother rising, all skin and bone, from the grave. Dane had tamed the spirit world. This was something else.

"Maw," he said softly.

"In the flesh." She fell against Fishmouth. "Sorry, honey— my, aren't you a cutie." Her arms hanging over his shoulders and legs angled backward, Mrs. Beneby placed the bible in her hand on his forehead and straightened up by pushing on the cover. She zig-zagged over to Dane.

"Home so soon," he said.

"Couldn't find your sister."

"She's at a friend's house."

"Forgiveness, Dane, that's Christ's mercy." Mrs. Beneby patted his cheek. "Actually, son, I stayed at the Revival longer than I expected. I was going to leave right after the healings—I do like watching the crippled walk—but suddenly, the air crackled with a cascade of amens and hallelujahs, the hymns thundered, and I heard shouts of praise. At that moment, I felt the Holy Spirit's energy wrap me in its radiance and lift me from my chair. In front of all those people, young and old, white and colored, I gave witness to the Lord. 'I hear you Jesus. I surely do. This poor sinner of a woman, once even worse, has been snatched, through Your grace, from the very portals of Hell. Take me, Lord. I'm ready to receive your Glory.' So, there I was, standing and shouting with everyone else, and just like that, another charge shot through me as if I'd just put my finger in a wall socket. I had been touched by the very hand of God Himself. Slain in the spirit, I fell down in a heap, stayed there afraid this time I'd gone too far in my praise and asking for salvation, the Almighty listening and taking me before my time. Of course, I want to go to heaven, just like anyone else, but it doesn't make a bit of sense rushing matters. So, I was afraid, but when looking up I saw all those shiny faces of the saved smiling down at me and heard their sweet voices call me sister. It was so peaceful…so beautiful…you'd have thought with all that love in the room someone would have helped me up. I grabbed a leg and bit it. There's no better way of getting attention than having a preacher holler."

She flopped on the mattress.

"Yep, Dane, next time we're all going. You're wrong about your daddy. He won't hurt her. He's been redeemed and forgiven. Remember the Revival we went to last summer in Cincinnati? Nothing brings a family closer, improves it more, than stomping around together in a tent full of sinners."

"You're already too saved for me, maw," Dane said, his face in shadow.

"Anyone seen my medicine?" Mrs. Beneby went to the window and stuck her head out. "Jessie. Did you hide my medicine bottle?"

"Never saw it." Mr. Beneby yelled back from outside. "Goddamnit, Bea, there's no need to scream at me."

"This better?" She shouted even louder. "I just reminded Dane you were born again and what does he hear? Your blasphemy. Maybe hell is the best place for you." Mrs. Beneby popped back into the room and looked Dane in the eyes. "You can't give up on a person." She grabbed Fishmouth by the arm. "So, pretty boy, do you go to church?"

"Sometimes," he answered.

"Sometimes is no time." Mrs. Beneby thumped a bony palm against her bible. "Satan works overtime to steal your soul. You've got to fight him with every breath. Find out where he hides. Learn all his tricks. That's why you need to surround yourself with Christian folks. Will you do that? From today on? Forever?"

"Sure," Fishmouth answered.

"Good boy, good child," she gently put her hand on his head. "Blessed are the children."

Mrs. Beneby turned slowly toward me.

"And what about you?"

"He's a Jew," Dane said.

"You don't say. Hold him."

Dane pinned my arms. I didn't want to escape. Mrs. Beneby left and came back with a dusty wine bottle.

"Found it," she pulled the cork out with her teeth. "Kneel, child." Dane and Fishmouth completed the circle.

"Do you believe in Jesus?" Mrs. Beneby held the bottle over

my head.

Did I believe in Jesus? I knew where he lived; his black velvet face hung protectively in the hallway just outside Dane's door. Unafraid of Mr. Riley's ghost, Dane was the conqueror of Halloween. Except for the outer darkness inside mother's house where her buzzing never stopped and the occasional flare of her words when he wasn't around, Dane had managed to kill her voice inside me. I needed only him. But he needed someone, too. His God. Through Jesus I could get even closer to my best friend and the true meaning of the love he gave me in Mr. Petty's drug store when calling me a Jew. Dane had wanted me to become someone new. Now I would.

Did I believe in Jesus? Of course.

"I want to be reborn," I said. Mrs. Beneby's bloodshot eyes, large and shiny, beamed at me from a face so radiant I felt held in its warmth.

"You want to take on His pain. Become Christ-like and rise on the third day. Dear sweet Jesus. Thank you for letting me live to see this miracle of faith. Now I know why I was saved—to lead this poor, unredeemed Jewish child to your love and grace."

She poured the wine over me.

"Do you accept Jesus as your personal savior?"

I nodded, keeping my mouth closed. The wine burned my eyes. Mrs. Beneby took a drink from the bottle and continued.

"Do you renounce Satan and all false gods?"

"Yes," I answered quickly then held my breath so I wouldn't drown.

"Today we have witnessed a rebirth. A soul born again and lifted into the body of Christ." Her voice rising, the sound of it filled me with love for Dane. "When we're born we receive a name. What did they call you before, child?"

"Steve Goldlbatt," I answered.

"And-he-shall-be-no-more. The glory is upon you. You have emerged from the waters of baptism a new person with a new name—Christopher Barnabas Lee." She shook the last of the wine out. My wet hair no longer curled.

"Smells bad," Fishmouth said.

Mrs. Beneby tasted her fingers.

"I hadn't noticed. Guess it's gone sour." She hugged me into her small breasts and left. Dane told me to go home.

I hosed myself off at the boarding house. Mother didn't believe I'd fallen in a puddle and when mother didn't believe something, father loved me even more.

7

MISS SHERIDAN YANKED ME up by the ear, then grabbed Fishmouth.

"Still laughing." She pulled us to the door. Most faces blurred. The ones that didn't zoomed out at me extra clear: Molly smirked; Henry nervously ate more boogers; Tom had become all eyes. I heard Fishmouth breathe and couldn't stop laughing. Pounding forward, Miss Sheridan dragged us toward the principal's office.

Too warm and quiet, the hallway slid us into a netherworld of neither class nor recess, but a strange combination of both that I decided the beginning of summer would feel like if I knew I was about to die. Head down, afraid, my execution only a few steps away, I squeezed my sides and giggled.

Miss Jane, the principal's secretary, rested her long white fingers on the typewriter and looked up, her colorless face a death mask.

"I need to see her," Miss Sheridan said.

The secretary pressed a button.

"Miss Balsy, Miss Sheridan is here with two boys," to eat, I'm sure she added.

"Send them in," the crackling, echoing voice in the box answered. Miss Jane tapped a red fingernail on her white bread sandwich and leaned over to smell the flower in her vase. Each morning the principal gave her a pink rose. I was hopeful. Maybe Miss Balsy had a heart—Miss Sheridan pulled me past the desk. Fishmouth had stopped twitching. I knew I didn't have a chance.

Were there really claw marks on the principal's door, the embedded, fingernail scratches of those who, in a final, desperate effort to escape destruction, had clung to the wooden doorframe before being sucked into darkness? I knew one thing. In Miss Balsy's inner sanctum, a room of deep shadows, Miss Sheridan and Fishmouth had just vanished, and I stood alone. Five small green eyes stared at me—lights on the PA; the beast, hungry for the taste of the principal's breath, waited for her to tickle its switches and valves while announcing through its long winding mouth an important message: Attention. Attention Cloverdale Elementary. Today, I hanged two children for laughing in class. Their bodies will be on view in the cafeteria at lunchtime.

Miss Balsy stepped in front of me. She carried a noose.

"I'm surprised, Steven. I've never had trouble with you before." She swung the phone back and forth by its cord.

"Someone threw a pin at me," Miss Sheridan said. I was still amazed she had actually felt it through the protective layers of her fat ass.

"Do you know who?

"I know these two were laughing."

Miss Balsy looked at me, all shadows gone.

"I'm afraid, Steve, I'll have to call your parents."

"Fishmouth did it," I said.

"You mean Clarence?"

"Yes, Miss Balsy." When I heard Fishmouth jerk, I bit my lip to keep from laughing in her face.

"That's what I thought." Miss Balsy began dialing. "Your mother is usually home, isn't she?"

"But I told you—"

"You shouldn't have laughed—Hello? Mrs. Goldblatt?"

I slumped into a chair. She didn't know how loving father's red eyes could get.

They put us in a small room. Fishmouth sat in one corner, I faced the wall. No talking. No moving. We were supposed to do our school work.

"Hello over there," Fishmouth's said, his voice low and gurgling. "You got me in trouble."

It was the funniest thing I had ever heard.

"Stop." I cried and laughed at the same time. My sides hurt. It was a goofy, carefree fun, not requiring any thought or planning. I almost forgot Dane.

"Listen to this," Fishmouth put his hand under his armpit and made a farting noise. Wanting a funnier, more realistic sound, he cut a big one just as the principal walked in.

"Clarence," I said, pointing at him. Miss Balsy held her nose and again picked up the phone.

After school, released energy slammed lockers and doors while filling the hallways with happy, shouting voices. Peter. Henry. Lar-reee. Did you see him? Did you see her? What a catch at recess. What a day. Come over to my house and we'll play. I still feel, even now, on the outside of these sounds… maybe, that day, I imagined some of them and heard what I expected. There would have been joy as friends with busting-out-of-school legs moved quickly away from classrooms, the escape more fun because the tortures had been shared. I know what I did. I walked slowly down the hall.

Fishmouth wiggled his tongue, snorted, jumped toward me arms outstretched like Superman, but he couldn't make what Miss Balsy had said sound funny.

"Report to the office again tomorrow. I'll decide when you can go back to class."

"It stopped raining." Fishmouth kicked the school door open. The free time light smothered me. I felt better seeing Dane.

"Takes real brains to get caught laughing like a fool," he said.

"He laughed himself sick." Fishmouth said, his legs above his head as he began inching his feet up the basketball pole. "I thought Steve would barf right on Miss Sheridan's desk."

"He should have. You won't need these anymore," Dane took my books. "Come on, Fishmouth." They chased Molly Adams. It looked like fun. I crossed Treemont and found Tom, delivering his newspapers.

"Can I pitch?" I asked.

"Sure, pardner. It hasn't been the same without you."

I stayed with him as long as I could, but the bees, even when sleeping, never forgot me.

In the almost perfect silence of my slow footstep-by-footstep movement toward her house, I enjoyed the empty streets inked by darkness into a blur until I heard the incandescent crackling above the laundry room door call me when I was still three blocks away. Steve, it buzzed, Steve...I hoped mother had left the light on and was riding with father and the sister things, everyone locked up in the car.

Under a blaze of lights at the laundry room, mother welcomed me home.

"I get calls," she began even before I stepped inside. Following right behind me, she kept talking. "Calls from the teachers. 'I hate to bother you, Mrs. Goldblatt'—of course they do. They know I'm a quiet person who never gave anyone an ounce of trouble. Truth is, they feel sorry for me. They are smart, educated people. They see how hard I've tried with you, how I did my best and still ended up raising a no-good. 'I'm sorry, Mrs. Goldblatt, but your son laughs in class and makes stinks.' Laughs. Stinks up the school. Who would believe someone coming from a home like this would do such a thing."

Circling and waving her arms, mother talked to the walls and ceiling.

"Didn't I diaper him as a baby? Buy him the best clothes. This is too much for one person to take. The shame of it. I could die."

"No, mommy," the sister things said and each hugging a mommy leg, pressed their cream puff smeared mouths against her skirt. Hunched up on his rug, Munchkin growled and tried biting me. I hooked a thumb in my belt and leaned against the kitchen sink.

The buzzing isn't so bad, even in here. Dane is with me... Some cereal would be nice...

"It's the poor goyim he plays with. That's the problem. You associate with trash, you become trash." Mother turned, looked one way, then another while sharing her theories with the stove, refrigerator and chairs. "You have to have sense in life. Use your brain. Do what's right. Even as a little girl, I knew most people are two-faced. They say one thing and do another, go when they tell you they'll stay. Nice words don't mean a thing. I never threw my family over for strangers. My mother always came first."

"We love you," the sister things said, the cream around their mouths making them look like they had an extra pair of lips.

"I'm talking about him." Mother shook her hand at me. "He's like his father. No loyalty. Let Mr. Executive handle the problem. It's time he did something more around here than just open his wallet. He has a son who's headed for no good. I'm tired of being a single parent. This brother of yours needs a father who doesn't run out on his responsibilities. I called the Big Shot's office an hour ago. He was too busy to pick up the phone. I had to leave a message with one of his *shiksa* secretaries. You bet if I were some woman he just met he'd have found time for me. It's more than an hour now and he's still not home."

The dog clock with its tick, tick, moving tail and rolling eyes, watched me. I knew I was safe. It was only seven. Even when the sister things had gobbled down a box of chocolate flavored laxatives and groaned into the phone mother held for them, father didn't leave work until his usual time at eight. I had at least another hour and a half. I might even be asleep by then and father would have to love me in the morning.

Mother stopped pacing in front of the stove and the sister things quickly stuffed the last of their cream puffs into their mouths. We had heard the front door open and close. The clock's red, dog eyes spun wildly as father walked into the kitchen. The cold of his overcoat smelled good.

"Finally. Here he is. Mr. Businessman with his fancy suit and tie." Mother stretched up toward him by standing on her toes. "Your money won't buy you out of this one. They don't want him back in school. Who can blame them? He's being raised like a wild Indian. Not by me, of course. They know he has only one parent. Dollar bills don't make a husband or father. If truth were told—"

Father never enjoyed learning too much about himself. He kicked me. Dug his fingernails into my arm. Threw me down and twisted my leg. Mother pulled him off. The sister things cried. In the end, nothing unusual had happened.

Father loved me.

Dane loved me.

In my bedroom, I felt warm and protected.

After a few days in the detention room, Miss Balsy let me and Fishmouth back into class. School life returned to normal. Molly cried if she didn't get all As. Henry, Peter, and the other over-achievers like him in the class' plodding middle, struggled toward a college still eight years away by studying late and asking Miss Sheridan for extra credit work. Butterball and his slow learner friends read out loud in the basement; Tom tried and failed. I made Cs…effortlessly, without cluttering my brain…the perfect letter for escaping Coverdale's standards and rules. Mother no longer cared about my grades. My laughter had frightened her with calls from school. The principal might have wanted a meeting. She might have had to leave her house. Having escaped that, she didn't press me for As, and I kept up my end of our unspoken agreement by not causing any more trouble in Miss Sheridan's class. Mother didn't mind not having a son to brag about. She had the sister things. When talking to the milk man she showed off their picture coloring, some of it within the lines and only partially obscured by chubby fingerprints or smudges of chicken fat. Mother beamed whenever the things came home from pre-school with a gold star or certificate earned for using the bathroom.

Miss Sheridan moved me to the back of the room. After studying from my books, Dane played hide and seek in class—with each test he hid a little farther from me, eventually ending up in the front row next to Tom. That didn't matter. It was only a game.

The morning Tom flunked another math quiz, Miss Sheridan took him away. After school I found him waiting for me in the hall.

"They put me with…Butterball," Tom barely got the words out.

"You're kidding?"

"Can you help me?"

"How?"

He looked at me, his eyes no longer full of summer. For the first time, I saw the bright blue of him afraid.

"Let's go to the Little Store," I said.

"Sure, Steve." He managed a half-smile.

The Little Store was across Treemont in The Neighborhood near a bus stop. Before I met Dane, Tom and I used to sit together on the concrete curb outside the store, talk and eat pickles and peanuts.

"Like old times," he said.

I unrolled the brown paper and took a bite from the large pickle I'd scooped out of the brine barrel. The taste was mostly vinegar and salt. Tom had treated me to a red pop. We floated the peanuts in the bottles of our soft drinks and drank chewing on the soggy nuts.

"This is good," he said. It was, the fall day warm and drifting…. A cloud covering the sun chilled the air around me. Dane wanted me back.

"Time to go," I said. Sprinting into the cold wind, we raced to Tom's home. Because I had a face to draw, and I did it every day, I had again stopped helping him with his papers. I left Tom waving good-bye to me from his front porch.

"It's not so bad," he said the next afternoon as we walked toward Treemont. "The teacher goes slow and gives us time to think. Her voice isn't loud like Miss Sheridan's." Tom gripped his book tight. "I've got it all figured out. I'm going to study so hard they'll have to put me back up. I won't fail." He saw it first. The large black bird glided overhead. "What if I'm wrong?" Tom looked at me. "Remember the eggs."

"Yes." Just like today, in the river, he never let me forget them…

It had happened the year before, in the spring of 4th grade. On a sunny afternoon we'd almost finished delivering Tom's newspapers when he put the few remaining ones on the ground and after shimming up a tree, brought a nest down gently cradled in his hands.

"I've been watching this for a few weeks. I want to show it to you." His eyes widened and became bluer as he slowly tilted the nest toward me. "Three speckled eggs. Aren't they amazing? I wonder if the baby birds inside hear sounds? They wouldn't understand them. They probably think the creaks and shakes of the tree are just part of the shell, the wind the voice of sleep. This nest is so cool. Sticks and pieces of leaves stuck together by dirt. There's even a little piece of newspaper inside. Careful…"

I had moved closer to get a better look.

"I'm not a klutz," but just as I said it, I brushed against the nest, knocking the eggs out. They fell onto the sidewalk and cracked open.

"You jerked your hand," I said. "That's okay. We can make breakfast out of them."

Tom didn't laugh but instead kept looking down at the yellow glop. It was dark when he finally pieced the shells back together into jagged egg shapes and returned the nest to the tree. I would have left hours ago but I didn't want to miss out on my Friday night with Tom's mom. She'd smell of baked bread, and we'd sit together licking trading stamps in her kitchen.

"Some things can never be put back together," he said. A bird screeched from the top of the tree. "Do you believe in curses?"

"No," just ghosts, but I didn't tell him that. We walked to his home in silence...

Now he had again spoken about the broken eggs. I understood what they meant—for him. He might never escape Butterball and return to Miss Sheridan's class. Tom's life was in pieces but there was nothing broken in me. I had Dane and we would be friends forever.

At Treemont, I turned toward mother's house.

"See you tomorrow in school, Tom. Don't worry."

"Sure, Steve. Pirates always find their way back."

I hid until twilight, then staying low to the ground, crept into my secret place beneath the hanging branches of Dane's willow. I again drew his face on the hard ground. The sun's last light, a thin ray of scarlet, reddened the tree's skin of ice. I put my head on Dane's and rocked with him under the willow's blood color.

I knew the secret tap. Tom had left in my locker on thin brown paper singed at the edges, a skull and cross bones map with instructions written in wavy letters directing me to a note he'd put in my jacket pocket. Folded into a tiny square, the note when opened and read sounded like pirates and spies, Tom telling me he was hiding out but I could find him Wednesday afternoon if I followed the map and used the code he'd hidden in my shoe. So I did, tapping three times on one of the old boards leaning against the Little Store's back wall.

"In here. Quick." Grabbing my arm, he pulled me behind the lean-to. "I'm being extra careful. They came for me today."

"Who?"

"A special unit of the police. They wore black uniforms with a skull on the sleeve. You should have seen the dogs they used for tracking. Mule sized. Big red eyes and huge fangs— and you thought Mrs. Humphrey's dog was scary. Maybe the eyes were yellow. It was hard to tell for sure from where I was hiding."

"You've skipped a lot of school."

"That's why Miss Balsy called out the dogs. She wants me arrested. Those giant bloodhounds sniffed and snorted, and wanting to rip my throat out, yanked so hard on their leashes they pulled the policemen holding them along the ground. One dog was this close to me, Tom said, holding his fingers an inch apart. "It caught my scent and mouth foaming, started howling and shaking its big monster head. I got away by running zig-zags and jumping in the river. Instead of floating to Milford like the police expected, I waited under some ice and breathing through a reed, stayed real quiet and still until the search party left. You should have heard how that killer dog whined like a puppy when it found out I'd gotten away. I dried off and came here hoping you'd show up. You did. You're my best friend. It's been a great day." He kicked the boards down.

"We don't need them," Tom said. I guess I'd looked

surprised. "The police are at my house. I'd better go home and surrender. Mom could get hurt if there's a shootout. Think it'll ever be summer again?"

"Of course." It always was under Dane's tree.

"I've got a hearing tomorrow in front of a real judge. I'll be surrounded by guards the whole time. What would happen if I ran?"

"You're going to get a warning, that's all. Remember when they locked me up for a couple days at school? That was a lot worse than this, but I dealt with it. No big deal." I snapped my chewing gum." Except for the freckles under them and their blue color, Tom's eyes suddenly looked like Dane's.

"I'll go to jail if that's what they want but I'm never going back to that special class. Never." His face again became goofy and happy. "Wish I could have caught one of those killer dogs. It would have made a swell pet. Let's get a pickle and some peanuts. I'll probably be riding around for hours after they put me in the police wagon. I don't want to be hungry."

We went into the Little Store.

I never ate with him there again.

Tom did get a second chance, but not a third. The juvenile court sent him to a state school in Milford. His mom sold their home. I remember hiding and watching her move out. An unused piece of butterfly paper twitched around her ankle as she swept the porch the last time. Torn by the closing front door and jerked upward in a rush of gray air, the sheet twisting above the yard compressed by winter into a hard brown mat, blew into the Milford field and trying to fly, convulsed before falling on thorns. After locking in the dark, Tom's mom left without looking back. I wanted cookies. I wanted to sit beside her on Friday nights and feel my special places in her kitchen table. I whispered good-bye while digging my key over and over into the stupid bark of that stupid dead tree.

A young couple moved into the house. They didn't have any kids. Then some old farts bought the place. I think they died in it. Years later, after I'd bulldozed the farmhouse, I traded the lot for one much better, Dane's, and built my home.

Near the end of fifth grade, Dane and Molly stood talking at the drinking fountain. I watched them. They were too close. I continued to sit at the back of the class. When Dane tore my shirt, hit or tripped me, it was more than fun for both of us. By calling me a Jew in Mr. Petty's drug store, he had shown his love; love needed pain, just ask father. But Dane's continued kindness now made him hurt me for a larger reason. If I became satisfied and lazy, content to roll along in life blob-like and without suffering, I'd never transform into Christopher Barnabas Lee. It took me years to figure out who Dane really wanted me to become.

In sixth grade, Linda left a small paper bag near my locker.

Dog crap, I decided. The girls in school hated me. Linda had a crooked nose, tomato red hair and farted at her desk, but Dane walked Molly home every day so I needed a girlfriend, too. Because any girl was better than none, if I could make Linda laugh and speak to me by putting my hand in shit, it was worth the smell and mess. I opened the bag and reaching down slowly, touched…metal. I took out a pen, two burnt cookies with smeared, pink icing smiles, and a perfect birthday card. "To A Special Boy" it said across a laughing clown face. Only the words mattered. I was surprised Linda knew so much about me. I ate the cookies, every black crumb, and buried the card in my underwear drawer where I also kept my other secrets: the old key I had found in a gutter, and the green cigar Dane had given me the summer day we first met. The drawer was safe from mother. She never touched my underwear. At night, I clicked the pen until falling asleep.

Sometimes I said hello to Linda when seeing her in the hall. Mostly we just nodded at each other. I knew Dane expected more. A few days before the sixth grade graduation dance, I put on a black T-shirt and waited in front of Linda's house until she came outside to walk her little dog.

"Want to go to the dance?" I asked, the words rushing out. I guess I surprised her. She farted before nodding yes. Her dog peed on my foot.

We danced together…

Spirals of dust-filled light reflecting off a hanging aluminum ball, fell in soft circles to the gym floor. Overhead, crisscrossing purple and white streamers swayed in the updraft from an old rattling fan mixing the odors of sweat and sneakers into air doused with too much borrowed perfume. Slow music escaped a record player guarded by Miss Sheridan. She watched the clock and made sure no one left the room or danced too close. Holding Linda at arm's length and moving stiffly, I turned in the same direction at the same slow speed no matter what the song. Linda followed nicely, only once or twice stepping on my toes. Once, when the large amount of space between us accidently became a little less, her starched, pink dress poked me in the face. She wore red lipstick, most of it on her lips; her streaks of eye shadow made one eye look bigger than the other; she had scraped her knee jumping rope.

I saw Dane standing with the other boys on their side of the room. He pushed and jabbed them, laughed whenever someone slightly more daring in the group made a few hesitating, chicken-hearted steps across the no-man's land separating the sexes; laughed louder when the boy, losing his nerve, inevitably ran back. I danced closer to Dane. "Look at Steve," I'm sure he said. "That's how it's done."

"Time to go." Miss Sheridan boomed, scratching the dance over in mid-song. She held the phonograph arm up, squeezing it in case it still had life. Gold balloons fell. Fishmouth broke them all. Dane ripped apart a cardboard record with my name in the center and chased Molly. To make him laugh, I hit Linda over the head with a roll of paper towels.

Outside, a wagon full of Goldblatts waited for me.

"I'm glad we were able to straighten him out," Miss Balsy said while reaching in to shake father's hand.

"Thank you for everything," mother said, finding more to discuss on the topic as we drove away. "Did you hear that? Straighten him out.   Giving you all the credit. I'm the one who sacrificed to make him a *mensch*. Not that he is one, but at least I try. What do you do? Go to work, come home, eat, and go to sleep. You don't even know you have a son."

Father kept driving. He had excellent concentration.

Their heads hanging low toward their bellies, the sister things looked like they were using all their energy for digesting. The mention of eating animated them.

"We're hungry." they said, jowls jingling, their beady eyes predatory and merciless. "Can we go to Big Boy? Please."

"See what I mean?" mother said to father. "Who do they ask? Me. I have to feed them, dress them, you don't have any responsibilities." She glanced back at the twins. "Of course, babies, I don't want you to be hungry."

"Thank you, mommy."

"And another thing," she turned again to father but I didn't hear the rest. By tapping my head against the car's steel frame, I had again made her buzzing more pain than noise and could sleep. While looking out the back window at where I'd been, I spiraled down into a darkness, peaceful and dreamless.

Two months later, the doctors cut Linda's leg off. The operation didn't stop her cancer. Is that her beside me in the water? Where am I now? Seventh grade? Eighth? I didn't know it would take me so long to float out of here.

Peter Shapiro, who had started wearing a tie and sports jacket to school, told me my epidermis was showing. I didn't have to sit quietly in back of the room with Dane in front. I could be a class clown and make him laugh. I looked at my zipper.

"Moron," Dane said, throwing a spitball at me.

The math teacher moved my desk into the hall. At lunch, I went to the Little Store by myself.

ALAN KESSLER

8

SOMETIMES, ON STILL, SUMMER afternoons, as the air shimmered over Dane ground in my hiding place under his willow, I let Tom's shadows find me. When moving my foot, I heard the stones scraping under it speak, asking me to play. The smell of green leaves touching my face became long and blond. Tall weeds, with hard green berries, thick thorn bushes that protected and hid me better at the willow than snow banks in winter but didn't taste as sweet, formed Tom's smile out of thin, twisted branches. Then, he was gone. Even when my best friend, he had never stopped mother's buzzing. I didn't have to see Dane every day to know he gave me life. The ground and his face in it, filled with tree, were enough.

In that summer before ninth grade, Peter Shapiro in his fucking tie invited me over to watch how many times he could spin his dead turtle on its shell. We spent an hour together before he left with his family to get Chinese food. While walking down the street with his friends, Henry the Booger Man waved hello to me. I called Fishmouth once. He wasn't home. I didn't try a second time. I continued to let the emptiness of the hiding place fill me as summer descended into July. Then I met Dave.

"She's phoned and phoned for weeks. Doesn't have anything better to do. Believe me, if she worked like I do around here she wouldn't have time to be bored." Mother circled the kitchen. I was at the laundry room door, ready to visit the willow. "Come back here," she said and continued speaking to me, to herself, to the sister things eating chicken wings. "She moved from New York, doesn't know anyone. So? Is that my problem? Who needs friends if you have a family? What are we, in kindergarten? Your father. A real protector. Got me involved with her by telling her husband we should socialize. I'm not like Mr. Big Executive. I don't drink highballs and go on dates. Some people have no pride. They push themselves on you so long you can't say no. What choice do I have? I'll go with her. Bake my skin so you two have someone to play with."

"Thank you, mommy." the things said and waddled to the garage closet where an old army tent and their bright, pink and green bikinis took up all the room.

"You're coming too," mother told me.

"I have plans."

"I know, with *shiksas*. Forget about it. She has a boy your age. You might learn something from him.

"I'm sure." I almost laughed. Maybe Dane wanted me to go and have fun picking on a nerd.

"We're going swimming." the sister things yelled and banged into each other in the doorway in their rush outside. I thought they could have given the tops of their bathing suits a purpose by lowering them to partially cover their bouncing bellies. Mother drove us to the Excelsior Club—a gleaming white building with cabanas and a deep blue, chlorine saturated pool. While sitting on the hot concrete, killing ants, I saw two wide feet with red painted toenails flop up beside mother's chair.

"You're a hard person to pin down."

"Not so, Francis." mother said. "I'm here, aren't I? I've been busy with the house, that's all."

"Is this your son?"

"Yes. Steve, show some manners, this is Mrs. Suskind."

I stood and looked up at a large head with rectangle sunglasses and jet black hair piled high.

"My, such a handsome boy—this is David. David, say hello."

"Hello." Pale and bony, he stood to the side and picked his nose. What a dork. I had guessed right. Dane did want me to enjoy myself today.

"Why don't you two play. My Jackie is already with your sisters, Steve. David would just love having a nice little friend, too."

"Go," mother said.

The webbing under the chaise lounge strained, barely keeping Mrs. Suskind's ruffled ass from hitting the concrete as she sat down.

"We have to get together more often," she said while lying back and slowly swinging one of her beefy legs onto the chair. The other leg followed with a thud. "Do you play mahjong?"

Mother smiled, wrapped herself in another towel and pulled the blue and white umbrella closer to her face.

I walked away with the nerd.

Cloudless and hot, the summer afternoon radiated into a bright smooth pool absorbing the small ripples of children disturbing the seamless glare by wading in the shallow end. A few old woman swam, making sure the water didn't splash or touch their blue hair. Sometimes, if the sister things were spurting exceptionally large amounts of sweat in the house, mother took us to the Excelsior club. She and I never went in the water. Mother was afraid—I think her cousins once tried to drown her. Unlike now, I couldn't swim.

"We're members here," I told Dave. We passed a stand selling popcorn, snow cones, seltzer and shrimp. "I can come anytime I want."

"And use the golf course?"

"Golf course?"

"Guess your membership is silver. Ours is gold. When my dad joins a country club he goes first class."

"There's a basketball court—"

"I saw it."

Someone accidently splashed me from the pool and called Dave a creep.

"Get him back," Dave said.

"Who?"

"That guy yelling at you."

"He was talking to you."

Dave didn't show it, but I knew he wanted to cry. We continued circling the pool through its concrete heat.

There was a gentle place where softened sunlight blanketed

pink tiles. New mothers, holding their babies high, sat around the edge of a shallow pool and with a smiling, boo, boo, boo, dropped little plump baby legs into the warm water, each woman aware only of her little game. Lifted out of the water kicking and happy, the babies laughed. I wanted to stop and watch. Maybe they would eat. Eyes straight, I continued on. I couldn't let Dave know anything about me.

"You don't live far from Treemont," he said. "That's a busy street."

"Actually, I'm close to the schools. We have a five bedroom house."

"We bought in the Manors. On a canal. My dad's an engineer."

"My father owns a factory."

"Really? How many?"

"One."

"We have three. They build radar and missiles for the army. What does your dad make?"

"Clothes."

"Shirts? Pants? What kind?"

"Underwear."

"Hey, if there's money in it, why not? There's the basketball court. Want to play?" Dave took an imaginary jumper from the side.

"Sure, I'll take you on."

"Are you any good?"

Bounce, bounce, bounce, the basketball bouncing hard and low on the empty asphalt, black against snow, Tom had cleared so we could go one-on-one in the cold; a rainstorm game when we shot and ran laughing, afraid of lightning, our clothes soaked, Tom's long blond hair hanging wet across his face; the rim, our faces, a part of the court, all in lamplight on summer mosquito nights; Steve, Steve, Steve, Tom calling me through the sound of the ball bouncing on the street while he waited for me to come out of the house mother never let him in...

Am I good? Against a creep with glasses?

I checked out a basketball and threw it hard at his boogery face.

"Guess you want me to start." A second later, he had driven past me for a lay-up.

"Your turn." The ball hit me in the head. I feigned, dribbled—he stole the basketball and scored. Dave blocked my jumper, blocked another, swished a hook. His glasses hadn't moved.

"What do you want to play to?"

I fell, holding my ankle.

"We'd better stop." I limped over and bought a coke. Dave followed and winked at the girl behind the counter. Guess she felt sorry for him. She smiled back. Continuing to hobble, I made it to a picnic table and sitting down, elevated my leg. I hoped Dave would go back to his mommy. He plopped down next to me.

"My shot was a little off," I said.

"Think so? Probably we just play a little harder where I come from."

"That's a laugh. You should go against Dane. He'd cram the ball down your throat every time."

"Really? Is he here?"

"Are you kidding? This place is for nerds."

"Seems like it. Does your friend practice getting hurt, too?"

"Are you talking about my ankle? I sprained it."

"When you knew you couldn't beat me."

"Screw you. Who cares what you think."

"Who's those girls over there?"

"No one interested in you." I put my hand to the side of my face when Dave waved at them.

"Why don't you introduce me—unless you'd rather stay here and hide."

I curled my lip, Dane style.

"Man, you don't know who you're talking to. I'm not afraid of anyone."

"Maybe it's time you proved it." Dave walked over to Tania and Carol who snickered whenever they saw me in school. The sun burned hotter and I began to smell like the chemicals used on Cloverdale lawns as my skin absorbed more of the pool's chlorine. I tapped the empty cup. What would Dane do? I got up.

"You girls know Steve, right?" Dave sat between them at a round metal table, an arm draped over the back of their chairs. Dark with a mustache, Tania kept filing her long, fuchsia colored fingernails. The blonde, Carol, able to concentrate on only one mentally challenging activity at a time, stopped ratting her hair in order to yawn in my face.

"Sit down and join us," Dave said, acting the big shot.

"I'm fine right here," I told the nerd. Some snot-nosed kid running around with an inflated dragon tube around his middle, bumped me into the table.

"Careful with the ankle, Steve," Dave said. "So, girls, did I mention my boat?"

Tania and Carol looked at him.

What a lying ass.

"A boat?" Tania held her nail file suspended in mid-motion.

"Yep. Actually, it's a cabin cruiser."

"Cool," Carol said, snapping her chewing gum after freeing up brain cells by putting her brush down.

"Would you two like to go with Steve and me for a boat ride tomorrow? I have my own key. I can take the *Took-Us* out whenever I want."

"We'd have to ask our parents," Tania said.

"Okay, see what they say."

"I can't believe they fell for that crap," I said after the girls left. "What are you going to do when they find out you're a liar?"

"I'm not."

"You have a boat?"

"Right in the canal behind our house. My parents bought it after we moved into the Manors. Makes no sense to live on the water and not own a boat."

"And your father lets you drive it?"

"Of course not. He isn't crazy. It's amazing how slow you are. Is that an Ohio thing?"

Dave had a skinny neck. I squeezed, enjoying the sound of cracking bones.

"My mother did you a big favor getting us together," he went on, unaware I had just strangled him. "Hopefully, you're not too stupid to learn a few things. Look, If you want to score with girls you have to talk big. Impress them. I fed Tania and Carol's a line without risking anything. There's no chance their mothers will let them go."

"You think you're so smart—"

"I know if you stand there, head down, twisting your hair with a finger, chicks will think you're ugly."

"I'm really a blond," I said. Dave frowned, not understanding. How could he? He didn't know I'd been baptized. The girls came back before I could cut his throat with my rusted key.

"They won't let us," Tania whined, even her mustache drooping.

"Parents." Intellectually exhausted by articulating her disappointment but still angry, Carol spat out a wad of gummy phlegm. It hit my foot.

"Hey, no problem, some other time," Dave said. "Do you guys want to check out the pool?"

"Guess so," Tania said.

"If I don't get my hair wet," Carol smoothed her bangs.

"Coming?" Dave asked me.

Dane never backed down. I could stay in the shallow end.

"I'm a great swimmer," I said. "Our pool at home is almost as big as this one."

"Who cares?" Carol said, walking away with the others. I

didn't hurry after them and disturb the water by rushing down to play. That's how you drowned. I knew that as a child, and I know that now. Mother understood it, too. Once, there had been a murmuring liquid in her as I rested on her breasts until the playful and plump sister things bounced me off, drowning her dreams and hopes for me in displaced milk. At father's pool in mother's house, I once stood next to her and on the unusual silence between us, floated back beyond her breasts to the womb. While father swam, the twins jumped sending a tidal wave crashing over the deck and by this disturbance of water, mother remembered a familiar topic and drowned our one moment of quiet time together in words.

"Mr. Executive needs a swimming pool like I need a hole in the head," she said loud enough so father could hear. "What's he trying to do? Stay in shape for his shiksa girlfriends?" Then she left and closed herself off in another part of the house, leaving me alone with the sister things and their laughter.

Dave swam off. Admiring her fingernails, Tania waded out slowly. Carol put one foot in and quickly pulled it out.

"It's cold."

I sat at the three foot mark, my feet, dangling over the edge, almost touching the Excelsior Club's clear blue water.

"Chicken fight." Dave yelled. He dove down, came up between Tania's legs. Squealing, she grabbed his neck and held on.

"Chicken fight, chicken fight," Dave and Tania chanted.

"You're sure you can swim?" Carol asked me. She wanted my head between her legs, too. I wished Dane were there to see it. I took her hand and we stepped into the water. Like a mountain climber with spikes, she dug her sharp toenails deep into my back. When on my shoulders, Carol steadied herself by pinning her bony knees against my head.

The water warned me with its heaviness. I understood. I stayed at three feet and made Dave come to me. He and Tania attacked. Carol reached for them, missed and tried again, both arms swinging wildly. Slipping, she poked me in the eyes and jammed a finger in my ear. Taller than me, Carol tottered backward until pulling herself up by grabbing my hair. Her knees jabbed me even harder. I could hardly breathe. There was only one chance. I waited until Dave turned slightly then hooked my leg inside his and was ready to yank when he quickly twisted Tania around toward us. Lunging, she pushed Carol, who falling back, her legs tight around my throat, dragged me under. Unlike now, the water buried me in darkness without images or sounds. I sank, tasting death.

Dave yanked me out.

"Should have told me you couldn't swim," he said. Carol stood coughing and sputtering and when finally able to talk, screamed at me.

"You ruined my hair. I hate you." She batted a heavy, matted clump away from her eyes. It swung back in front of them. I wondered if my hair looked as bad.

Tania kicked me in the leg.

"You made me break a nail."

"Have a good time?" Mrs. Suskind asked when I came back to my spot on the concrete.

"Dave's fun," I answered. "Thank you."

"I knew you two would get along." She oiled the hanging flap of skin under her neck, closed her eyes and immediately began snoring. Beside her, under the umbrella and still wrapped in towels, mother continued to hide from the sun.

I picked up a rock.

"Kill," Dane said.

I found a colony of ants, smashed them all and sat counting Dave's bodies. Now *that* was fun.

9

"HOW'S YOUR MOTHER?" MRS. SUSKIND asked while opening the drapes in the living room to make sure I again got a good view of the boat and canal out back.

"Fine."

"Your sisters? Last time I saw them it looked like they had lost some weight. Did your mother take them to a diet doctor?"

"No." They couldn't fit in his office.

"Well, here's what I think. Not everyone in the world has to be skinny. The twins are big girls, good for them. What law says they have to look like David's sister? Sure, she eats and doesn't put on a pound, but in their own way, your sisters are very pretty, too. And how's your father? Still working late?"

"Yes."

"I'm sure he'd like to spend more time with his family. What's important is that you know he loves you."

I touched a scar on my hand.

"David. Come say hello to your little friend. We just went shopping, Steve—Here he is. Bright and shiny. Don't you just love David's new clothes."

"Yes." He looked like a scarecrow.

"I'm always telling my friends at the club what a nice boy you are." Mrs. Suskind squeezed my cheek. "David, your lunch is ready." Leading the way, she marched into the large marble and copper kitchen.

Grease from steak frying on the stove coated my skin. The maid served Dave meat in blood; my cereal was clean and cold. Dane had been right. By hanging out with Dave on summer afternoons, I'd been able to study the differences between me and a nerd. It was education without reading a book. Dave cut his steak lengthwise as if slicing open a belly.

"Rare, just the way you like it," Mrs. Suskind said, standing behind him and watching every bite. Dave continued to methodically slice and chew, each piece of meat he swallowed dipped in the fat laced gravy on his white china plate. I knew his routine and prepared myself for its disgusting finish. When he washed the last of the steak down with a glass of milk, I wanted to vomit. Even the sister things, in the middle of one of their feeding frenzies, never mixed meat with milk. We weren't religious. By lighting Friday night candles and herding us to temple once a year on Yom Kippur, mother tried expanding father's spirituality beyond the ascension of money. But basically, Goldblatt orthodoxy was defined by the dentist next door who had put on a large addition after killing our tree, the proctologist's three cars down the street, and my future Bar Mitzvah party. Our rituals involved wealth, not dietary laws. Even so, drinking the insides of something you ate was wrong unless, for me, the body and blood were Christ's.

I sipped pale iced tea from a Mickey Mouse mug.

"A Danish? Some cake?" Mrs. Suskind asked Dave as he pushed away from the table.

"Got to go."

"Thank you for the drink, Mrs. Suskind." She looked different. At the Excelsior Club she had squeezed into a ruffled ass bathing suit; for the past two months, when visiting Dave, I had seen her in an assortment of shorts so tight they ripped at the seams. Now, standing near me and wearing a simple black dress large enough to cover a stomach any baby would have enjoyed being inside, Mrs. Suskind looked pretty. It's strange, but at that moment I felt there could be some leftover affection from her large and overbearing mothering of Dave; an overflow so maternal and powerful, just my closeness to it might make her want to hug me.

"Such a polite boy." Mrs. Suskind turned away from me and walked out of the kitchen on thick, ugly legs I noticed were crisscrossed with blue veins. I went outside.

With its bumpers tied too loosely and misaligned, nothing prevented the boat's hull from scraping along the metal dock. I picked up pieces of the wood and turning them in my hand, knew Tom would have spent a whole summer afternoon making ships from splinters like these. And as for having a real boat to play pirate on—he'd have sailed off with me into his dreams…

Dave kicked the boat.

"This river is so boring. There's nothing to see in it but some old mills."

"We could fish."

"Wow. What a great idea. Maybe catch an old toilet or some garbage bags." He brushed the sleeve of his suede jacket and flipped up the collar on his shirt. "There's a party tonight. Why don't we go? You could get lucky."

"You have a one track mind."

"Don't you like girls? Are you gay?"

"No, jerk-off." He'd never understand about Dane.

Dave shook his head.

"If I didn't already have you figured out, I'd swear you are a nut case. How about some pool?"

"Gee, that's different." We played pool whenever I came over.

His maid, scrubbing the kitchen floor, sounded like Mae and all the other maids I'd known except she said everything twice.

"Is mother still here?" Dave asked her.

"Went to the beauty parlor to get your sister. Went to get her."

"Thank you, thank you." Dave circled his finger around his ear when she wasn't looking. The maid scrubbed harder.

In the center of the large game room, well-lit compared to the rooms in mother's house, the pool table filled time. I don't remember what the table looked like. Dave always won when we played. Today, he didn't.

"See what you can do if you give yourself a chance," he said, talking in riddles.

"You boys having fun?" Mrs. Suskind asked, the smell of beauty shop chemicals following her into the room.

"Hi, Steve," a smaller painted and dyed version of the woman said.

"Can you get Jackie out of here?"

"Your sister's just being friendly, David. She's not bothering anyone, is she Steve?"

"Am I?" Jackie winked at me, the heavy weight of her varnished, black hair tilting her head to the side.

"We're leaving," Dave said. Mother and daughter quickly closed ranks. Somehow I managed to push through.

The summer ritual at Dave's house continued. After more of his theories and bullshit talk about girls, we played Home Run Derby, another game I never won. There was only one rule—anything not hit over the fence was an out. His yard was too big and neatly trimmed for a ball field so we used his concrete driveway. I threw a baseball at his head. Unfortunately, he ducked. He swung and missed my next two pitches, barely dribbled the third one to my foot. My turn.

"You probably need thicker glasses," I told him and smashed his slow, fat pitch into the street. "Go get it, sucker." I beat him, ten zip.

"Hurt your leg?" I asked.

"Hey, what can I say?"

"That I creamed you."

"Yeah, guess you did." We sat on his driveway, only a couple of our toes touching the grass. Dave stopped cleaning his glasses. "Shows what you can do when you want to. You just need confidence. So, what about that party?"

Although he was ugly, Tania and Carol had kind of liked

him. Why shouldn't I go?

"Where is it?"

"Randy Flynn's house. He lives on the other side of Cloverdale."

"I know. In The Neighborhood."

"Where?"

"You wouldn't understand. I'll meet you there."

"I'll come get you at seven."

"No—"

"David." Mrs. Suskind called from the front porch. "Time to go look at some new coats."

When half-way to the front door, he turned and hit the ball over the fence.

"Just luck," he said while casually swinging the bat.

Jackie smiled at me from her upstairs window.

I wandered around town and after spending twilight at the willow, waited in the dark on mother's laundry room steps. I had to time it just right; leave as soon as Dave got there.

10

WHAT MONOLOGUES KEPT MOTHER riding?

"I don't like the way the butcher looked at me today. I'm sure he knows you and you've filled his head with stories. Other women go in, buy, no one bothers them. I have a husband who complains to the world about his wife. Well, if you think I'm going to stand for it—turn here—you've got another think coming. Let me tell you this—"

Or,

"I feel like a criminal every time I call your office. 'I'm sorry, Mrs. Goldbaltt, Mr. Goldblatt's at a meeting.' Do you think I'm a fool? I should come down there and make you show your true colors. Embarrass that secretary of yours and you. But I won't. I'm a quiet person, not like your sister, the snake. Remember when she—"

Effective as these topics were in prolonging mother's drives—the sister things lucky because they could drown out most of the noise with their constant chewing—nothing matched the subject of *shiksas* for keeping us all trapped in the station wagon for hours.

"Why do you look at them. What do they have? Gold

between the legs? You see a blonde and you become an imbecile. Of course I'm not exciting enough for you. I don't go to bars. I'm busy raising your children. I'm not a floozy. It's only a matter of time. You'll run out on me. Go on, I'm used to it. I know all about men."

Mother could give examples of this all night.

If *shiksas* were tonight's topic of choice, I'd still be locked out when Dave came over. I'd have to go to the party dirty and unable to fix my hair. If the butcher or father's office were in the car, I'd probably have time to change and then wait on the stoop for Dave. The worst case was if mother didn't talk at all. The length of those rides was unpredictable. She might arrive at her house right before Dave. Not really worried about this possibility, an outcome so remote it could only happen if I were very unlucky, I began to relax.

Car lights blinded me ten minutes before seven.

"It's early." Mother said, unlocking the laundry room door. "Why did you rush home on a Friday night? Is someone coming over?" Her hard eyes flittered at the edges. In her list of deadly sins, inviting a friend to the house was even worse than marrying a gentile.

"No one's coming." I ran past her and up the stairs. If I were quick, I might make it yet. Shirts and slacks went from closet to floor. Dane had started wearing sweatshirts. I found a gray one. It looked too fancy on me. Another I'd torn in the wrong places.

"I want you down here," mother yelled. Tick by radioactive tick, the alarm clock moved Dave closer to me. I had to hurry.

Reaching under the pile, I grabbed the jeans and shirt I had just taken off and splashed father's Old Spice on the areas most likely to smell.

"What are you doing up there?" Mother's voice got even louder as she climbed the steps. Sleeves up, sleeves down, up again. In the bathroom, to see better I swung the vanity mirror in front of my face. Time for the hair. I parted the right side, then the left. Swept it forward and combed it all back hoping I'd look like father. Maybe I'll go natural, just a shake, muss, mix and scramble—ta da. My hair stuck out like wire struck by lightning. The Watcher's eyes and the invisible, nameless girls waiting at the party, made me sweat. I could almost hear Dave knocking on the front door. There was one technique left, an old one. I plastered my hair down with water.

God, I look like Hitler.

"What's happening? Where are you?" Mother was now at the top of the stairs.

Don't panic, don't think, I told myself. I'll press a small curl over my forehead and I'm done. It's over. I can leave. No...it looks bad. Real bad. I'll pull everything straight—Oh, Jesus. I can't go out like this.

She pounded on the bathroom door.

"I'm coming in."

Two curls, a long and short, two long ones, two short... Finally, a mass of hair centered perfectly on top of my head—if I didn't move. Grinning, I was as cool as Dane and ready to go...almost. A section of hair had kinked behind my ear. I needed just a little more water to flatten it out and by holding the clump down—

The doorbell rang.

Mother's knocking turned frantic.

"I knew it. You asked someone over then disappeared. Out of there. *Now.*"

I turned off the lights and in the dark, took a last look.

"You're a no good." Mother yelled at the back of my head while following me downstairs where Munchkin snarled, then ran yipping and snapping between my legs, the fury turd trying to trip me. "If you think for even one moment I'm going to let someone in—" She picked up Munchkin and opened one of the front doors half-way.

"Hello, David. So nice to see you."

"Hi, Mrs. Goldblatt. Is Steve ready?" He tried looking inside. Mother blocked him.

"He's right here." Without opening the door any wider, she pushed me out.

"You look very nice, David. My son could look nice, too. He has a whole closet of clothes from New York City and this is how he dresses. Well, what can a mother do?"

"I like your mom," Dave said as we walked to our bikes. I heard the lock in the oak door click. "Think you'll ever let me in your house?'

"No," I answered. We rode together for half a block, then Dave shifted gears on his English racer. I stood and pedaled harder, giving my hair-do to the wind. When I couldn't keep up with him, I coasted, realizing it didn't matter. He was a nerd riding a piece of shit. By taking my front fender off and pinning black Aces to the spokes, I had customized my bike into what Dane wanted it to be, a motorcycle speeding me through the dark. In the buzzless quiet, I left Cloverdale's big houses and mother behind.

"What took you?" Hands in his pockets, Dave leaned against a light pole, not a drop of sweat on his pimply face. The music of blonde, cheerful, pretty girls like Molly Adams drifted from the house. My hair hurt. It had dried into a frizz ball. I knew the girls were waiting to spit on me. Was this part of Dane's plan to help me grow?

"Are you going to stay out here all night?" Dave asked. "Let's go in."

Looking down, admiring the crabgrass, I followed him.

"Glad you came." Randy Flynn greeted us at the door. Shorter than me—and he never grew—he reached up to slap Dave on the back. "The party's in the living room. No one's going to bug us. My parents are upstairs watching TV."

He had decorated the small room, about the size of the sister things' bathroom, by replacing the ceiling's light bulb with a red one, the color turning the party-goers into indistinct, crimson and grey shapes full of sound. I heard them talk and laugh. Soon the girls would see me. I took a folding chair and sitting behind the snack table, built a small wall in front of me using off-brand pop bottles and potato chip bags. Safe here, I let the light's blood color warm me.

"Hiding?" Gladys' huge breast slapped me in the head as she plopped down hard on my lap. "Don't worry, I won't bite." When she leaned forward to grab a handful of peanuts I could again feel my legs, the numbness returned as she shifted her full weight back. I had known Gladys since kindergarten. She was the fat girl in school no one saw.

"Great party." Gladys crunched peanuts in my ear.

"I can get you a chair."

"Oh, no, Steve, I like sitting right here."

I wanted to rip the long black hair out of her chin.

"I see you two are hitting it off," Dave said, walking over holding the hand of a bright faced blonde. "This is Tammy."

"And he's mine." Gladys' hug smothered me.

"What knockers, get some tit," Dave whispered before he again disappeared into the red haze. The music played louder. Crushing my balls, Gladys bounced to the song.

"Why don't we go for a walk," she said.

"Good idea." But I made the mistake of trying to stand before Gladys got off. Twinges of sharp pain shot through my groin. Slowly, in inches of movement marked by foul breath and rolling lumps of heavy skin, the load of her lifted. I was free. Gladys pulled me into the pumpkin patch.

"Don't be afraid," she said, moving closer. "Do you think I'm pretty." I touched her hair. Not bad. No fungus or rot. Strings of frosty air in a late summer chill wrapped our fingers together. I smelled the willow. Gladys' wet, drippy lips smacked off-center against my mouth.

My first kiss.

Circle, circle, evening stars. The bright full moon wore a cap of shimmering starlight. Moonlight covered each gourd, giving them masks of silver and silvery voices saying, nicely done,

Steve. She likes you. Feel the warmth. Jolly young pumpkins rocked on legs of green vine in reborn earth telling me that I, too, at thirteen, was part of the promise of renewed birth.

We walked back holding hands.

"A quickie," Dave said. Tammy punched him in the arm and Gladys giggled. The warm queasiness inside me from Mrs. Humphrey's black stockings mixed with the shame I'd felt when mother saw me sitting on the toilet, spread from my stomach to my legs. The party continued. Gladys again sat on my lap. The pain returned. She was a pig.

Mother quietly let me back into the house.

"I'm glad you have a Jewish friend," she said. "It won't last."

After gargling with mouth wash to kill the taste of Gladys along with her germs, I went to bed. Lying with eyes open in the dark, I stared at the ceiling and waited. When would Dane let me know I was like him? When would my transformation be complete? Tonight? Tomorrow? Before I died? Falling asleep I thought about Dave. What a creep.

Looking back now from the river, I know most people I met were like Gladys. They became shadows, a fat girl I once kissed. I don't know what became of her. I don't care.

ALAN KESSLER

11

THE YELLOW BUS PARKED outside Cloverdale Junior High didn't wait quietly. Engine running, the bus clanked, vibrated, changed into backfire and black exhaust smoke, the shudders sent from the dented hood in front to the emergency door at the back. Louder than all the other sounds the bus made were the words on its side, Milford Hebrew Academy, the name, in billboard sized letters, announcing Here Come the Jews. The bus didn't embarrass me. I was a Christian.

"Hey, Stevie." Dane called out from the street corner. "How's that nose doing?" His group of friends laughed.

"Great." I yelled back, and while getting on the bus, laughed with them.

"God is love," the Negro bus driver greeted me.

I sat beside Peter and to offset his proper white shirt and blue tie, ripped a page in my prayer book.

"God will strike you dead for that," he said.

"Hope His aim is good." I stuck bubble gum in the pages.

Peter scooted to the other side of the bus.

I might have hesitated to mess up a bible but a faded, backward turning prayer book printed in Brooklyn meant nothing to Dane and me.

Because of cheap rent, the Hebrew Academy had relocated a few years ago from Cloverdale to an old mill building in Milford. The Hebrew school, with its drafty windows and cracked floors, survived on donations. The purpose of its existence was to prepare a boy for taking on sin in order to redeem his parents. I figured this out my first day of Bar Mitzvah classes. The process was structured like a banking transaction. Before a boy's thirteenth birthday, God directed His wrath at the parents if their son stole, blasphemed, or ate a ham sandwich. The lavish party after the Bar Mitzvah celebrated the parents' increased line of credit with Jehovah. Withdrawing a child's sins from their spiritual account, allowed the parents to sin more without risking reaching the limit where God closed the books—killed them—because of an overdraft. It was all a neat plan of debt forgiveness that had nothing to do with me. If I ever sinned, I knew Jesus would save me.

The bus, hitting a hole in the school's parking lot, bounced me up, then down on the metal insides of my busted seat. Although painted over, I could still see the swastika's outline on the Hebrew school's front door. No one hated me. I'd been baptized Christopher Barnabas Lee and was blond, like Dane, except my color was underneath.

Mr. Cohen took my hand.

"Come," he said softly, his fingers bony and crippled. For a year I'd gone to class with the others but this last month Mr. Cohen tutored only me. Across from me at our little wooden table, he spoke about God and faith, and I saw in his eyes the same love Mr. Petty showed when selling me a comic book for twenty dollars. I didn't understand why Mr. Cohen cared about me. I wasn't Jewish, and I'd never given him a dime.

Lights. Action. Friday night. The performance began with mother in her most challenging role, sitting quietly in the car. Father drove us on ice; the sister things slurped down the lox on top of their toasted bagels. At the synagogue, men in dark suits surrounded me thinking I might try to escape. Father shook hands, mumbled a few things, but, of course, I didn't actually hear him talk. Radiator steam, mixed with the smells from perfume and closed in piety, made mother's mink coat droop and melted the sister things who left behind a trail of tallow as they waddled across the worn wooden floor. The pine box holding yarmulkes spoke to father by rattling on uneven legs:

'Take one. Bow before God. Thank Him for letting you deliver your son up to his future sins. You're free. He's responsible for what he does. Just think of all the *shiksas* you can date now."

With its peak too high and resting precariously on top his black pompadour, the yarmulke made father look like he was pretending to be Jewish. We had never been closer. In the chapel, inside the heat and candles and where, above the Torah, an eternal light burned orange and dim, men swaying back and forth filled the room with the rising and falling cadence of their prayers. The rabbi stood before the congregation and lifting his hand, summoned me forward. At the end of his prayer shawl, the blue strings separated the world of flesh and cloth from spirit. Mr. Cohen had taught me this; Dane told me what it really meant: I was here, in temple, in a Jewish place, while actually, through Dane's love, I'd been made a part of his velvet painting and the spirit in it, not old man Riley's, but that of the Holy Ghost. My new prayer book slipped in my hand as I walked to the altar. I wasn't nervous; the book knew my true identity and wanted to get away. In front of the ark, I sang in a clear voice the prayer over wine. It was a nice tune. Dane would have enjoyed dancing to it and playing along on his comb. From the silver and shiny goblet, I drank Christ's blood.

Bent over and arthritic, Mr. Cohen, a kind man full of misplaced faith, managed what for him must have been a smile.

That night, lying on the floor, I studied for the next morning's Torah reading by flipping through one of the comic books I'd bought from Mr. Petty. It was a biblical story about Jesus sending demons into pigs. When buying the comic I had seen a soft, otherworldly light from the gumball machine reflect off Mr. Petty's hand reaching for the money.

"I hope you're not sleeping up there." mother called out. "We've spent plenty of money on this Bar Mitzvah. You should be getting ready for tomorrow."

"I am." I yelled back while shifting my legs more comfortably on the *tallit* I had tied like a small hammock between the door and bedpost.

"Do you hear how he talks to me?" mother said, I guess to father, but her voice wasn't shrill enough to get his loving eyes rising. She was skilled at keeping father's love in check when it might ruin a special occasion. Mother didn't want to do anything that could jeopardize tomorrow's sacrificial rite offering me up to sin.

I opened another comic book and read about Jesus feeding the multitude with fish and bread. So little food, so many people. A miracle. I wondered what He would have done if the sister things had been in the crowd.

"...and my cousins, Ida and Edith, I love them so, the imbeciles. But I wasn't raised to be ignorant, so I invited them today. Did they ever once ask me to one of their functions?" Mother adjusted Munchkin's Star of David bow tie while father continued reading the paper.

She wouldn't let me go to the bathroom.

"We'll be late. You should have thought about that earlier."

With the car heater blasting and the sister things singing, Old MacDonald, I hunched over holding my stomach.

"Phew. Steve farted." the things yelled, scrunching up their flat little noses even more.

"No matter how much I try with him, I can't make him into a decent human being." Mother lifted Munchkin's perfumed body to her face. Given this chance to release a little gas of his own, father rolled down his window. Mother made him again seal it tight.

In temple, she kissed Ida and Edith on the cheek. The Rabbi proclaimed God is One. I didn't have a problem with that. I read the Torah section flawlessly, my face reflected in the silver filigree of the pointer I dug into each word. At the Excelsior Club, the three-piece George Lewis Orchestra—

drums, clarinet, George in his pink tux playing the accordion and singing—entertained with Bar Mitzvah favorites. The celebrants, whirling in a circle, bounced me higher and higher on a chair near spears of ice thrusting up from a blood red bowl of jumbo shrimp. I escaped and even managed to endure mother not holding me while we danced—her body stiff and angled away, her fingertips barely touching my hand. In his thin, cracking voice, George sang, *My Yiddishe Momme*, while I kept my head suspended in air at the level of mother's chest. The party continued. After a while, everyone forgot about me. I was small looking up. Maids' legs served food. Everyone's belly ate.

"Nice party," Dave said. "Too bad there aren't any girls."

"I'm here," Jackie said. "I'd love to dance."

"Oh, Steve's probably too tired," Mrs. Suskind said while pushing Jackie closer to me. "Are you too tired, Steve?"

My pain from the morning returned. I hurried to the bathroom.

When George's toothy smile, as phony as his hair, dimmed into a dull grayness the shade of a herring, I knew the party was over. Borscht had spilled across the white tablecloths; its bones and glistening head on a platter, the whitefish winked up at me. I carefully lifted a small ceremonial loaf of yellow bread and plunged it under the melted, icy water that three hours earlier, in its sharp, Old Testament form, had wanted to impale me among the shrimp. Because of mother and, of course, Dane, I had come of age through my Bar Mitzvah and entered an even clearer, Christian life.

"Thank you," I said to her.

"You're welcome," she answered. "None of this was cheap." Arms around the sister things, she hustled them toward the car. Father walked in front of me. He didn't seem in a hurry until I tried to catch up.

The cold wind blew my yarmulke off. I'm sure it floated toward thorns.

ALAN KESSLER

12

INTERSECTING DARK PASSAGES, ITS original color, green, still visible in flecks and streaks along both sides, the high school's main corridor showed in its worn, distant middle, an undercoat of unreachable gray. I kept in my own track near the lockers where dirt caked along the walls embedded ancient pennies and hairballs. In the hallway's middle, friends talked and laughed together. At the edges, where I walked, no one looked at me. I could stay isolated and alone.

I noticed shoes. Father had nice ones—Italian leather with the designer's name on a small brass plate attached to soles soft and shiny. Only the heels were hard. Years of father's love had made me an expert on footwear. In the middle of the school hall, the style of shoes changed during the year. Sandals became sneakers; the boys wore camouflage boots in winter; the girls, boots of fake fur laced neatly to the ankle, the Zebra patterned ones the nicest. Spring brought out cheerful colors in rubber and ridged plastics. A little off center from the hallway's middle, the less popular kids stayed in solid browns. I wore black with a tap at the end taped over so I wouldn't embarrass Dane by clicking down the hall. Each morning, after leaving the house,

I changed into his shoes.

"You're hideous," he said, sometimes adding a swear word or other important comment. I agreed with him. My pimples and glasses hadn't made me into a very good Christopher. I needed more refining through pain and Dane was always willing to help. Tenth grade, 11:35 lunch, and waiting with his friends were he always did, near the lunchroom door, Dane taught me a little more.

"You're disgusting," he said. Head down, I laughed, too.

Under the cafeteria's bright lights and pulled down by the weight of the sandwich in my brown bag, I followed a familiar pattern of old spills back to the last table in the room. Their strange eyes blinking, the slow learners waited for me. Butterball said hello and handed me a salt shaker. As she did every day, the albino girl scooted over, making room beside her. I looked around. The other tables were still full. I had no place else to sit.

Because the sister things loved egg salad I had to eat it, too. Mae had squeezed the sandwich together when making it but now, hours later, a large mound of yolk and mayonnaise levitated the white bread and saturated my lunch bag. By stretching my mouth carefully into the sandwich's middle, I tried to bite and chew with minimal leakage. The lumpy yellow mixture oozed out and slid down the front of my paisley shirt. A plum and peach, both big and extra juicy, probably grown under a farmer's radioactive, alarm clock light, fell through the bottom of the bag and landed with a splat on my lap.

"Here," and I handed the white-haired girl my cream filled

cake. At least I had outsmarted it. When I got up, my elbow brushed against her chocolate milk, knocking it over.

"Let me help you." Before I could push her away, she began blotting the milk on my leg.

"Look. Stevie's getting a hand job." Dane yelled from his table full of nicknames: Stash, Flash, Beetle, Jinks, and, of course, Fishmouth. "Rub him good, cutie."

The warm, crawling Mrs. Humphrey chill, crept down from my stomach. I left the cafeteria and wandered the halls, not noticing until the bell rang for class that there was cake smeared across my crotch.

The next day I went to mother's house at lunch.

"What are you doing here?"

"Someone stole my lunch bag."

"All that good food to waste. Mae spoils you. Who did it?"

"Some guy. I don't know his name. I think he's a Baptist."

"Come inside."

The maid served me egg salad. My story didn't work twice.

"Stole your lunch again?"

"Yeah, a new kid. Benedict Christianson."

"Tell the teacher."

I stood looking at her closed door, the day windy and cold.

The French bakery downtown kept a nice, fat woman inside who let me buy stale rolls. I'd eat one, then hungry and lean, run back to school, most of the time getting there on time. When I didn't, Watcher eyes in Art class stared at me.

"Here's your paint and brushes," the teacher, Mr. Aquaviva, said while putting a hand on my shoulder. He wasn't afraid of my paintings. Too bad he was queer.

The Chicken Hawk of tenth grade...

I knew Dane liked uniforms. I'd watched him play army with his friends. So, I joined the band determined to wear a cape, blazer and stripped pants while marching banging cymbals. Instead, the director made me the school mascot. Before home football games, I took the giant, papier-mâché bird from its pit in the band room and after struggling to get the large, beaked head balanced on my shoulders, tottered outside. I waited until the band hit the first notes of Cloverdale's fight song, *In December We'll Dismember Milford High,* a team we hadn't beaten in fifty years, then yelling "caw, caw," flapping my wings while running onto the field. The crowd ignored me. Unfortunately, so did Dane until my last game.

"Hey, asshole." He shook the Chicken Hawk as I stood inside it in a dark corner of the stadium beside one of the thirty-six luminescent chicken scratches forming a Victory Pathway no one knew was there. "You don't need to dress up like a freak. You are one." He slammed his fist into my purple belly. The punch felt good. Everything he taught me always did. 'I can't believe you forgot,' is what he really said. 'Why wear a mask when you have me?'

It was just like in the bible. I was always angering Dane and repenting.

The sound of teenage boys and girls talking together, laughing brightly in cold air, floated toward me and from the unvented darkness of the Chick Hawk, I answered, "caw, caw," but softly, so no one would hear.

13

AFTER THREE YEARS WALKING cheerfully alone down the edges of the high school hallway with Dane waiting to give me a big, lunchtime hello disguised as an insult, I heard someone call out Steve without laughing. I looked up. A man standing in silhouette against the window's bright, fall light waved at me.

Tom. Son-of-a-bitch. I tried to stand taller.

Disregarding hallway etiquette with its placement of students according to social status, he bulled down the middle and smiling, gave me a big homo hug. I hoped Dane wasn't watching.

"I'm back."

"Smelling like gasoline." I pushed him away.

"Comes with the job. I'm a mechanic at Import Service."

"You can fix cars and speak German?"

Tom laughed.

"I like your glasses, Steve. They make you look smart."

"I was never dumb."

I could tell by the way he looked at me that he saw how I'd changed. He didn't know there was more of Christopher to grow.

"Do you have plans for lunch? Why don't we go somewhere and talk. I've got a lot to tell you."

"There's a table behind the school no one uses," I said. Sometimes I'd sit there and eat my rolls. We walked together down the center of the hallway.

Outside, Indian summer air from the schoolyard carried the murmur and cries of games trapped in the past. We sat across from each other at the rotted picnic table chained to a pole. I remembered eating pickles with Tom at the Little Store.

"I wrote," he said.

"I know. I wrote back."

"I never got the letters."

"Really? The mail stinks."

"Or maybe they just didn't give them to me. Milford was bad but the state school they sent me to in Toledo was worse. You'd have thought I killed someone instead of just skipping school. I had a label—habitual truant. I did screw up a little, got into a few fights, and there was this kid, Nick Foley, completely nuts. One night he snuck some beer into the dorm and after getting drunk, pissed out the window on the headmaster's car. It looked like fun, so I did it too. You would have liked Nick."

"I'm sure. I hope you didn't drink too much. You can't afford to lose many brain cells."

"Steve, you'll never change."

I'd been wrong about him. He didn't see Christopher. What a fool.

Tom folded his large hands together and leaned closer.

"The counselors planned it so I'd go to the Voc—Milford Vocational. They figured I'd get two years of auto mechanic training and when I dropped out at sixteen, at least I'd have some skills. Can't blame them for thinking that way. That's what most of the kids did, drop out. Nick got his parents' permission and joined the Marines. I went along with the counselors because it fit my own plan. I got a part-time job at a gas station in Milford and saved enough money so mom and me could move out of her small apartment. I transferred back here. I'm done with special classes forever. I'm taking English, science, and math. I'm going to college, just like you. And get this—do you know where we're living?"

"No—"

"In The Neighborhood. At Mrs. Humphrey's. Some old people bought my home. I knocked on the door but they wouldn't open it. That's okay...I can look over from my window at the boarding house and see my old bedroom. The field hasn't changed. Wonder if there's any butterflies still in it. Is Fishmouth around?"

"Yeah, and he hasn't killed anyone—yet."

"What about that friend of his, I forget the name..."

Of course he meant Dane, but Dane wasn't Fishmouth's friend, and Dane wasn't a name anyone should forget. I didn't say anything.

"Dane, that's it. What ever happened to him?"

"He's great. I talk to him every day."

"Want to go butterfly hunting?" he asked, half smiling.

"We're too old."

"I know. All grown up. When did that happen?"

"When you moved away. How's your mom?"

"Couldn't be better. Working hard, like always."

"Still baking those chocolate chip cookies?"

"All the time. Hot for September, isn't it? There's the bell. Just like old times. You and me hurrying together so we won't be late for class."

In front of the school, Dane stood talking to Fishmouth. Usually there were other nicknames around him. They had probably gone inside at the first bell. Jerks. I knew Dane appreciated my loyalty. He reached into his back pocket. I had my treasures. I saw he still kept the comb he had taken from the drug store the summer day he showed me he was stronger than Mr. Petty.

"That's Dane," I said proudly. "The one combing his hair."

"Yeah, I could have guessed. Well, time to say hello."

Tom had actually gotten dumber. He'd once believed killing butterflies and pinning them to pieces of paper showed his power to create beauty out of death. I never said anything to him about that lie. Even before I met Dane, Tom's dream world of butterflies meant nothing to me, and what he felt about it didn't matter. But by sneaking up behind Dane and pushing him, Tom profaned the power and beauty of my friend who loved me. I wanted to hurt him.

"What the fuck—" Dane spun around, fists ready.

"Wanna fight?" Shuffle stepping like a fool, Tom threw a few jabs in the air. Dane frowned then slowly shook his head.

"Tom. Finally out of prison."

"They needed room for you."

"I see your little dog is still following you around."

"A man's best friend."

"Hi, Tom," Fishmouth said. "Remember me?"

"You're talking to a general now," Dane said. "After graduation Fishmouth's joining the army. He'll be a perfect fit. Running, jumping—killing."

Tom and Fishmouth shook hands.

"Are you going to school here?" Fishmouth asked.

"Yep. Enrolled on Monday."

"Hey, Tom, guess what? I'm dating your old girlfriend." Dane looked especially beautiful, his face fresh and smooth in the soft sunlight. "Molly's having a party on Saturday. You can even bring Tiny Tim. Let him fix you up. Stevie's real popular with the girls now."

The second bell rang and Dane's legs rushed in while his head, bobbing and smirking, showed he was too cool to worry about being late. I didn't hurry either. Tom and Fishmouth ran down the hall.

Although Dane had been going out with Molly since the beginning of 10th grade, I wasn't jealous. In elementary school I worried when they stood too close; over the years, I realized this connection for Dane was only physical. She was an accessory, something useful like his comb. Still, I had a problem. I didn't want Dane to worry about me. He used pain in a kind way, to teach me so I'd change; he believed his relationship with Molly made me sad, but sadness without a purpose. To show me how important I was to him, he'd invited me to her party. I wouldn't let him down. I'd go because I was too shy to tell him that of course I knew Molly was just a piece of ass. And since he wanted me to bring Tom along, I would.

In English class I used the inside cover of *Moby Dick* to make a list of the ten ugliest princesses in school. I would have preferred tramps but on the weekends they booked up first. I actually admired the ones I'd selected. Although short and festooned with pimples and bumps, this never prevented these girls from striding importantly down the middle of the hallway. Unaware they looked like trolls, these ugly princesses, stuffed by mommy and daddy with self-importance, exuded a confidence that made their stupidity seem like someone else's fault.

"I don't see that, it's just a fish story," Tania whined to the teacher. For her, tragedy meant shopping with only one credit card. Carol snapped her gum while ratting her beehive hairdo higher, a difficult combination of activities she would never had attempted when younger. Even now, the effort mentally exhausted her and she fell asleep, jerking awake in mid snort. Tania and Carol were terrific. Just what I needed. Two dates. If they refused because they didn't want to be seen with someone like Tom, a mechanic living in a boarding house, there were still eight other uglies I could call. The odds were with me. Molly's party was going to be great.

At night, after a bowl of corn flakes, I went slowly down the basement stairs making sure they didn't creak. Dropping to the floor, I slid under the mahogany desk. In the dark paneled office father never used, I was Tom, hiding from the cops on shag carpeting. Only one part of me stuck out, my arm, reaching up to pull the metal desk lamp over the edge and toward me. Dangling by its cord, the light made the faces in the *Chicken Hawk Squawks* yearbook open on my lap glow. I dialed my number one choice. Carol was a close second but I had once drowned her.

"Hello, may I speak to Tania?"

"Who's calling?" the man asked. The phone slipped from my hand and rattled to the floor. "Is this a prank?" I heard his tiny voice inside the carpeting.

"N-no," I said, bending down and speaking into the mouthpiece before lifting the phone back to my ear. "My name is Steve, Steve Goldblatt."

"I'll see if she's home."

I held the silent line in a death grip.

"Okay, Rachel, I know it's you. Big joke."

Tania's voice, expected, yet too suddenly there, startled me into something worse than speechlessness. I made a sound. The only one I could—heavy breathing.

"Who is this? I'm going to report you to the police."

"Don't hang up. It's Steve. Really—"

"Making an obscene call?"

"I—"

"What do you want?'

The words tumbled out.

Molly. Party. I have lots of money.

"I'm busy."

"Right. I'm sorry. I should have—"

Click. I'm sure I was the one who hung up first.

I studied the wart on Carol's nose. It gave me hope. Besides, what were the chances she'd remember the swimming pool? That had been years ago.

"You got my hair wet," she said. "Drop dead."

After removing the pencil from Tania's face and poking out Carol's eyes in the yearbook, I worked my way down the list then added more names. In the end, I had mutilated fifteen pages of photographs. I had to call him.

"Steve Goldblatt. My, my, isn't this a surprise. Why just the other day, I asked David if he ever saw the little Goldblatt boy in school. I used to call your mother, invite her to the club, but she was always too busy, so I gave up. Who would have guessed you and her have so many friends and are that independent. I'll see if David wants to talk to you."

I drummed my fingers on the floor—stopped when I thought I heard a sound from the basement steps.

"What do you want?" Dave asked.

"I need two dates for Saturday."

"Is that all? How about if I throw in a goat, too."

"I'm doubling with someone."

"And both of you are losers so you call me—unbelievable. You really have nerve. I tried to be your friend, get you out of your shell, and what happened? You wouldn't even say hello. Now, after all these years, you're asking for a favor. Fuck off."

"I couldn't compete with you, Dave. You've always been so confident and good with the women. It was too painful." Yep. Feed the pig, stick the pig.

"Well, yeah, I have a certain talent." Did he actually click his tongue. "So you're apologizing?"

"Yes."

"Because you need something. You're a horse's ass, Steve, and I'm not a fool. But what the hell. There's worse crimes than helping out a jerk. It just so happens I have a couple names. The girls live in Milford. Diane's a friend of mine. I'll call and make the arrangements—you take her out. That way I know the kind of creep she's getting."

"Thanks, Dave."

"Spare me," and he hung up.

After turning off the light, I crawled out from under the desk and put the lamp back in place. No one would know I'd been down there. At the stairs, mother emerged from shadows.

"He thinks he can keep secrets from me. Sneaking around. Making dates with *shiksas*. Just like his father."

"I called Dave about my homework."

"Homework? Since when?"

I needed father.

"Since I decided I wanted to be smarter than you."

Mother's dark little body started shaking. The sister things behind her gasped and for the first time in the lives stopped eating while still holding food in their hands. In its frothing, snarling, lurch toward me, Munchkin almost shot out of mother's arms.

"Listen how he talks to me." mother shouted through the ceiling. "No respect. He treats me like dirt. And it's because of you, Mr. Big Executive.

Father bounded downstairs just as I had planned. After he knocked my legs out from under me, I fell backward, hitting my head. Five minutes, tops; his loving never lasted very long. When he finished, everyone disappeared into a dark part of the house, and I could move freely, protected by the gentle, quiet afterglow from his beating. I walked out the laundry room door without mother telling me to stop.

Down the wide sidewalk of Cassidy Boulevard the scratching little sounds from bundles of dead leaves circling my feet kept me company by repeating my name, Christopher. All the Watchers' eyes had gone blind and Mother couldn't see me. I was free even before crossing Treemont into The Neighborhood.

I'd been back many times but only to Dane's willow. Now I noticed the change. Beware of Dog. No Trespassing. Keep Out. On streets with abandoned homes and ones for sale, metal signs warned anyone who didn't belong here to stay away. Of course, the residents remaining in The Neighborhood wouldn't turn their pit bulls loose on me or shoot in my direction. I was family. Whistling, I cut across lawns.

Mrs. Humphrey's boarding house looked the same: white clapboard and red tile roof, each window a different shape, the building tilting to one side; slender brown flowers and a tomato plant twisted up through the gravel of the front yard. Fishmouth had moved out years ago, his family buying a small house on the other side of Treemont. I never thought I'd be back here.

When I saw her name, Elvira Madison Humphrey,

engraved in the brass plate on the front door, the queasiness I'd always felt when near her black stockings, reached down from my stomach. Inside the boarding house, the Negro statue in tuxedo and top hat waiting patiently for umbrellas, looked at me as if to say, 'I'd feel the same way you do if I weren't just plaster with a smashed-in face.'

At the end of a narrow hallway, hazy pink light seeped under Mrs. Humphrey's door. Starting there and stopping at a row of mail boxes beside the staircase, the red slashes and splatters of violet and green on the doors and walls looked like the work of an artist who had died before finishing his abstract art or gone insane while painting it. Before Mr. Wolf from Cincinnati moved out, the hall had been all white.

Below a dangling six missing a screw at the bottom, I found Tom's name. Fishmouth had lived upstairs, too. I'd always enjoyed climbing up the dark, steeply pitched steps leading to the second floor. The higher I went, the greater the love I imagined father giving me down a staircase like this.

When I knocked on Tom's apartment, Mr. Aquaviva, the queer art teacher, opened the door.

"Steve. What a pleasant surprise."

"You live here?"

"Three years. Ever since…it's been three years." His large, liquid eyes saddened.

"Tom and his mom moved in with you?"

"Oh, no. They are across the hall at number nine."

"Sorry, thanks," and I started to leave.

"Tom isn't home," Mr. Aquaviva said.

"His mom will let me in."

"Uh, she's probably sleeping. You can wait in my apartment if you like."

I smelled lilac perfume. His hand tightened around the belt of his satin robe. In school, Mr. Aquaviva wore a beret, ascot, and double breasted striped suit, but dressing normal wouldn't have helped. The way he acted showed everyone he was gay. After a brother drowned, Randy knew he still had a whole family of midgets left. Embarrassed at the attention, his face puckering up, he grimaced when Mr. Aquaviva put his arm around him and talked in a low, sickening voice. And why should a great painting, even if mine, make a man cry?

The creep leered at me from inside hallway shadows. It wasn't fair. I had always been careful in public toilets.

"I have to go," I said.

"Too bad Tom missed you," then before I could run or shut my eyes, Mr. Aquaviva removed his robe. I blushed at what I expected to see: blubbery, naked flesh.

"Think I'll take a stroll," he hung the robe on the back of his door. Dressed in his double breasted suit, Mr. Aquaviva adjusted his ascot and locked the apartment. "In case you change your mind, there's a spare key under the mat. I don't have a television. You can play records. Most of mine are opera, but I have a few jazz albums you might enjoy. I made an excellent apple pie if I say so myself. Help yourself. Teenage boys are always hungry, right?"

You should know, I wanted to say, but he had already walked away. I wondered, as I heard him going down the steps, if he really thought I'd fall for his trap—step inside his apartment so he could rush out from hiding and lock me in. Didn't he know that keeping constant Cs required more brain power, imagination, and planning than making all As? I was way too smart for him.

I knocked on Tom's door, jingled the handle and kicked the old wood. How could his mother sleep through all this racket? Ready to knock harder, I whirled around after hearing Mr. Aquaviva on the stairs. His mask was off. He had come to get me. Now there would be no more pretending. Ready to swing, I held Dane up in the steel tip of my shoe.

"What?" Tom said, looking confused.

"Bees," I said, swishing my arm in the air. "They're gone now." I put my shoe back on.

"Mr. Aquaviva said you might be waiting. Look, Steve, I'd invite you in but mom's real tired at night. Maybe tomorrow."

"Sure, no sweat. I have a mother, too. I just want to tell you about your date."

"Date?"

"You didn't forget, did you? Saturday night. Dane invited us to Molly's party. He asked me to fix you up and I have."

"I didn't tell him I was going."

"You didn't say you weren't. I've made plans and everything. It'll be fun."

"I'm working and then I have to get home."

"Call in sick."

"I can't do that."

"When's your day off?"

"Sunday."

"So switch shifts with someone. I don't see the problem."

"Maybe some other time, Steve."

Unlike Tom, I hadn't wasted my childhood hunting butterflies. I knew the sound of excuses given to keep me locked out. Tom had a secret and it was inside his apartment. I'd find the key.

"Can I have a glass of water?" I asked. It might have worked but became unnecessary. We heard groaning and Tom quickly unlocked the door.

"Mom, what are you doing out here." Cradling her under his arms, he lifted his mother from the floor and carried her stick body to a rocking chair. After gently propping her head on a pillow, Tom covered her shoulders in a shawl and turned on a small lamp.

"Your dad woke me getting out of bed so I got up, too," she said. A few wisps of her remaining hair fell across eyes too bright for her skull like face. Despite the shawl's iridescent script, *Souvenir of the Arkansas Turnpike Authority*, and its brightly colored highways, on her it looked like a shroud.

"Look who's visiting, mom. You remember Steve."

"Sure do." The skull turned slightly in my direction, its eyes growing bigger while looking farther into the past. "I'm sorry. We can't afford having milk delivered anymore. My husband's out of work but he has a lead on a night job. We'll be fine. I'll get something too when Tom starts school. Take a plate of my chocolate chip cookies home to your family. I know how much they like them."

Staring at the wall, Tom's mom rocked back and forth.

"Steve Goldblatt," Tom said.

"Do I know him? Oh, dear me, I've spilled tea on my lap. There's no need to help me, boy. I've always taken care of myself." She tried to stand but fell back, the effort pushing her thin bones deeper into the chair. Tom bent down and after placing her arms around his neck, stood up slowly. Unsteady, but on her feet, Tom shielding her from me, his mom shuffled toward the bedroom.

I sat near a sagging card table and waited. On one of the dark walls, a calendar with a spark plug in the center advertised auto parts. From the living room, I could see the hotplate and small refrigerator in a kitchen without pots or pans. When Tom came back, he stood in shadow and spoke quietly.

"She's sleeping again. I don't know what happened, how she got out of bed. Mom had a stroke a year ago. It was harder when we lived in Milford. Now I've got help. Mrs. Humphrey watches her during the day and Mr. Aquaviva checks in when I'm at work. She usually sleeps through the night. The doctors want me to put her in a nursing home. She…forgets things…"

"Hey, so do I. What do doctors know? They're just like all those teachers who thought you should be with the slow learners. Now look at you. You're in Cloverdale High and getting ready for college. Nothing can stop a person if he's determined and has a force inside him that won't let go."

"Maybe some things are just too broken." Of course, Tom said that. He had always tried to wreck my plans with Dane.

"Those goddamn bird eggs. When will you forget them.

This is your mom we're talking about. She never gave up on you. Know what I think? She came out for a glass of water, slipped and fell. It happens. People get disoriented. No big deal. She remembered I liked her chocolate chip cookies, right?"

I saw hope in Tom's eyes. That's all I needed.

"Mr. Aquaviva wants to help out even more."

"Why do you say that? He does so much as it is. I hate imposing on him."

"Are you kidding? He's lonely. He told me that. Did something happen three years ago?

"His friend died."

"You and your mom are now the only family he has. He's hurt you, don't ask him to do more. Like this Saturday. I mentioned I got you a date and you should have seen how happy that made him. He's already planning the evening. He wants to play some records for your mom. Jesus, Tom. Don't you think she deserves a little respect? You're making her feel like an invalid, that without you around to hold her hand she doesn't even have permission to get out of bed at night for a glass of water. I'm sorry to say this but I can't lie to you. You're taking away her will to live. You heard what she said. She wants to take care of herself. She hates feeling dependent on you. It's humiliating.

"Your date is cute, too."

Tom looked toward the bedroom door. I heard the eyes of the dog clock in mother's kitchen spin. I talked about our childhood and the future. I bombarded him with words. Tom wasn't me. He didn't know how to get away.

"Okay, okay," he finally said, "if I'm back by ten."

"No problem. Leave everything to me." I got up and shook his hand. It didn't matter, but I would have liked to see him smile.

Mr. Aquaviva wasn't home. I let myself in. When he returned, we ate pie together and laughed. He was as pleased as punch to babysit on Saturday. I told the old queer I'd visit him often.

That night I slept in mother's driveway until father, retrieving his morning newspaper, bumped into me. For a moment I was surprised he wasn't dead. The dream had been so real. In it, he had again walked around without a head.

So there wouldn't be any last minute screw-ups, I told Peter I needed his car for three days. He adjusted his tie and charged me $100. No problem. I had my Bar Mitzvah bonds and they weren't doing crap. After I paid him, he licked the end of his pencil and asked for the tax. On Thursday, I parked the rusted junker outside Mrs. Humphrey's boarding house. Friday night, I informed mother I was sleeping over Dave's.

"David Suskind? I'm supposed to believe that?"

"Call him."

I stared right back at her while I reached behind me for the laundry room door. Steps, driveway, streets, lights—I had escaped again. I ran to The Neighborhood and after getting into the car opened the bag of rolls I had bought earlier in town center from the silent, flour dusted fat woman who, although tired, was always happy to see me. I appreciated her kindness and for the last two years, repaid it by buying and eating more rolls. The twenty-two oily croissants glistening from the bottom of the plastic bag now on my lap would be a new record. I breathed in the soft and empty taste of bleached flour, the smell leaving no place in me for emptiness even before I finished the last roll. Dinner over, I folded the bag neatly and put it in my pocket next to the old key. In my room, in the drawer of treasures—the rusted key when I wasn't carrying it; Dane's green cigar; Linda's birthday card and pen—I now had an important addition: the greasy bag marking the night I left mother behind speechless. To keep on winning, all I had to do was stay away from her until Sunday.

It had gotten cold, the night air creeping like fingers through holes in the car's sides and lifting up the few rags I had draped over my shoulders to keep warm. I wondered if Mr. Aquaviva was home and immediately knew it was Stevie asking. Christopher wasn't a pussy. Glasses and curly hair dragged me upstairs.

"Hi Steve, nice to see you again," Mr. Aquaviva said, his small bright teeth as sharp as a cat's. "Come in."

We talked. I drew. He again learned too much about me.

"Did you ever think about studying art in college?" He lightly tapped his arched fingers together, the pink flesh of them plump and food like. "You have real talent. Your work is emotional. From some place deep inside. You don't just use colors. You make them explode."

Dane drew stick figures throwing bombs. Now that was art.

"It's late," I said.

"And I should check on Tom's mom." We shook hands. He held on too long. I wanted to bite his fingers off and swallow them.

Back inside the car, I found more rags and made a blanket out of them that smelled of oil and dirt. Under it, I slept protected from the cold in a piece of shit car wrapped by ice.

On Saturday, The Neighborhood again let me walk inside it. I traveled in circles around other people's homes and in the afternoon went tired and hungry to Mr. Aquaviva's room. When I knocked there, Tom's door opened.

"Hello, Mr. Steve," the woman said, her long black stockings disappearing into her short red robe. "My, how you've grown."

"Hi, Mrs. Humphrey." I touched my stomach—quickly moved my hand away.

"Maybe you just seem taller. It doesn't matter. Follow me." She clicked down the hall in her high heels.

The streets again? The car? Mr. Petty wanted to see me but he was two miles away. After writing a note on one of the blank checks I'd stolen from father, I left it wedged in Tom's door and went downstairs.

"Shut it, please, Mr. Steve, and come over here."

I closed her door behind me. In the pink light, everything looked distant and forbidden. "Sit down there, on the couch. Doesn't it have a lovely pattern?"

Across from me, in her high back, fan-shaped wicker chair, Mrs. Humphrey took a long drag from her cigarette, neatly crossed her black legs and blew a smoke ring in the air. A spring in the spotted couch poked me. I scooted forward to the sofa's edge and feeling too close to her legs, slid back quickly. The spring shifted and jabbed into the back of my knee.

"So, Mr. Steve, how are you?"

"Fine," I answered.

"Fine? That's so tepid. It's a lukewarm baby bath. What does that word mean to someone your age? I think nothing. I'm sure you are hotter than that."

I did feel warm. The cuckoo bird in her clock sprang out, missing a head.

"Excuse me," Mrs. Humphrey said. "I have to wash my hands."

After she left, I turned and tried looking in her bedroom. Was it pink too? And what about the toilet…

"Have a piece?" Mrs. Humphrey asked. Startled, I knocked the box of chocolates from her hand. She caught it, one of her long, white fingernails piercing the top of a bon-bon. "Oh my, I'll have to eat this myself." Her face close to mine, she licked her finger slowly. I caught a glimpse of her white breast and couldn't breathe.

"Guess you're not hungry," Mrs. Humphrey pulled her robe closed and hips swaying, clicked back to her wicker chair. She crossed her legs higher and tighter than before. A trace of cream glistened on her hand. Mrs. Humphrey. Mother seeing me on the toilet. The queasiness that rolled from my stomach to my groin. Dane. It was somehow all connected…I pressed a pillow over my lap.

"Good, but messy." Mrs. Humphrey washed her hands again and returned wearing a yellow leotard with tiger stripes.

"Like it?" She spun in a circle in front of me. "Of course you do. Men love animals. That's why they leave them behind as gifts. You remember my dog don't you, Mr. Steve?"

"Wolf. Too bad he stopped eating."

Mrs. Humphrey smiled.

"Is that what happened?" Her gleaming eyes and twisted mouth made her look as if she'd swallowed something wonderful but disgusting. "Here's my advice to you, Mr. Steve. If you want a long life, walk for hours on a short leash and starve. Minutes will seem like days. Isn't that great?"

I realized then how much she had loved and hated the boarder from Cincinnati who had given her his dog. I'd always known love required pain. Now I knew it could also kill.

"Want to play?" Mrs. Humphrey got down on all fours. "Isn't there a game where no one leaves or gets hurt?" She softly bumped my leg with her head.

"Cards?" I suggested.

"Cards. How clever." Her expression didn't look like she thought the idea all that great. Mrs. Humphrey taught me whist and except when she left to visit Tom's mom, change into an orange and yellow moo-moo or wash her hands, we spent the afternoon together. It was fun and peaceful. She didn't talk.

At six o'clock, the cuckoo sang four times from its headless throat and dropped over dead. Mrs. Humphrey knew Tom's knock.

"Come in, dear," she said.

"Hi, Mrs. Humphrey, Steve." In his white shirt and dark pants, Tom looked all neat and clean, not a trace of grease monkey on him. I was impressed. He had even slicked his hair down. "Mr. Aquaviva's with mom. I hope everything will be okay."

"Don't worry," Mrs. Humphrey said. "Nothing's as bad as losing a pet. Care for a pickle before you leave, Mr. Steve? You must be hungry."

I shook my head.

"Have a good time, boys." She kept shuffling her cards.

"Aren't you going to change?" Tom asked as we walked to the car.

"Into what? I'm cool enough." It made no sense to tell him I was Christopher bubbling to the surface through Steve. He wouldn't understand how part of me was already perfect. A sudden wind whipped my hair into spikes. I pulled them down and knew I'd made a mistake not planning better. I needed water, or an hour with one of the potions I'd developed, in order to fix my hair like Tom's. Now it was too late.

Tom frowned, looking at the car.

"Whose is this?"

"Peter Shapiro. He owed me a favor."

"A small one. Does it run?"

"No. I had it towed here so we could stand around and look at it. Hop in."

I turned the key. The engine cranked weakly and stopped. I tried again. This time, not even a sound. It was as if the motor had discharged all its energy on purpose, the wires, spark plugs and valves, tired of pretending they wanted to help me, settling back into the natural state of inertia formed by cold and steel.

What had happened? The car had run fine. Damn Shapiro. He had destroyed my party and would make Dane sad. I didn't want my money back. I wanted to take something from him he couldn't replace. Shapiro had a dog. I knew what Dane would do to it.

"Let me check the battery." Tom got out and opened the hood. He jiggled a few wires. Dane whispered to me that he'd fix the car if I scratched his face into the window shield ice. I did it quickly.

"It should work now," Tom said when back inside. The engine started right up. "A loose connection, that's all. Hope you're a good driver, Steve. It's icy tonight. Don't brake too fast."

"No sweat."

Tom lurched backward against the seat as I punched the gas pedal down hard. With the car fish-tailing, spraying up slush and pebbles, we skidded inside the sweet smell of smoke and wet, burning rubber.

"Christ, Steve, you're going to get us killed."

"Not me. I'll never die." *Christ, Steve*—Tom, always a little slow, didn't know how right he was. The velvet Jesus held me in its protective hands while Dane's gray eyes of ice continued to smile down from the window. When Dane touched the engine he made it run better. Drawn into the mystery of his grace, that night, in the dark and snow, my love for him deepened. He'd shown compassion toward Peter Shapiro, someone he didn't like. How much greater then was his love for me. I forgave Peter and decided I wouldn't kill his dog. Apparently Dane liked animals.

I drove faster.

"Slow down." Tom gripped the dash. "What's wrong with you?"

"I'm nuts." I rolled my window down and howled into the night.

"Okay, Steve, what the hell—" Tom stuck his head out his side and started howling, too. I'd never had so much fun.

When a child, I played with Tom in a confined space of stupidity, the small part of the field near his home where he ran after butterflies and found, at a pit, a treasure chest top that didn't exist. Now, driving by it, I saw the field expand. Its garbage and old tires reached far into Milford toward the Hog River. Wrapped tightly in black ice and tied with moonlight, stunted trees sinking gently into the black ground guarded a stardust covered bog and an old truck half submerged in stagnant water. The field was beautiful and mysterious, exactly what Mr. Aquaviva wanted me to see and paint. Damn all fags.

"Nice over there, don't you think?" Tom said.

"It's a dump. That's all that field's ever been. I'd pave it over."

"Do you have the addresses?"

"Of course—" While reaching into my back pocket, I accidently veered the car toward a ditch. Tom quickly grabbed the steering wheel and turning it, saved himself.

"I'll take that. It's safer with me." He read the directions. "I know this area. Once we cross the bridge, make a right on First."

"I can find it," I said. Dane wouldn't let me get lost.

Five tall spans over the Hog River supported a ribbed floor of steel that played a thickety-thick-click rhythm as we drove across, the sound becoming the word "party" spoken in a joyous and incessant metallic voice. Daylight on the water painted it green but now, at night, the river's true nature made it a willing part of the dark. Below us waited the black hole of a fifty-foot drop.

"By slightly moving my hand, no, less than that, if I just twitch the tip of one finger, I can turn this car and send you crashing down."

"Me?"

I laughed, seeing his face. "Don't worry. You haven't bought your dream boat yet." Tom didn't relax until we left the bridge.

"First is right after that old mill," he said. "It's been abandoned for years."

Half the mill had crumbled into piles of bricks. I saw a light in one of the remaining rooms. When we drove past it, the light vanished, darkness again erasing the riverfront at our side.

"Imagine all the people who once worked in there and got chopped up in little pieces but didn't even know they died," Tom said. "I'll bet there are all kinds of secret places in that mill where cut off arms and legs are still doing their jobs as if it were just another work day."

"Do you believe in Christ?" I asked.

"Yeah, I guess...I used to go to church with mom."

"Then you should know there aren't any ghosts He can't

throw into the belly of a pig. All you need is faith."

"Wow. Where did you get that?"

"I see things. I learn. I have a friend…" I took a breath and let Tom into a small room of stained glass. "My grandmother wanted to kill me after she died. I thought I needed a mask to hide from her. Dane taught me not to be afraid of ghosts. Old Man Riley never hurt him. Through Christ, the dead disappear forever."

Silence in the car. I had never been closer to Tom…He put his thumbs in his ears and wiggled his fingers at me.

"Ghosts. Monsters." His laughter in rolling bellyfuls of pounding sound crashing down around my head, slammed the door and locked him outside my skull forever. "Good one, Steve. You really know how to tell them.. Look, over there. Ghosts in the mill. They're coming to get us. Help, Dane, save me."

He laughed and laughed, the flames of it growing stronger even in me. I was again in Miss Sheridan's class except this time the laughter scorched my throat. Tom had rejected what was inside me and blasphemed Dane while dragging me along. I wanted to tie Tom to a stake and as he burned, cut his head off and listen to his confession gurgle out the neck. Instead, we just kept laughing. I screeched the car into a sharp turn.

"Keeeeeee-rist," Tom yelled. But it was too late for him. He couldn't be saved. "Go left at the next street, pardner."

Pardner. It did sound kind of funny. I pounded the car roof with my fist and alone, always alone, cried silently.

"That's the house," he said.

The car's wheels slowly grinding on gravel, I stopped in front of a chain link fence propped up by boards. The light on Diane's porch leered at me. An old Ford on concrete blocks in the driveway made Steve's pimple's hurt. Yes, I was becoming Christopher, but the blond part of me remained mostly hidden. Fathers with oil and grease on their hands and who worked on cars in their front yards would see only a Goldblatt.

"Aren't you getting out?" Tom asked.

'What's he doing here?' I heard a man with a smashed nose ask staring at me while I waited outside his front door for his virgin daughter. And what if I got by daddy and Diane took one look at Steve and thought him ugly? By making fun of what I had told him about Dane and ghosts, Tom deserved to die but Dane had tied him to my party invitation. I believed the reason simple: he just wanted him there. Now I understood Dane's real purpose for bringing Tom tonight. Even a sinner could be useful.

"I'm not going in," I told him.

"What? I don't understand."

"Parents know I'm an ass-man. I've got that reputation. Whenever I pick a girl up, I'm put through the ringer. I'm surprised they don't ask to see if I have notches on my dick. I'm tired of all the questioning. Why don't you go? Tell Diane you're me. That way I won't have to deal with her parents. You won't get hassled either. No one would think you're dangerous."

"But Diane knows you, right?"

"Of course she does. It's like this—a friend of mine, Dave, the one who gave me directions, met Diane first. We were at a party and he was talking to her, then she saw me and told him I was cute. She called me a few times. Asked me over to her house. I didn't have any time for her until now. She won't remember what I look like—good thing. You're not as handsome. After she's in the car," and I lock the doors, 'I'll tell her the truth."

"This is the craziest thing I have ever done," Tom said, and got out. A song, mostly static, played on the radio's one station. When I touched the knob, the radio sparked and fizzled out. I tapped my fingers, picked my nose. Two dark splotches moving quickly to the car brought the cold inside. Diane scooted beside me.

"Hi Steve." she said. Tom gave me a pathetic, 'Gee, I'm sorry' look. What an asshole. I glared at him and the rat, slinking down, sat pressed against his door. Diane lightly touched my shoulder. "Don't be angry. It's okay to be shy."

"That's what Tom told you?"

"He's a good friend."

"We're best buddies." he said, pretending we were still eight and that I didn't hate him.

"I'm just not comfortable around parents."

Diane's big green eyes made me shiver.

"Cold?" she asked.

"No. Malaria," I answered.

She laughed and a curl of her long, brown hair glided across my hand. I took a deep breath.

Who do you see? I asked her.

Christopher, her green eyes answered.

"My mom and dad are great. You'd feel right at home. Is this your car?"

"Borrowed it. I know it's a rust bucket but I didn't have a choice. My convertible's in the shop."

"Where?" Tom asked.

"I like old cars," Diane said.

I gunned the engine.

"Hold on, Diane. Steve thinks he's a race car driver."

I drove away slowly. I knew his plan. Tom had scooted close to her hoping those in the passing cars thought she was his date. Worse, he wanted to show Diane how much he liked her.

"Tom can't wait to meet Vita," I said.

"She's a swell girl, Tom, and a good friend of mine. You'll have a great time."

That's right, Tom, Vita's your date and Diane wants you to know it. She turned back to me.

"How long have you known Dave?."

"Since seventh grade. We met at the Y. I worked a summer painting houses and saved up enough to buy a membership. I love swimming."

"I never knew you had a job," Tom said, still turning the knife.

"How could you. You were away in reform school."

"My brother works construction."

"I've done that, too. Shoveling, carrying bricks. I never want to sit behind a desk."

"Dave's a funny guy and so sure of himself. He said you were nice. I don't usually go on blind dates."

Tom started to say something.

"Dave's my secretary, that's all—where should I turn?"

"Right at the stop sign," Diane answered.

"Would I like him?" Tom asked, not letting it go.

"Probably not. He doesn't hunt butterflies." My arm hurt from keeping it locked at my side. My nose itched, but I didn't scratch it. I was afraid if I changed positions Diane might think I was trying to put the moves on her. She had stopped talking. Tom looked out the window. I had never ridden in a car with so much quiet. Please, Jesus, don't let me fart.

"Dark this time of the year," I babbled.

"Dark and scary," Tom said. "Steve's afraid of monsters."

I wondered why he hated me.

"We're almost there," Diane said.

On a street where all the houses looked the same, unpainted and rundown, I pulled over to one a little different because of the tires, rusted bicycles and old refrigerator for sale on the brown lawn.

"Vita's dad is out of work," Diane said.

"I'm a little nervous," Tom looked at the house.

"Go on, don't be a baby." It was payback time.

The door closed—Alone with Diane. In the dark car. All of me, skin, brain, bones, became a pounding heart. What should I do? What should I say? Do I smell? My leg's shaking. Is that okay? I wanted Tom back...

"My father lost his job once," I said, trying to again fill space. "We had a hard time after that. There wasn't much food in the house. We ate a lot of turnips." I jumped. Electricity shooting through me as Diane took my hand.

"You have nice long fingers but you shouldn't bite your nails. Do you play an instrument?"

"The violin and trumpet…the piano."

"I'm not musical at all. It must be great to be so talented."

"I paint, too. My art teacher thinks I should study sculpture in New York City next year."

"Wouldn't that be something. I'll probably never leave Milford. It's neat the way you're interested in art and music. Most of the guys I know only want to talk about their cars."

"You'd like my convertible. It's bright red."

Diane looked into my eyes and gently squeezed my hand. We could have kissed…

"Deeeeeeee." A bulbous face surrounded by spikes of bright orange hair yelled looming toward me.

"Vita." Diane answered.

The blob leaned over Diane.

"Hi, Steve, glad to meet you—you've got a good one here, D." Climbing into the back, Vita pushed the front seat forward crushing my chest against the steering wheel. Tom, looking lost, followed her.

"Hope this is fun," he managed to whisper. He'd gotten what he deserved. I had Diane. He was out with a freak.

"Vrooooooom." Vita yelled in my ear. "Let's see what this baby can do."

I burned rubber, the car shaking and groaning in one last spurt of energy before settling down to a slow, constant speed no matter how hard I pressed on the gas. Even with Dane's repairs, Peter's junker acted like an old mule that would do what it wanted. I knew, of course, this was just my imagination. Engines didn't make decisions to run or break; cars were machines, engineered and soulless. I didn't learn until a few months later about the one exception—father's Buick where Mr. Beneby's spirit in the car became my dad and in the back seat I saw a shadow across time.

We laughed and sang on the way back to Cloverdale. Launched over the front seat after we crossed Treemont, the blob's thick, meaty arm careened?? Check spelling\ off my head as she pointed out the window.

"Look at all those houses, D. They're humongous. Big yards. Probably all have pools with diving boards and everything. How much does one cost, Steve?"

"How should I know?"

"You live in one, right?"

"No—"

"Bigger," Tom said.

I wanted to believe in hell for the wicked and damned.

"Wow." Vita said. "It must be great being rich."

"I'm not," I said.

"I'd love it." Diane said. "Think of all the clothes we could buy."

"And jewelry. I saw a swell pair of rhinestone earrings at Blade's. The dangling kind Danielle wears."

"Not everyone in Cloverdale has money," I said.

"I live in a boarding house," Tom knowing just what to say to make himself look good.

"Any interesting neighbors?" Diane asked.

"The landlady is friendly and Mr. Aquaviva across the hall is a nice guy."

"For a fag," I said.

"Aquaviva—what a pretty name."

"Sounds Italian. Makes me hungry." Did Vita actually slap her stomach? "I had a boyfriend once, Guido Pucella. Remember him, D? Had a wart on his chin and walked with a limp but was really handsome. His mother loved me. Said she'd never seen anyone eat so many meatballs at one sitting. Boy, could she cook. Guido Pucella. Too bad about gangs…" She actually stopped talking.

"My dad loves Italian food," Diane said. "I remember once when I was little, he took me on my birthday to this restaurant that had checkerboard tablecloths and candles in bottles. A man with a large, yellow mustache and smelling like cheese played the accordion and smiled. He had big teeth. I ate and ate but the pile of spaghetti in front of me just kept getting bigger. They brought out a cake. My dad got pink icing on his nose—I'm sorry. I know I'm boring you with all this."

"I like cake." the blob said.

"My dad once bought me an ice cream soda at the drug store," I said.

"My dad's dead," Tom again wanting to steal Diane's heart. But he had a point. His dad was a skeleton in Arkansas. My father was alive and full of love.

"That's sad," Diane said.

"Tommy," the orange thing blubbered.

"Anyone want a piece of gum?" I asked.

While still a block away, I saw the light from Molly's house illuminate the night sky's black clouds. When we drove up, the light became even brighter, rows of spots along the front yard turning the house and its block shaped trees all white.

"I didn't know we were visiting the President. What a house."

I glanced back and saw Vita press her face against the window—perfect, if I were decorating the car for Halloween. This was different. I had friends here.

"Sit back, Vita," I told her. She kept staring.

A jumble of cars crowded the street and lawn. Dane was waiting for me. I parked on the sidewalk and opened the door.

"Let's go, Tom. Time to party." The blob shoved me into the steering wheel again as she and Tom got out.

"Don't do anything stupid." But I knew Vita wouldn't listen and I'd have to hurry. "Come on, Diane."

"Fabulous cars. Fab-u-losa.", Vita's ability to express herself limited by the overpowering emotion of touching something beyond her world of retreads chained to a tree.

"Hands off." I pushed her arm away from the shiny hood Dane had probably brushed against, Vita's fat fingers streaking orange sweat over his cells. I trailed behind and when no one was looking but the fountain's stone angel, went back to the car and breathed on its steel. By rubbing gently with my sleeve, I cleansed the hood of corrupting blubber. It was a fair exchange. Dane had also breathed into me. The angel approved. The last time at Molly's, when Dane taught me the beauty of his dirty words and revealed, only to me, how he could transform any pool table he touched into art, the fountain's angel spat in my face. Why not? I had been Steve. Now, seeing the almost-Christopher I had become, it slowly turned its face to me in respect and homage as I marched past.

"Everything okay?" Diane waited for me on the marble walkway. Tom and Quasimodo were already at the front door.

"Yeah, I just wanted to make sure I'd locked the car even though you'd probably have to pay someone to steal it. The owner's a friend of mine and was nice enough to loan it to me. The car's all he's got."

"That was thoughtful," Diane said.

"I try," I answered.

"Let's go in. What are we waiting for?" Vita looked back at me and tugged on Tom's sleeve.

The yelling and laughing from inside told me to hook my thumb in my belt and holding Diane's hand, saunter in while keeping Tom in front of me. So, I did. One light, cafeteria hot and bright, rotated toward me. I blotted my face with the piece of toilet paper I always carried in my pocket.

"Hey, everyone. I have an announcement. There is a God and He does perform miracles. Goldblatt's here with a date." Dane came over and slapped me on the back. "Is this your sister?"

"I'm Diane."

She didn't sound friendly. I hoped Diane wouldn't embarrass me.

"You aren't bad looking. What are you doing with him?"

"That's a rude thing to say."

"Oh, Stevie doesn't mind. He and I go way back. We have a special relationship. Right, buddy?"

"Right, Dane."

"See what I mean. Hi, Tom. How's it going? Whoa. Who do we have here?"

"Vita's my name, don't wear it out." I think all her teeth were orange—maybe not... "I really like your name, Dane. It sounds like a Viking. I remember this movie once—"

"Hey, Jinks." Dane called out. "Throw me a brewski. Tom needs something to deaden the pain."

Whether it was Jinks, a Stash, Flash, or Mash, one of the nicknames playing a chugging game launched a bottle toward Dane who held his hand in front of my face to protect me. I didn't need Tom to push me away. The bottle missed anyway, smashing a hole in the wall.

"Dane." Molly screamed, rushing over to look at the damage.

"Hang a picture over it," Dane said.

"Good one," I said.

"Shut up." Molly glared at me then spun around toward him. "This whole thing is out of control. Why did I ever agree to let you have a party here?"

"Have you ever told me no?" Dane blew her a kiss.

"You'll never change," Tom said.

"Why should I? See you around, Tom. I'm out of here. I don't like being bitched at."

Molly looked all teary-eyed—how sad.

"Don't go," she said quietly.

"Okay," Dane patted her on the ass but spoke to me. "I'll do anything for love. I need a drink." He joined his friends who were busy stacking empties on the mahogany dining room table.

"Good to see you, Tom. It's been a while."

"Thanks for inviting us over, Molly. Sorry about the wall."

She half-smiled and was about to say something else when she saw Dane talking to a girl.

"Excuse me," Molly made a beeline toward him. Dane had it right. What a bitch. Sniffing after him like a little dog in her brown leather pumps, size four and a half, $69.95. Didn't she know by now who he really loved?

"These are your friends?" Diane asked me.

"Not all of them. Dane's a good guy."

"Are you kidding?"

"You don't know him."

"I know enough." The green fire in her eyes should have warned me. But Steve was a weakling always choosing new books.

"Let's get some food, Tom." Vita said. "Hear that? Great song. Let's dance." She yanked Tom into the crowd. Sometimes when Dane wanted me to do something, he said it. 'Come to the party,' and, of course, I did. Other times, because he knew I was smart, he made me figure things out myself. He had grown up in a home of beer. Beer was his family's food, warm and nurturing, as comforting to the Benebys as bacon, eggs and biscuits were to a Christian family who, despite their supposed belief in Jesus, didn't recognize the spirituality in alcohol. Mother had been wrong again. Booze didn't kill brain cells, it expanded them into a higher level of consciousness. I had seen the magnificence of Dane's mom and her saturated religious transcendence. Dane had killed the buzzing. My skull only hurt when mother actually talked to me. I knew—could smell and sense it—that beer would not only bring me closer to Jesus but through the sacrament of drinking, let Dane transfuse into my blood his power over mother and her bees. He wanted me to get drunk.

"Excuse me," I left Diane and grabbed a bottle.

"I don't drink," she said when I returned. "You're driving."

"It's just one beer," I said and finished it. The bitterness tasted good because it had a reason. "Let's talk." I slid into a corner on the floor and taking Diane's hand, pulled her down next to me. "You'd think Molly would have gotten some of the imported brew." The bottle became a spy glass and peering with one eye through the glass neck, I turned Diane amber. "I don't like the domestic stuff. It's got lousy hops. Hop. Hop." I bounced two fingers up and down her leg. Diane was so funny.

"Do you have any brothers or sisters?" she asked.

"I had sisters. Twins. They choked on salami."

"At the same time?"

"They always did everything together and were hungry. The dog's still alive." I pressed against Diane's shoulder and using it to get up, wandered into the light no longer harsh but softly blurred. Another beer was easy to find. I took it from inside a cluster of joking nicknames.

"How's it going, Stash. Mash. Trash. Yo, Beanie." I slapped them on the back, noticing, for the first time, the interesting slope of their foreheads and how all had large and wonderfully bright, colorless eyes. It didn't matter that the nicknames pushed me away. I was one of the clan, clever enough to finish the beer before my easy going, mingling style at the party brought me back to Diane.

"You've had enough," she said after I banged my head against the wall while sitting down. The top of my skull floated up but I grabbed it by Steve's kinky hair and yanked everything back in place.

"Tom will drive home," Diane said.

"Christ, D—"

"Let me have the key."

The key?

I gave it to her.

"You don't have to impress me," she said.

"I'm not trying to. This is who I am." The room was too hot. Was she a bitch, too?

"What are your parents like?" Diane asked.

"Full of love. Father has red eyes and can't talk. My mother's a queen bee." Then I told her more about me than even Mr. Petty at the drug store knew.

"Should I believe you?"

"No," I answered. "I'm crazy."

"Deeeeeee. Everyone is so friendly. And they all love Tommy." The blob had returned to place her hairy orange legs in front of my face. I stood, needing air but didn't want Tom to keep the world from spinning. When I pulled away from him, Dane gently caught me and poured beer down my throat. Diane kicked him. There was some scratching and yelling; Molly screamed about her rug. My stomach pushed up but I had practice holding my insides in. Bent over, someone strong helping me—Dane, I'm sure—I told Diane I loved her and made it to the bathroom. Cool water in a cool porcelain bowl, I lowered my head into the toilet. The gurgling swirl of flushed water mixed with vomit beckoned me down into the sewer where, cleansed by scrubbing powder, I'd be saved. I toppled backward and cracking my head on the marble floor, thought about Dane. He was my friend. He loved me. We'd enjoyed a beer together. Dane banged on the door.

"Steve, are you all right?" he asked in a girl's voice.

"Yeah...great..." the words crawling weakly out of my mouth. I pulled myself into the bathtub and slept until feeling Dane over me. When I opened my eyes I was happy to see he'd changed into Diane—alcohol, quieting and spiritual, also distorted values.

"Is that better?" she asked, putting a damp cloth on my forehead.

"Yes. Thank you."

"What's going on in there?" Molly yelled.

"Hey, Shithead. Let someone else in."

I had a nickname, too. Relaxed and holding Diane's hand, I walked into the light.

"Creep," Molly said, looking at me.

"Hope you invite us over again real soon," Diane answered.

The nickname pushed past and slamming the bathroom door, knocked a photograph of Molly's mom from the wall breaking the frame and scarring the large, coiffured face with shards of glass. Fish-like, Molly's mouth opened and closed soundlessly.

The party had split off into make-out corners. In the living room of overturned lamps and busted chairs, Vita circled with Tom on a smear of potato salad, her orange head buried in his chest while her foot dragged a strip of toilet paper.

"We should go," Diane said.

"Oh, Deeeee. I'm just warming up." She hugged Tom who choosing to speak instead of breathe, squeezed out a couple words.

"I'm—ready—"

So was I. Fishmouth had arrived late and taken Dane away.

By turning Tom, we managed to steer Vita to the front door. Before leaving, I thanked Molly for the good time by grinding a jelly doughnut into her carpet.

Arm in arm with Diane, I let the night air fill me. It was clean and undemanding; just a temperature: cold. I didn't think about Dane. I didn't think. Tom drove and I sat in the back seat, resting my head on Diane's shoulder, my hand barely touching her knee.

"I know a secret place," the blob said and giggled.

"She wants to park," Diane whispered to me. My head suddenly hurt.

"Tom, it's getting late. Your mom might need something."

"Is she sick?" Vita asked.

"No," Tom answered. "Where do I go?"

Diane held my hand. Steve's glasses slid off.

In Milford, Vita directed us down a narrow back road near the mills. Large cobwebs strung between fire-blasted old trees trapped drops of red moonlight. I heard the tiny screams of insects, their insides slowly liquefied by spiders having dinner. A branch scrapped its fingernails along the roof. Jagged shadows cast through fissures in the broken walls of the mill where I'd seen the light, loomed over us and made Tom stop.

"Listen to this," Vita rolled her window down. Machinery squeaking and shuddering and run by the skeletal hands of ghosts formed out of ancient, milled dust, rattled the mill's missing windows. Their arms outstretched, zombie grandmothers looking for little boys to eat, thudded into walls and left behind glowing shreds of their decomposed skin. The wind formed a mouth with teeth. It howled. Tom had been right. There were monsters here. I could feel them pounding at the front door of my skull.

"Nice," Tom said.

"And peaceful." Diane kept looking at the river.

"I just love listening to the water. It's so romantic." The blob oozed, taking over most of Tom's lap.

I took a deep breath. I had backslid…No, the weakness was Steve's who had always been afraid of ghosts. I had Dane and his Jesus for protection against the undead. Unfortunately, Diane was alone.

"Close the window," I told Vita.

"Afraid?" she asked.

I didn't answer or feel insulted. Vita was inconsequential. I locked the doors.

"Let's go for a walk, Tom."

At first I liked Vita's idea. She would make some half-man, half-lizard a tasty snack. As pleasant as this thought was, I didn't live in a fantasy world. I heard Diane breathing next to me. This was reality. If Vita and Tom left, I'd be alone with her. I had told Diane I loved her. She might want me to prove it. Love was in short supply. There was never enough to go around. What I gave her I'd have to take from Dane. That didn't seem right—or wrong. I decided it was best to keep everyone in the car. Or maybe not...

Looking back, I see all this as the typical confusion of a teenage boy.

"It's too dangerous," I said. "You girls could fall and get hurt. And what if there's some creep out there?"

"I know this place like the back of my hand." Vita said.

"I'm sure about that—"

"We'll stay," Diane said.

"Okay, D. No problem." The creature pulled Tom down on the front seat and ingested him.

Tick, tick...two torn plastic strips hanging from the ceiling and hardened by age, moved back and forth. Contacting, tired metal, rasped a last shallow breath while rust, flaking off the dome light, floated down like brown snowflakes. I heard and saw everything so clearly, the nearness of Diane heightening perceptions. She moved her thumb an inch. Her shoulder dropped and her elbow clicked. I could tell from these signs she wanted me. Steve gave in.

He put my right hand on her left breast. It was as small and soft as a wet kitchen sponge. Where were the plump, milk filled sacks the sister things took away when replacing me in mother's heart? The crawling chill crept in again. I was on the toilet for mother and Mrs. Humphrey to see. Shivers made me sweat but there was no escape. I wondered how long I should sit feeling her breast. Would Diane give me a signal to go farther? To where and do what? What were the rules? My arm fell asleep.

"You can kiss me," she said. I did. It wasn't wet and sloppy like the one with Gladys in the pumpkin patch. Our lips barely touched and I was a little boy of summer before the bees…

Tom yelled and sat up.

"You bit me."

"No, I gave you a hickey." Vita said. "I like to mark my men."

"How can I go to school like this?"

"You could cover it with a Band-Aid," Diane suggested.

"Don't tell him that, D. I want everyone to see it."

I saw the man first. Grateful I could finally take my hand off Diane's chest, I leaned forward and pointed.

"He's coming toward us."

Diane screamed.

"I'm good at handling perverts." Vita whipped out a long fingernail file from the top of her white plastic boot.

"Zombies." Tom squealed the car backward, spun us away from the mill and getting that old clunker to run fast, accelerated to the road. I put my arm around Diane and held her close. She stopped trembling.

We let the blob off first.

"I had a great time, Steve. Thanks for everything," the car rising on its springs after she got out.

"I'll call you," Diane said to her.

Tom walked Vita to the door. No problem. I now knew exactly what to do—hand on breast, feel, squeeze, count ten, kiss and start again. Steve's weakness in me had won and I didn't care—copping a feel and kissing Diane was awesome. Dave only pretended to be an ass-man. I was the real pro. I told Diane a joke and she laughed. When Tom returned, he continued serving me.

"Home, James."

"Yes, sir."

He was my chauffer and pet. I could almost trust him again.

Cleverly supported by boards, Diane's fence glistened in moonlight. The antique car on blocks in her driveway seemed ready to fly. Behind the front door her father smiled at me and said, 'nice face, Christopher. I'm glad Steve's pimples don't hurt you anymore.

We stood close to each other on the porch.'

"What are you thinking about?" Diane asked.

"You," I answered.

"It's been quite a night."

"Not bad," and I flipped my collar up. "I'll call you next week."

"I'd like that." Diane kissed me on the cheek and went inside. With my thumbs in my front pockets, I swaggered down the sidewalk and when sure she couldn't see me through the window, jumped, and fist in the air, quietly said, "Yeah."

I drove back.

"Do you believe my neck?" Tom said, twisting the rear view mirror toward him so he could examine the bite.

"It'll heal."

"By Monday?"

"No. Sorry Vita was such a pig."

"I like her."

"Then I guess you owe me a favor."

"Looks like you and D hit it off."

"She's okay," I said.

At the boarding house, Tom asked me if I had some place to go.

"Of course," I answered. "Home."

He stood in the street watching me drive away.

By parking in an alley near Dane's home, I showed him how much I wanted to be near him and hoped he wouldn't be mad at me for kissing Diane. After all, he had Molly. Lying back on the rags I'd formed into Diane's body, I looked out the window as drifting clouds, filled with night, ate the moonlit sky. It was so peaceful and quiet. I slept without moving and would have felt even closer to Diane if the springs in the back seat of Peter's

crap car had let me dream.

14

AGAINST MOTHER, I THOUGHT a lie worked best when it engaged father and got his love filled, red eyes flashing. I knew she'd have figured out I hadn't slept over at Dave's. Perfect. I could arrange a beating whenever I wanted to see Diane, escaping to her through the soft glow and silence created after father kicked in my sides. It was a foolproof plan. Awakening stiffly, the morning gray and drizzling, cold metal in my bones, I drove around Milford for a couple of hours before returning the car.

"I said, Sunday morning. You're late."

"Am I?" I stuffed a twenty into Peter's shirt pocket. "I'll call you when I need the car again. Have it ready."

The day had cleared. Frozen blue and smiling down on me, the sky above Mr. Petty's drug store welcomed me back. I returned to medicinal smells and the warm taste of stale gumballs and pickled eggs in a place where Mr. Petty's ointment on his bald head made me feel more thankful than did all the whip cream on pumpkin pies served by our maid at Thanksgiving in a house silent only during the holidays. I could share secrets with Mr. Petty father might have heard had he learned to speak. Through the door's brown glass, I saw the old man slowly counting sticks of gum. The rusted bell clanged once. Mr. Petty looked up quickly, his blood shot eyes ready to help a customer.

"Hi, Mr. Petty. It's just me."

Spit dribbled from the side of his mouth. Before cracking up, Tom's mom kissed and hugged. Father used his Italian leather shoes. People showed love differently. Mr. Petty drooled when seeing me. I hopped on the stool I'd used since childhood and after spinning around once on its ripped, plastic seat, ordered the usual.

"A banana split, please." Over the years I'd developed an immunity to Mr. Petty's gray ice cream. It no longer gave me cramps. He shuffled to the rusted cooler and dumped a load of his homemade specialty on a brown banana. Once again, when he put the dish in front of me, I almost touched his fingers stained red by the gumballs and twisted from years of hard work into beautiful spirals and knots. It wasn't easy being a druggist. He quickly took the money.

"Your toothpaste display looks great—that's okay, Mr. Petty, I don't need the change." I never did with him. I could show love, too. While stuffing the twenty into a drawer of poisons, more spit ran down his face. He was such a good man. I liked making him happy.

"I don't think I've told you yet. Tom's back. He wants to go to college. Can you believe it? What a fool. He had a hard time getting out of elementary school. He's still big and clumsy. You've seen how much I've changed."

196

I'm sure Mr. Petty nodded while struggling to lift a canvas bag to the counter. His stiff, arthritic fingers barely moving, he didn't give up trying to untie the bag, eventually opening it, the pennies spilling out. Carefully and slowly, he placed them in stacks of ten. Mr. Petty was amazing. I admired his determination and concentration. Whenever I talked to him, he listened, cared about what I was saying while continuing to count money, fill gumball machines, or do any of the other important work that made his drugstore so special.

"I had a date last night." I said. Although Mr. Petty didn't look up from his pennies, I knew he was proud of me. "Remember when girls thought I was a toad? Not anymore. That was someone else."

Over the years, I had let Mr. Petty become part of my summers and school. He had played pirates in Tom's field and been with me and Fishmouth inside the principal's office; we had traveled together on the Hebrew school bus; the high school hallway wasn't a mystery to him, he understood the rules about who could walk in the middle and what shoes to wear. Mr. Petty also knew about mother. But because of love's limited patience, I couldn't tell him everything. I had never mentioned Dane.

"We went to a party. The girl's name is Diane. I'm going to ask her out again."

Using both arms, Mr. Petty pulled the pennies toward him and bagged them tight. He started counting nickels. Because I knew kindness, like breast milk, dried up quickly, it was time to go.

"I'll try and visit again tomorrow." When at the front of the store, I glanced back and saw Mr. Petty spray disinfectant on my ice cream dish getting it ready for me to again use. He already missed me.

Outside, the boy stepped closer.

"Thought it was you," he said, his eyes still large and bright behind the battered glasses that had always been a part of his face. Although he didn't twitch, he still created movement. Old candy wrappers swirled around his legs. I wanted to laugh.

"Fish—" I stopped. We hadn't spoken in years.

"Fishmouth is fine, Steve. You were at Molly's, right?"

"Yeah, with a girl."

"Tom made it there, too. He seems the same."

"He is."

"I can't believe Molly let everyone mess her place up like that. Remember the time her mother threw us out as kids?"

"She always liked Dane," I said. The wind blew harder.

"Cold today," Fishmouth put his hands in his pockets.

"Yeah…" We stood looking at each other.

"Well, I've got to go. Tell Tom hi for me."

"I will." I forgot about Fishmouth as soon as he left. I hurried over to Dave's.

"Want to know how far I got?"

"No," he said, standing at his back door. "And keep it down. My mom will hear you. What are you after now? Make it quick. I've got homework to do."

"On Sunday?"

"That's right. Unlike you, I want good grades."

Oh, Dave, stupid Dave, can't appreciate the beauty of perfect Cs, but I didn't want to argue with him.

"Tit," I said.

"What are you talking about?"

"That's how far I got with Diane. I squeezed her bare tit."

"She doesn't put out like that."

"She did for me. Vita went even further."

Dave stepped outside and shut the door.

"Are you going to ask Diane out again?"

"Sure. Let's double this Saturday. Take Vita and you're guaranteed to score. I'll call her for you."

"That's a switch. Why?"

"To return a favor," I said.

"And your friend?"

"Tom? No problem. He already got what he wanted."

"Something about this smells. Who's driving?"

"You are. In your bright red convertible."

"So that's it. You are such an asshole. But I have to admit, you've developed a little style over the years. All right, it's a deal. Where do I pick you up? I learned a long time ago I'll never penetrate the inner sanctum of the Goldblatt home."

"I'll meet you in the parking lot at school after last period."

Dave stepped closer.

"Your mother called Friday."

"Did she?"

"If you'd given me a heads up, maybe I could have gotten to the phone before my mom."

"Gee, Dave, how nice, you wanting to help. But I'd never

ask you to lie for me."

He shook his head.

"You are one strange fucker. I was wrong. I'll never figure you out. Well, I've wasted enough time. Back to the books."

With hours left before I needed a bowl of cereal, I walked around The Neighborhood and wondered who it should be: Mr. Aquaviva or Mrs. Humphrey? I needed to piss. After a quick unzipping in Tom's dead field, excitement and shame brought me to her.

I tapped only once. Mrs. Humphrey's door swung wide open.

"You look tired, Mr. Steve. But isn't that why I'm here? To help little boys and men sleep? Come along, you know your place."

I sat on the couch. She swung one leg over the other and leaning back in her wicker chair, slowly rotated her foot.

"Do you like dogs?"

"No," I answered. "I hate them."

"What a shame. They make such fascinating friends. Mr. Wolf loved Cincinnati and couldn't wait to get back there. He-went-away," Mrs. Humphrey barely opened her mouth, "but-the-dog-stayed. Now sit up and listen, Mr. Steve. I've got something important to tell you. Dogs are selfish and not very bright. They get on top of you, slobber and grunt instead of talking so how can anyone really know when the poor things need to eat? I'm not a mind reader," and she giggled. "Here's my advice. Give them a small piece from time to time, a thin slice quick and dirty you don't mind losing. Dogs like to sniff each other and run away, so why do too much? It's all stomach anyway. They haven't a heart. It's better to starve bones, keep a dog leashed for as long as you can and take him on walks. Brittle legs snap apart. Pain endures. It lengthens life and companionship. If you watch a dog die slowly, seconds of its life become days. The longer the animal suffers the less time you'll be alone. Nod your head, Mr. Steve, if you understand. Excellent. You're not only a tepid boy but a smart one, too."

Mrs. Humphrey reached down beside her.

"This is Mr. Wolf from Cincinnati. Isn't he pretty?" She wiggled a pink poodle made of yarn. "He loved dancing fast but I wanted it slow." With the poodle straddling her knee, she swung her legs apart. Heat and the crawling chill rushed through me. I grabbed a satin pillow and covered my lap.

"What have you done." Mrs. Humphrey snapped her legs back together. "I think you've been very naughty." She threw the poodle against the wall and marched over. "The pillow."

"I—"

"Let me have it. What does anything matter now? You're finished." She yanked the pillow away and pressed the fabric against her cheek. "Time to leave, Mr. Steve. Make sure you wash before eating, then wash again. Proper hygiene is essential for good health."

Hunched over in the hall, I stayed a part of Mrs. Humphrey's soft pink light until she kicked the door shut sending me back into the real world of red slashes and violet green paint.

In twilight outside the boarding house, I no longer crouched but stood tall and called down the remaining light from the sky. Strong and proud, Christopher marched toward mother.

"Out a whole weekend and you look like a bum. Come in, I'll toast you a bagel."

Was it poison? Why was mother in a good mood? Had one of her cousins died? She held the laundry room door open for me.

In the kitchen, father read a book. The sister things colored. Mother hummed while washing the dishes. Had I been transported into a parallel universe? She turned from the sink.

"You lied to me. I know everything."

Excellent. This was the house I knew. With a few words I could light a match in the heel of father's shoe and explode it into my side. On Friday, father would be at work. If I wanted a fool-proof way to escape mother, determined to lock me in, I needed the afterglow freedom from a week's worth of beatings. That meant I had to start now.

"I'm eighteen and a senior in high school. I'll do what I want."

The sister things dropped their crayons and father lowered his book. I was ready for him…

His eyes stayed clear. The twins began munching carrots.

"Here's your bagel, nice and warm," mother said. "I used to eat cereal, too. It doesn't stop anything."

Father read his mystery.

I looked around lost.

Two days of mother's friendliness packed my head with so much unaccustomed affection I knew the pressure from one more, 'How's the soup?' or 'Did you have a good day at school?' would splatter my brain against her kitchen walls. Because of her new found love for him, Steve couldn't think. With time running out, on Wednesday I cleared my mind by giving him the headaches and finally called Vita.

"I don't understand," the blob said. "We had such a good time."

"Tom's my friend and I hate hurting you, but it's better you found out now than later."

"He told you he didn't like me?"

"That's right. Said you weren't his type. Tom's not very nice when it comes to girls. I'm sorry I ever fixed you two up."

"I thought your friend Dave did. He knows D."

"That's what I meant. Dave's a great guy and he wants to go out with you on Friday. You like cars. We'll pick you up in a red convertible."

"I like Tom," Vita whined. I wanted to reach through the phone and grab her orange neck.

"Maybe if you play hard to get he'll become jealous and call you."

"Think so?"

"Trust me."

After Vita, Diane was a snap.

"Sounds great." she said. "Where will we go?"

"Does it matter? Wait to you see my car. I'm going to let Dave chauffer us around, he's been bugging me for weeks to let him drive it. Pick you up at 4:30."

"See you then, Steve."

Christopher had gotten his first date.

Mother stood at the top of the basement steps.

"Calling someone?"

"Yes," I answered. "A girl."

"How nice. Are you hungry? I made soup."

The eerie quiet in her house continued. I didn't take any chances. On Thursday, I hid my tight jeans and white T-shirt in the gym at school and on Friday morning walked straight ahead as mother waved good-bye from her open, laundry room door. I waved back. Nothing could stop me now.

The hours dragged on under the weight of useless information, a fire drill, assembly, and my lunch of white rolls. When I finally made it to my last class, English Lit, I thought how foolish the clock's second hand looked trying to tease me by inching along. It was a slug with Hamlet's face—excellent. The slower it moved, the better. I used my experience with stomachs and pain. The teacher thought I had cramps and gave me a bathroom pass. Now I'd have the rest of the period to myself.

In the locker room where I'd never undressed for PE, I enjoyed the privacy of tiled emptiness and showered, rubbing my face hard. The steve hair took a little tugging, but I made it perfect. Christopher smiled back at me from five tall mirrors. When the school bell rang, the middle part of the hallway with its cool kids, parted to let me through. In the parking lot Dave sat in his car, the top down. An icy wind rattled the trees. He honked once, again, then two times more. Didn't he see me walking toward him? The car horn blasted. It sounded like angry bees…

"Steve," mother called through her window. "Come here, dear. We have to go." Father raced the engine. The sister things made monkey sounds while jumping up and down on the seats. Packed into the station wagon and loud, the Goldblatt family waited for me.

"Stevie, listen to your mommy," someone behind me yelled. The out of school crowd laughed, the sound cascading over me in a roar. steve was a coward and the world stared at him. He took over and choosing new books, moved my legs as if they were on strings.

"That's a good boy," mother said. "Giving up a shiksa isn't easy. You father never has."

"Pretty clothes," the sister things said.

I crawled into the station wagon's last seat and sat facing Dave's flashing lights. After a few minutes, he screeched past us.

We ate at a take-out specializing in fried fish. I chose a hamburger and ordered it rare. The dripping blood and fat formed interesting patterns on the wax paper. Alone in the back of the car, I gobbled down the meat and licked my fingers. I wanted to feel bad. I wanted to poison steve.

"It's better this way," Dave said. "I'm finally rid of you."

I stood there expressionless, a stone, the words running off me.

"Sorry, Diane, Steve couldn't come. He decided to ditch you and go for a ride with his parents. That's what I should have said but I'm a bigger idiot than you. I actually made up an excuse. Of course, I didn't know then that I'd spend the whole night trying to get Vita's bra off. Action my ass. She's in love with that friend of yours. You are such a liar."

I wasn't careful. I could have tricked the answer out of him. Instead, I let Dave hear steve's heart.

"What did you tell Diane?"

"Fuck you." He went to class.

There were teachers in the hall. I didn't start running until out the door. No one followed. I realized then how few people cared about steve or even knew he was in school. At the Little Store, now selling only booze, I paid a man to buy me a beer. I drank it quickly and feeling calm, in control inside the phone booth, called Diane, willing her to answer. I wanted her home and sick. The phone kept ringing. No problem. I'd track her down in school. A rim shot sent my books tumbling into a garbage can.

A half a block from the Little Store, I stood to the side trying to ignore the woman who, holding the hand of a little boy, paced the sidewalk in front of the bus stop. The boy looked at me, his eyes large and afraid. I knew immediately he'd been kidnapped. Humming, kicking a stone, I glanced around casually, pretending I hadn't noticed anything. I could already describe the kidnapper: skinny, dirty yellow hair, small eyes and a smoker's cough. I sat on a bench and poking two holes through a pigeon stained copy of the *The Beacon*, kept her under surveillance. I would save the boy the same way Dane had saved me from ghosts and bees. I was Christopher,

Defender of the innocent.

With belches and diesel smoke, the bus pulled to the curb. The kidnapper, yanking the boy toward her, got on. All I had to do was tell the driver…The bus drove away, the boy looking back at me from the window. I waved good-bye to him. I'd decided he was going to a better home, someplace where his new mother, although a hag, would hold and hug him and keep him protected by never locking him outside. He'd be her only child. Besides, I didn't have time for the police. Diane was waiting.

I flipped past the comics to the only section of the *The Beacon* I enjoyed. The obituaries. Isaac Burnbaum. Thomas Kelly. Karl Ripple. Howard W. Schwartz. Jeweler, golfer, family man, veteran, Rotarian, patron, saint—the small paragraphs in black ink neatly summed up what others thought the dead had been. The death notices were all grins and clown paint; tidy, shorthand descriptions never once taking the reader into the inside world of shadows and dreams where even old men went to again taste their mother's milk. The obituaries always made me laugh.

The D bus pulled up. Why D?

I got on and held out a twenty.

"Can't you read?" The driver tapped the exact change only sign above the coin drop. "Are you trying to be a wise-ass?"

"No, sir. Can you chan—"

"I don't have time for punks. Get off."

The accelerating bus splashed slush on my pants and shirt. Of course the clerk in the Little Store didn't want an underage stud like me inside but by stuffing a twenty into his hand I got all the dimes and quarters I needed. My pockets sagging with coins, I went back to the bus stop and stood waiting in the cold drizzle. Shivering, I sneezed before my sleeve was ready. My wet clothes stiffened and the wind blew harder. Finally. Lights. Another bus…Even though the driver impatiently gunned the engine as I slowly pushed my numbed fingers into my frozen jeans, I managed to fumble out at least $5 in change. I dropped a few coins but shoved the rest into the box.

"Sit down," he said.

"That's right. I will." I had done it. I was on my way to Diane. The sudden lurch of the bus stumbled me back into a seat. I rode resting my head against the window. I was warm and safe and riding without any voices, not even Dane's.

"End of the line," the driver said, his grin all I saw in the long, rear view mirror.

"So soon? Is this Milford?"

"Not unless it moved."

I recognized the station. Instead of driving past The Neighborhood and over the Hog River bridge into Milford, we had stopped at the concrete Municipal Transit Building on the other side of Cloverdale, near the town dump.

"I want to go to Milford."

"Then get a transfer."

"Okay, wait here."

"Sure, sonny, anything you say."

On the ground between broken railroad tracks, a maid's frozen white sock and hair pick puffed themselves up. The station was the way domestics entered Cloverdale. I'd always disliked the loving, caring way maids held the hands of their sons when coming to mother's front door to collect a holiday turkey or Christmas bonus; I resented the ingratitude the maids showed by quitting as soon as they got the extra money, these women not appreciating the freedom they'd been given when mother, with the power to lock them out of her house, didn't use it. Mae had been with us the longest. Periodically she needed extra money to fix her car, pay the rent, help a brother, or for some other 'Mae-Calamity'. Mother always opened her pocketbook. It wasn't that she had become more kindhearted over the years. Mother simply reconciled herself to the fact that having someone cook, clean, and make sure the plastic was always in place, was worth writing a few more checks.

I smashed the sock with my foot and stomped the comb into slivers of plastic.

Inside the transit building, under a lopsided, hanging ticket sign, the man ahead of me unzipped a pocket in the sleeve of his leather jacket and took out a couple dollars. After buying a ticket, he turned and facing me, wiggled the cigarette lodged between his two broken front teeth. I quickly looked down and walking ahead, bumped into the counter.

"Need something?" The agent wore a green visor pulled low over his forehead.

"I'd like a transfer—to Milford."

"Why didn't you get one?"

"I'm sorry. I don't understand."

"Guess not," and he spat on the floor. "You were on the

bus that just came in. All you had to do was ask the driver for a transfer. They're free. Too late now. That bus left."

"I can't go?"

"Do I look like your mother? Go anywhere you like just as long as you pay. A ticket to Milford costs a buck fifty."

"I need two. I've got to come back."

"What we professionals call a round trip."

I began counting my lint covered change. The man's eyes narrowed even more; he crinkled his nose as if smelling something unpleasant.

"I wouldn't have suspected someone like you would be paying in nigger money."

My face turned hot and red. What did he know about me? I was Christopher Barnabas Lee. Without father, I'd be as poor as anyone else who took the bus. Making sure he didn't touch the coins, the agent raked them into a drawer using the side of his gray, Municipal Transit pencil. He tore off the tickets—snatching them back when I reached across the counter.

"What do you say?"

"Thank you?" I answered.

He drummed his fingers.

"Thank you—sir?"

"That's better." The agent inched the tickets toward me. I could tell by his steely eyes what he wanted. It was a gunfight and I had to be quicker. I flexed my fingers and striking suddenly, like Mr. Beneby's cobra, my hand shooting out so fast he hadn't had a chance to move, I grabbed the tickets and pressed them against my chest. I'd beaten him.

"Want a safety pin?" he asked.

On a metal bench a safe distance from the ticket window, I sat in front of dirty windows and not wanting to see or think, didn't, my eyes turned inward into the quiet blankness of an empty skull room. Suddenly, a streak of white, piecing light lit up the inside of my head and I jerked up straight. What if I took the wrong bus.

"Excuse me," I stopped before getting too close. The man in the leather jacket leaning against the wall continued to comb his long, greasy hair. I read his name, Chico, four blue letters, *h i c o*, each tattooed over a knuckle, a crude capital *c* inked into the base of his thumb. His cigarette glowed red.

"Uh, would you happen to know which bus goes to Milford?"

"Uh, yeah," Chico said. "Come here and I'll tell you."

When I did, he blew smoke in my face.

Back on the bench, I decided to gamble on the next bus pulling in. A few minutes later, when one arrived, I hurried outside and got on.

"Do you go to Milford?" I asked the driver. "I have a ticket. Two of them."

"Express all the way. Let me have one of those. Okay, you're all set."

"Get moving," Chico said, shoving me from behind.

"Sorry." I took the first seat.

"That's mine—" Chico's black leather hovered over me.

"Don't start anything I'll have to finish," the driver told him.

"No problem," I said getting up, "it's too drafty here anyway. I have asthma." I touched my throat and coughed. The bus's empty middle section seemed safe. As soon as I sat down and stretched out my legs, two large, old women closed in.

"Hope you don't mind a little company." Pushing through, her flowered ass in my face, the woman plopped down next to me and her friend, just as fat and missing teeth, sandwiched me in from the other side. I tried to make myself smaller. Toothless took out a long salami.

"Care for some?" she asked, hitting me in the face with it. "It's kosher. Can't get this kind of meat in Milford, that's for sure. Right, Hilda?"

"Right you are, Phoebe." In her bright, flowery shorts, her gray legs, the size of small dead bodies, looked like they had been decorated in preparation for burial.

"No, thank you," I said. There wasn't any air. The bus barely moved.

"Too bad," Phoebe said, "it's tasty." She gummed and slurped on the end of the salami.

"We've been visiting Cloverdale," Hilda said, her face inches from mine.

"We like to see how the other half lives," Phoebe said. "You from there?"

"No. My name's Christopher, Christopher Lee."

"Lee, you say?" Phoebe stopped eating. Despite her small eyes and heavy, clown-like make-up, she looked thoughtful. "I knew some Lees once. Blond folk. None wore glasses."

"They must be from a different tribe," Hilda remarked.

"Probably they're his cousins."

"Distant ones, from the looks of it." Phoebe dropped the remaining piece of salami into her purse. The smell of sweat from the women's armpits floated up like poisonous gas.

Please, Dane, help—

Hilda pointed a bloated finger at words scraped into the back of the seat in front of us.

"'Jane sucks dead toads.' Now what do you think that means?" Her face did more than squeeze together in merriment, it shriveled inward like something gleeful but rotted. The sweat and airless space combining with the warm, crawling chill of mother's toilet and Mrs. Humphrey's legs made me want to rip my skin off.

"Aw, leave the boy alone, Hilda. Can't you see he's as innocent as punch." She pinched my cheek, scratching me with a dirty fingernail.

"Got any more of that taffy?" Hilda asked.

"Let me see," When turning quickly to look in her purse, Phoebe elbowed me in the head. Somehow, I managed to lift my arm above these mounds of flesh smothering me between them and pull the cord. The bus stopped.

"Leaving so soon?" Hilda asked.

"Just when we were getting to know each other. Say good-bye to Christopher." Yanked from her magical purse, melted taffy and a piece of string sticking to them, Phoebe clicked her dentures at me.

I fought my way up and over the women and by pushing down on Phoebe's head, made it to the aisle.

"Rude, ain't he," Hilda said.

"What else can you expect from someone who lives in Cloverdale," Phoebe answered.

I was almost off the bus...

Chico stuck his legs in front of me.

"Okay, you can go," he said.

When the door opened, I jumped out and ran straight ahead as fast as I could, stopping only when I'd reached the center of an empty lot. I was Christopher. Alone, and again in control. But I didn't know how to get to Diane from here. I walked back to the street and found Chico waiting for me.

"I said you could leave, but not for nothing. How much money do you have?"

"I don't know," I answered. "I always have enough."

"Hand it over."

He let me keep my ticket. I thanked him and again ran. One of the large gray apartment buildings lining both sides of the littered street represented through art the warm little homes inside all of the clustered buildings towering above me. Inside a nicely fenced yard of stones, the granite sculpture of a woman holding a baby welcomed me to Milford. There was life all around. I could feel the energy it had taken to smash the fence inward, paint a white bull's-eye on the mother's breast and cut off the baby's head. This street was just like The Neighborhood. The invisible people of Cloverdale, ducking down when rushing across their chemical lawns toward the wombs of their cars, weren't capable of understanding the feel and taste of simple, life affirming joys. Instead of jumping and spiraling forward like I was doing to absorb the gusto of warm cooking smells seeping through the apartment bricks, those from Cloverdale, lost here, would have locked their car doors and speeding away, adjusted the climate control switch on their dash.

I ran faster.

In Milford's unpretending downtown of small, shiny glass buildings separated from each other by vacant lots, the driver of a pick-up probably didn't see the faded pedestrian crossing, but was polite enough to warn me with a small, simple blast. In Cloverdale, the owner of a Cadillac would have run me over and put in an insurance claim. Turning right, then left, I followed the sound of banging signs hoping they would lead me to Diane. At Joe's Hardware, four old clocks in the window showed different times. It was getting late on all of them. I hurried inside.

A plump man wearing red suspenders stood behind the counter.

"Is the high school far from here?" I asked him.

"Let me show you." After licking the end of a stubby, yellow pencil, he began writing down directions, stopping and contemplating each sentence. The clocks ticked. "There, that should do it—no, might be a little confusing." He took the paper back just as I reached for it. "I think I'll send you across Seventh. Yep, that's better. You're all sweaty, son. How about a glass of water?"

"Do you have the time?"

He took out his pocket watch, wound it, and finally clicked

the cover open.

"One fifteen."

I grabbed the directions from the counter and ran, banging the door open.

Alley wire tangled my legs, hobbling me so a hairless dog with bulging eyes could bite my ankle. I kicked him away; fought through the cuts and blood and again running, crossed over Seventh to Courthouse Way and finally School Street. There it was. The High School, simple and complete. No ivy. Few windows. The clanking metal doors welcomed me inside. After straightening my clothes and pulling steve's hair down, I wiped my face with toilet paper and walked into the principal's office.

"May I help you?" the secretary asked.

"I'm Diane Foley's cousin. I have to see her right away. Her mom sent me. They're at the hospital and her grandmother's gotten worse."

"Oh, dear. Why don't you sit right there, I'll call her class."

The woman used a PA system with friendly, green and red blinking eyes. I couldn't keep my leg still. Finally, I heard her. Echoing through the empty corridor, Diane's footsteps banged louder inside my head as she came closer. I couldn't wait any longer. I rushed into the middle part of the hallway where I'd always belonged.

"Steve? What are you doing here?" Her eyes made me shiver.

Stay calm, I told myself, you've come too far to blow it now—

"What did Dave tell you Friday?"

"That you got sick. Is that what this is all about? I know you didn't stand me up. Dave said you like me."

"I've never liked anyone so much." I heard the words as if spoken by someone else. "I wasn't sick. Dave just lied. He can't handle anything serious. My grandmother was killed in an automobile accident on Friday. We buried her this morning. She made the best chocolate chip cookies in the world and took me Trick or Treating every Halloween. Everything's happened so fast. I can't believe she's gone."

I saw the tears in her eyes and knew I'd won. But steve always wanted more.

"When I was small, I poked a stick in a hole and bees flew out. They covered my face and I couldn't scream. Grandmother brushed them off not caring if they stung her. She held me and rocked. Even when my sisters cried for her, she didn't let go. I was her favorite. Her voice never hurt.

"I've always been scared and alone."

steve had pushed me out of my skull. I stood naked.

"I have to go back to class," Diane said. She kissed me on the cheek. "I love you."

The secretary looked at us.

I didn't think about anything until back in Cloverdale. It was as if I had been suspended unconscious inside a moving cloud. I picked up my books from the garbage can and returned to school before the last bell. Outside when it rang, I called to Tom and we walked together toward my house. He mentioned Vita only once. I had outsmarted everyone.

I was tired. I didn't mind sitting on the stoop and waiting for the laundry room door to open.

Peter's car died rusting into the ground. That didn't matter. I learned the bus routes and stored them in my head. Some I used to meet Diane whenever I could sneak out of school or fool mother. The others were just for fun—to travel to the Milford Cemetery or City Waterworks nearby while drinking a beer behind the Little Store, all I had to do was imagine myself in Cloverdale taking the Hilda and Phoebe bus where after a twenty minute ride to Twentieth and Brick Street in Milford, I'd transfer to the K line and get off at Dead End Road. I liked my mental trips. I loved Diane, and she carried me far away from my skull home.

We ice skated and made snow angels. I took her for a ride on a sleigh. There, floating now above the river, is the red Santa balloon she gave me and I let slip away. I bought her a book about butterflies. Did she ever read it? We talked, I think a lot. On May 10th, her birthday, I surprised Diane with a picnic in the park. Under the twilight filled leaves of an old tree, on a red-checkered tablecloth, candles in bottles burned around the lopsided pink cake I'd baked at Mr. Aquaviva's. I took my hand away from her eyes. I don't think Diane liked surprises. She cried. I made up for it by scaring her in the dark. Funny how these memories nibble like little fish at my fingers and toes. They want to eat me—and maybe should. By loving Diane, I had betrayed Dane.

Because spending time with Diane and figuring out ways

to escape mother took up most of my time, I could help Mrs. Humphrey around the boarding house only two days a week. That seemed enough for her. I painted and cleaned. She taught class. One evening, the lessons suddenly ended. Wearing her leopard skin, she opened the door and after I'd taken my place on the sofa, told me good-bye.

"I don't understand." Was it because I no longer needed a pillow and the warm, creepy feeling had drained away?

"You are a great artist," Mrs. Humphrey said. "No one else would have had the skill needed to paint Wolf's head and skeleton on my garbage can." She got up and lightly touched my throat. "So thoughtful...But an artist must be self-contained. A kiss is a stone. Fleshy pods dumping seeds make jack-o-lanterns inside stomachs but why grow a crying, ugly little pumpkin when you can cradle a dog of string? In you is all the heart you'll ever need. Be special. Be careful. Paint as you see the world using pink and blood. Never let a handsome witch steal your soul unless he won't leave or is dead. There's nothing left to say."

Mrs. Humphrey took her clothes off.

"Am I wrong, Mr. Steve? Tell me I'm beautiful."

I had to look away from her shriveled breasts and patch of thin, gray hair. I ran from her screams.

I sat with Diane beside the Hog River. Over us, cars crossing the bridge from Cloverdale patterned the air with gently billowing exhaust fumes. Tires circling on pools of iridescent oil floated past while birds sang. One crapped on my head.

Diane laughed, her breathing becoming short and quick as in suddenly covering silence I settled back with her on a soft bed of weeds and old hamburger wrappers. I unbuttoned her blouse. No sponges here. Diane had beautiful round breasts. I used both. Thorn bushes along the river bank cut the lapping water and mother apart. The heat was milk and it flowed through me in a nourishing, flowing rush. I didn't touch Diane's short skirt.

It was a Saturday morning when the fever began to break. After joking with Hilda and Phoebe on the bus and giving them a box of chocolates, I paid Chico more money than he wanted, transferred, and two stops later, walked whistling the half a block to Diane's home.

Her father greeted me with a smile.

"Hi, Steve. How's it going?"

"Good. No complaints. Is Diane around?"

"No, went out early this morning job hunting. She wants to earn some money over the summer."

"Yeah, I know how that is. I'm lining up work, too."

"Saving money for college, huh?"

"Couldn't go otherwise."

"You can wait for her. I could sure use some help in the backyard."

"I'd like to," I said, "but I have an interview in an hour. I just wanted to stop by and say hi."

"I'll tell Diane you were here."

I had come all this way and Diane had shot me down. Christopher didn't take shit from anyone. I decided to make her pay. I rode the buses until I'd been gone long enough for mother to let me in. On one of the jaunts back and forth across Milford, I had seen Dane's sister, Karla, standing on a corner, her skirt hiked up. What a whore. I would never have polluted his blood.

"Diane's called your house, she's called me—why won't you talk to her?"

"I have my reasons, Dave. It's really none of your business. I was a lot happier when you weren't talking to me." It made me sick thinking I'd ever asked him for a favor. I didn't need him—or Tom. Although I still loved Diane, she had to learn. I turned and walked into the schoolyard grass where I sat and ate my lunchtime rolls with Dane. Unfortunately, he didn't know he was there.

"You've been such a good boy lately," mother said. "That girl keeps calling and you ignore her. It shows me all my hard work over the years has paid off. You have values. Now I've made a decision and I don't want your father taking any credit for it."

He didn't try. At the table, as the sister things slurped chicken soup, he turned the page of his newspaper—the thick, Sunday edition he'd recently subscribed to for added insulation.

"I'm going to give you a car," mother stated.

"Stevie's getting a car." the things shouted, their exuberant happiness for me quite touching despite the shower of broth and chicken parts that came with it.

"Red or white?" I asked, knowing mother had followed Cloverdale tradition and bought me a sports car for graduation. Diane would be impressed.

"Black," she answered. "It's your father's old Buick."

"You're kidding, right?"

"It was good enough for me. I went on my honeymoon— such as it was— in that car. Now you can have it. But make no mistakes. I'm not doing this so you can drive around tramps. The car's transportation to college in the fall. I've spent enough of my time playing nursemaid. I'm not going to be your chauffeur, too."

I'd been accepted to Carlisle, a private college in southern Ohio that welcomed the average students of wealthy parents. My first choice, Holy Cross, had rejected me.

"Stevie has a car, Stevie has a car," the sister things chanted. Munchkin, begging at his dish, barked with them. Holding their hands up like paws, their tongues hanging out, the twins whimpered behind their soup bowls.

"Look at you two girls, playing so cute with the dog. There's a key on the table," she told me. "Don't lose it."

A key.

From mother.

I squeezed it tight and went into the garage.

The Buick waited, dark and parked in a corner far from father and mother's cars. Unlike their cars, lumps of dead metal in this large, unspotted space of empty walls and shelves, the Buick knew I was there. I sensed a presence in it. Although I struggled to open the heavy, driver side door, once I got inside, the door quickly slammed closed. When I touched the steering wheel it said hello by shocking my hand with a thin sparking line of blue static. I sat on turkey bones and melted chocolates left there by the sister things encouraged by mother to picnic in the car. For a moment, while looking in the back seat and seeing a shadow, I almost knew the reason why mother hated the Buick. Then the secret slipped away…until now…

The river around me remembers. Mother and I float together silently inside our own memories but the strands tangle and I see into her. She lies on rose petals covered with virgin blood. Father made her bleed in the Buick and from her honeymoon the shadow stained the back seat forever. I'm glad, as an 18 year-old with his first car, I didn't know that whenever I drove it I carried with me the stain from my conception. I wasn't mother. I couldn't keep all my rooms neat and uncluttered. Even when young, I already had too much inside my head…

A sliver of sunlight through a crack in the garage wall, elongated across the pitted dash to form the head of Mr. Beneby's tattoo snake. While backing out, I tested the turn signal. Its clicking blinked a loving red eye. On Treemont, the sudden downpour following one deep rumble of thunder, blinded the car windows inside a sheathing of gray rain. The wipers didn't work, sparks shooting from the switch. When I leaned forward to wipe the glass, the Buick swerved toward two blurry, oncoming lights. I yanked the steering wheel just in time to avoid the crash. The other car passed in a quiet swish, its blaring horn muffled by the heavy weight of water splashed up and over me from the street. Leaks in the roof converged, dripping a cold, wet line down the back of my shirt. Maybe Tom could help.

"Sounds like a short." He looked almost competent in his Import Service Centre overhauls. "Isn't this your dad's old car?"

"Bought it from him. Can you fix it?"

I scooted to the side and he looked under the dash.

"Yeah, the wiring's all screwed up. We're really booked, Steve. I'd never be able to squeeze you in today. Come back tomorrow after we close. I'll work on it then." He got out and stood in the rain, his matted hair making his eyes as blue and butterfly stupid as they had been when we were eight. He had let me down again.

"Thanks. See ya."

"I wouldn't drive it this way."

What did he know? I accelerated out of the lot, maybe splashing his uniform. I couldn't tell. He was already wet.

The rain hit harder, striking the Buick like metal pellets. I fiddled with the wiper switch, rubbed condensation off the window and still not able to see, opened the door and leaned out. The wipers went on. Door closed, they stopped.

I understood.

The snake on the dash; the turn signal's red eye; the way the Buick had showed me its ornery streak by swerving into traffic and joked using its funny wipers—the Buick had something more in it than an indistinct presence inside metal. It held dad. The loving spirit of Mr. Beneby who, through wires and steel, would not only listen to me but even better, speak back demanding I include him in my life.

"We're going to mother's," I told him. "I'll get you all fixed up tomorrow."

Dad liked that. The wipers swish-swished across the window. He didn't once try driving us head-on into traffic. In mother's driveway, while waiting for her to return, I told dad a few dirty jokes. I'm sure they made him laugh.

The next day, Tom rewired the dash and tuned the engine. If the rest of the work hadn't taken a week, I would have paid him even though he didn't charge me. But Tom's slow, plodding laziness, made me break my promise to dad that he'd be in tip top shape in a few hours. Because he was incapable of understanding the difference between a burned out taillight and dad intentionally accelerating on a curve or stalling when passing a truck because I'd made him upset, I never told Tom how dangerous he'd made a week of my life by dicking around with the car repairs.

"It's been seven weeks." We crossed the bridge on a spring day quiet and blue white. Dad hummed along, listening. "I'm sure she's learned her lesson by now." A ball and bat rattled in the trunk. Someday I planned to drive with dad to the park. steve was a little nervous so to calm him, I opened a tube of Mr. Petty's head ointment and sniffed the clotted green ooze. I turned on to Diane's street and just as I had expected, saw her walking.

"Hi," I said, my arm draped over the steering wheel, a tooth pick in my mouth. "Care for a ride?" She didn't stop. "I, uh, know I haven't been by—"

"Or called me back." Her green eyes looked through me.

"I had to make plans for college. Get a job. Work on this car. It's an antique."

"Is it?"

steve would have eaten a whole tube of Mr. Petty's ointment by now. I stayed in control and kept pace with her.

"So, D, the prom's next week. We can double, if you want. I'll get Tom to go with Vita." I could tell Diane appreciated that. Her lip trembled.

"Has anyone ever told you you're a nasty bastard and a liar?"

"I don't understand—"

"Neither do I, but I'm done wasting my time trying to figure you out. It's over. Stay away from me."

Maybe a minute passed, or two. steve sat, unable to think. When I saw her again, she was half a block away.

"Should I run the bitch over?" I asked dad. He was smart. He made me decide. I floored the Buick and with the toothpick sticking in my lip, grinned at her when speeding past. I left Diane behind in fumes and poisonous smoke while giving dad a good 'ol ride.

At the Hog River, we parked under the bridge where I had polluted myself with Diane's tits, the thought of them an actual taste curdled and sour in my mouth. The day had gotten hot. I rolled up the windows and took my clothes off, letting steve absorb the heat and pain of his betrayal of Dane. Christopher knew. Love existed in rationed amounts given by father, Mr. Petty, even dad, but one love formed a baby of sunlight inside me. In the heat and sweat, I thought about Dane and touched my stomach. The baby slowly rocked…

Dane took Molly to the prom. Tom went with Karla. Dave, Peter Shapiro—wearing a gold tux—Henry, the Boogerman, nicknames, nerds, Fishmouth, even some parents bringing along pets, showed up at the Cloverdale High School gym turned into a castle and peasant village for the evening. The cafeteria staff, dressed like serfs, served turkey legs and pizza. I watched through a window, then went back to mother's house and played checkers with the sister things in their frilly, lavender and lace bedroom.

"You're such a good boy," mother said, checking in on us. "Keep off the beds."

The next day, in the hallway at school, Dane smiled at me.

"You're hideous," he told steve, who after piecing together into jokes a few of the words he could hear from the cafeteria, giggled to himself.

ALAN KESSLER

15

THE END OF HIGH SCHOOL, and I planned to leave free. Mr. Aquaviva was the first. He had trapped me during the year using hot cocoa and a kitchen table full of art supplies. It was time to pay his kind, liquid eyes back.

"Please, boys, I need you to listen," he said while lightly clapping his soft hands. Hidden behind Peter, I laughed the loudest when Dane farted. "Remember, when the band plays—"

"How about playing this." Dane yanked on his crotch. Girls giggled. More pushing, laughing and shouts in the hall as Mr. Aquaviva tried to organize us into a proper, marching formation. Those seniors he managed to line up near the lockers made faces at him as soon as his back turned and rushed again into the middle of the hallway where I stood, proud in my new, mean, black shoes.

"Look for my signal," Mr. Aquaviva pleaded.

The noise became louder—ending suddenly in a heavy, almost visible quiet full of nervous anticipation. From the gym, the band had played the first few notes of *Pomp and Circumstance.* Slowly, in hard cadence, the senior class marched beyond the corner where Dane had waited for steve outside the cafeteria. The legs, in step, sounded a unified acceptance of Cloverdale values held by yawning, sweating parents cooling their faces in the gymnasium by using the graduation program as fans. These bored parents were present only because Harvard and Yale's graduation ceremonies were still four years away. In their business suits and tailored, tweed dresses, they listened smugly to the uniform thud of legs reaffirming through their conformity the importance of Ivy League connections, country club membership, and golf. I deliberately tripped. I had rejected everything mother and father believed in. I was going to college a new man. The only thing I needed to take from Cloverdale was Dane.

We sat in folding chairs. When I wasn't watching the clever way Dane pared and cleaned his fingernails using a pocket knife, I heard some of the principal's drivel about accomplishment and remembrance, the words sounding as if they had been stolen from greeting cards and the obituaries of old men. Back straight, Tom listened to every word.

The principal handed me the wrong diploma. Hats filled the air. I stepped on mine.

"We won." Tom said, holding his certificate tight. He was one big grin. "Can't wait to show mom."

"Too bad about college." I looked around for Dane.

"Next year. It will give me time to save some money."

Mother walked over.

"Your sisters are hungry."

"Hi, Mrs. Goldblatt."

She looked at him.

"Tom," I said.

"Yes, of course. Congratulations. Tom," and she briefly shook his hand then turned back to me. "Your sisters."

"There's someone I have to see."

"Good-bye, Mrs. Goldblatt. Check you later, Steve." The room swallowed him.

"It's not like the school will miss you," mother said. "Who are you waiting for? Have a little pride. Why are you always throwing yourself at people? Your father's already plopped himself down in the car. He's relaxing. Job over. Typical. That's how much he cares about anything having to do with his family. My feet hurt and I want to leave. You have two minutes to get outside or we're going to the restaurant without you. I'm not waiting around here all day."

In the crush of bodies with happy faces and cheerful voices, mother left me alone in space too free and clean of her. I saw Dane waiting for me, his head bobbing above the crowd—his mother cut me off and yanked both of my arms toward her.

"Am I too late? Where is my child? I'm here to bless him in the name of God, Almighty." She squinted, studying my face. "Who are you?"

"You know," I answered. "Christopher Barnabas Lee."

"You look like a Goldblatt to me. Dane. I'm coming boy. Don't worry. Your mother's here." After tripping on her long pink boa, she yanked it up and looping the feathers around the principal's neck, pulled him close and began talking about Jesus.

Fishmouth saluted me from the end of the hall.

Outside, brightness on the Buick's grill moved dad's pitted chrome mouth. He was blue collar and grease and didn't liked being parked between two shiny Jags driven there by rich, snot nosed kids. He told me what to do to the cars. I took my old key and scratched deep into the paint.

"St-steve," the albino girl from the cafeteria tapped my shoulder. "Good luck." She reached out and because of her eyes, the caring in them I could almost feel, I wanted to hold her hand…

Instead, I put the rusted key in it and drove away just as one of the Jag owners came to get his car. That key wasn't important. I had already started my collection of duplicates.

"How much money can you get me?" Mr. Petty asked, his trembling hand knocking a section of the caked ointment from his head.

"Is two hundred enough?"

He licked his lips and his bald head sweated even more. I liked that about him. He never hid his emotions. Mr. Petty handed me the rat poison. I could tell from his nodding and shaking he wanted to get back to counting gumballs.

"Take care of yourself," I said and hopped off my stool making sure it didn't squeak or spin. "Have a good summer."

After closing in his kind, merry heart behind the drug store door, I drove at night into the narrow space Mr. Aquaviva had left for me by always taking his walks at the same time. The spare key under the mat almost jumped into my hand knowing

I had to act quickly. But I was surprised how much I could break in so little time. Standing among fragments of the small things he had gathered in his fag life, I heard the needles of moonlight through the lace curtains scratch *Chris, Chris, Chris,* from the wobbling record pieces decorating the floor. That's right. I didn't have to come here anymore. It was steve who had drawn his insides out at the kitchen table showing thoughts too personal for anyone, let alone a queer, to see. I tore apart steve's framed paintings and all his drawings except one, the skull with red eyes taped to the refrigerator. It wasn't that I liked this piece. To make sure Mr. Aquaviva didn't think I'd been there, I had to be clever. No vandal would have destroyed everything or replaced the key under the mat. I dropped it at the door and left, right on schedule. Mr. Aquaviva didn't suspect me, and Mr. Petty kept my secret. You couldn't buy a better love than his.

Tom's mom finally died.

We crossed the road and walked past indentations in the ground where the fence had once stood. I ate poison berries with Tom and we watched, in silence, white butterflies fill the blue sky. Then I went to the willow.

Someone had hacked up the ground and put dog shit where I sometimes still sat to draw Dane's face. The desecration had been a fool's errand. Dane had grown inside me. When he whispered, I listened. His roots were in my heart.

The next day, after feeding Munchkin, I left for college.

ALAN KESSLER

16

IT WAS A GREAT ADVENTURE. An hour south of Cloverdale, Ohio farmland separated by wire fences turned into hills; rusted plows, tractors, wheelbarrows, tire swings and flowers in tin cans decorated the front yards of old farmhouses; sagging walls narrowed barn windows into sly, little eyes that blinked. I winked back. Miracle Mile seemed a lifetime ago. I was already part of the land.

For safety reasons I described everything to dad.

"There aren't any big cars out here, dad. No Jaguars, that's for sure. The kids playing in haylofts know I'm just like them." In preparation for college, I had read one book and from it, learned about crop rotation. "Go on, Jeb," I said when passing another barn, "don't be bashful. Climb down from there and ask me anything you want about alfalfa and beans." I opened the window to smell manure and in an epiphany caused by the cow shit's sharp, acidic smell, understood why the barns and some farmhouses had cupolas. They were bell towers to warn about flashfloods and tornadoes. The sky darkened. Weather vanes on the roofs spun wildly and a little girl, her blonde hair in pigtails, pulled her pet hog by its back legs toward the root cellar.

"There ain't no time for that now, Betty Lou," her pa yelled, straining to hold the shelter door open for her, the swirling wind blowing his long white hair and beard back from a weathered, wrinkled face. "You've got to leave him." His blue eyes, kind but intense, had the look of a man who, from a lifetime of storms and loss, knew when to fight and when to hide underground. He yanked his daughter in just before the funnel passed overhead sucking squealing Penelope into the air. Bong, bong, the bells rang while gusts behind the tornado beat down the barn roofs even more. Inside the ground, the farmer's family ate turnips and prayed until the howling outside stopped.

Dad drifted across the center line, swerved back, barely missing an on-coming bus.

"Sorry-about-that," I took a deep breath. "It won't happen again." My daydreaming had almost gotten us killed. I had to remember and never forget: dad didn't like being left out.

"The bell towers protect like the alarm system buried in mother's walls but things still get destroyed," I explained. "That's part of life out here. Country kids grow up seeing their animals die. Too bad Munchkin wasn't someone's pet pig. Well, that doesn't matter now, right dad.

"I'm looking at a barn that's different. Postman Pouch Tobacco is painted on the side. The farmer makes money by doing nothing except sell advertising space. He's smart enough to be your friend."

Cows with heavy udders made me remember how Dave's

mommy filled him with meat and milk. Soft bovine eyes gazed up at him from his china plate full of cow parts; the largest chunk, a pink, thick-lipped mouth, grew fangs and leaping from the table bit Dave's nose off.

A jolt, then loss of power on the hill, dad's anger pushing us back toward where the shoulder of the road had caved in leaving a fifty foot drop to the farmland below. I floored the accelerator and stroked the dash.

"You're right. Why waste time thinking about an asshole. Come on dad, not here, not today."

He again forgave me. We crested the hill and I wanted to say thank you, but hesitated and immediately realized my mistake in the shrill sound of air rushing over the weight of the Buick's sudden brakeless drop. Images shot past, shallow and sparse, unlike now. Dane stole a comb. I drew his face in dirt. Smiling Mr. Aquaviva handed me a piece of apple pie, and Tom held up a white butterfly. I saw Jesus and Diane... By pulling the handbrake hard, I managed to skid to a stop outside a one pump gas station. I wiped my face and got out.

"Fill it?" a freckled faced, red haired boy my age asked while unscrewing the gas cap.

"Yeah, thanks. Would you mind checking the brakes? They feel a little soft."

"I'll take care of it." He watched the gallons ring up.

"Weather's been good," I said.

"Too hot for me," he answered.

"Sure enough. The corn could use some rain." I chewed the end of an oil splashed weed. "How's the chow in there?"

Behind me, the front of a small wood house collapsing in back advertised with peeling letters on cracked plate glass, grandma's home cooking.

"Try the chili," the boy said.

"Thanks, brother," and I went inside.

The restaurant had one table. I sat at the counter once a large tomato sign.

"Watcha have?" the waitress asked, her large breasts in a small, grease stained halter top flopping toward me as she leaned forward. I used my deepest voice and tried looking only at her face.

"Chili, please."

"How do you want it?"

"With a spoon?"

She had a nice laugh but not many teeth.

"I mean, do you like it hot or regular?" Her breasts rolled even closer.

"Hot," I answered.

"Hey, Louie," she called over her shoulder, "one acid. Need a drink with that?"

"No—I'm fine."

The waitress walked to the end of the counter and sat waiting to ring up my bill on an old iron cash register with a crank at the side. I knew this register was just the type of practical machine an Amish family would buy. After working hard for many years in the field, these simple farmers had saved enough to open a gas station and restaurant at their Amish homestead and hire the waitress and a chef. The owners were gentle people who had told their employees never to ask even those with honest, freckled faces like mine to pay in advance. But I didn't want anyone to worry. I touched my wallet to make sure I hadn't lost it.

"Something else?" The waitress stopped filing her fingernails.

"I'll pay now in case you think I might skip out."

"My, ain't you sweet." The woman cracked her chewing gum and adjusted her chest. "We've got insurance for that. Right Louie?"

"Right you are, Flo—acid's up." Ambidextrous, the chef used one thick, hairy hand to push a bowl out the kitchen's pass-through while the other hand pointed a shotgun into the room. I went back to my stool.

"Enjoy." The waitress handed me a cracked bowl and brown metal spoon. The gray liquid bubbled with bits of green shimmering meat. steve would have nibbled but I ate a heaping mouthful and caught fire. I immediately knew exactly what Munchkin had felt when I poisoned him.

"Water," I whispered.

The waitress didn't hear me. After I'd stopped sweating and could sit straight without my insides feeling like they were burning away, I paid the bill.

"Hope you enjoyed your lunch."

I nodded and didn't leave her a tip. Farm boys never wasted their money.

"The gas is ten fifty and I looked at the brakes like you asked," the kid at the pump said, his bright face and quick darting eyes showing his eagerness to please a fellow landsman. "Gave them my special eighteen point going over. Didn't find a thing." He pulled a rag from his back pocket and wiped a squashed bug off the window shield.

"I didn't expect you would." On the death ride down the hill, dad had just been dad.

"Yep, crawled all the way under there," the boy said, waiting.

"And I appreciate it." I gave him one of my twenties. "Corn's high."

Driving away, I watched in the rear view mirror as his eyes became the shape and color of mine.

At the scenic view above the Little Miami River, I parked and looked down into a valley forest of mottled grey sycamores whose color and thin trunks made the trees appear as if they had been dappled on the air by an unimaginative artist using the wrong sized brush. I didn't like the leaves either. They sagged under the weight from too much light. The river added depth and prospective to the scene but wasn't reptilian enough. Just beyond the woods, the sameness of the sun-cast shadows on Carlisle made its buildings blend together. I would have shaded them differently, made each appear to have façades of wings and soaring spikes. After backing out, I turned and headed into this valley twenty miles from Jackson, the town closest to the university. Down here, the forest was perfect.

Thick woven branches of the forest changed the large farmland sun that had followed me on the road above into a small yellow eye. It wasn't a Watcher's eye bulging from the face of a Cloverdale mother looking out her window, but Dane's talisman welcoming me into this sacred forest of trees and stone where an ancient, vestigial darkness hidden from the bulldozers that had built Carlisle, promised power over the university to the beautiful and truly Christian. Five minutes later and while singing a hymn, I drove onto campus.

Spread-eagle, a girl in shorts landed on the Buick's front window, crawled over the roof while boys wearing beanies and fraternity shirts threw buckets of pink, soapy water at her and dad. The girl slid down the back and ran. The fraternity guys surrounded her and after making sure they drenched her T-shirt, pushed her back and forth. Two sports cars sped past, followed by a convertible full of waving, laughing blondes. Screams made me look up. Hanging out her dorm window, a redhead in a robe yelled at beanie wearers running away carrying a ladder and a stick with a pair of pink panties flying from the top. The frats, holding their flag high, charged the campus pond where another group of them splashed girls in bikinis. I knew what every high school senior in Ohio did about Carlisle's Hi-Jinks Day. In the *Why Come to Carlisle* brochure I received at the beginning of my senior year, the ivy bordered page highlighting the school's expanded library and academic improvement followed pages on fraternity life with special mention of Hi-Jinks Day, the day before the start of school when students were allowed to 'blow off steam before commencing the rigors of Carlisle's academic life.' I knew the truth. Carlisle recruited the rich and spoiled. They shopped on a hundred main streets with names similar to Cloverdale's Miracle Mile. I wore overalls and didn't need a party school but

I had come prepared to help Dane transform me.

"Phi Gamma, pale face. We scalp all freshman nerds." The face in war paint whooped in my ear before joining a band of warriors dancing around their fraternity house. Caught in the cross fire of an egg fight, I turned left and saw the sign for Cormick Hall. I didn't want dad to feel bad. The cars in the lot were new.

"They're not interesting, no character or dents, just shiny paint. You'll outlive them all." He seemed happy. The Buick didn't speed up and smash into one.

I parked and unloaded. Because I might need a change of costume, I had packed well. Under the heavy weight of bundles and bags—I now knew how the sister things felt every day—I trudged toward the dorm, slipped on grease and fell, sending everything flying.

I met Billy.

"Let me help you. Just stuff it all back in. Doesn't make any difference, right? It's like eating. Steak or cream puffs, they all came out the same end. Billy's the name, Billy X. Kelly. Careful, one of my friends lost his thumb that way, buckle cut it right off at the bone. There. Done. All it needed was a good stomp. Hardly left a mark. Actually, the suitcase looks even better than before. I'll carry it for you. Have to watch your step around here, the parking lot's a mine field. What's your name?"

"Christopher."

"Glad to meet you, Chris." He used his free hand and shook my arm. "I've already checked the school out. It's great. Plenty of big windows. Excellent targets."

"For what?"

"Rocks."

"I just got here. I've haven't had a chance to see much—"

"Sure you have. All that's important. The eggs. By the way, your car's a beauty. I came by bus."

Billy was shorter than me. He wore plaid shorts and a green shirt; his black hair stuck up in back. Two girls on their way to the tennis courts, laughed at him.

"I can take it from here," I said, reaching for my suitcase. Christopher didn't need a nerd for a friend. Billy held on tight and turned toward the girls.

"You, there. Blondie. I hoped you locked your car."

"Excuse me?"

"The corvette, right? I saw you park it. It's nice, too nice for this school. My friend here, Geoffrey Christopher of the Avon-on-Hampton Christophers, London, England, had his antique roadsters shipped to Carlisle from his family's country estate in Cheshire, and now look at it over there, covered in yolk and egg shells. Unbelievable. What kind of a person would do that? Vandalize a gentleman's car right outside his dorm room. The campus police are working on the case. Geoffrey's father is personal friends with the police chief. They both went to Cambridge together. Make no mistake about it, this matter will be settled to everyone's satisfaction. Keep your eyes open. Report anything suspicious. My name is William. Geoffrey and I are in room 250. Come by anytime. If you want, I'll watch your car. Treat it just like my own. What's your name?"

"Bug off, creep," the girl said and glanced over at me

sympathetically. I managed a weak smile. Although pretty, the blonde and her friend reminded me of high school princesses. How did I fit in?

The girls continued on.

"What was that all about?"

"Fun." Billy answered. "What else is there? Well, time to go." The fucker ran off with my suitcase. I bumped along after after him.

In Cormick's lobby where golf clubs, record players, guitars, trunks covered with stickers from European vacations, blankets and oversized pillows, cluttered the floor on both sides of a line of nervous freshmen, the girls wearing dresses, the boys, polo shirts and pleated pants, I sat on my bag and waited. Billy pulled me up. He tapped the boy in front of us on the shoulder.

"I know Mrs. Fisher. We have an appointment."

"What?" As soon as the boy turned, Billy pushed me past him.

"We're from maintenance. There's a serious problem with the binary indicator on the top floor air valve. We've got to tell Mrs. Fisher right away. Yes, it is that important. People are suffocating." Billy kept talking and we kept moving closer to the front. Of course everyone knew it was all bullshit, but in this room of anxious, sweating freshman, Billy's crazy performance filled time. He was entertainment. The line propelled us on.

"Sure's crowded. Place like this is probably full of deadly germs. Hope that doesn't kill you." Standing on his toes, Billy looked up into the face of a fat kid about to eat a candy bar. "Seems okay, but you can't really tell. See the curly haired guy with me? Looks the picture of health, right? Truth is," Billy lowered his voice, "he's a carrier. If he sneezes on you, you're dead." Billy shoved my knee from behind, crumbling me to the floor.

"Oh, God. What's happening to him? Someone get his legs. You two, grab his arms. Careful, now, lift." Pointing and yelling, his eyes crazy bright, Billy directed the show.

"Put me down." I said, twisting to get free.

"He's delirious. I knew this would happen. Hang on Christopher. Just a little longer and we'll be home."

Carried to the sounds of whistles and cheers from those in the lobby, I reached the front of the room where a small old woman, hunched over and surrounded by stacks of papers, only glanced at me before turning to Billy. My student porters held me tight.

"Hi, Mrs. Fisher. I'm back." Palms on his chin, he learned forward across her desk. The woman's eye twitched; a section of her well-kept, blue-white hair unhinged and flopped down across her face.

"Yes. William." She lowered her voice. "I thought I'd taken care of that little problem."

"You did." Billy making sure everyone could hear. "I went right to health services. It's amazing what a little cream can do for puss and a rash. When I scratch my balls now it's only recreational."

Mrs. Fisher's proper, rouged and dusted face, puckered up even more. She fanned her face with her hand.

"So, William, this gentleman with you—"

"Christopher. We've been friends for years. We're from the same town. You can tell he's sickly. Hemorrhages. Not all the time, thank goodness, but when he bleeds it doesn't just drip from his ass but clots in his leg. He either limps along or, like now, if it's too painful, needs a wheelchair. Do you have one handy?"

"I can—"

"That's okay, Mrs. Fisher. We've come this far, we can do without it and just carry him to my room. His parents want me looking after him."

"What's Christopher's last name?"

"His last name? Hm, strange. All of a sudden I can't think of it." He looked at me.

"Steve Goldblatt," I said quietly. "I'm adopted."

"Did I mention he also vomits blood?" Billy said. "There was this time—"

Mrs. Fisher made a mark on her list and without looking up, motioned us on.

Applause followed me upstairs.

"Watch his head," Billy said. "Turn right and dump him on the bed. Thanks boys. Have some gum." After they left, he jumped up and down across the mattress until bouncing me off. "So, Roomie, what do you think?"

"That you're probably nuts and Mrs. Fisher's a fool."

"Probably?"

"I haven't decided. Did you have friends in high school?"

"Tons."

"With nicknames?"

"Does Stinky and Psycho count?"

"Your dad—any tattoos on his arms?"

"No, but he has a big burn mark from the time he tried to deep fry a turkey on our porch."

"Does he drink beer?"

"All the time. This is great. It's like being questioned by the FBI." Billy slapped me on the back. "You and I are going to be great friends."

"Why am I so lucky?"

"You don't care what people think. I knew that after taking one look at your car. Where are you from?

"Milford. My dad's a minister and my mom works in a factory."

"Reverend Goldblatt?"

"He's half-Jewish. My real parents were missionaries. When I was four, they went to Africa and didn't come back."

"Wow, Africa—know where Buckley is? An hour from here in the real Ohio hills. It's even smaller than Jackson." Billy hopped up on the window sill of our open window. "The local bird is a buzzard and the picture show plays grade B horror flicks. I never planned to go to college. I figured I'd be lucky just graduating from high school. Then some coach from Carlisle saw me play baseball and decided I should get a scholarship. So, here I am."

"I wrestled, but I don't have time for that now," I said, while carefully putting my folded clothes into all the drawers of the room's only dresser. "I'm on a scholarship, too. An academic one." Overalls were good on my farmland drive but in school

I needed variety if Dane wanted me to overpower Carlisle's social order. I liked what I had chosen to bring, wondering, as I finished unpacking, what went better with wool slacks, alpaca or leather.

"We both better make grades or they'll boot our asses out of here," Billy said and was gone, leaving white open space as he fell backward through the window. Was he dead? I walked over to check.

"The porch has strong railings," he commented matter-of-factly while looking up at me. "That's important for anyone who gets drunk at one of our parties. Give me your hand."

"So you can yank me down?"

Billy looked like I'd hurt his feelings. He crawled back through and sitting Indian style on the floor, spoke of revelation.

"When it comes to fun, my home town's buzzards and flicks taught me all I need to know. Buzzards are goofy looking but each in a different way. You can get a girl to scream just by putting on plastic fangs and jumping out from behind a bush. One Sunday morning, outside the Filmore, while standing in front of a movie poster for Dracula from Outer Space, I watched two buzzards stick their heads inside a dead rat and speaking through the sound of their eating they told me the three great commandments: never have fun the same way, use the simple things in life like a scary face and disgust to make people shit their pants, and a lie isn't wrong unless you tell it to a friend." Billy got up.

"You can have either bed, Chris. I sleep on the floor."

He said Chris. He saw my true form. Did he also believe

in Jesus?

"The X in your middle name—is that for Xavier?"

"Yep. I'm a sainted one. Here's your key."

Billy, religious with nickname friends and a father who drank beer, had just given me a key. To my home. Did it matter that he thought buzzards talked?

"Thank you," and I was close to letting him grow inside me.

"Let's swear a solemn oath." Billy took my hand. "In honor of the nymphs living in the forest, we offer our bodies filled with all the cheap wine we can drink, to you, oh gods of fun, promising that when we graduate from this noble institution we'll forget everything we learned and leave no unsacrificed virgin behind." He opened his pocket knife. "Time to seal it in blood."

Ritual and initiation into a new life…

I pulled away.

"Maybe later," Billy said. "We've got four years. I like the leg thing. Mrs. Fisher spooks real easy. I'll tell her you need a nurse."

"How about looking around campus?"

"Sure. Let's get drunk." Billy shot by me. In the hall, I practiced locking and unlocking the door.

"Think someone will steal our clothes?"

"We have a whole room of beautiful things," I said and laughed. "Race you downstairs."

"Don't forget to limp."

I dragged my leg outside.

Laughing blondes on the large grassy oval in the middle of campus teased fraternity men who goosed each other while heat lightning flashed in the clear blue sky. Freshmen, their sagging shirt pockets full of pens, carried shopping bags full of new books and walked heads down along stone footpaths.

"That won't last," Billy said.

"What?"

"The studying. They'll learn cheating is more fun."

"I say do just enough to fuck the system."

"I like that, Chris. Are you good at it?"

"It's always worked for me."

We came to Mirror pond. Boys still splashed bikinis. The sign read, *No Swimming.*

"I used to follow all the rules," Billy looked across the water. "Then, in 10th grade, I made a mistake. That's the problem with goodness. It demands perfection or someone dies. Trouble's different. It stretches like a sack of shit. There's always room for more. I feel safe with devils." He unzipped his pants and pissed in the pond.

At Eve's Asp, the campus bar located conveniently at the end of fraternity row, Billy stacked our empties. I liked drinking. It rested me.

"A masterpiece." He stuck a straw and napkin flag in the top bottle just as a frat boy bumped the table.

"Hey. Numbnuts." Billy called out and jumped up, his hands in fists.

The boy didn't stop and turn around until his friends almost convinced him he'd been insulted. I'm sure in his whole life no one had ever called him a name.

"Are you talking to me?"

"You fit the description. Apologize."

"For what?"

"For almost knocking over my work of art."

Over six feet tall and muscular in a cut-off T-shirt, his crew-cut bright blond, the frat guy's expression changed from slight uncertainty in a mostly vacuous face to contempt, his little mouth twisting unpleasantly.

"Art? That's shit, just like you." Acknowledging the applause, he lifted his clasped hands above his head—bent over gasping, holding his stomach after Billy charged into it head first.

"Run," Billy said calmly. So I did. Out the back door, I fell over a garbage can, scraped my arm on a brick wall and kept going until reaching Mirror pond. It was dusk. Tired and hungry, I wanted cereal or a bag of rolls. I went to Cormick where I stood outside the dining room with freshmen showing what they had learned their first day—how to wait in line. The thick, hot, food smells made me sick. Billy joined me. He had cuts and a black eye. I wondered if I should care.

"Why are you here?" he asked.

"You told me to run."

"You bet your ass. No sense both of us getting beat up. I mean, why are you in line?"

"To eat?"

"God, Chris, how did you survive without me? Come on. Oh, Mrs. Fisher."

At the oak, dining room doors, Mrs. Fisher stood smiling

until hearing Billy call her. Suddenly, she looked even older, new crevices cracking the rouge on her face.

"Hello William…I hope there's no problem…What happened to your eye?"

"Ran into a tree. No big deal. But you can help me." He told Mrs. Fisher that because of my bleeding and leg, I had to eat on time. She looked back at the forty hungry freshmen watching her.

"I'm sure Steve—"

"Chris," Billy corrected her.

"Oh, yes, sorry—I'm sure Chris won't have to wait long. Once we open the doors—"

"He needs to go in now," Billy said. "The ambassador will appreciate it."

"The ambassador?"

"Chris' father. The family's very well-connected."

"Well…" Mrs. Fisher looked at me and bit her lip.

"Bullshit," the thick necked jerk behind us said, his pock marked face turning bright red. "I'm first."

"Yes, you were," Billy said. "Now Chris is."

"I remember you from earlier. You're an asshole. You look good with a black eye. I've got half-a-mind to give you another one and improve your face even more."

"Half a mind? Are you sure you want to do that? You'll have nothing left."

Standing with his arms down and speaking softly, Billy seemed so calm, almost peaceful. I knew he was about to attack.

"Please, boys, no fighting," her hands fluttering, Mrs.

Fisher turned to the Negro attendant at the doors and nodded. He let us in.

"Thank you, Stuart," she said.

"No, thank you, Mrs. Fisher," Billy called back.

Bubble and rattle; tentacles of warm, greasy steam from stainless steel containers full of baked chicken, fried chicken, brown rice, wild rice, asparagus tips, white and brown gravies, glazed carrots, fish and lobster stews, wrapped my stomach and pulled tight. A slab of rare roast beef glistened near pitchers of milk. In their smell, cinnamon sprinkled squash reminded me of the weed killers used on Cloverdale lawns. Mrs. Fisher trailed behind me, offering suggestions.

"Try the prime rib. Or maybe you'd like a piece of liver?"

"Is there any cereal?"

"For breakfast. Ha. I see you have a good sense of humor." She stabbed a thick steak and dropped it on my plate. "Can't have your father thinking we don't feed you." I was back in high school, my lunch bag leaking egg salad. The hot food in the room pulled me down. I not only limped, but walked bent over.

"Nice touch," Billy said while throwing another drumstick on his plate. I waited for him as he piled more food on. The room filled with bodies and clatter.

"There's an empty table over there." I said after he grabbed one more cupcake.

"Naw, that one's no fun. Let's sit with Mrs. Fisher."

Stuart had carried her tray to the front. The glob of fat in the center of my meat wobbled back and forth and stared at me as Billy and I crossed the room.

"Chris…and William. So nice of you to join us." Mrs. Fisher knocked over her china teacup, spilling tea on the table cloth. Silent and efficient in his white shirt and bow tie, Stuart leaned over and, after placing a linen napkin over the stain, poured her another cup.

"Thank you," Mrs. Fisher said without looking at him.

"Yummy food," Billy said, taking another big bit out of his turkey leg and smacking loudly with pieces of skin dangling from his mouth.

"You're a slob," the pockmarked boy from the line said.

"Now, Harvey, don't be unkind," Mrs. Fisher said.

"That's right, Har-vey," Billy said. "You have to have manners in life. Would you be so kind as to pass me a roll."

The rolls. White and dry and nicely clumped together, waited wanting to fill me…Billy took the basket and dumped them in front of him.

"Hey." Harvey yelled. "Maybe someone else wants one."

"I like to make sandwiches."

He stuffed a pad of butter inside each roll, mortared the sides with mashed potatoes and peas and poured ketchup over the top.

"That's disgusting," Harvey said. "He's wasting food, Mrs. Fisher. Look at his plate."

"Now William—Stuart, may I have two aspirin."

"My family's poor, Harvey. Sometimes this was all we had to eat."

"Yeah? We'll how can you afford to come here?"

"Athletic scholarship."

Harvey laughed.

"That's more bull crap. You're a shrimp."

"We shouldn't call people names," Mrs. Fisher said, "and we shouldn't make assumptions based on how someone looks or care if he's rich or poor. That's what education is all about. Tolerance. Accepting different customs, religions, and social backgrounds. When you graduate Carlisle, you will have developed the sensitivity and maturity needed to treat everyone as your equal. More tea, Stuart, and another aspirin, please."

"Mrs. Fisher, you hit it right on the head with that customs stuff." Billy pointed a steak knife at her. "There's this tribe in Africa. Whenever someone special visits the village, the tribesmen trap a few monkeys, tie them to the table and slice their skulls open, just like this." The blade swished close to Mrs. Fisher's mild, well-mannered sipping. She rattled her cup and saucer down.

"Very interesting William, but perhaps this isn't the time to discuss it. Chris, you're not eating your meat."

"But it gets even better." Billy used a sliver of chicken bone to pick a piece of lettuce from between his teeth, then leaning closer to Mrs. Fisher, continued. "The monkeys twitch and jerk even after they're dead. It's a delicacy to catch and drink the spraying blood and eat the eyeballs. The main course is served when the Chief gives everyone a spoon so they can scoop out chunks of the warm monkey brain. The really neat part is after dinner. The guests put coconut oil on their penises and—"

"Excuse me," Mrs. Fisher got up and with Stuart rushing to

open the door, quickly left the dining room.

"Something I said," Billy's eyes big and innocent. Everyone at the table laughed, except Harvey.

"I don't have time to hang around with losers," he said. "In high school I just beat the shit out of them. I'm out of here."

"Before you see me eat these?" Billy held up one of his sandwiches.

"I'd like to see you choke on them. Twenty bucks says you're a liar."

"How about fifty?"

Harvey's flabby hand that would someday adeptly use a gold pen to sign a pink slip but never have grease under the fingernails, or help install a rifle rack in the back of a pick-up, folded into a fist. He hit the table and took out a fat new wallet.

"Anyone else want a piece of the action?"

The bets went against Billy. I stayed neutral and held the stakes.

"The deal is this," Harvey said, glaring at him. "You eat all of them in three minutes. Spit anything out, and I win. No water. Nothing to drink. That shouldn't be a problem, right? After all, you were raised on this shit."

"I don't like the terms."

"Too late now, asshole. I've got you by the balls."

"Well, Harvey, here's what I think. I'll eat the sandwiches in *two* minutes and if I do, you pay everyone back."

"How much you got?" Harvey asked me.

"$164." I saw sweat on his pockmarked upper lip. He nodded and watched the clock.

"Go, go," those at the table chanted. One minute. A minute and a half. Billy just sat there.

"Just as I thought," Harvey said. "You're a pussy."

"Guess you called my bluff," Billy poured hot sauce on the sandwiches and stuffing three at a time into his mouth, finished all of them with five seconds to spare. Applause and whistles; glasses banged the table. I was the first one to slap Billy on the back.

"Knew you could do it."

He gave me half the winnings. After muttering something about shitheads and dildos, Harvey sulked off. Head down and ugly, he reminded me of steve.

Billy was still eating my steak when Dave walked over.

"I didn't know you were going to Carlisle," he said. "We could have been roommates."

"Damn. I can't believe I missed out on that. Well, time to split. See you around, Dave. Come on Billy."

Still chewing, he stood up first.

"Hi. I'm Billy X. Kelly. If you're a friend of Chris, you're a friend of mine."

"Chris?"

"Or Steve, whichever's most fun at the time."

"I'm not sure I understand what's going on."

"It's simple. Chris gets special attention. The best of everything. All he has to do is limp."

"Limp?"

"That's right. Isn't it great?"

"I guess acting odd gets easier the more you do it."

This wasn't the first time I'd wanted to kill him.

"I think Chris has natural talent," Billy said. "Are you from Milford, too?"

"No…Cloverdale."

"We met at a swim club," I said.

"To me, one small town is the same as another," Billy said. "Nothing makes sense anyways. So, Dave, what's your idea of fun?"

"Girls."

"Figured that. Bet you and Chris raised some hell back home."

"I fixed him up once."

"Yeah, and after I was done with her she became a nun."

"Isn't this guy the coolest." Billy threw a couple of fake punches at my stomach. "With him around we'll never run out of laughs."

I agree, I thought Dave would answer, but he didn't. He just kept looking at me.

"There's a freshmen mixer at the Student Union tonight," Billy said. "We should all go."

"I'm sure Dave is busy."

"Not really. I could use a laugh."

"That's the spirit. I'll get my party duds from under the mattress. How about meeting back here in ten minutes?"

"Sounds like a plan," I said.

Dave started to say something to me, but I walked away and at the vending machine in the hall, bought an Italian sub of cotto salami and sausage covered in mayonnaise and white cheese. I didn't believe in voodoo or spells. I wasn't steve afraid of ghosts. I couldn't get rid of Dave by pretending there were demons who would drag him away If I burned a piece of his hair together with this sub of flesh and milk while chanting, under a full moon, just the right incantation. I wanted to kill time and make sure Billy wasn't in the room when I got there. The sub's ingredients required destruction. This gave me the perfect reason for taking a five minute walk up the street to a garbage can.

After stomping it flat, an act gratifying but not supernatural—Dave would have enjoyed eating the sandwich but I wasn't really smashing in his face—I threw the sub at the metal container and left.

Once again at the dorm, I slowly climbed the back stairs and outside our room, knocked once. He didn't answer. I tried the handle. Billy had been a good boy and locked the door tight. It was pleasant using my key and hearing in the smoothly turning tumblers the sound of rolls dropping one by one down mother's throat. I peeked into the dark and felt the cozy emptiness. He wasn't there to ask any questions. Without switching on the light, I took my oldest shirt and pants from the dresser. These clothes matched Billy's personality and by tearing the shirt pocket I would make the outfit even better. To finish dressing, I went where I'd find what I needed—water, a mirror, and secrecy.

In the bathroom down the hall, the glare from twenty sinks and urinals spotlighted me only briefly. I escaped the light by ducking quickly into the dark enclosure of a stall. After tearing the shirt's pocket, I scuffed my black shoes, a pair not fashionable or hoody, but a safe, nondescript style that could fit in anywhere. When dressed and at the mirror in the still empty bathroom, I saturated steve's goddamn kinks and pulled on them, letting go only when I heard footsteps in the hall.

"We've waited a half hour," Dave said when I joined them. "What the hell took you so long?"

"Your shirt's ripped," Billy said. Neat and pressed, he had even parted his hair.

"Yeah, I'd better change."

"I'm leaving," Dave said.

I returned wearing alpaca and wool.

"Look what I found." Billy waved the battered sandwich. "A whole sub. Can you believe it? Want some?" I shook my head. He chewed, his teeth squishing into the little pieces of heart in the salami. I didn't mind. Dave hadn't gotten any.

Illuminated by flood lights angling up from a garden of Bonsai trees and black pebbles, the Jacob Gotlieb Student Union with twenty decorative silver beams piercing its sides, rotated, at its apex, a large crystal globe of the earth pulsating red light from inside. We passed two sculptures, one a pile of bronze legs and arms; the other, a little girl welded onto the drooping shoulders of her parents. The building's architecture, meant to make me feel small, did the opposite. I would stand on top of Carlisle's world and its red eye would be mine. I liked the sculptures. I'd always known education was violent and by waiting, even a child could get revenge.

As soon as Billy and I entered the music filled room with

its overhead banner welcoming Carlisle freshmen, he headed straight for a fat girl standing alone. Dave bumped my shoulder.

"So, Chris, when did you get a new name?"

"Same time I got this," and I showed him the cross around my neck.

"You're Christian now?"

"Have been, for years."

"Okay, whatever. This is ridiculous."

"What do you know? Have you ever seen Jesus?"

"No, I guess not, Father O'Malley. But I wasn't talking about your remarkable conversion that I'm sure makes your parents very proud. Being here, with all these freshmen dorm rats, won't get me anyplace. It's stupid, just like I thought."

"Know what's stupid? All those beanie wearers on campus."

"Becoming a Baptist sure didn't make you any smarter. Those beanie wearers, as you call them, are fraternity pledges. And at Carlisle, if you're not in a fraternity you're a social zero."

"Like you?"

"Until Saturday. I'm going to a rush party. I'd ask you to come along but I can see you're too busy making a fool of yourself."

"Hi, Chris, Dave. This is Gloria. We arm wrestled in a corner and I almost won twice. I'll bet she could bend metal." As if in the presence of some powerful and mysterious force of nature, Billy looked up at her, his eyes wide and shiny.

"I'm an actress," Gloria dramatically raised a palm to her forehead. "I suffer for my art."

"Let's dance." Billy said.

"Why not, indeed." She pulled him against her and pinning his arms, lifted and swayed. "You move divinely for a professor."

"Every gentleman should know his way around a ballroom," Billy's voice muffled by Gloria's stomach, only one of his legs able to reach the floor.

"Care for a roll?" she asked Dave. He ignored her.

"Think about what I said, Steve. Maybe, by some miracle, a fraternity will let you join. Wouldn't it great to be a little less fucked up? There's Perry." Dave pushed through the crowd.

Billy and Gloria circled back toward me.

"I'll have one," I said. Smiling, she reached into the fringed pocket of her long, calico dress. In a corner, away from other people's voices, I stood and nibbled on the lint covered, white roll. It tasted full. Inside the Jacob Gotlieb building, in my small space, I dimmed the music until it faded into silence. While everyone danced, I would have enjoyed a stroll through the cemetery where Dane had buried the bees in little graves but I couldn't shut out Dave or what he had said. He'd always wanted inside of me.

I left the mixer and outside listened to the distant sound of a basketball bouncing on asphalt; I saw Tom's blond hair flying as he dribbled and jumped high to catch a butterfly and shoot toward the sky. If only he'd been stronger…

Beside Mirror pond, I knelt and swirling my hand through the moonlit water, fractured my reflection into opaque pieces of white unable to swim or fly—

Moonlight floats around me now but I'm no longer eighteen and the pieces of my skull fused together long ago.

What is this place? What sacrament do I take by drinking the oil and rotted fish in this river of the decomposed? I was always a C student who knew everything. What did Tom think he could teach me today?

The dance is over. I am eighteen and the water of Mirror pond has released me into the night...

Of course, I saw Billy waiting to jump out from behind a tree.

"Whoa. You got me there."

"I am a shadow. Invisible, until I strike." He curled his fingers into claws and hissed. "How about a pizza? We could drive to Jackson."

"It's late—"

"Yeah, you're right. They're probably closed. What if we make our own? We'll sneak into the kitchen, steal some cheese and dough and fire up the ovens."

"I'm not really hungry."

"Me either. Let's do something else. You know, Chris, Gloria is perfect. I told her the truth, that I'm not a physics professor. She likes me even more. She already hates her roommate and wants to move in with us."

"I don't know—"

"Who does? That's the fun of it."

Trusting Billy, I climbed blindfolded up Cormick's fire escape. We wrestled, ate peanut butter crackers while sitting together in a broom closet and at two a.m., banged on doors. Finally, he let me go to bed. Even with Billy's desk lamp shining in my face and the mattress hard, I was almost asleep.

"Always sleep with a light on," he said from the floor. "Gus was afraid of the dark. Goodnight, Chris. What should we do tomorrow?"

"'Night…" I barely heard the word while drifting off thinking about mother crying over Munchkin's stiff, poisoned body.

17

THE NEXT DAY, SUNDAY, Billy continued to take me along on his adventures. When summer finally ended that night, it left a malevolent piece of itself behind, Billy, on the floor, punching the air as he slept. When I reached to turn his light off, he opened one eye and stared at me.

At six a.m. on Monday, two hours before my first class, the radioactive alarm clock I'd stolen from mother's house, rang. Mother no longer told me how long I could sleep. I controlled time and the clock now worked for me. Curled in a ball, Billy kept snoring.

Just as I had planned, the bathroom was empty. I went to work on the stubborn places where steve still lived. Day to day, his ugliness moved. Leaning close to the mirror, I saw that overnight he had grown twisted black whiskers on my chin. I scrapped at them, cutting myself and cleansing the space with blood. Although by the end of high school Christopher had pierced through steve replacing most of him, the nerd still persisted; an infection I chopped at and bled and at the place he had always loved most, his hair, attacked using an arsenal of household remedies: eggs and beer; tomato juice; coffee grounds, yogurt, mud and various chemicals. Sometimes, after shampooing, I'd wear a nylon stocking on my head for thirty-seven minutes then use tongs or pliers to yank any stubborn curls straight. Even with a two hour start, all these techniques required more privacy than I had now. Unlike in mother's house, here in Cormick I couldn't be sure I'd remain alone. So, again, the best system was an old one. I plastered my hair with water and waited for any sign of rebellion. Water dribbled over my eyes. A kink twitched and I killed it. The battle won, I peeled toilet paper from my cut chin and, with skin and hair healed, put steve's glasses on after first turning away from the mirror.

"How's it going guys?" I asked, not waiting for an answer as two laughing, towel slapping freshmen chased each other into the bathroom. With my shirt collar pulled wide, I limped back down the hall.

"What time is it?" Billy asked, invisible under his sheet.

"Seven-thirty."

"Wake me in thirty minutes. I have a class at eight."

I left him a note: make sure you lock up.

Outside, morning fog streaked by drizzle turned the buildings into water-color paintings while making the pathways near them indistinct blots of shimmering grays. At the bottom of an old oak, on a few leaves, caught inside beads of water along the top of an iron fence, then ahead, at the center of two overlapping spider webs spun across Carlisle ivy, light through a hole in the sky led me on. The quickening rain soon turned everything decently black. After all, I wasn't Mr. Aquaviva who saw the world through fag eyes.

"Where am I?"

Thunder and darkness turned me in circles. I had a map, the only paper I'd saved from the *Welcome to Carlisle* information mailed to mother's house. I tried finding Jason Hall. It became a splotch of orange. The Stone Science building next to it stained my hand red, the map dissolving in rain that burned my shaving cut and caused steve's curling hair to pull up on my scalp.

Broooom. Broooom. From someplace in the storm the bell at University Tower solemnly tolled the hour. Christ. I'd gotten up two hours early and was still late. I looked into the dark sky and asked Dane if he would help. An explosion of thunder answered. Shivering, I crouched low under an old telephone pole.

"It was his leg," I heard Billy tell the college reporter. "Poor fellow couldn't out swim the lightning."

A small light, not moving toward me or away, floated in the rain. An upperclassman. Who else would have such a large umbrella? But what if he laughed at me? I didn't need him. The rain would stop, it always did, and I'd find my way. I always had.

I ran to him.

"I'm lost."

His face hidden by the umbrella, he guided me under its cover to Jason Hall. I didn't thank him. Again cold, I hurried up the steps. Both he and I made an odd choice that day, but I forgot about that until now.

In a small room crammed with fifty freshmen taking Health 101, heads nodded while a pimply teaching assistant showed slides of venereal diseases. No one noticed me. From my seat in back of the class, I looked out the window. The storm over, I rested in the quiet that had absorbed the rain and felt the power of Christopher again flow through me.

After a day of classes, I found Carlisle as easy as high school. Without studying, I'd be able to buy another diploma with Cs. On the way back to Cormick, I stopped to give my accounting and economics books a tasty dunk.

I didn't have to touch it. I could tell the door wasn't locked. Goddamn him. Billy sat with Gloria on my bed and dangling a slice of pizza from between his toes, feed a rat faced, one-eyed dog bouncing in circles on its hind legs.

"Hi, Chris. Meet Bucky."

"I asked you to keep the room locked. Why can't I trust you?"

"Sorry. I forgot."

"He forgot." I said to the walls and slammed the door shut.

"Why lock the door when we're in here?" Billy asked.

"That's not the point."

"You're right. My mistake. So, how do you like him? All he can do is eat, shit, and beg. We found him when hitching to Jackson. He took to us right away." The pizza gone, the dog snapped at the air, toppled over and immediately fell asleep, snored butt up while drooling on the floor.

"This is a dorm. We can't have pets in here."

"Right again, Chris. We'll hide him under the bed."

"I thought you said your roommate has style," Gloria shook her head. "He's a dud."

"Chris? Are you kidding? You saw his car. Wait until he hears our plan."

"Plan?"

Billy hopped off the bed.

"Gloria's a nurse. Show him, Big G."

With a hand on the back of her short, frizzy hair, Gloria modeled the Red Cross hat she'd pulled out from under her ass.

"We found it at the Salvation Army store in Jackson. Gloria and I decided to skip class. It's only the first day and I needed a waffle iron. I wasn't looking for a dog or a way too keep Gloria with us, but now we have both. We'll tell Mrs. Fisher the ambassador hired her."

"I'll feed the hungry, help the downtrodden, friendless and oppressed." Gloria crossed her hands over her chest. "I want to heal the sick. You are the first. Give me your wounds and running sores, your sad, limping leg. Tell me your secrets." She reached her greasy fingers toward me.

Gloria was bulky but probably didn't have good balance. I wondered how hard it would be to shove her out the window.

"Mrs. Fisher isn't stupid."

"If she were, what fun would that be?" Billy put the nurse's cap on. "Gloria will walk you to class. Eventually she'll push you around in a wheelchair. I might even get one myself and race you downhill."

"I won't take much room. Bucky and I can eat scraps, the food of misfortune left for us on the table of life." Gloria sighed and the dog farted.

"Do you believe any of this?" I asked him.

"No," and for a moment there was nothing in Billy's eyes.

"It's obvious Christopher doesn't want me," Gloria threw a long, paisley scarf over her shoulder. "Well, Gloria von Ortwomp never begs." With a huff, she marched out pulling the dog who, abruptly awakened, managed to bite into the pizza box and drag it along.

"Gloria likes you. Don't worry, she'll be back," Billy touched my arm. "I'd better go help her and Bucky down the fire escape."

Lying in bed, I watched summer shadows, still alive in September but shapeless, float into the room. Dave was a mommy's boy but he might be right.

Visible from the street, large Greek letters tilted below an attic window. With Dave on the passenger side, I drove the Buick down a cracked driveway and into the pit where I saw the rest of the old, two story house.

"Hello, I'm Myron," the smiling head said, leaning through my open window. "Welcome to Phi Delta Omega." Myron opened the car door for me and after I got out, shook my hand, his smile becoming even brighter. He hurried over to greet Dave. "Follow me, gentlemen."

"Pays to have connections," Dave whispered to me. As we walked through the yard of tall weeds, Myron, squat and strong, held my arm tighter.

"Hello. I'm Ziggy. So glad you came." The second Active,

tall, with a small head and also smiling, welcomed us at the front door. "If there's anything you need, just ask Ned, your party host."

"That's me." He peeked out from behind Ziggy. Ned smiled too. With Ned in front and Myron behind us, we went inside. Ziggy closed the door.

A candle on a milk carton and a pole lamp leaning for support against the wall, cast pockets of dim light in the small, shadow filled room. A few freshmen, their pocket liners left home for the night, stood surrounded by laughing and joking Actives offering them beers.

"Great party, don't you think?" Ned asked, pressing even closer to me. "Lots of Rushes, plenty to drink. As you can see, we've got a whole keg."

"I'm David Suskind. I think you know my aunt."

"I do. You're from…"

"Cloverdale."

"And you?"

"The same," I said.

"Excellent. Over the years, some of our best frat members have come from there. I'm sorry. I don't think I caught your name."

The music played. Ned and Myron looked at me.

"Steve Goldblatt," Dave said. "We went to school together."

Ned stretched his thick, hairy arms over our shoulders and after looking around, lowered his voice.

"I don't usually do this, but sometimes you just get a feeling about people, know what I mean? With you two, there was an instant connection. Let me tell you something in confidence."

"Excuse me," Myron said. "I see someone who needs a little help." He intercepted a freshman about to leave.

"It isn't easy getting into Phi Delta Omega," Ned went on. "For every twenty Rushes we might pledge one. The key is Perry. He's the Rush chairman. If he talks to you, try to make a good impression. You'll only get one shot. I'd love to see both of you with pledge pins on. If you're looking to have a good time in college, it starts right here—with us.

"Do you drink?"

"Sure," I answered.

"Then let's get some suds."

At the keg, Actives and the freshmen Rushes now stood arm in arm, singing and belching while beer splashed from their mugs. A short, two hundred pound Rush, encouraged on by bald Active twins, chugged out of a pitcher. When he collapsed onto a long black chair, the frat members laughed. I wondered if any of them had nicknames.

"Here you go guys," Ned handed us beers.

"Maybe later," Dave said, putting his down.

I finished mine quickly, the warm smoothness of it flowing through me.

"Do you guys like girls?"

"How many have you got?" Dave answered.

Ned and the Actives near us laughed. It sure was a laughing crowd.

"We just started a movie," Ned pointed to a hanging sheet, backlit and with moving shadows. "Every Saturday we get together and watch people fuck. It's tradition."

After getting another beer, I followed Dave and crawled under the screen.

"Hey. Watch it."

"My hand."

"Get down, goddammit.."

"Sorry…" I crouched lower and after scooting across the lint filled light, sat leaning against the metal legs of a long folding table. Single grunts; nervous, jittery laughs; snickering about balls and tits; horny breathing and worse, the quiet of thirty leering eyes with one thought, crept around me on sweaty, hairy, spider legs that wouldn't let me pretend I was sitting alone in the dark. The audience of boys mimicked in their awkward motion and sounds the stiff bodies on screen duplicating the strange shapes, but not the silence, of the two times mother and father had sex together. More terrible than watching the camera dip, rise, twist, and stand on its head searching for more distortion in filming bundled flesh, was the personal surrender I saw for the first time. This wasn't the pitted nakedness of Mrs. Humphrey in her apartment of satin pillows and pink light. Fucking left no barriers. It perverted love, which was singular and internal, by destroying its oneness and remixing it in humping chunks that looked like the bed had vomited. I squeezed my stomach and stumbled out.

"This one's really drunk. Good show." An Active slapped me on the back.

"The bathroom?"

"Down the hall." Of course, he smiled.

Stubby and narrow, the hallway ended at a lopsided trophy case with a yellowed, plastic front. To the side, under an overhanging pipe dangling insulation, the small, toilet paper strewn bathroom smelled of piss despite the pine tree deodorizers nailed over its doorway. Phi Delta Omega had one trophy: a one-armed man held a ping pong paddle above his head; his other arm, broken off, lay across a tarnished plate on the trophy's base, the words, Second Place. Intramurals engraved in the metal.

An award of excellence. My stomach felt better.

"Lost?"

I turned around quickly.

"You too can be a member of Phi Delta Omega. I still am." Unshaven and unsmiling, the Active swayed in front of me.

"Are you Perry?" I asked.

"Am I?" he answered.

"Kevin. Quit pulling Steve's leg. He's looking for me. Hi, Steve. I'm Perry and you've just met Kevin. He's a legend around here and very funny. I mean, how can anyone be lost at a Rush party when there's always someone around to take your hand? Let's go back. All the fun is in the other room."

I saw charm and calculation in Perry's blue eyes. I liked that. I could play, too. He walked behind me. Kevin had disappeared.

Near the pole lamp, Actives rolled shelled peanuts with their noses while Rushes placed bets and cheered. Myron showed off the letter jacket he had earned in high school playing golf. In this room of good fellowship, farts added their aroma to the smell of burps and spilled beer.

"I hope you're having a good time." Perry stood close to me.

"Everyone seems friendly," I said.

"We don't pretend here. There's too much bullshit in the world. Phi Delta Omega is a brotherhood. Why don't we go somewhere a little less noisy and talk."

In a corner of the room, behind a bamboo screen, we sat on chairs positioned so we'd face each other.

"So, you're from Cloverdale."

"That's right."

"Ned likes you. Say's you're sharp. You made a good impression."

"Thank you."

"What does your father do, Steve?"

"He owns a factory."

"And your mother? I assume she's a homemaker."

"That's right. She takes care of the house."

"Any brothers or sisters."

"Two sisters. Twins."

"Sounds like you have a great family. Phi Delta Omega is a family, too." Perry scooted his chair closer. "We care about each other. Most freshmen have difficulty adjusting to college life. Sometimes it's hard making new friends and the ones you do may not be the right kind. Everyone in Phi Delta Omega shares the same values because we all have a common background. Our fathers are doctors, lawyers, and businessmen. We forge bonds that last a lifetime. Many successful partnerships started right here, in this room."

"Do you have cereal," I asked.

"Any kind you want," Perry answered.

"Nicknames?"

"Funny ones. During Initiation Week we make up a few more."

"Who gets a key?"

"A key?"

"To the front door."

"All members. After all, this is our home."

"Is there any land around here for sale?"

For the first time since my interview began, Perry looked confused.

"I, uh, don't know—"

"That's okay, I'll check it out myself. My father's looking for a place to build his new assembly plant."

Perry reached into his pocket.

"As Rush Chairman of Phi Delta Omega it's my pleasure to offer you membership into our fraternity." He held out a tin pin. "Do you accept?"

"I do." This was the new Bowie Knife Club.

"Let me do the honors."

I'd chosen a gray shirt like Dave's to wear. The pledge pin slid right in.

"There, perfect." Perry shook my hand. "The palm tree represents the oasis of Phi Delta Omega, the eye, our wisdom." He snapped open a pocket sized ledger. "Where should I send the bill for dues?"

"To me. I'll take care of everything—brother."

We both smiled.

Long after drinking into lightness, I said good-bye to Ziggy, Myron and Ned at the front door and climbing out of the Phi Delta Omega pit, grew into a giant, my footsteps shaking the night. Wanting dad to feel part of my new family right from the beginning, I left him parked at the fraternity. I had forgotten about Dave hours ago. Good thing, for him. I crushed small people.

Billy stopped snoring as soon as I stepped into the room.

"Have fun tonight?"

"I joined a fraternity. I won't limp anymore."

"Great. A fatal illness is better. A frat house, huh? That was a good idea. You can never have too many brothers." Before I could say anything he was back asleep.

In bed and relaxing, my new home life about to begin, I had more important things to think about than Billy. Still, I wondered why I felt sorry for him. It's steve again, I decided, the part of me pimpled, needing glasses, and weak.

"Good night, Bill." I giggled from under my covers, it was good being Christopher.

Five hundred miles away, Fishmouth trained for war.

ALAN KESSLER

18

MRS. FISHER WAITED IN front of the line for me.

"Hello, Chris. You can go right in." Her make-up and red lipstick on extra thick, her blue hair particularly bright, she didn't look bad for a corpse. It was time to bury her.

"I won't be eating here anymore."

"Oh, my." Even her hair dimmed.

"Has someone been mean? Done something to upset you?"

I pulled my tennis sweater, straightening out a crease so she could see my pledge pin.

"Don't worry. Billy won't be leaving."

"William," Mrs. Fisher touched a few trembling fingers to her neck.

In the hall, Gloria, carrying Billy on her back, pranced in circles.

"Ride 'em cowboy." I yelled, and went to visit Stuart who had the day off.

At 9:00 that night I went to my first pledge meeting. Ned had asked me to bring a toothbrush. I figured it was a sleepover.

"Drop your pants," he screamed. We stood at attention in our underwear. "Suck in that gut, Rothstein, you fat pig."

Rothstein, the pledge at the Rush party who had fallen down drunk on the black chair, took a deep breath and held it. Ned punched him in the stomach. Myron and Ziggy laughed.

"Any more babies here?" Ned asked, walking down the line. I could smell the fear. The others didn't understand. All they heard was Rothstein crying.

"You did the right thing," I whispered to Ned when he was in front of me.

"Who the fuck said you could talk?" The veins in his neck bulging, he stuck his face right in front of mine.

"I know you care about us," I said.

Ned stared at me before turning toward Myron and Ziggy. "Do you believe this shit?"

They did a good job looking pissed off.

"Give me the wood." Ziggy handed him a thick paddle. "I was going to let all of you have a taste of Phi Delta Omega's Big Bertha, now you can thank Goldblatt for saving your asses. Pull down his underwear. Hold him."

Ziggy and Myron pinned my arms, but it wasn't necessary. I had never tried to get away from father.

"Thank you," I said when Ned finished. I saw the love in his eyes. He hit me again.

"Listen to this, you stupid, sacks of shit. I'm your Pledge Master and no one is going to make a fool out of me." Ned swung the paddle in the air. "Goldblatt thinks he's funny. We'll see who's laughing in the end. Get going, all of you. Into the fucking kitchen and start cleaning the floor. If you forgot your toothbrush use your tongue."

Pants still around our ankles, we hobbled into the room of long tables where they'd shown the porno flick.

"They'll hurt you, quit pissing them off," Dave said and quickly moved away from me. Harvey, who had lost the sandwich bet with Billy, called me a name. I guess he thought I was making things worse.

"Thank you," Rothstein said. He was a fool, too.

After brushing more than my section of the floor, I smeared cooking grease on the stove. Ned grabbed a heavy skillet. I knew he wasn't planning to fry eggs.

Billy and Gloria were out. Although almost asleep in the afternoon quiet, I heard two polite knocks.

"May I come in?" Perry asked after I'd unlocked the door.

"Sure," I went back to the bed and lying down, arms behind my head, waited. He put a purple and yellow beanie on the table.

"This is yours. It's our tradition to give each Pledge a Pledge hat after his first meeting. I wanted to present yours personally."

"Thank you." I kept looking at him.

"So, Steve, about last night. How did things go?" Perry stood tense against the wall.

"We cleaned up a little. Ned taught us about fraternity life."

"He is a dedicated Pledge Master. He wants every Pledge to become an Active. Sometimes he cares so much he could be misunderstood, especially by those outside fraternity row. Most people who go to college aren't fortunate enough to become Greeks. They don't understand fraternity traditions or how working through something difficult creates unity. A good Pledge would never make the mistake of telling outsiders the secrets of our brotherhood. Why get someone in trouble who's only trying to help you?"

I picked lint from my pants.

"Have you spoken to your parents lately?"

"No."

"The dorm mother?"

"Why should I? The fraternity's my family—isn't it?"

"I knew I wasn't wrong about you. You're going to make a great Active." The shiny blue of Perry's eyes held me, reflecting back my Christopher face full of hope. I put the beanie on, kept spinning its propeller long after he left.

The Pledges never went to the fraternity unless summoned. How stupid they were not to want the warmth inside. In cold twilight I stood at the pit's edge and looking down into the light felt the happiness and caring waiting for me inside my home. I need only open the unlocked door and the Actives would touch me. But that wasn't enough. I wanted a deeper love. To be truly part of Phi Delta Omega I had to show Ned, Myron, Ziggy, and the other Actives, I understood that love, through pain, made us a brotherhood. If from my suffering the pledges learned that by suffering together we became a family, the Actives would love me even more. Getting kicked or paddled was love in a vacuum if the other Pledges weren't there to see it.

I left the fraternal voices and singing behind and in starless dark, crossed the campus to a hated place, the warehouse of other's thoughts. The old, stick boned librarian with spidery veins, searched for the sound but couldn't find me. I continued ripping pages. Back behind her desk, she stacked and stamped in a flailing, frustrated movement of spindly arms unable to tramp me. Startled from her useless spinning, she looked up afraid, her expression quickly changing. I saw how much she and mother hated the girl standing there in white who would graduate from Carlisle and like me, shit on everything taught.

I followed the girl home to an apartment two miles from campus and waited in the woods. Just before sunrise, I returned to Billy's room and sitting, watching Gloria sleep, wondered if farmers felt anything when they slit the throat of a pig.

For the last few months, I'd spoken to Billy only when necessary—hello, good-bye, lock the door if you want. Now, he'd cornered me.

"How about a little privacy." I gripped my bundle of clothes tighter.

"I know. This place is a zoo." He closed the stall door behind him. "I'm wondering if I should drop out of school and marry Gloria. What do you think?" Billy wore his baseball cap backwards and was missing another tooth.

"Do what you want. Just get out of here."

"So, that's it. I knew I could count on you for good advice. It's swell being your brother. You might not believe this, but I was pretty depressed when I first came to Carlisle. Then I met you. Fun's great, but it gets a little lonely if you don't have a brother to play with. Gloria made things even better. But I've been thinking. Maybe when a buzzard eats a dead rat that's all it's doing. What if fun isn't a commandment but an excuse for giving up?" Billy looked past me, his voice distant. "Gus and I liked to hunt. I climbed over a fence at a No Trespassing sign, tripped and the gun went off. He never got up. After that, I figured if you have to be perfect and follow all the rules all the time, why follow any?"

Billy blinked. An eye peered at us through the crack between the stall's wall and door.

"After I marry Gloria, I'll join the Rotary, donate blood, print business cards with my name, William Xaiver Kelly, Esquire, and become a Republican."

I kicked the stall open. I didn't have room in my head for him.

"Goddamn fags," the blond boy said, rubbing his nose where the door had hit it. Billy jumped him. In the Buick, I finished combing steve's hair, then drove for hours with no destination until heading to Jackson and buying rolls. The bag of them had oil drops at the bottom. Dad enjoyed the familiar smell. With the doors locked, I ate inside the car then, at night, slept in the backseat on the shadow of the unknown. I knew Billy would be gone by morning. He was. I read the note he'd left on my bed.

> Hi Chris.
> Here's a four-leaf clover and
> rubber. I've carried both for a

long time. One is new. When
Gloria and me get our double-
wide I'll write with the address
so you can join us.
Keep limping, even if it's only
on the inside.
Your Friend,
Billy

Although neatly printed, the writing grinned. I carefully refolded the paper and kept it next to the key to his room.

On the day before the start of Initiation Week, I sneaked into the basement and poured coffee in the fraternity's hot water tank.

"Bastard, son-of-a-bitch." Ned yelled, rushing out wet and brown from the shower. Other brown, angry Actives followed him. He knocked me over, grabbed steve's hair and yanked up. The few Pledges upstairs huddled together afraid. I wanted them to watch. But instead of beating me, Ned pinned my arms and pushed me down the hall to a ladder.

"Let me show you, Goldblatt, where assholes in this fraternity go to die—climb up, jerk-off, and meet your fellow turd."

In the attic, a door without hinges leaned against a low opening in the wall. I walked over and knocked.

"Fuck you." the voice said, followed by coughing. After brushing away a cobweb, I ducked through the hole and entered an alcove littered with newspapers and empty cans of beans. Cold wind billowed out a torn sheet hanging over the open window.

"Didn't you hear me?" Kevin asked. Head on the floor, his legs draped over the back of a ripped sofa, he stared at me, his upside down eyes large and bloodshot. "Do I know you?"

"We met at the Rush party."

"Yesterday?"

"A few months ago."

"Did we smoke dope together?"

"No."

"Then you're a nothing like all the others."

He rolled forward and crossed his legs under him.

"See these?" Kevin opened his hand. "Each pill has a different altitude. You can tell by the colors. Maybe I'm wrong about you. How do you fly?"

"I drink."

His face turning bright red, Kevin's hoarse laughter filled the room. He jumped up, and running to the window, kicked the Omega on the ledge while shouting into the pit.

"Fraternity. Brotherhood. Bullshit. I'm a legacy, fuckers. I pay my dues. You'll never get me out of here." Kevin turned toward me. "Will you be my friend?"

"We can't all be family," I answered.

I turned and left him standing at the open window, his outstretched arms forming on the wall in front of me the shadow of jagged black wings. After I climbed down, Ned poked me hard in the chest.

"Get the point, Goldblatt? One way or another, Phi Delta

Omega gets rid of its freaks. Don't fuck with me."

"I won't, Ned. I like you."

It hurt when he kneed me in the balls but the warmth afterwards was worth the pain.

"Grand Master Frater. Keeper of the Ancient Book of Rites. First Stacker of Beanies. Brotherhood's Key Holder. Most Supreme Carrier of Light."

I glanced up. Ziggy sat on a stool covered with blue satin and as President of Phi Delta Omega, nodded acknowledging each title Myron read from a black book. The two bald Actives, the Gartangle twins, crossed paddles above Ziggy's head. Heads bowed, the pledges knelt beside me.

"Nose down, Goldblatt."

Ned kicked me in the side. Six a,m,, Saturday, the first day of Initiation Week, and he had again chosen red eyes.

"Entering through the scared portals of Phi Delta Omega requires a courageous heat," Myron continued. "With courage there is no fear. Without fear, brotherhood replaces the dark."

"Pledge Master." Ziggy called out.

"Yes, Master Frater," Ned answered, stepping forward.

"Have these searchers for truth shown good courage."

"They have."

"'Tis good," the Actives said.

"Has any been afraid?"

Rothstein's trembling made me sick and bow even deeper.

"No. All possess fearless hearts."

The Actives again voiced their approval.

"Then who can we welcome into the brotherhood of Phi Delta Omega?"

"The seven I have brought." Ned said. He lifted me by the arm and shaking my hand, squeezed hard. "Welcome, brother."

"You're an Active." Myron slapped Dave on the back.

"Come on, smile," a Gartangle said while his twin pulled Rothstein's fat cheeks apart into a twisted grin.

"I don't understand," Dave said.

"It's simple," Myron answered. "There is no Initiation Week. We were just having a little fun scaring your asses. The paper work's already been sent to national. You've been Actives for weeks. Let me show you the secret fraternity handshake."

"And here, Rothstein, is the fraternity pin." The Gartangle held a blue box close to Rothstein's sweaty face. "Go on, take it."

"Rothstein, Rothstein," the Actives chanted.

"What's wrong," the other Gartangle asked. "Don't you want to be an Active?"

Slowly, Rothstein reached out his shaking hand.

"Don't." Dave yelled.

When Rothstein hesitated, I grabbed the three small Greek letters made of white stone and silver and held them tight until Ned slapped my face. The blood tasted sweet.

"You stupid piece of shit." he screamed. "Haven't you learned anything, Goldblatt? A Pledge should never touch the Frater pin. Now, I guess we'll have to have an initiation after all. Wonder what we should call it? I know—Hell Week."

The Actives cheered and stomped their feet.

At the barber station, a line of wooden chairs in the hallway upstairs, a Gartangle sheared steve's hair off down to the scalp, the coarse kinks refusing to unwind even when lying dead on the floor.

"Let me help," Ned said, digging the shaver in deeper. Fed by blood, my blond hair started to grow.

"Like what you see?" Ned asked after dragging me to the bathroom mirror.

"Thank you," I answered. He punched me in the back.

The Pledge class stripped.

"Get down, you fucking maggots."

"Rothstein has tits."

"Harvey looks like a toad. Squat, froggy. Jump."

Good natured and helpful, the Actives shouted advice while we crawled through green muck on the bathroom floor. I got as much on me as I could. When Ned poured the sludge in my eyes I knew why.

"I'm blind." Jumping up, I bumped into Ned who slipping forward, pushed Myron against Ziggy. Ziggy grabbed a Gartangle who grabbed his brother. Arms flailing, I stumbled around smearing. Actives dressed perfectly for this lesson in their white tennis sweaters and white pants. When finished, I stood in the hallway and looked at the Actives and Pledges lying together in green glop. We were all one. Exactly what Ned had wanted me to do.

He loved me for it.

Still naked, we ran to the kitchen.

Ned's rules for Hell Week hockey were simple.

"Sit on a block of ice. Keep your dicks hanging over the edge. The first team to score wins a prize for the losers." Harvey immediately had a break-away.

"We've got them." he shouted after I scooted alongside. With his scurrying legs dragging an ice block abdomen, he looked like a large insect. He didn't have time to show shock. I kicked his ice out, sending him tumbling hard into the wall. The Actives whistled and pelted us with ice cubes.

"We're all in this together," I told the Pledges. Ned let Harvey jump me from behind. I went down hard and knowing this was another lesson the Pledge Master wanted taught, I didn't fight back. By hurting me Harvey cut himself off from the body of our brotherhood. He might survive Hell Week, but when an Active, wouldn't have a nickname or any friends in the fraternity. He'd eat alone while watching my brothers pass me rolls. Ned had shown me Kevin so I could show the Pledges the next outcast of Phi Delta Omega.

Harvey kept punching my face. I stayed down, in control and thinking. I'd always been able to separate my body from its skull. Father had taught me that instead of how to catch a baseball or fish.

"Stop it." Dave pulled him off. Ned let me rest for a few minutes in the bathroom next to the trophy case. Then there were more games. The Actives loved playing bombardier with me.

"Lie on your back." Myron said.

"Open wide." Ziggy instructed.

"Bombs away." Ned stood on a ladder and dropped a raw

egg into my mouth. "Perfect shot."

Rothstein's face, still streaked by the bathroom swim, turned darker green as he watched another yolk splash in followed by the slow pour of egg-white snot. I chewed and adding spit, made the eggs gush down my chin.

"The chair," I gurgled, "do it there."

"I'm going to throw up." Rothstein said, rushing toward the living room.

Myron grabbed a leg and held on. A Gartangle hopped on Rothstein's back; Ziggy put his arm around the fat neck and pulled down. Reaching greatness for the first and last time in his life, Rothstein dragged them all and when at the sacred, black Fraters' Chair no Pledge had ever touched, hurled himself on it and vomited. No one in the room moved or spoke. His face sweaty and covered with puke, Rothstein looked up in horror, then at me, his pleading little eyes hoping I could save him. Grotesque and weak, he wasn't someone I wanted in my family. That's why I had sent him to barf on the active chair. Like Harvey, he didn't deserve a key.

Ned trusted me. He knew I'd do what he asked. When everyone left, I made the Active chair again shiny and black by soaking up the vomit in my shirt. Hell Week's first day continued until late at night. I was disappointed when Ned locked us in the cellar. I wanted more.

"Sleep tight, pussies," he said through the door.

We gathered rags and bundled up against the cold. Rats pitter-pattered across the concrete floor or watched us from rotted beams, their eyes yellow spots in the dark, their long tails swinging. Dave sat next to me.

"I never thought it would be like this," he said. "Ned's a sadistic bastard."

"He's just trying to teach us about brotherhood."

"By hitting you? The guy's nuts. I'm thinking about quitting. I don't need this crap."

"It's your choice. I'm staying until the end."

"And that's where I hope you get it, right up the ass," Harvey said, kicking an empty paint can at me. "Forget Ned, I'd love to beat the shit out of you myself."

Although I knew he didn't realize love and pain were connected, I was surprised by how much he hated me.

"If it weren't for Steve taking the heat, we'd all be punching bags for the Actives," Dave said. He actually sounded grateful. Of course, he didn't understand me either.

Rothstein looked up from the dog bowl of undercooked spaghetti Ned had left for us.

"You've helped me big time," he said, rigid noodles poking spike-like from his mouth. The other Pledges thanked me, too. I liked having friends.

"Fuck you all." Harvey took more than his share of the rags and went off into a corner with the rats. After waiting until everyone was asleep, I covered Rothstein in an old blanket. He was soft and fat but maybe I'd keep him around.

Sunday, the Actives gave the Pledges six official Hell Week nicknames: Bullshit, Pigshit, Horseshit, Dogshit, Dumbshit and Shitass. I stayed Goldblatt. On Monday, as instructed, I wore my vomit and blood stained clothes to class. The giggles and whispers made me sit straighter. I was in a fraternity. How I looked the proof of my status. Two seats down, a pretty girl, soaped and scrubbed, her shiny blonde hair combed straight, glanced at me and turned back quickly, crinkling her nose. In less than a week, I'd be a member of Phi Delta Omega, a fraternity man whose smell she'd want all to herself. Feet on the desk, I leaned back and gave the propeller on my beanie a hard spin.

"Goldblatt run."

"Goldblatt dance."

"Goldblatt's ass isn't red enough. Paddle him again."

The Actives made the rest of Hell Week fun…

At week's end, I waited crowded with the other Pledges inside the small downstairs bathroom. Too tired to feel anything or even smell the piss, I rested my head on Dave's shoulder until hearing Ziggy's booming voice:

"Steven Goldblatt."

After blindfolding me, Ned tripped me only once while leading me into the kitchen.

"Who have you brought to us, oh, Guide of the desert?" Ziggy asked.

"A journeyer seeking the oasis of Phi Delta Omega," Ned answered.

"Does he have the eye of wisdom? Has he accepted our rules?"

No answer.

"Pledge Master?"

"Yes," Ned said quietly.

"Does he understand our traditions? The meaning of brotherhood and fraternity?

"Yes," and Ned mumbled something else.

"Then let him drink."

Ned poured hot sauce spiked ketchup into my mouth.

"The shock."

They attached wires to my leg and plugged them in.

"And now, the final stroke."

I remember the sound of Big Bertha swooshing through the air and how, when the paddle hit, I couldn't breathe.

"'Tis good," the Actives said.

"'Tis very good," Ned said. Welcoming me as a brother, he let me sleep where I fell.

I smelled cooked meat. Above me, Dave drank milk.

"Well, look who's returned from the dead. Sleeping Jesus." Ziggy laughed and so did the others. I sat down at the end of the kitchen table.

"Me want more eggs." Rothstein jabbed his fork into Ned's plate.

"You'll pay for that." Harvey grabbed the ketchup bottle and squirted Myron back.

"How about playing some ball after breakfast?" Ziggy asked.

"Good idea." Ned said. "It'll help get these lazy-ass Pledges back in shape."

"Fuck you." Harvey said. "We ain't Pledges anymore." He belched and pounded the table. Shouts and backslapping, chairs toppled over, then Ned and Ziggy picked sides.

"What about Steve?" Dave asked.

"Next time," Ziggy said. "The teams are even."

"Let's get together later, Steve, and hang out." Dave left with the others.

At the door, Ned and Harvey looked back at me, their faces blank.

Alone, I reached for a roll.

After breakfast, I wanted to feel the specialness of Phi Delta Omega. At the trophy case, I tried looking into the gilt sealed eyes of the one armed ping-pong player.

"Quite an ordeal, wasn't it?"

The yellowed plastic made the reflection of Perry's smile in it dim and small.

"Were you looking for me?" I asked, turning around.

"Of course, congratulations." His fraternity handshake felt weak. "We're having a meeting tonight at seven. You need to be there."

"Why?"

"Economics. Membership is down. The fraternity can't survive unless we find more Pledges. Every Active has an obligation to troll the mixers and recruit. You'll learn more at the meeting. Again, welcome, Steve, to Phi Delta Omega."

I heard Dane whisper.

My nicknames were cool. You fooled yourself with Billy

and these fraternity nerds...with Diane...You forsook me three times. Aren't I enough? Go outside. Hide. Wait for night.

So, I did while listening to the Actives play basketball...

In the pit, the rattling branches of an old tree scraped the icy, moonless sky making it bleed and cover me in warmth. Indians from their fraternity out there, in the dark, Actives and former Pledges, sang together around a fire, their voiced lies floating toward me on hallucinogenic-tinged smoke I refused to eat. At the pit's bottom where I stood, tumors of frozen potato peels and smashed bean cans also sang, crackling away as my foot melted the ice around them. The ice flow, caressed with rot, and a blast of wind reverberating gently inside my head, cleansed me. Grown among other crystalline thorns, one long icicle, black and shiny, snapped off, the sound calling me to it. I made a mark on skin and pressing the ice pick into my forehead, stuffed steve and his weakness down the hole forever.

"There you are." Dave said. "Where were you today—God. What happened to your face?"

"Slipped on ice," I answered.

"Careful. The fraternity needs you. The way I figure it, when Perry becomes the next president, you and I will have some real power around here."

"Hey, Assman." Ziggy yelled from the front door. "You gonna fix me up or what?"

"Coming. Well, time to make a few calls."

"You'll never change."

"But you have. See you at the meeting. Don't fall."

Someone above me moved. I watched Kevin walk along

the attic's ledge. Exactly at seven, I left the fraternity and never went back.

That winter, I visited Stuart, ate rolls and laughed whenever I saw Dave head off to a fraternity meeting or party. Each morning I crushed more of the Farter's pin until finally there was only powder and slivers left. When April's brightness let me feel summer early, I swallowed Phi Delta Omega in a Carlisle coffee mug one-third filled with a mixture of water, metal, and blood. After locking the door, I again went to the places where I could watch the girl in white.

* * *

I read in the college newspaper they found Kevin's body in the pit, below the attic window. Some thought he fell; others said he jumped. I knew the truth. Kevin was a fool who believed he could fly.

19

TWO HOURS OF HIDING and searching brought me back to Mirror pond. I'd spent the last few weeks again watching her. Now she'd disappeared. I believed that serving me, the convergence of time and space would make the girl appear. It did.

She liked white. Although wearing a white, ankle length robe, it didn't hide her beauty from me as she strode on long, slender legs across The Oval, each step shredding colors. With a disdainful shake of her head and in a spray of droplets, the girl shook the gaudy sunlight clinging to her black hair. I had decided to run to her. The wet, slippery grass sent me sprawling. Legs in the air, a sprinkler head ripping my pants, I skidded to a stop across her path. She clapped once.

"I'm Christopher," I looked up at her through muddy glasses.

"You already know me," she said.

"No…"

"My mistake then. Good-bye."

"Maybe I can walk you to class."

She stepped over my head. I got up and hurried after her.

At Stone Science, she climbed two steps before stopping and glancing back at me.

"We've had our walk. Now what?"

"A little more time?"

Her unblinking, almond shaped eyes made me want to look away—or stare into them forever.

"Isn't it interesting how sometimes things fit together so nicely it seems as though they were planned. I'm Dawn."

"Pretty—"

"It wasn't meant to be."

Out of breath, always behind her, my feet making a distressingly frenetic, pitter-patter sound, I followed Dawn into the classroom of white men. I noticed how they looked at her. Were these idiots blind to beauty? If so, then they were also incapable of seeing how my shaved head made me completely blond.

"Ah, Miss Johnson. so glad you've decided to join us again." From his podium in front of the class, the professor looked over the top of his horn rimmed glasses. "A week without your keen political observations has left us intellectually parched."

A derisive, low sound tittered through the class.

"Were you away on business?"

"Yes, professor, I was."

"And I see you've brought a guest. How delightful. Is he interested in politics, too?"

"It's hard to tell exactly what he is," Dawn answered.

"Congratulations, young man. You've done the impossible by making our Miss Johnson admit there is something she actually doesn't know."

More snickers. The professor adjusted the one strand of hair on top of his head and tapped the lectern with his chalk. We sat in the back.

"So, to continue—this is Economics, graduate level, the market system and the welfare state. I'm sure, Miss Johnson, you remember the course title—" He turned and slashed two intersecting lines on the blackboard behind him. "The federal government's interference in the economy through deficit spending to fund entitlement programs creates a negative impact on growth." The professor scribbled a few words in broad strokes. "Deficits can't continue indefinitely. Eventually, taxes increase, reducing the business sector's ability to invest in capital improvements and fund R & D. Productivity declines. To save costs, businesses reduce the work force. The economy spirals into recession. Making matters worse, the government finances some of its deficit spending by borrowing from foreign governments. Welfare payments are, if you follow the source of their funding downstream, a threat to our national security."

He again faced the class.

"Any questions?" The professor looked at Dawn who sat hands folded on her lap. "No? Hm. All right then." He cleared his throat and continued. "The government's heavy handed involvement in the supposedly free market economy isn't limited to the revenue and expenditure side. There's the issue of regulation. Our domestic corporations, faced with overburdening rules, can't compete with foreign industries in partnership with their governments. Profits decline, a business' only *raison d'être*. So, what happens? U.S. companies go out of business or relocate overseas, creating jobs for foreign workers at the expense of our own labor pool. Axiomatic is the inverse relationship between regulation and full employment."

Gripping his wide lapels, not looking at his students, the professor continued lecturing while walking back and forth in front of the class.

"A contracting national economy means a shrinking GNP. So-called social legislation, take, for example, the forced hiring of marginal units of labor, is self-defeating. Instead of creating a robust economy, quotas injected into a market system where profits are a function of productivity, and productivity dependent on competence, lead to stagnation or, in a worst case scenario, total economic collapse. Taxing corporations twice. Keeping artificially high tax rates on capital gains. Deficit spending. Regulations aimed at avoiding any injury or even the smallest environmental impact. Unions. All this affects our ability to compete in the world market. But worse are laws giving education and employment preference to the euphemistically labeled socially disadvantaged who are, in fact, simply the underachievers and poor who make up a statistical percent of all societies. To help these individuals is reverse Darwinism with the result that our economy selects for traits that destroy not only prosperity but the American way of life."

"Professor Harris," Dawn said, not raising her hand. The class moaned. Reminded by her he wasn't dictating a chapter for his next book, the professor blinked, and again aware of the classroom, readied himself for Dawn, showing in his hardened expression no intent to use sarcasm, which, I'm sure, he thought was his most benign and humorous way to convey contempt toward her.

"I'm a little confused by your terms and logic."

"And why is that, Miss Johnson?"

"Who is a marginal unit of labor? You or me?" Harris' face turned red. "If welfare is bad and you don't want to train the poor and provide jobs, what's left? Slavery? Extermination?"

"I am not a bigot or fascist, young lady. Name calling isn't very productive, especially when you need a grade in my class."

"You are a proponent of a totalitarian system run by the wealthy," Dawn stated calmly. "Capitalism isn't democratic. Just ask anyone who's been fired."

They went back and forth arguing about the rich and poor. I liked having a pocket full of money and understood hunger and pollution because of all the time I'd spent in The Neighborhood and field. So, I tuned out, concentrating instead on catching a glimpse of Dawn's breast.

After class, standing to the side in the hall, she passed a note and book to a red haired, pimply boy who quickly hid them under his jacket and hurried off as if afraid of being caught carrying state secrets.

"That's why I like chatting with Professor Harris," Dawn explained. "Sometimes I meet a person who understands. I'm going to the library. Want to come along?" She didn't wait for an answer. On our way across The Oval, I felt a surge of manhood, my leg, bloodied by the sprinkler, touching the edge of her robe.

Hidden by stacks of books and without mentioning Dane, I told Dawn about me. She listened for an hour, then handed me a copy of the *Communist Manifesto*.

"Read this. We'll discuss it tonight."

I already knew what she wanted me to believe.

In a suitable place, on the toilet, I buzzed through the yellowed paperback, finding it interesting only because I knew what mother would say.

"Dating a Negro wasn't enough. She had to be a communist, too."

I read the book again, this time enjoying every page.

Knowing it was a special night for me, Stuart washed more of the Buick than he usually did—he cleaned the windows. He didn't ask for it, but I paid him extra.

"Dancing and wine." I told dad as we drove toward Dawn's building. "You'll really like her. We're going to a restaurant in Jackson. Maybe she'll let me hold her hand. The sky's gray. It looks nice." Happy to be included, dad made the wheels hum.

Dawn let me into her small apartment above the boarded up bulkhead.

"This is Panther."

Peter Shapiro sat crossed legged on the floor. Instead of the new suit his mother probably bought for him to wear in college, he had on pressed army fatigues. He glanced up and looked down quickly.

"He's a pet," Dawn said. "I taught him a new trick. Go on, Panther, show us."

Peter pulled nervously on his matching headband and still looking at the floor, recited in a monotone.

"Because Carlisle serves the aims of a decadent and imperialistic social order by holding stock in companies that belong to the industrial-military complex, I am withholding my tuition to protest to the Board of Trustees the university's participation in acts that exploit the proletariat."

"Excellent." Dawn patted him on the head. "Maybe next time I'll have you sit up and beg. Finish your cookies and milk, Panther, and make sure you lock the door when you leave."

"I know him," I said as we walked to the street.

"Really, Steve? How interesting. I like your car."

Dad moved us smoothly on Sycamore shadows, the soft, rhythmic sound of tires merging into the quiet night. Whispering and silver, the trees swayed above the blue black river to our side; moonlight, starlight, pieces of shredded, luminescent cloud, touched the forest leaves and shriveled magically into nothing; the forest air through the Buick's open windows smelled of resin, needles, dead animals and moss. Motionless and calm, her neck and fingernails glistening with specks of the moon, Dawn watched the road.

"Turn here," she said. We drove down a narrowing, dirt path.

"Is the restaurant this way?"

"Yes. Stop the car." She climbed into the back seat. My heart pounding so hard it hurt, I followed her. Dawn stripped me quickly. Even naked she looked dressed and untouchable. She slid me into her wonderful, constricting cold.

"Is this really what you want?"

"Yes—no—I don't know."

"Your father owns a factory."

"In Milford."

"Does he build things for the government?"

"He makes underwear."

"Why did you come to Carlisle?"

"Everyone goes to college."

"You've been watching me."

"I wanted to meet you."

"Why?"

"You're beautiful."

"I'm not even pretty. Playing the wrong game can be dangerous, Steve Goldblatt. Why are you here?"

My skull cracked open.

"I've always been alone…"

"Did you read the book?"

"Want me to explain it?"

Dawn rocked, each motion bringing her closer to me. Our flesh shaped smooth lines, nothing projector fed and ugly. I tried to kiss her. Dawn turned away and leaning over the front seat, tapped the horn twice. A jeep without lights sped out of the woods and past us.

"I'll drive back," she said, already dressed.

Shrunken and empty on the blot shaped shadow I'd seen when mother first gave me the car, poked by springs and bounced around, I stayed in the back seat imagining the soft taste of Dawn's lips—

I thought about Diane…

We never ate in Jackson, drank wine together, or kissed, but when she was home and if I'd waited long enough for her, Dawn loved me in the cellar of her building where I'd lie pressed against pieces of old coal and glass. In late spring, her meetings started lasting weeks instead of days, so I spent more time with Panther. We ate cookies, discussed politics and listened to each other recite poems about the working class. Once, when talking about his old car, we even laughed.

Dawn told me to meet her outside the student union. I went early.

"You look nice," I said, happy when she arrived but keeping my distance. Except when we were together in her basement, she didn't like me too close.

"I'm pregnant. There's a chance you could be the father."

A son. Made from parts of her. A perfect container for my blood.

"I'll buy him a butterfly net. We'll play catch. I already have a ball and bat. You'll breast feed…" I wanted to hold her and cry. Her voice was ice.

"A collection of cells isn't a him. By Sunday, this problem will be over."

"I don't understand."

"Then it's time you grew up. I'm getting an abortion and I want you to pay your share."

"Hi Steve," Dave said, each cheerful, cow-gut layered piece of him showing how much he enjoyed the bright spring day now pressing down on me with blocks of light. He nodded at Dawn.

"Hello, David," she said. "How's fraternity life?"

"It'll be a lot better when I move into the house," he answered, looking at me. "It was tough having to spend the whole year in Cormick but that's what dad wanted and he's paying the bills. Next semester I finally get to live with my friends."

"How exciting for you," Dawn's eyes darkening even more. "Hanging out with all those future CEOs who will someday live in big houses and earn millions by dumping chemicals in lakes."

"I wasn't talking to you."

"And you'll never learn. What a shame."

"Perry's the Master Frater now, Steve. We've got twenty new Pledges and the Spring Formal's this Friday. You might want to check it out. Well, time for class. See ya."

"Tootles, Dave." Dawn turned back to me. "I'm waiting."

"I'll give you all the money. There's one condition."

"I didn't come here to bargain with a shopkeeper."

"We go to the fraternity dance."

She laughed. It didn't sound pleasant.

"What a great idea. Wonder what I should wear?"

I remembered when I had first seen her. In two days, she could be a June bride. Dawn sat on the steps of the Jacob Gotlieb building and lifted her hospital gown. Steel went in and my blood spurted out.

"White would be nice," I said.

Dawn never showed emotion. I wasn't surprised when she didn't react after we drove past the lights from the fraternity and into the forest. At a small, dark pond I parked and turned on the radio.

"Let's get out."

"Why?" she asked.

"To dance. Just that."

Dawn took her hand from her purse.

Perfume on smooth brown shoulders matched the scent of the wild flower I put in her hair. Trembling, I lightly touched her waist. She spun circles of light inside the circle of candles I had lit on the ground. A petal, playfully splashing in the water, called to me before suddenly disappearing without a ripple.

"It's late," Dawn said. The commercial for a toilet bowl cleaner had ended the flow of songs. The sycamores guarding us gave me the power to kiss her. I didn't. I could have hugged her too but my son would have cried. I drove Dawn home.

In my room, I finished the dance by spinning, spinning with shadows.

The day after the cells not my son died, I drank and took a few more of Stuart's pills. Lying on the floor, I traced the colors swirling above me in the air. *Nothing's wasted. Someday we'll make a real baby together...* Dawn agreed and floated back into the wall.

A week later I stood hidden in rain and watched her leave.

Dave only lied to girls.

"Of course, I called them," he said, turning around from his desk and looking up unafraid even though I stood over him. "I'm an idiot for getting involved. Why should I care? You've always acted like a jerk. But I can't stand to see you screw your life up. You don't like the fraternity. It's too normal for you. okay, that's your choice. And you enjoy cutting your hair off. Well, that's not the oddest thing you've ever done. But your obsession with some nut who thinks she's Madam Zedong is crazy. I don't understand it, even from you. What's the attraction? She's ugly. I had to do something."

"You did what you thought was right."

I remembered mother sounding on the phone just as desperate as I had imagined she would.

"A *schwartze* and communist. And who should tell me? David Suskind. His mother's big mouth will broadcast it all over town. She has a son, someone who goes to school, learns, and does what's right. I raised a murderer. Does Mr. Big Businessman care? Does he take even one minute out of his precious schedule to deal with the problem? No. And what's more—"

I held the receiver away from my ear but listened again when hearing the faint, alien sound of father actually speaking.

"I've frozen your bank accounts and you won't get a penny more from me until you terminate this relationship. I'm cutting you off as I would a useless finger."

In the background, mother talked to the walls while Munchkin, immune to poison like Rasputin, barked at the phone.

"No hard feelings," I said to Dave and shook his hand. "She's gone. Lost her scholarship. Everything's worked out for the best."

"I'm glad you feel that way, Steve. And who knows? Maybe next time you'll aim a little higher and fall in love with an anarchist."

I laughed.

"Actually, I was thinking about taking your sister out. I heard Jackie's visiting this weekend."

"Jackie—"

"Sure, unless she has other plans."

"The only thing she wants to do is bug me. What's the catch?'

"I've always treated her and you like shit. I admit it. I figured it's time I stopped being such a prick and remember how nice your mom was to me whenever I came over. She made the best ice tea. But you're right. Jackie's your sister. You should show her around."

"Hey, I never said I'd do that. I've got a test on Monday. Okay, I'll ask her. You know Jackie's only fifteen…"

"Come on, Dave. She's your kid sister. Trust me."

He did.

Squat, big chested and precariously balanced between the forward pull of her tits and the heavy counter-weight of her black, beehive hair she had kept sprayed and stiff since childhood, Jackie looked as laced up and protected as I had expected.

"Hello, Steven," she offered me her gloved hand. "David

told me about your invitation to dinner on Saturday. I'm happy to accept. Would you get my bags. There's five of them. A girl can't have too many outfits."

I dragged the bulging suitcases into Cormick's small guest apartment while Jackie, sitting on the bed, examined each of her fingernails.

"You are such a gentleman. So, Steven, what are you doing tonight? I'll bet there are a lot of great parties at Carlisle on Fridays."

"There are Jackie, but I have some studying to do."

"Oh, what a shame. You could bring your books in here."

"That'd be great except I don't think I'd get a lot done. Know what I mean?" She giggled. "Tell you what. I'll stop by tomorrow afternoon and we'll spend the whole day together."

"Wonderful, I'm so looking forward to it. Until tomorrow then." She fluttered her hand at me from the doorway.

After paying Stuart for the meat and pills, I jimmied open Dawn's door and put a new white sheet on the bed. I took a couple ludes and washed them down with beer. Although the light hurt my eyes, after my fingers and toes went numb and the mattress started floating, it was easy sleeping on a thousand nails. I'd told Peter I would break his neck if I ever saw him near Dawn's building. She had left me only her silence. I wanted it to myself.

Each brief walk we took the next day ended with Jackie back in her room freshening up by changing her clothes and putting on more mascara. Instead of a clock, I measured out the afternoon by the number of slacks, shorts, culottes, skirts, monogrammed jackets and blouses she wore. Used to primping and studying herself in the mirror, at night it was easy to get her to try different dresses until I found the one I liked.

"You don't think it's too short?" she asked.

"No. You have nice legs. Why not show them off?" The pimples on her knees matched the dress' red color.

"I think I'll—"

"You look great," and I pushed her into the hall.

"You're so strong."

"If you're good, Jackie, I'll let you feel a real muscle."

"Oh, Steven."

I think she blushed. It was hard to tell with all the make-up on her face.

Because dad still loved Dawn and I hadn't told him my plan, the Buick blew a tire.

"I can't believe, after all these years, we're actually on an official date," Jackie said, hanging over me as I changed the flat.

"Back in the car now, I don't want you to get hurt."

She smiled.

"I've always liked you, Steve."

That mattered to me, so I didn't go directly to Dawn's apartment but instead, bought Jackie a slice of pizza and a coke at a gas station then drove around for a half-hour before parking at the building.

"No one knows about this place," I said. "We can dance."

Inside, I took her sweaty hand and led Jackie into the bedroom.

"I've never gone all the way," she said, her voice like a little girl's.

"I know," I said, guiding her backwards. I looked down into her eyes. I knew what I should do. Dave had fucked me over by calling my parents. But I stopped and gave her a chance.

Jackie tried kissing me. I lifted her skirt, went in, out, and felt the sheet. Crying, she reached for my hand. I got up and turned on the light.

The next day, I brought Dave his Sunday dinner.

"What's this?" he asked, looking at the tray.

"Just the best steak you ever had. I know you're sick of dorm food so I had Stuart make you something special."

"Is it poison?"

"Very funny. Let me tell you about the gravy—it's Dawn's recipe. One thing about that bitch, she could sure cook. When's the next fraternity meeting? I want to go."

I watched Dave cut then dip into my special sauce. I poured him a glass of milk.

"I'm still wondering what I did to deserve all this."

"Well, since you asked—maybe you could call my house. Tell them I broke up with Dawn."

"Now I get it. You always have an angle. okay, Steve, no problem."

And just like that, I made father's money again flow.

Dave took his classes seriously. He'd already turned back to his books. How convenient.

When leaving, I slipped one of his fat, neat notebooks under the tray. In the basement, after wrapping the notebook and his plate in the shredded sheet from Dawn's bed, I opened the incinerator and pushed the bundle in. Staring into the flames, I smelled the steak sauce I'd made using bouillon cubes, a touch of garlic, oregano and Jackie's blood. The flames tasted yummy.

Dave passed his course. He always shook my hand when we met. His sister started dating a lot of older men. What I had done I saw as vengeful but nothing more serious than a college prank like putting coffee in the hot water tank at Phi Delta Omega. In the end, no harm done; everything washed away.

It seemed so clear...then....

ALAN KESSLER

20

I COULDN'T BLAME EVERYTHING on steve. At 13, I had wondered when I would transform completely into Christopher. Now, at the end of my senior year, I sat in Stuart's room and looked back on the lost dead things—Diane, Billy, Dawn, Phi Delta Omega—Christopher, in his imperfection and betrayal, had tried to substitute for Dane. Less weak than steve, Christopher was a fool, too. The forest trees didn't completely love him. Through grace, I'd been delivered from his sins but not yet reborn. Stuart had passed out drinking with me. I tucked two hundred dollars into his pocket and walked out into the night. At Mirror pond, the water promised rebirth. I waded to the center knowing Dane wouldn't let me drown.

On the day of graduation, I locked my room for the last time, closing in my bed and little desk, the walls I'd never decorated and the cold, smooth floor without plastic. Behind the door, I heard Billy jumping on the mattress.

"I'm going to miss you," Miss Fisher said when I gave her the key. I'd kept a duplicate for my collection. "It seems like only yesterday you were a freshman and now, my, my, off to law school. I'm sure you'll make a wonderful attorney."

"I will." I had decided three years ago law was the perfect profession for me. To make the grades needed to get into Warren Harding, the Ohio law school that billed itself the Harvard of the Midwest, I compromised my Cs and studied two hours a week.

"I hope I can meet your father today at graduation."

"I'm sorry, Mrs. Fisher, I don't think that's possible. My whole family's here and he'll be busy. He wants you to know that he appreciates all you've done for me, especially the meals. He's mailing you a check."

"A check. Oh, Steve, how thoughtful of him. Quite unnecessary, of course…"

I walked away feeling good. I had given her a special kind of hope, one that would renew itself each day as she waited at the mailbox for father's money to arrive.

At two p.m., I opened a beer and leaning against the slope of a small hill, my feet propped up on a rock, unfolded Billy's letters and postcard. In the distance, dressed in orange and green robes and sitting in lines on a platform floating in Mirror pond, Dave and the others like him graduated.

Chris—
Things going great in South America. We love Missionary work. Think of you often and smile. A croc ate Bucky. Talk about bad luck for us. Please

write.
Your Friend,
Billy

Chris—
Good News. We've almost set the date. Gloria wants to get married on back a garbage truck but that could be a problem if she decides to wear white instead of purple. Brown's my choice. I've told everyone at the sanitation department about you. Keep the next two months open. Here's my address. Please write.
Your Friend,
Billy

Chris—
Just another note to tell you where we are—Cali-fornia's definitely out, not enough earthquakes and smog, and we've put off getting MARRIED UNTIL my arm and Gloria's leg heals. The trailer still smells like the dump

but I've got all the holes fixed.
See you here <u>next</u> <u>week.</u>
Your FRIEND,
Billy.

Chris—
Got back in the country a month
ago and boy do I have stories
to tell you but I'm saving them
for when I see you here. Gloria
started acting again because her
career at the Pig 'N Poke didn't
work out—she was in charge of
the lettuces and asparagus tips
but the manager's girlfriend,
in a bloody, coup d'etat, took
control of all the vegetables.
What a shame. No one could
display lettuces like Gloria,
she's an artist when it comes
to arranging wilted leaves.
I'm singing in the park, the
pay's not great but the work's
steady and it beats garbage—
remember that job? I miss you,
no, we're not married, and yes,
you're still not writing.
Your friend,

Billy.

Although I had heard Billy dart in and out of time, the last page was his final words.

> Hello Christopher—
> Sad how fast life goes. Maximilian isn't a baby anymore. One year old and he's changed so much. We do everything together. He's a wonderful teacher. Did you ever look at people from the floor? All you see are long arms and legs, a piece of chin. No wonder kids stare up at us and scream. Gloria's back. She left the butcher. This weekend we're going for a drive in the mountains. I'm worried. I think Gus is coming too. Have fun Chris for as long as you can.
> Your brother in blood,
> Billy X.

I smelled the collection of papers, the typed and printed messages from someone crazy. I liked his postcard the best, the one he'd sent from South America showing on the front, Sister Maria Rosa Consuela standing next to the world's largest cross made of feathers. All Billy's letters but the last were on notebook paper. For that one he'd used thin, skin colored stationary to say goodbye.

The sky split in the middle, summer flowing red and warm into my last beer. When the metallic echoes from graduation finally faded, I buried Billy's words, clover, and rubber under the rock. Even steve had never played with ghosts.
I returned to Cloverdale tall and no longer wearing glasses.
I came back a man finally ready to find Christ.

21

LOCATED IN MILFORD AND chosen by father by glancing out his car window while driving past it on his way from house to factory, the small apartment building isolated behind a high security fence, welcomed me to the best part of town.

"Pleased to meet you, sir," the manager greeted me and with a big smile took my bag. "Your father has filled out all the paper work. You can move right in. I'll show you the apartment. It's large and tastefully furnished."

I gave him money. His teeth grew even bigger.

Although full of furniture—red brocade couch, upholstered chairs, console TV, bookcase and a long, dining room table— the apartment smelled empty. I liked that. It made the rooms inside me even nicer. Through the large windows I saw the roof of the old mill. In three days, I'd start the job father had chosen for me that would absorb the rest of my summer. For now, there was still time to visit old friends. I didn't lock up when leaving.

How bright The Neighborhood's tumbling in homes looked. How alive without people. Boarded up, Tom's old house was as dead as his tree. At the boarding house, Mrs.

Humphrey, wrapped in black and standing stiffly, watered a shriveled tomato plant. After she left, I ran upstairs and knocked on Tom's door.

Dane's sister, Karla, opened it.

"Yes?"

I wasn't surprised she didn't recognize me.

"I'm sorry. I'm looking for a friend of mine. I guess he moved."

"Is it Tom? He's at work. And you are—"

"A name he knows. Steve Goldblatt."

"Steve." and the chain slid off. "Of course. Tom's told me so much about you. I think you know my brother, Dane. Please, come in." She rushed ahead to pick up a newspaper and straighten the pillows. A stove had replaced the hotplate. I smelled something baking.

"Apple pie?"

"How did you know?"

"Matches the daisy curtains."

"Tom told me you were clever."

"Not really. He's just easily fooled." I flopped down on the sofa. "Have you lived here long?"

"A few months."

"Did I miss the wedding?"

She blushed.

"Tom thought it would be a good idea if we saved some money first—can I get you a muffin? I made them this morning. Or some cookies?"

"What kind?"

"Chocolate chip. Tom's favorite."

"Sure, I'll try one. Have any beer?"

I watched Karla in the kitchen. She took a few pills and after moving busily about the counter, carried back a bright steel tray.

"Are you okay?" I asked. "You look pale."

"I'm fine. The doctor thinks I might be a little anemic."

On the spot where a wonderful old card table once caved in under its own weight, Karla served me with metal and china.

"Interesting," the beer made the cookie bitter enough to swallow.

"It might taste better with tea."

"I don't think so," I said. "I remember the ones Tom's mom made."

"I keep trying."

"That's the spirit. I like what you've done with the place, everything so cheerful. How's the bedroom?"

"Fine…"

"So you're trying to put some money away."

"Mrs. Humphrey's been great. She keeps the rent low."

"How nice. Someday you and Tom might buy a house with a picket fence. Get a dog. Have a baby."

"Maybe. We haven't thought about any of that yet."

"But you're in love. That's what's important. Does he know you're a whore?"

Her tea cup and saucer jingled together, a quaint, polite sound at odds with her violent shaking until she dropped them on the floor.

"I—" But what could she really say?

"Don't worry, Karla, I won't tell him. It'll be our secret. I'm sure Tom's still working at the garage. Let me know his hours, and I'll visit you when he's not here. It'll be just for the summer. I'm going to law school in the fall. You can't be the only one with a good profession.

"Your pie's burning."

Dad understood perfectly. Karla had corrupted the Dane blood inside her by selling it on the street. Tom couldn't purify it. I had to. Also, she had wanted her blood as close to Tom as Dane's was to me, a diminishment of my special relationship with her brother I couldn't let happen. On the way to Milford, dad let the Buick run sweet.

Although Diane's street looked the same, her house had changed. Two cars with all their wheels on the driveway had replaced the one on blocks. In the front yard, a father, playing catch with his small son, laughed when the child caught sunlight instead of the ball. I closed my eyes.

"That's it," Dane said. "Don't feel anything."

I again drove across the bridge into Cloverdale. Downtown there were fewer stores between Cavanaugh and Taggert's expanded buildings. I had stayed in Carlisle during the summers, happy in my dorm room. I knew Mr. Petty had missed me. I decided to make it up to him with money. In his alley I found an empty lot where the old man had once stood counting sticks of gum and loving me. I rolled down the car window. Even the air had changed. I couldn't smell his ointment. The silence listened but it wasn't him, so why open my skull and talk? Where the kickball field at Cloverdale elementary still ended in weeds, the old log I had stood on with Dane when he made me King-of-the-Hill, whispered, wanting me to stop and play. I drove on.

Outside mother's house, two large blocks of chrome and crimson steel used brightness, color and size instead of Molly lights or a fountain spraying dollar bills, to shout, *Look at Us. We're Important. We're rich.* Each of the twin cars in the driveway seemed big enough to carry one sister thing and a tiny boyfriend.

"Of course the Buick's better," I told dad and lightly stroked the dash.

White butterflies circled above Tom's field, scattered there by a Plymouth Development bulldozer excavating through the stickers and summer burned brush. Against nature, Tom's dead, rotted tree still stood strong; Dane's home had been torn down, his willow only a stump. Filling summer hours with motion, not knowing what else to do, I drove to the old mill. The man fishing at the river looked promising.

"Any luck?"

He lifted his cane pole and swung the worm toward me. The hook gleamed through the dark and shriveled body.

"Seems like all I'm doing is drowning them. Can't catch anything if you use the wrong bait."

I liked his eyes, shiny and as black as the velvet in Dane's painting of Christ.

"I'm new in town," I said. "Know anyone who could do me a favor?" I took out my wallet.

"Money doesn't mean a thing to me."

I wondered what did. All I wanted were a few uppers.

"I am a collector of souls," the fisherman said. He propped the pole against a rock and reaching into his shirt pocket, took out a small bible and began reading. I saw the bright red underlings on the page.

"'The Jews then disputed among themselves, How can this man give us flesh to eat? So Jesus said to them, Truly, Truly, I say to you, unless you eat the flesh of the Son of man and drink his blood, you have no life in you.'

"Do you understand?"

"No." I'd already been baptized and given a new name. But Christopher had failed…Could this man help?

"God doesn't visit us on temple mounts," the fisherman said. "His home place is in our souls. The Lord never uses thunder. He whispers. And what does he say to those who listen? What Jesus did. Eat the flesh. Drink the blood. Love me."

I had moved closer to him. The dead worm swinging back and forth at the end of the fishing line called my name in a still, tiny voice. I turned away.

Back in the apartment, I drank watching folds of darkness through the windows envelop the room in velvet.

22

DRINKING NEVER GAVE ME a hangover. The next morning, my eyes popped open right on time. Before leaving Carlisle, I received in the mail typed instructions from father telling me where I'd live and work. Also included was advice about today's meeting with Bert Smith: Look sharp. Don't act like a fool. Using a sharp kitchen knife, I sliced through the plastic over the suit left for me in the closet, cutting in two with the same stroke the typed note attached: For Your Interview. I wasn't worried. The job was already mine.

I dressed and after a breakfast of cereal, orange juice and vodka, gargled mouthwash at the bathroom sink while examining my short hair for any black roots. Ready for the day, I clicked my polished black heels and deciding to use my new key, locked the apartment door. Of course the manager rushed to get the car for me. I only had to ask. Dad didn't complain. He admired success and liked having a chauffeur.

Milford's stunted office buildings tried with steel and glass to stand proud and ignore the trash and dust swirling in front of their lobby doors. But the steel had dimmed and peeling tape covered cracks in the windows. When I still loved Diane and took the bus to Milford, I thought the city full of life unlike the chemically preserved, synthetic people and houses of Cloverdale. Now, driving toward Bert Smith's building, the tallest in Milford, I saw in the EZ Cash outlets and liquor stores on the ground floors, the external symbols of failure for what was inside these buildings: offices where little men with dead dreams sat crumbling away at their desks. I didn't want Milford's poverty—or Cloverdale's wealth, extractive and weak. I wanted success, power, and Christ, and knew, when I combined all three, I'd finally become perfect.

I appreciated Bert Smith's doorman and the efficient surge of pressure shooting me up to the penthouse inside an elevator whose mirror-like, polished wood and brass multiplied my face. The door glided open on a large reception area. From behind her high, carved desk, the woman waiting for me watched as I strode Dawn-like across the tile floor. I no longer put my thumbs in my belt. I didn't have to. When I entered a room, everyone noticed.

"May I help you?"

"I'm Steve Goldblatt."

"Do you have an appointment, sir?"

"Of course." Obviously this skinny woman with a small chest was an idiot.

"I'll buzz Mr. Smith's office. Please have a seat, Mr. Goldblatt. Would you like some coffee?"

"No. I already ate." I walked away.

From my chair of high, thick leather in front of a wall of glass, I looked down on Milford and the dot people below moving through a miniature world. Even with all his imperfections, Christopher had never been small or afraid of heights.

"We are above everyone," Dane said.

I propped my feet up on a teak table decorated with a Chinese vase in the center and leaning back, relaxed.

"Hello. I'm Miss St. George, Mr. Smith's executive assistant." The woman in a business suit extended her hand and without looking away from me, moved it slightly to the side to steady the wobbling vase I'd jarred when getting up quickly and bumping the table. Taller than me, she had high cheekbones and wore her dark hair pulled back tight from her face. She shook my hand, her grip strong.

"This way, please." A leather binder under her arm, Miss St. George clicked away on expensive shoes with two inch heels. To the side, steps led down to a large pit where women worked surrounded by stacks of files. We stayed on the main floor. At a brass door flanked by palms, she knocked once and we went in. The carpeting was even thicker than mother's.

Legs crossed on top of a large, uncluttered desk, the phone cradled under an ear, Mr. Smith leaned back in his chair and while doodling on a yellow legal pad used his free hand to motion us forward.

"Of course I'm listening. Now, I need you to listen to me. I'm going to attach your husband's business accounts. I have the motion right here. He knows I'm ready to file it. That's why he's worried and is talking settlement. If he were really serious about this, he'd have made the offer through his attorney instead of calling you. The pattern's always the same. Cheat on your wife and when the financial heat is on, try to manipulate her some more. Here's my answer to your husband—forget it, buddy. My client's done being a sucker. She's going to get the house, permanent alimony and your business, too. I've been practicing law for over thirty years, Mrs. Hendrick, and I've seen it all. Your husband will regret the day he left you and started screwing around with that tramp."

Mr. Smith flopped his legs down and after tossing the pad and pen on the desk, pried out a nail clipper from his vest pocket squeezed closed by the pressure from his large stomach.

"Uh huh, mm, mm, yeah, that's right." Clip, clip, then his eyes opened wide as he gripped the phone tight. "Reconciliation!. My God, what does he take you for? A fool? She has her hooks in to him too deep for that. Now don't cry. I understand, I really do. I'll see you through this. Trust me. Why don't we get together for lunch and go over the file. I'll show you how I'm going to cut your husband's balls off and serve them to you on a plate. That's better. It's good hearing you laugh. There's a little restaurant on Canal Street I think you'll enjoy. I go there all the time. How about tomorrow at one? I'll even buy. Great. It's a date. I'm looking forward to it, too."

"It's only business, Joan," Mr. Smith said after hanging up. "Is that a new blouse?"

"This is Steve Goldblatt," she said.

"You don't say? Myron's boy. Your father told me you want to be a lawyer."

"Yes, sir."

"Are you smart?

"I am."

"I don't mean with books."

"Neither do I." I thought the answer clever. Mr. Smith got up and while pacing with a putter under his arm, dictated a letter. Joan took notes.

"This is to Ralph Peterson, Hendrick's attorney. Dear Mr. Peterson, Mrs. Hendrick has advised me to terminate all settlement negotiations and immediately schedule—no, strike immediately—to schedule a final hearing in this matter. Paragraph. I plan on taking the deposition of your client and his employees and seek an attachment of his business and personal accounts to prevent any dissipation of assets. In addition, I will soon send you written interrogatories and a Request to Produce all tax returns and financial records for the last five years relevant to Mr. Hendrick personally and his corporation, Global Securities, Inc. Paragraph. My client continues to suffer from a chronic back condition that prevents her from finding gainful employment. Consequently, I will file a motion with Judge Newton for an increase in temporary alimony. Paragraph. If Mr. Hendrick continues to harass my client by contacting her I will immediately seek a restraining order against your client with costs and attorney's fees taxed against him. Mrs. Hendrick has no interest in reconciling with her husband. She intends to move on with her life. Finally, as per the court order regarding my fees in this matter to date, please have your client issue to your trust account within the next two days, the sum of three thousand dollars. I expect you will then forward this amount to me forthwith.

"Okay, Joan, that should do it. Usual ending. Let's get it out today."

"Should I have the pleadings prepared?"

"Yes, and schedule the depositions but don't file anything in court. When Hendrick gets my Notice of Deposition and Request to Produce, he'll shit a brick. There's no way he's going to let me nose around in his business records. He's made a fortune through insider trading and other shady deals—good for him. More money for us. He'll cave and I'll be able to wrap this case up. Make sure I log in extra hours on the billing sheet. I'll need the file when I meet Mrs. Hendrick for lunch. Reserve a table for two at DeMoto's."

"I understand," Joan said, snapping the binder closed.

"Maybe it's the suit. You look terrific today." Head down over his gold golf club, Mr. Smith putted, missing the cup by a foot.

"Thank you—sir," Joan glanced at me and clicked out.

"Don't know what I'd do without her." Dragging his putter along the floor, he scooted the ball in. "Golf's not a hard sport. All you have to do is adjust the rules. Why the law, Goldblatt?"

A thin line of sweat trickled down my armpits. What if this *was* an interview and I gave the wrong answer? Mr. Smith wore a gold watch like mine. He practiced putting in a penthouse. He had stuffed himself fat.

"Power and money," I said, leaving out Christ.

"As goddamn a refreshing answer as I've ever heard. Well done. I'm so fucking sick of all the bullshit I get from the morons who come in here looking for a job. Of course they all want money, why else go to law school? But what do they tell me? Gee, Mr. Smith, I love the law and I want to serve the community and make a difference in the world. It's all I can do not to puke. Don't get me wrong. I admire selfishness and greed as long as the person's not trying to fuck me over. Most of my interviews don't last five minutes. I like you, Goldblatt. You're your father's son."

"Thank you," I said.

Mr. Smith threw his putter toward the bag, missed, and with a heavy thump, sat back down behind his desk.

"Since we're being so honest with each other, let me tell you why you're here. I make a lot of money as corporate counsel for your father's company. Your daddy's rich and someday I'm sure you'll be worth a few shekels, too. But I wouldn't be interested in hiring you if you weren't a Jew."

I nodded and crossed my legs.

"I believe in the American way of life, our freedom to choose," Mr. Smith continued. "With everything else being equal, people would rather do business with their own kind. It's a tribal thing. Cloverdale is 40% Hebrew. Your name on our stationary will open a lot of doors for me. You'll be the nice, Jewish boy, rich old Jewish women will want to see when making out their wills. Interested?"

"I am."

"I heard what you said about the books. Any chance you'll flunk out of law school?"

"I've never had to work very hard for grades. If I study a little, I'll make all As."

"The less effort, the better, huh? Fine, just as long as when you're in here I get 100% of your soul." He pushed an employment agreement toward me. "There's no sense reading it. Every word was written for my protection."

I signed the last page.

"Joan. Show Goldblatt to his office. He's starting work today."

But there are still two days of summer left, I wanted to tell him.

Summer? What the fuck is that? I knew he'd say.

Located between a bathroom and broom closet, the small, windowless room trapped more dust than air. My pitted desk shared space with a broken copier, discarded plastic plants, and decorations from a New Year's Eve party five years ago. The overhead light flickered.

"I'll tell maintenance," Joan said.

"That isn't necessary, I'll take it from here," Mr. Smith said, his large body blocking the small doorway. "Like what you see?" he asked me after Joan left.

"Yes, sir."

"Are you fucking nuts? This room is a pit and you're not in the military. I don't want any of that yes, sir, crap." He poked a chubby finger into my chest. "Look around, Goldblatt. It's a warning. If you don't learn what I teach you, you'll end up in some dip-shit government agency or working for the Public Defender. Or maybe, if you're really lucky, you'll get a job with a firm that defends insurance companies. You'll write memos to the file, sign out to take a piss and wait for the guy one rung above you to drop dead. Every time you step into this office, think about all the fools who spend their lives inside little boxes they can't escape."

"That won't be me," I said.

"Don't be so sure." He adjusted his diamond cufflink. "Let me show you the operation." Puffing, swinging his short arms back and forth, Mr. Smith moved briskly down the hall. I hurried to stay up with him. "I do a lot of PI, that's personal injury. The girls handle most of it. I sign the client up then turn the file over to Mable, that's her over there, the old broad with the big jugs. She sends out our standard demand—Dear so and so, this office represents Joe Schmuck in reference to his accident of such and such a date. Our investigation has determined your negligent operation of a motor vehicle caused the permanent injuries suffered by our client. Please forward this letter to your insurance company. If you are uninsured, contact us immediately. Govern yourself accordingly—this letter starts the ball rolling. When we find out the amount of coverage, Mable ships the client to one of our doctors. I want lots of medicals. The more medical expenses a client has the higher the final settlement. Unless an uninsured is wealthy— highly unlikely—we don't waste our time with those cases."

"That makes sense," I said.

"Glad you approve." Mr. Smith pinched the ass of a girl carrying files.

"Mr. Smith."

"Sorry, honey, nothing personal—so Mable, have you opened the McKenzie file?" He had circled behind the older woman and stood looking over her shoulder.

"I'm in the middle of it, that and the hundred other things dumped on my desk." She scribbled a note on an index card, poked the pencil back into her frizzy gray hair and pulled another file toward her.

"What would I do without you," Mr. Smith patted her hand. "This is Goldblatt. He might be here a week or two."

She glanced up and didn't look too friendly.

"Have you found out the amount of coverage in Blinkman?" he asked her.

"100,000/300,000."

"Good. We'll keep the case. Send the kid to Fletcher for treatment."

"I already have."

"That's my girl."

Her phone rang. Someone called her name. Another secretary came over and waited, wanting to ask her a question.

"Come on, Goldblatt, Mable's got work to do."

In the pit, Mr. Smith introduced me to the girls. They filled out interrogatories, prepared motions, answered clients' questions, and spoke to the judges' secretaries. Even though I didn't understand all the details, I realized this system of dividing up a case saved Mr. Smith time and allowed him to concentrate on trial strategy. I told him this. He looked at me like I was an idiot.

"Trials cost me money, Goldblatt. If I'm dicking around in front of a jury I can't be on the phone settling a case. Do I tell my clients I never go to court? Fuck, no. Lawyers have one thing to sell—these." He yanked on his crotch. "Always act like you have the biggest ones in town. That's how you earn respect. Law is a business. To be successful in it you have to convince those who stand between you and the money—clients, insurance adjusters, opposing lawyers—that you will do anything to win. Sometimes that means acting like a son-of-a-bitch. Other times you need to schmooze a little, grease the pig, and socialize with slime balls. What I do is an art form, a little of this, a little of that. You can't just throw shit on a canvas and expect to sell it. This is your first day, so I don't expect too much from you. But spare me your insights on how you think I earn a living. You don't know dick. Well, time for lunch—Joan. I'll be back in a couple of hours. I'm taking Goldbaltt with me."

"Enjoy yourself, sir," the receptionist said when we passed her desk.

"Thank you, sweetie."

Thumbs in his vest pocket, he hummed as we rode the elevator down.

Even had others parked their cars in the private section of the building's garage, I would have recognized Mr. Smith's by its long black body and the license plate, SA UNCL After wedging his stomach under the steering wheel, he barely glanced behind him before backing up. Tires squealing, he accelerated onto the street.

"PI, divorces, they cover my nut. The gravy comes from putting deals together. Real estate, that's what it's all about." He drove even faster, his diamond pinky ring flashing in my eye. "Your father has made some nice investments with me over the years. I hope you're hungry. The club has excellent steaks."

Two miles outside Milford, Mr. Smith turned toward the river and after driving a short distance along a stone wall, ignored the brass plate marked *Private* embedded in rock at the entranceway and sped through open iron gates. Oak shade trees lined both sides of the upwardly winding driveway. The grass, neat and trim without visible cut lines, appeared self-maintaining, a plant whose sense of duty required that it never exceed a certain height. Located in an old Victorian mansion on a hilltop above the Hog River, the Stonehill Country Club offered comfortable chairs and an excellent vantage point from its back porch for members who wanted to sit and sip brandy or smoke a good cigar while looking down at Cloverdale.

"Hello, Mr. Smith," the tall boy said opening the car door. He wore striped pants and a dark jacket with gold buttons, the uniform in contrast to his simple, open and honest face. By hurrying around to get my door, he welcomed me into this new farmland. The club had rich soil inside. I just had to figure out how they grew their corn. I wondered if the boy checked brakes.

"Getting any lately, Phil?"

"I have a girlfriend, sir," he said, blushing.

"Good, then you won't fuck with my car." Mr. Smith threw him the keys.

We climbed the steep steps. Out of breath, Mr. Smith rested a moment, his hand on the wood railing, he smoothed his silk tie and with a nod to the doorman, hustled inside.

Chandeliers burning miniature, candle-shaped bulbs

dropped beads of light down shadowy bookcases and across the staring busts of the club's founders lined in rows. Mahogany furniture and deep rugs muffled the sound of our footsteps.

"Your table is ready, Mr. Smith."

"Thank you, Murray."

"It's Maurice, sir."

"Of course, sorry."

The maître d', a twig thin man with a large mustache and luminous eyes, bowed slightly.

We sat at a small round table decorated with an orchid in a crystal vase. Mr. Smith put the vase on the floor.

"Who wants flowers when you eat," he said.

Except for a murmur from behind me and the occasional faint click of silverware on china, there were no other sounds in the room.

"Nice place, right?" Mr. Smith pushed a pad of butter into the center of his roll. "Good food. Plenty of hired help around to kiss your ass. So what if it's expensive? I can afford it. I like being pampered." He ate half the roll in one bite.

"In Cloverdale, people make money by belonging to the Excelsior Club," I said.

Mr. Smith hit the table with his fist. Even the murmuring stopped.

"Goddamnit. You are smart. You understand what I told you. None of this would mean shit if I didn't make connections by coming here for lunch. This place is a gold mine. I've always known that. That's why when they opened the restaurant to the public, I jumped on it. But I'm not done. I'm going to parlay this into full membership. The club's hurting financially. I've got money, I know which members to finesse, and I'm not a Jew. Sorry, Goldblatt, but those are the rules. This place isn't for you, anyway. What would you do? Sit around in your tweed jacket and smoke a pipe?" He laughed.

"Your food, sir," the waiter said.

"They know what I like," Mr. Smith said. "I ordered the same for you."

Blood oozed from my steak.

"You don't drink do you, Goldblatt?"

"No."

"That's good. You can't go around shit-faced if you expect to make money in the law. People are either sharks or fish. If you're weak, you're dead meat. Eat your lunch. I've got two people I want you to meet."

Mr. Smith ate quickly, his face inches from the plate.

"Done?" he asked me. I swallowed the last of it.

"Yes."

"Cream in your coffee?"

"Thank you."

Cup in hand, Mr. Smith motioned for the bill.

"Drink up, Goldblatt."

So, I did.

In the library, I recognized the men sitting in armchairs by the fire. With silver hair and blue eyes, they looked the same as they had twelve years earlier when, strolling downtown in Cloverdale, they stopped and each in turn patted me on the head. Taggert read a newspaper folded neatly down the middle.

Cavanaugh smoked a pipe.

"Good morning, Mason. Patrick." Mr. Smith stood at a respectful distance. Taggert took out a pocket watch.

"Afternoon as I see it."

"Lunch must have been good," Cavanaugh said and turned toward me. "And who is this young man?"

"My new associate. Steve Goldblatt."

"Someone you've left standing in the middle of the room."

Mr. Smith quickly found two folding chairs. He moved his close to the men.

"So, Mr. Goldblatt, what law school did you graduate from?" Taggert asked.

"I'm starting Warren Harding in the fall."

"Starting?"

"And Bert has already hired you? How remarkable." Cavanaugh looked at Mr. Smith. "Is there a chance our Mr. Goldblatt here is Myron Goldblatt's son?

"I've known his father a long time," Mr. Smith answered.

Cavanaugh smiled and settling back in his armchair, puffed his pipe. Taggert turned his newspaper over.

"So, Mason, Patrick, how is the redevelopment project going?" Mr. Smith leaned toward them as far as he could without risking toppling forward.

"Plymouth Development has acquired some property. Not as much as we would like." Cavanaugh tapped his pipe on an ashtray.

"Someone representing an unrecorded Trust apparently believed now was a good time for the Trust to exercise its option to buy the Carmichael parcel, a tract of land in our projected path of construction. An unfortunate miscalculation, I'm afraid." Taggert folded his paper into a neat square and put it into his suit pocket.

For the first time, I actually noticed Mr. Smith's features—not old or young but indistinct, more like a bladder, and sweating.

"Why is that, Mason?" he asked.

"Politics," Taggert answered. "You know how unpredictable that can be. Patrick and I were having lunch with Mayor Cox just the other day. He informed us he will soon ask the Cloverdale City Council to roll back zoning on the subject area to single family residences. A number of homeowners have organized and want a moratorium on apartment development in town. These people are rather well connected, which is important considering the Mayor and a majority of his councilmen are up for reelection in the fall. I'm not a betting man but my guess is the rollback will be approved. That will, of course, make the land purchased by the Trust, unprofitable. The public records show—I'm right about this, aren't I, Patrick—"

"Yes, Mason, you certainly are."

"That the price paid for the property was predicated on multi-family usage. No money will be made by building individual homes. The Trust has bought some very expensive park land."

"Any zoning change will also hurt Plymouth Development, won't it?" Mr. Smith wiped his face.

"Come now, Bert, you're an attorney. You must know that

once building permits are issued they can't be rescinded. What's the reason for that Patrick?"

"It would be a taking without due process of law," Cavanaugh said.

"When buying for development in this area over the years, our company always had the foresight to acquire authorization for the building of apartments on all parcels it owned even though construction regarding certain phases was years away. Because of the pending zoning change, I believe if the Trust now applied for multiple dwelling permits, the request would be denied. What a shame."

Taggert and Cavanaugh looked at Mr. Smith.

"In light of what you have just said, from a business and legal point of view, it would be in the Trust's best interest to sell its land to Plymouth Development."

"That is probably its best option," Cavanaugh said. "Too bad no one knows who represents the Trust. He could certainly use your advice."

"I'll make a few calls," Mr. Smith said, "see what I can find out."

"In your representations, Bert, don't forget to include the fact that our ownership of the Trust property won't change what the city council plans to do with the zoning on it. If the Trust intends to sell the land to us the price must reflect this political reality. Patrick and I aren't known to be imprudent or wasteful, especially in matters of business."

"I understand," Mr. Smith said.

Although concluding the arrangement successfully by

screwing this Trust to the club's oak wall, both store owners, in a show of good breeding, nodded only slightly. Taggert picked up another newspaper. Cavanaugh filled his pipe.

"Well, I'd better be getting back to the office." Mr. Smith stood but didn't leave. "I was wondering…Has the membership committee had a chance to review my application yet?"

"In due time, Bert, in due time," Taggert said. "The committee wants to be thorough. Character is so important. Membership isn't just dependent on past acts but what we can expect a member to do for us in the future."

"It's a lot like land," Cavanaugh explained. "You research its value ahead of time so you don't get stuck with something worthless."

The old men smiled at me.

"Warren Harding. Yes, a solid school."

"Our grandsons are starting their study of law this year at Harvard."

"Good luck with your plans, Mr. Goldblatt."

In this room of fire and smoke, these crimson tinged guardians of class and wealth tried, with one voice, to make sure I knew my place. Taggert and Cavanaugh thought their blood superior to mine. I almost laughed. All I had to do was make one small cut and they would see Dane, not a Harvard inbred, bleed out.

Except for the sweat still beaded on his face, Mr. Smith didn't look worried. He smiled, stayed controlled and calm until we were outside, waiting for the car.

"Bastards." He yanked on his tie, loosening it from his

neck. "I knew something was up but I never guessed it was a roll back of zoning. And the Grimm brothers are behind it. They have their claws so deep into Cox he'll do whatever they want. The Trust is fucked. Taggert and Cavanaugh will get the land for nothing and make a profit on it because once it's owned by Plymouth Development you can bet your sweet ass this whole zoning brouhaha will evaporate like piss on one of the goddamn flowers in there. They'll be able to build a whole city of apartments. Brilliant, goddammit."

"Why should you care?" I asked.

"You should, too. I'm the Trust's attorney and your father is the beneficiary."

"And you knew Taggert and Cavanaugh were out to get the land?"

"Did I say that? How are they hanging, Phil? Here's five bucks. Buy yourself some rubbers."

Mr. Smith drove away slowly. He didn't talk, but that was okay. I was beginning to understand.

In my small office with its flickering light, when I wasn't sorting paper clips or folding letters into envelopes, I watched the clock until it was time to take orders for lunch. A lot of the girls liked egg salad sandwiches. Sometimes, after work, I visited Karla. I kept her secret from Tom—it was easy. He never called me to play basketball. Summer lived without him or me. I always left Karla a little money. I think the pills she took were for her heart.

Power and money through Mr. Smith but I still needed Christ to complete my transformation. I knew where to find Him. I returned to the mill.

"I am John," the fisherman said standing by the river, his dark eyes burning into me. "Jesus appeared on the road between Emmaus and Jerusalem. Here he comes again, straddling a flying saucer. Isn't that what people want? Christ on a tortilla? A God they can touch and eat. Zap. And his face materializes on a cheese cracker. Rattle. Drip. Look, children. The statue bleeds.

"'If we love one another, God lives in us and His love is perfected.'"

The Fisherman reached out.

"I am not an illusion. I am the flesh. I am the blood."

He was the man I had seen years ago when parked with Diane and Tom at the mill. His room in it held the light of Christ that had searched for me from Dane's velvet painting. I took the fisherman's hand and went with him down a long wooden hallway adorned with relics: broken machine parts, fly wheels, twisted metal and nails. Wind trapped inside the crumbling building moaned an ascending hymn as he stood in front of black curtains that flapped in the night. The fisherman taught me. Finally, Jesus could abide deep within my skull.

Mr. Smith twirled his putter and tapped it hard on my desk.

"Six weeks working next to a copier. Like your job?"

"I'm learning," I said.

"Good. I'm going to give you a chance to step up. I need a signature. No big deal, really. It's just a formality. Take this power of attorney to your dad."

"So he can sign it?"

"That's right."

"Is this about the Trust land Taggert and Cavanaugh want?"

"It's so I can unload property that's worthless."

Now I understood.

"If I get the signature, you're protected."

"I'm not sure what you mean."

"Why do they call it a Trust?"

Never particularly jolly toward me, Mr. Smith now looked even less pleased.

"Do we have a problem here?"

"No, Mr. Smith. I know the real reason you hired me. You weren't exactly sure what Taggert and Cavanaugh were planning but you knew it involved the Trust land and my father. I might be useful. I am. I'll do anything you want. I just need a better office."

"Holy shit, Goldblatt, you're one scary, mother fucker. You'll make a great lawyer. Bring the power of attorney back signed, and we'll talk about your future."

After he left, I took my flask out and slowly unscrewed the top. I had forged father's name many times and could easily do it again, but I wanted everything legal. No ticking bombs. I called his secretary and got a five minute appointment for that afternoon.

He stood examining the fabric draped over his black desk.

"Find something cheaper that looks the same," father said.

The worker nodded and carried the sample out. Father walked to the large glass window behind him and arms folded, peered down on the rows of women sewing below.

"Production's off. I can hear it. Get Chester in here."

His secretary, now old and fat and because of this reluctantly removed by mother from the categorized list of women she thought father screwed whenever he had the chance, left me standing in the middle of the steel and concrete warehouse room. Father remained with his back to me. Footsteps pounded up the stairs.

"What's going on with three and four?" father asked, turning to the foreman.

"New girls, Mr. Goldblatt, but hard workers." Chester wiped his face. "I'm sure they'll be up to speed in a week."

"I don't pay for learning. Let them finish the day."

"I—yes, sir," Chester gave me a quick, nervous smile and hurried out.

"They come to this country and don't want to work, that's the problem. Everyone expects a free ride." Father looked at me. I could tell by his eyes—not red, but still, deeply caring—that he wasn't done speaking; that now, after all these years, he was ready to say something personal and important to me.

"Fuck them all but six."

"Excuse me?"

"You heard me. All you need in life are six people to carry your coffin. Fuck the rest. How's the job?"

"Good…"

"Learning how to be a lawyer?"

"I think so—"

"Why are you here?"

"Mr. Smith wants you to sign this." My hand actually trembled.

"What is it?"

"I'm not sure."

"You've got to be smarter than that, Steve. Good thing Smith called earlier and filled me in. This is a power of attorney. It gives him the authority to sell some land I own. I'll take a loss because I should have known better. I make underwear. I'm good at it. What do I know about real estate? The whole thing's not worth my time. I'll let Smith handle it. That's why I have him. He does the leg work. Now he has you to do his. Do you trust him?"

"No," I answered.

"Maybe your mother didn't give you too much tit." Father opened his mouth as if to chuckle or maybe even laugh, I couldn't tell which. I knew only what the red in his eyes meant. Deciding against both, he just went on speaking. "I always thought you were weak. Maybe there's hope for you, yet. You're right. Smith's a snake. That's why I'm putting your name on the power of attorney. I know you won't fuck with me. There's some documents in that cabinet over there you might need." He went back to his glass wall. "Goddamnit. All the machines are slow today. Chester's gotten soft. I'm going to fire his ass and hire a new foreman. Someone with balls. Anything else,

Steve?"

"No, father."

His strong fingers pushing hard against the glass, he continued watching the women sew. I took the file from the drawer and leaving, closed the door quietly behind me.

Outside, the smiling sun rained light in large burning drops. I sat in the Buick and giggled. Dad laughed too. When looking through the file, I'd found stuck between the pages of a lease an old excavation permit for the land the Trust had just bought. It'd been issued to the previous owners, the Carmichael family. Apparently, father or Mr. Smith misfiled the permit and forgot about it. From what Taggert and Cavanaugh had said about property rights and building permits, I knew this one made the Trust land valuable. But dad and I weren't laughing because of that. Also in the file was a bright and beautiful mortgage. I drove away singing, the wipers keeping time by scraping merrily across the dry glass.

When Smith walked into his office he found me putting into a cup. Every ball went straight in. His gold putter had a nice feel. He stood looking at me, probably thinking I'd cracked up.

"Golf is easy if you have control," I said. "A copy of the power of attorney is on your desk. I have the original."

Still watching me, he went over and picked up the form.

"Your name?"

"Father thought that best. He gave me a file, too, with something in it that might interest you. Ten years ago,

Cloverdale's Zoning Department issued an excavation permit to the Carmichaels. It was probably once attached to the Option to Buy. Remember that now?"

"I didn't represent the Trust back then," Smith said.

"So, it was father, not you, who misplaced it—I should have guessed. You're too sharp a lawyer to forget about something that could make you money. The permit's still good. I already checked that out at Town Hall. I'm keeping it safe and locked away with the power of attorney. Maybe Taggert and Cavanaugh will look at you differently now. You have buildable land in their way. With a little negotiation, you might get into their club. Wouldn't that be swell?"

"Do you know what you're doing?" Smith asked.

"Oh, yes. I understand how father thinks, and you've taught me a lot. I used to hunt butterflies in that field. Apartments there would be spectacular."

"All this so you can get a bigger office?"

"That's part of it. You work with me, I work with you. Right now, to show your good faith, I want you to adjust the payments on a mortgage the Trust holds. It's a small one."

"What mortgage?'

"The Humphrey one."

"The old woman with the boarding house?"

"That's right."

"Sure, we can reduce the interest rate—"

"No, Bert, I want her to pay more."

Of course, he didn't understand.

"Has she done something to you?"

"Not at all. I like Mrs. Humphrey. We used to play cards together, but I don't want her tenants saving money at our expense. Their rents are too low. She'll have to raise them. For me, Bert, it's just business."

"To increase her interest rate I need to—"

"Look at her payment history? I already have. She's always late. If you have time today, why don't you send her a letter with the new—what would you call it?

"Adjustment?"

"That's it. A simple adjustment." I twirled his putter. "Yep, very nice. I think I'll buy a few."

When I left, Smith looked, despite his large body and diamond ring, too small and unimportant for his office. Outside, on the Milford city street, I stood in front of a used clothing store and widening my eyes, melted the lopsided mannequin in the window. Squeezed by free time constricting gently around me, I grew even taller knowing Karla would now never be able to save enough to buy her little dream house and set up housekeeping with Tom. I was doing all I could to protect Dane's blood.

Feeling age nine again, I raised my arms to the sun and hobbled after butterflies. I had power, money, and Christ. I was Barnabas.

23

IF THE WARREN HARDING Law School had been built on the Ohio River's other bank, in Kentucky, I would have smelled blue grass and horses, and studied with blond, Kentucky farm boys instead of Wendell Geets, a Cloverdale faced rich kid from a suburb of Cleveland.

"This is my girlfriend," he said, holding a photograph I thought would bark.

"You two fit."

Wendell of the small head, legs and dreams, stretched a little taller.

"Beth's an artist. She did these." Iridescent seascapes, flat and emotionless, crammed the walls of Wendell's room in a dormitory of seminary students. Each year, the church rented out a few of its dorm rooms to law students. I wanted to live there too under a wooden cross. I never got in.

"They're nice," I said. Can I have one to wipe my ass?

"Would you like a cookie?" Wendell carefully opened a tin box lined with foil. "My mom made them. I'll be getting a package from her every week. Beth's mailing cakes."

I shook my head. He quickly retied the box and put it back

in its place at the end of a shelf used mostly for his bottles of vitamins and laxatives.

"Think I'll shave before dinner." Wendell stroked the sides of his face permanently darkened by coarse, black stubble. Hairy from head to toes, constantly in heat over Beth—he drew pictures of himself with horns—I figured nature had compensated him for his diminutive size by providing an excess of testosterone packaged inside an overactive dick willing to fuck anything that seemed alive.

The shaver moved wonderfully close to his neck.

After shaving, Wendell selected new clothes sent by his mother, dressed, splashed on cologne and hearing the dinner bell, disappeared into the smell of hot food coming from the meal plan mommy had bought him. Sometimes I waited for him. If I were hungry, I walked to my apartment in a tall building where I never saw anyone. I no longer enjoyed cereal and rolls. Barnabas craved meat. The Lumberjack Frozen Entrée came out perfect every time unless baked at more than 350°. At a higher heat, the peas shriveled and turned brown, the pod of chocolate pudding bubbled and the dried out, toughened sinews protruding from the thin steak made it look as if it'd been electrocuted. White-haired Miss Gurdy in her apron and oven mittens served from her stove-ready aluminum tray, a nice chicken leg and muffin. On Thanksgiving and Christmas, Wendell went home and I spent the holidays drinking vodka with Dane while Bing Crosby sang, promising me sleigh bells in the night.

Never breaking his routine, Wendell always took a shit

after dinner. Then I'd read his notes and case studies out loud so he could type the information into outlines. I hated him. He was a baby ingesting cookies and milk his mother sprayed from her tits into the ordered universe she had created for her little poopsie away in law school. He lived with priests and although he couldn't be me, I thought he should at least learn a few parables. He never did. His skull was too small. Wendell had one redeeming quality. He groveled for As. I knew from the first day of law school, he'd be useful. So, I sympathized when his father got sick, gave him advice about Beth, put up with the way he swallowed, breathed, scratched his ass. In return, the little fur ball shortened the time I had to waste studying lies. With its twisted ivy and a library packed full of so many nervous, hunched over students my stomach cramped up every time I went into the room, Warren Harding taught a distorted version of what I had learned from Smith. My law professors spoke about the Constitution, our jury system, common law, statues, and justice; over the summer, Smith had shown me what really mattered: in criminal cases get the fee then plea bargain; in a tort action, run up the medicals and settle; always represent the woman in a divorce; let Mable handle the pleadings. Because Wendell took excellent notes and knew from brown nosing every teacher in school what cases we should concentrate on, I could wait until a few days before exams before filling my head with garbage by actually studying his outlines. The system worked. I graduated near the top of my class.

I paid Wendell back for all his help.

After his father croaked at the end of our senior year and

the associate position once planned for Wendell in the family's high powered law firm went to a cousin, I called Smith who had a connection in Cuyahoga County. The Cleveland Animal Control Board hired Wendell to investigate complaints about barking dogs. He got a badge and a nice basement office. When I left Warren Harding, I again had no debts.

24

AS EXPECTED, I FOUND everything I wanted had a reasonable price, especially partnership with Smith. But there was a loose end. Father. He could swoop down at any time and by revoking the Power of Attorney, end my deal making even though it kept him well stuffed with money. So, I waited, and in the meantime, married Esther, the daughter of a rich client. She was a plain woman and a lousy cook. She never learned how to fry steak or keep the meat from touching the potatoes on my plate. I hit her. We must have been in love.

Tom and Karla had moved away. I didn't hear from him until today...

Plymouth Development tore down Dane's home. The Trust held title to Tom's house. I exchanged properties and with Esther moved into a home on Dane's old land I built exactly like the one he had grown up in. I stacked beer cans in the sink and planted a black willow out front. Jesus hung in the hallway. On moonless nights, it was fun sneaking through Mrs. Humphrey's vegetable garden and, when hidden behind Tom's dead tree, hack it closer to the ground. Sometimes I left work early to bring toys to dying children in Milford General.

Of course, the restrictive Stonehill Country Club let Barnabas in. I sat between Mason and Patrick, smoked a pipe and talked about money. Eventually, they let me buy the development project. I transferred the properties into my new company and on the old butterfly field, built apartments designed in the one small room I kept inside my skull for art. Each of my buildings had a façade that reminded me of Mr. Petty's twisted old fingers. With its snake logo on the side, the venom shiny in sunlight, my bulldozer smashed Tom's farmhouse apart. I lived in a great home; his house had trapped too many ghosts.

My power kept Smith out of the office.

"Joan." I liked to yell.

One morning, the old fart actually came to work.

"No golf today?" I reluctantly let him sit at his desk.

"A meeting. Taggert and Cavanaugh have some hot shot marketer working for them. They want to bump up his salary, give him a new employment agreement."

"They didn't tell me about it."

"Probably thought you had more important things to do. I have his name here—Dane Beneby. Says he knows you."

The clock ticked. Smith finished another cheese danish. A white suit and face full of smiling teeth glided into the room.

"Steve. Mr. Smith." The man touched my hand, his fingers boney and cold. "Steve and I have been friends since elementary school. We were wild kids, weren't we? He was always smart. It's great we can work together now."

I got up and left. Esther acted happy to see me. I even looked at her while we fucked. It was such a beautiful afternoon. Later that week, I told Mason and Patrick that the man in white was a fraud. I didn't know him and he'd lied on his resume. I'd highlighted his misrepresentations in red and also the ones I'd added. The old men liked me. We puffed together, the imposter's new employment agreement going up in smoke.

"Esther's worried about your drinking," father said. "Look at this sink. You have a painting of Jesus in the hall. What's wrong with you?"

I'd just come home from a peaceful drive with dad.

"Esther's worried?" I looked at her. She rattled her tea cup down and left the kitchen table. "How's business, father? I have another check for you. Care for a drink?" I poured myself a scotch.

"There's no talking to you." he said.

Along with speech, father had acquired a sense of humor. Through the prism of my glass I watched his face fracture— how funny. To keep from laughing I downed another shot.

"I'll take these," he picked up the Buick's keys. I'd parked right behind him. "You're going to kill someone with that car. Why do you live here? You can afford better. Didn't we teach you anything?"

I looked at him, my red eyes smiling.

A few minutes later, I heard the crash. It had been a long time coming. I'd dreamed about it as a child. Esther only glanced at me when running from the bedroom and out the back door. After washing and drying my glass, I waited until the sirens called me. I knew what I'd find. By occupying the same space, dad, the Buick, and father, had to die. It was a law of nature with a well-known corollary: love killed. Making sure I didn't get blood on my leather shoes, I crossed the street and stood on the corner watching red lights spin. Esther tried talking to me, but she was only noise. In the road, father's crushed body didn't have a head. Tilted against the curb, the head didn't have eyes. When they took the pieces of him away and I was alone, I walked slowly to the wreck. Head bowed, I gently touched the broken shadow of a snake on the dash and said good-bye. The car key, added to my collection, jingle jingled in my pocket.

At the cemetery, mother, clinging to her cousins, Ida and Edith, tore her clothes and moaned.

"He left me. He left me. Men. What can you expect." She placed a cold finger on my cheek. "You're a good son." I noticed she had two buttons missing from her blouse.

Behind the circle of family around the grave, a blonde woman stood holding the hand of a dark haired boy who looked like me when I was steve. I walked over to her.

"Did you know my father well?"

"Yes, for many years."

I nodded and patted the child's head.

Still crying, adjusting their breasts, the sister things pulled skinny husbands toward their cars for the short ride to mother's house where tables of hot mourners' food had finally unlocked the doors. I ate spaghetti at an Italian restaurant in Milford, then top down, drove father's convertible to work. The radio, sounding like a voice, crackled nicely between channels, but I missed dad.

The cold wind helped.

The sister things were soft and stupid. They didn't give me any problems. I controlled father's estate and all the money. I never again had to worry about him taking away who I was. Powerful and rich, I was also generous. I bought father's blonde mistress and her dark son a small annuity and sent it to her, marking the policy, *for services rendered.*

25

"I ALWAYS KNEW YOU would turn out a *mench*." Mother smiled at me from the rocker I had bought for her at a rummage sale. "You're not like those sisters of yours. The ingrates. Do they ever come over? Do they even know I'm alive? I love your hair. It's so blond."

"Thank you. I put cereal and rolls in the kitchen. They're behind the dog food."

"You're so good to me. I know how busy you are, but maybe tomorrow, when you visit, if it isn't too much trouble, you could bring me some chicken soup…"

"Of course," I said, "a bowl full, nice and hot."

The next day, Dr. Blank made a house call.

"Just something to calm you. A small sedative." I held mother's hand. "You've been through a lot. We have to be careful with your heart."

She winced as the needle went in, then her trusting black eyes glazed over. I paid Blank in cash. After he left, I stood over mother watching her sleep. She looked so peaceful…I kissed her drooling mouth. Sitting on her thin legs, I moved her heavy arms around me in a hug and unbuttoned her blouse. In the dark silence, no crying sister things pulled my mouth away. I was again her baby.

I knew the judge. The competency hearing lasted ten minutes, my experts testifying that older women often sink into dementia when they suddenly lose a husband. I found mother a bed in a wonderful nursing home run by nuns. She didn't complain about the cross I nailed into the wall above her head. She didn't complain about anything.

It wasn't easy finding the white haired girl from high school. She had a different supplier. But all drugs deals eventually intersect. She liked the idea, plus, I paid her. She pissed under the plastic; we broke crystal together and blackened the walls with smoke from the stacks of wood we torched in fireplaces that had never been used. I fucked her in every room of the house. In the living room mother's paintings of little girls stared down at us through the holes I'd poked in their big eyes.

All bones and rotted fur, toothless, blind, but somehow, still alive, Munchkin lifted its head and tried biting me. My arm outstretched, I carried mother's pet by the neck and in the back yard dropped him into a hole. After planting my sapling I stamped down the moving dirt. Through the kitchen window, I saw the albino make herself another ham sandwich.

Despite a law suit by the dentist next door and petitions from all the neighbors, I let mother's walls crumble and her doors and roof cave in. She had worried about mice. Her weed filled yard attracted rats. Sometimes, at night, I would go back and, sitting outside the laundry room, listen hoping to hear the sounds of demons trapped within the collapsing house. I never did. Only Dane buzzed…

Moonlight continues to float around me. Can I raise myself by the sacrament of drinking in the oil and rotted fish in this river of the decomposed? I was always a C student who knew everything. What did Tom think he could teach me today? Nothing. I will always be Barnabas.

Except…Jackie haunts me and I hurt Tom.
Maybe there were others…

I am not five or forty…or Barnabas. I know that now. I am dead and the water won't let me go. Is this because tonight is Halloween when souls are judged and damned? Or did my Bar Mitzvah chant my sins into the river for me to see? Is this the message of Christ—search for me and find pain but no redemption? Was the tattoo right? Am I the girl on the snake and the destination, hell?

The cross is so heavy around my neck.
I hear Munchkin bark.

Sometimes, for a vacation, I left my skull behind. Tonight, before Tom, I sat in the oblivion of not thinking. Is that eternity? A peaceful one without noise? I am ready for it. I am waiting—
I still hear Dane…

Mother is with me. She has been, from the beginning, floating here in silence. She is like me. We didn't want our bodies pinned to paper. We wanted to fly. Can a lost soul be forgiven? Is there still hope for the damned? If not in this universe then another? Why else show pain? Is that love? A light so powerful it can pull me through darkness and beyond to a place where it is the only Friend? A tree of starlight branches holding me gently in space…

I am stardust.

Will God again plant me in the cosmic wind?

Is that umbrella holder mine?

Not everything can be changed, but can one change make a difference?

We were children.

I loved her but she was a bee.

What choice did I have? Or she?

Did I ever love anyone else?

"Call for you on line one, Mr. Goldblatt. Says he's an old friend."

I put the glass down.

"Friend?"

"Yes sir."

"What's his name?"

"Tom."

I repeat it, the sound full of summer and broken things. What did he want from me?

"Line two, Mr. Goldblatt. Diane. She didn't give a last name."

I look at both flashing lights while trying to decide which one to answer.

Sarah

IN SHADOWS, SARAH SAT in her bedroom on a rug woven by her grandmother in shades of brown and yellow yarn. Black branches of the maple tree in her small backyard shredded the winter sun, ice webs on window glass trapping all but one strand of the feeble light. The child cupped this light in her hand and spilling it into the rug felt the brown fibers soften, the yellow turn oil gold. Resting her face on the warm rug, she went inside it to the long gray hair and wrinkles of her grandmother. In summer, the old maple Sarah had always known, moaned happy wind songs and shaded her under its leaves as she watched her grandmother hang clothes or bring out trash from the small grocery store at the front of their frame house. Shaking down pieces of tree, the maple let her play with its raining smells and colors. She breathed in its leaves and bark, felt warmed by the smell of flour and chicken fat absorbed in the old wood. The tree loved her grandmother...

Except in winter. This November, Sarah noticed for the first time the maple's large size, how its branches covering the sky with a thick tangle of black veins drained light from the grayness before snow and, on cloudless days, ate the clear, blue cold. Inhaling light and color into its bark, the tree grew toward greater darkness.

Sarah pressed her cheek into the rug's center, into the small place where her grandmother smiled as yarn. The winter tree didn't matter.

"You won't go away," the girl whispered. "I feel you combing my hair." The brown and yellow ridges of the rug became a metal brush. Sarah rubbed her hair along the yarn to the *swish, swish* of her grandmother's bent hand soothing her with each stroke while the cream tone of the old woman's voice chanted, *ba-a-baby*. Memory transformed the yarn into days of baking. Sugar topped apple strudel, onion rolls with hot centers of butter, the smell and feel of the old iron oven near the window where everything good cooled facing the tree, all merged in Sarah's heart as she lay in small, beating sunlight on her grandmother rug. Through the floor's wooden planks, she tasted fresh bread and heard her grandmother singing in the kitchen. Closing her eyes, Sarah slept dreaming of summer and green shade.

Long finger shadows of the maple's branches crept through window ice and tightened around the girl's neck. The light died, the rug turning black.

He had visited her again. Her first father. The dark one who looked like her.

"Shhh," the grandmother said, "there's nothing to be afraid of. It's only a dream." She had carried Sarah from the floor and now, sitting on the child's bed, held her and rocked. Sarah nestled against her grandmother's breast. The deep, quiet voice of the grandmother heart sounded weak and alone. Sarah tried giving it strength by breathing when her grandmother did.

"I have too much air. Take some of mine." She willed her grandmother a new, unbreakable heart made from the iron of stove and pots. Still tightly gripping the rug, the protective yarn curled into her hand, she released it. When night hid in the house, or winter day followed her grandmother, leaving behind dark shadows, Sarah needed the rug for protection. Now, the world was again safe. It had only one smell, work fed and full of soft, enveloping flesh. But rising dough had holes, so, too, could her grandmother's heart.

"Where did Harry go?" Sarah asked.

"You know, *tatula*," her grandmother said. "I've told you so many times."

"I want to hear it again."

"To heaven. He's with God."

"Did Harry love me?"

"Of course, like a daughter."

"Then God has enough blood from me and doesn't need you," Sarah thought while staring at her grandmother until the old woman's silver hair changed into brown curls and her heart banged pots of thunder.

Sarah locked the bathroom door. Looking in the cracked mirror, she saw Harry and stroked her chin the same way he did his. They reached together for the brown tin of shaving powder on a shelf above the iron sink and tapped the container three times against the rim of a blue mug with an Indian face on front. Harry knew the exact measure of powder and water they needed and how to stir it. Three taps worth, never more or less. One quick turn of the faucet. Ten whisks of his ivory handled brush. Sarah lathered her face.

"I'll shave around my mutton chops," she said.

"Just like me," Harry said. "Careful with the razor. I don't want to cut myself."

"You won't. You once put a dab of shaving cream on my nose."

"Not anymore, where I am, nothing is funny."

Only Sarah remained in the mirror. Her small hand squeezed the razor's handle tight. Dust fell over her eyes. Harry had been blond with blue eyes. She was dark.

"I can change how I look," the straight edge gleamed close to her face. She rinsed the blade off and placed the razor exactly where Harry had left it when alive, to the right of the sink next to a long black strap with a brass hook at the end of the worn leather.

"How many sharpenings were inside this before Harry used them all?"

She washed and dried the mug and brush then carefully positioned them two finger lengths from the left side of the faucet. Sarah put the tin back on the shelf and took a last look around the bathroom. Everything again in place, she stepped into the hall and with two hands, pressed the door closed.

Whispers from the kitchen below found her standing in shadows.

"Here."

"Take."

"Have some more."

"A tragedy. He stepped on a nail. What can you do? Life goes on."

The voices of those who had visited her mother two years ago when Harry died again buzzed inside Sarah's head. She remembered how the whisperers downstairs had used the kitchen for mixing her grandmother's baking smells with food for the dead; the meat and potato knishes, brisket, kasha, fish and yellow noodle kugel, brought on good plates, not the best, but ones anyone with a little sense would know to return. Drifting up, wanting to seep into the grandmother rug, the sweet steaming odors left by strangers had told Sarah to eat them, enjoy, if not now then later when they returned after her grandmother died. She had wrapped herself in the rug and cried. A week later, Sarah answered the food.

"You don't like my strudel anymore?" the grandmother had asked, her hands covered in flour.

"No," Sarah answered. She breathed in the smell of metal milk. By eating cold cereal in an iron bowl she would keep death and its warm food away. Sarah saw her grandmother's sad face become stronger.

Two days after Harry died, the mourners still came to feed her mother and themselves. They hadn't noticed Sarah standing alone in a corner of the living room. Now, in the hallway upstairs, the gray colors of the whisperers again moved through her, ghosts carrying food seasoned with darkness squeezed from Harry's closed eyes. The faded wallpaper and old wood he'd touched no longer smelled of brown tin powder or the truck grease always under his fingernails. She couldn't remember the sound of him pacing outside the bathroom door, brush and razor in his hand, his face half leathered. The shadows disappeared, turning the hallway where he had walked into a nothingness of dust and silence.

Sarah slowly opened her mother's bedroom door. The waiting darkness pulled her in. Small candles burning inside blue and white glass etched with death prayers, hissed.

"We are the winter tree. We are warm food and your grandmother's weak heart. It's been two years. We are again hungry. Look into our eyes." The candles flickering light winked at her with blackness.

Sarah climbed onto Harry's side of the tall bed where she had bounced with him and hid, watching him sleep. Pressing her hand into the thin, grandmother-made cover of almond shaded squares, she tried to outline his head and the one leg he always kept mattress still while the other one dangled over the edge. The cloth didn't hold her lines.

"Too weak," the candles said, "too tired. Like your grandmother."

Sarah pressed harder. Harry's head grew large. His narrow chest wasn't strong enough. Only his arms seemed right. Lying inside them, she whispered his name then listened for the bell on the store's door to ring. It didn't. No customers.

"Grandmother will be worried. Mother's job doesn't pay much. I'll help by eating less."

The closet door rattled, kicked from inside by Harry's brown shoes. They had taken his other ones away, the narrow-toed, shiny black dancers that moved lightly on holidays and in temple. They squeaked when speaking. The brown pair Harry wore while driving his coal truck were round and heavy in front. Never quiet, they now banged for attention. Sarah opened the closet door.

"Is this what you want me to see?" she asked them. Their tired, sagging faces nodded. Sarah lightly touched the empty hanger. Harry's only suit, the black one he wore with his black shoes, was gone along with his striped green and yellow tie. "I know where. The shadows passing through here on their way to important places of crying, carried his poisoned leg, carried him dressed for a party. God will know him by his brown shoes, I would have told them. No one looked at me. They had dressed him, buttoned him up with all the notes in his pockets he'd written for me that day. He always had something funny to say. They buried his last words."

Sitting inside the closet, Sarah held the brown shoes to her face and smelled the old leather. One by one the candles blinked out.

"Nothing remains of us or him," they said, the ghost-like wisps of smoke forming small mouths in the black air. "No shadow. No eyes. Don't you feel it? His brown shoes are as cold as winter tree ice. You're almost eight. He would have worn shiny black on your birthday and danced."

"Grandmother," Sarah called into the darkness. Reaching for the hanger, she tumbled forward and felt herself falling through a hole in the floor; heard, behind her, the brown shoes snapping at her neck.

"How are you feeling?" the grandmother asked.

"Full," Sarah answered. She swallowed, tasting metal.

"You can't live on cereal. Try some of my chicken soup. There's not a bit of fat in it." The old woman smiled.

"It's too hot."

"I'll cool it off—"

"I don't eat soup for breakfast."

"Maybe later, after school," the grandmother said.

"Maybe…" Sarah swirled the milk around in her bowl. Blond Harry was in heaven. She hadn't seen her father's dark face in a week. Her grandmother still baked and made soup; the winter tree would soon bleed spring. Elbows in, knees together, Sarah sat not wanting to take up space at the small kitchen table; she waited until her grandmother wasn't looking before nodding at the pots hanging on the wall. They again had voices. If tapped with a spoon, the dented skillet sang high notes. Shutting the door made the rust speckled, deep boiler rattle its liking for apples bubbling in cinnamon and brown sugar. The smallest, blackest pot cried when placed on too hot a flame. This morning her grandmother cooked with other pots. They, too, had their songs. After her stepfather, Harry, died, Sarah couldn't hear the pots speak. Using chicken fat, she had started to draw a mouth on the hanging skillet until her mother, with a hard slap, twisted the half-formed lips into deformed silence. For two years, the pots hung mute in their place between the icebox and stove or simmered voiceless on the fire. Now the world again safe, her grandmother's heart plump and strong, kept that way by cold cereal filling the space the warm, dead food wanted, Sarah heard all the pots speak using her grandmother's kitchen words eaten by these kettles and pans during their days of cooking and baking.

"She's a baker, fryer, chicken skinner, too strong to leave you. Don't worry. Metal makes the best hearts."

Sarah almost ate another spoonful of cereal.

"I heard you, mama," Sarah's mother said, hurrying into the kitchen, her frizzy hair flying, dark circles under her eyes. "You're not doing Sarah any favors babying her. If she's hungry, she'll eat." Her hand shaking, she drank a glass of water.

"Sarah's so skinny," grandmother said.

"Should I feel sorry for her? God knows, you and I work plenty hard to make sure there's food on the table. I feel sorry for those who don't have anything to eat. It's time Sarah realized what life's about. Out there, no one is going to hold her hand."

Sarah stared into her bowl.

"Have some eggs, Bess. here, they're already made."

"I'll be late. You don't know that boss of mine. He'd fire me without thinking twice. And why? Because I don't work hard enough? He should have fingers like these. Remember what they looked like before I started dipping chocolate? How everyone said I had beautiful hands and should play the piano? Piano. Who could afford that. I'm not blaming you, mama. You did your best. Your husband wasn't around either."

"He died."

"Died, left, it's all the same. If we'd had more money I wouldn't have ended up married at seventeen and to a no-good besides. He wanted to be a movie star, said he'd send for me. The bastard. The drunk."

"Bess, the *maidel*..."

"Sarah isn't too young to know the truth. It's a plain and simple fact. Men run out on you and leave nothing behind. The sooner she understands this, the better off she'll be. Look at Harry. An accident, and he got lockjaw. I'm sorry for him, and I'm sorry for me. As men go, he was okay, but he didn't have any insurance. Not a dime. So, here I am, again struggling to get by. I have to go."

"The store will do better, wait, you'll see." The grandmother gently touched her daughter's head.

"Even if it does, will that give back all the young years the movie star stole from me?" Holding her thin coat tight against her, Sarah's mother walked out into the cold wind.

"Thank you for making me this new school dress," Sarah said. "Do you think mother likes it on me?"

"She told me you look beautiful. Your mother loves you very much. Who wouldn't with such a face?" She squeezed Sarah's cheeks. Sarah wore the long blue dress her grandmother had sewed; her black hair, braided by the old woman and tied off with velvet bows, hung neatly over the dress's starched, white collar.

I feel new. Sarah wondering when her eyes would grow dark circles like her mother's. Bent over, breathing hard, her grandmother moved slowly around the kitchen. "Nothing's different. She's full of ginger snap cookies and spices and still plays the stove."

Adjusting the stove's fire, the old woman opened and closed the damper and used a soot blackened poker to maneuver the pieces of wood. She stirred her chicken soup simmering in the pot she always kept filled with warm water. After taking the thin pan with fried eggs off the stove, she lifted the lid of the kettle and checked on the beef, onions, and garlic boiling together and almost ready for the white horseradish she had ground fresh that morning. In the afternoon, when she wasn't in the store, she would bake on top of the stove by putting dough in a pan and covering it with a big iron bowl. Sarah liked the metal sound of her grandmother's baking. The other good smells from kitchen cooking with their overpowering mourner sadness born in fire made her stomach hurt. She fought the sickness as she always did by secretly chewing another small piece of the dry, horsehair plaster she'd broken off the kitchen wall and hid. The wall had absorbed food vapors and the sweet smoke from wood cracking apart and dripping resin inside the stove's firebox. By eating the plaster, Sarah tasted the mummified layers of her grandmother's cooking; the entombed, once-warm flavors now as tasteless and safe as cold cereal, yet able to invoke memory. She remembered Harry spilling gravy down his shirt and the lumpy head of mashed potatoes on his plate he gave pea eyes and a string bean smile when her mother wasn't looking. All the thick, greasy warmth using up air had become baby cookies of plaster easily swallowed and dense enough to choke the stomach pain inside her that wanted to rise on dark wings and fly into her grandmother's heart. Sarah felt better. She touched the webs of flour her grandmother could never completely clean from the old wooden table.

"You are a beautiful child," the grandmother said, ladling soup into a bowl. "Have some. It's cold out. This will warm your insides."

Sarah let the chicken soup steam her face.

After gathering her books, she waited at the door for enough kisses to take to school.

"Keep safe, *tatula*," her grandmother said. "Eat the lunch I made you."

"I will," Sarah always fed it to the same old dog.

The day burned cold. While walking along the cobblestone street, she decided that when she got back home she'd nibble the wall at a different place under the hanging pots. Sarah warmed her hand by touching the piece of plaster in her pocket.

"Dirty Jew," the boy on the playground yelled, already forgetting what he'd said as he ran past her to join his friends. The teacher looked the other way. Sarah stood alone by the swings and watched Rachel jump rope with a group of girls, the wind blowing their voices and laughter to her. Rachel used to visit. Dressing up, they would put on big hats and feather boas, pose in front of the mirror, make tea and play with dolls. But that was when Sarah could speak to someone other than her grandmother. Sarah knew Rachel would like her again when she understood why some girls with dead step-fathers stopped talking. Kisses unlocked words—lies killed them. Harry couldn't kiss her anymore in the morning and he had lied by promising to never go away. The school bell rang, ending recess. Head down, arms wrapped around her thin body, she walked back slowly toward the gray building and remained silent even when the teacher, upset at the insolence of a student not answering her, smacked Sarah's knuckles with a ruler. After school and again huddled in, Sarah watched herself float liquid and smooth through a puddle of slush. A blond face smiled at her from the water. Harry? Glancing up, Sarah saw the policeman's double line of yellow buttons, his gold mustache, the amber eyes under a blue cap. He stopped traffic for her. Dark clouds took his face away.

At the sagging store front a part of her old wooden house, Sarah pulled the tired door open and heard the dull sound of the bell that had lost most of its voice during thirty years of dutiful service between mezuzah and sign.

"Shut that. Do you think it's summer?" A big woman wearing a faded brown scarf over her head gave Sarah an angry, backward glance.

"Your grandmother can't afford to heat the whole neighborhood," a second woman added. Her thin and yellowed skin dotted with age spots, she pointed a bony finger at the cracked glass of a display case one third empty. "Two Kaiser rolls. Three bagels. I want them fresh."

"Make sure you trim the cornbeef close," the first woman said.

"Fanny, Bertha, I've known you so many years. Would I cheat you?" Sarah's grandmother hurried back and forth behind the counter. "What else can I get you?"

"Nothing,"

"We're not Rockefellers."

Sarah saw the warm bread and cocoa her grandmother had left for her on the kitchen table. She wasn't hungry, even for a piece of wall. Carrying her doll by its long blonde hair, she went upstairs to the bathroom. Her dark father, the one who scared her in dreams, had run away to Hollywood, so he could keep himself alive inside movies. She knew he was still out there, one small face in a crowd scene stored in the canister of a forgotten film. With Harry, it was simpler. He was gone, buried in black shoes. Her grandmother didn't understand. She made soup but it was full of sadness and needed special seasoning. God wanted an old woman in it, not men who vanished leaving behind wives with used up, chocolate covered hands and daughters haunted in nightmares by the dark and the dead. Husbands and step-fathers died, but it was an afterthought. God enjoyed a hot bowl of mourners' soup made from the stock of a grandmother's boiled and simmered old heart. He didn't eat liars like her father and Harry. They were both the same except Harry was worse. Blond, with blue eyes, he had pretended to be Jewish and to love her. She liked dolls. He had bought her a blonde one.

Sarah picked up Harry's razor. The metal's cold warmed her. No golden Harry face in the mirror told her she would grow up with yellow hair like his. His blue eyes were gone forever, only her black ones lived in the glass. She had cut the doll before. She did it again, smoothly and deep.

"Sarah looks like him more every day," her mother said, dipping a piece of rye bread into her soup. "It's a curse. Mamma?"

"I'm fine, Bess, nothing to worry about. I'm tired, that's all." The old woman lifted her arm off the chair she now kept close to the stove and brought Sarah a bowl.

"She should be serving you." Bess finished the bread.

"Eat, child, eat," the grandmother said.

"Is there anything white in it?' Sarah asked.

"I made the soup just the way you like it. Only dark chicken."

Sarah dug into the meat with her spoon. A week ago, she had put her cereal away and believing she could absorb the darkness always waiting for her grandmother, began eating all warm mourners' food not blond. "When I get stronger, grandmother will, too. She won't need the chair by the stove. Mother sees it. I'm almost as dark as father." The stringy chicken tasted good.

"Sarah should be grateful we have food and not ask if it's white, black or purple." Bess said.

"I want a dog," Sarah said to her grandmother.

"And I want to be Mrs. Vanderbilt." Sarah's mother hit her small fist on the table. "Is she crazy? A dog? That's all we need around here, another mouth to feed."

"We'll talk about it later," the grandmother stroked Sarah's head. "I'm just happy you're eating."

"Sure, go ahead, mama, promise her the moon. Did you

see her doll?"

"The eyes fell out," Sarah said, looking up at her grandmother.

"More waste. I'll tell you this, you're not getting another one."

"Bess, don't upset yourself—"

"No? All this about a dog, and I don't even know if I'll have a job next week. He wants me to work longer hours and for less pay. He's taking advantage of a widow woman with a child. Do I have a choice? Men. And the goys are the worst."

"The store—"

"Never made enough. Not now. Not when I was growing up. The bills, the rent...I don't know what I'm going to do."

"We'll manage," the grandmother's small smile and her hand on Sarah's shoulder told the girl not to worry.

"You're not helping her. She doesn't speak to me, hangs all over you or is upstairs in her room. She's old enough to do her share around here."

"She does—"

"Go on. Keep protecting her. But no good will come of it, mark my words. You can see that now. Where are her friends?"

"Sarah just needs time."

"All the time in the world won't change anything. Harry died. Her father left her—may he get leprosy and go blind."

Sarah rolled the eyes of her doll around in the pocket of her long, blue dress.

"The other children don't understand," the grandmother said. "I'm going to invite the Blumberg girl over and Bertha's niece. Make some strudel…"

"They called her a dirty Jew, mama. I heard her tell you."

"Children say things. They give everyone a name. If you're Italian or Greek. If you have red hair or freckles."

"A *Jew*, mama. I know how that feels. But what can you expect where we live? Bertha will shop here, why not? You practically give her the food and who else would put up with her complaining? Just don't fool yourself. Make all the strudel and pies you want. She isn't going to let her niece play in this neighborhood, especially with someone who won't talk.

"Mamma, are you okay?"

"It's nothing. Don't worry. I'll just sit and rest for a second."

Sarah smelled burning soup.

"May I have some more?" she asked, holding up her bowl.

Summer in the maple drifted through Sarah's open, bedroom window. Lying on the grandmother rug, her hands behind her head, she watched the curtain float toward her on the yellowed scent from marigolds growing in the backyard. Expanded with air, the cloth suddenly exhaled and snapping back against the window frame, rested before again dancing to the maple's high pitched wind song. Sarah felt the rug's old heart beat on her fingers and head. She closed her eyes… opened them and knew.

Something was wrong. Out of place. Sarah got up.

The doll's head was still cut off and the bed perfectly made. Her black street shoes and laced fancy ones were just the way she had left them: toes against the wall by the lamp next to the dresser of small drawers she kept as organized and tidy as the rest of her room. On laundry day, after carefully folding her every day clothing, Sarah put her bloomers and woolen stockings in the top drawer and used the drawer under them for her cotton school tunic, shirt, blouse, and pair of overalls. She opened the bottom drawer only when it snowed and she needed to take out her snowsuit and the gloves her grandmother had crocheted.

Behind her closed door, Sarah felt safe when nothing changed or was taken away.

What was wrong?

"I'm ready. You can wear me again today. I'm fun after school, too." The new blue dress said, swaying on its closet hanger.

"That's not fair." the pink chiffon beside it protested, its triple collars moving like three mouths. "She's always going places. I only get out of here on the holidays. I like to play, too."

Sarah shut the closet door turning the dresses' voices into whispers. Like candles and faces in mirrors, dresses could talk. Nothing unusual about that. The disorder she felt came from someplace else. Drawn to the window by the sound and motion of play, she watched the girls in the alley behind her maple release their jacks-hopscotch-leapfrog laughter into the wind. The children chased soap bubbles, sat in a circle and made necklaces out of red and blue pieces of broken glass. Fun had donned singular colors—the sky and air and walls of sheds looking as if the girls in their bright pinafores had colorized themselves and the alleyway by using just three crayons. Although these girls had never asked her to play and if they had, she wouldn't have known how to answer, Sarah loved them. They lived in a pretty world just beyond her yard where everything sparkled. There were no bad words there. No boys or men. She kept watching.

In mid-dance, the curtain gasped, shuddered, hung limp and still. Sarah understood. The summer tree had poisoned it. And the death was traveling…through her bedroom and out the door, creeping to the store below where it would grow its black roots into her grandmother's heart. For the maple, all seasons were winter, the cold living in summer leaves spreading down to twisted roots that rattled their laughter and killed. Iron pots for a grandmother heart. Eating only dark things. A tidy, controlled bedroom. None of this mattered if she left the tree inside. By pulling the curtains closed and tight, Sarah blocked out the light. She wanted to barricade the doors and windows and cover the furniture with a protective layer against death.

"Someday I'll have a key and lock everything inside to keep it safe. If a tree comes close to me, I'll chop its legs off."

Sarah let the tired old curtain slip through her fingers. Her face again in the rug, she cried into its slowing heart.

Her father visited her one last time in dream.

"When you are grown, I will bring you flowers and put the petals on your bed. We'll kiss. I'll be your husband and never leave. I love you. Who needs movies?"

Smiling, Sarah floated toward a tree of thorns.

Had it really been a whole day since she died?

"A lovely woman."

"Her whole life she worked hard."

"They'll have to sell the store, the house. Such a pity."

"First Harry. Now this…" Sad expressions…deep sighs…

They left. The uneaten pieces of mourners' food on nice dishes cast shadows that dripped from the edges of broken mirrors as Sarah walked alone through the house. Days merged into continuous night.

"Has it been a month? There's still time, still a chance the tree will give back grandmother's heart."

Bess sat on the edge of her bed. Downcast and unmoving, she stared at the floor.

"If we leave, she won't know where to find me," Sarah said.

The woman's head snapped up, her eyes red and swollen.

"God in heaven. It's like talking to an idiot. Don't you understand? She's dead and that's the end of it. Everything's settled, sold, and we're leaving. Do you think I'll enjoy living with my cousin? Tessie isn't that big hearted. She's not thrilled with taking us in."

"I don't like Edith and Ida," Sarah said. "They have faces like dolls."

"Are you a *meshugganah?* Start with her girls, and we'll be out in the street. Be polite. Don't get in their way. Maybe you can learn from them how to act normal. Go to bed, we're taking the bus early in the morning."

Careful to step lightly, Sarah went quietly down the stairs

and into the kitchen. Silver dust, turned to ash, drifted down covering the stove. Iron pots hung mute and blind. Her mother had been right. No more foolish talk about the dead returning to bake and cook and laugh. The dark felt good. Breathing deeply, she filled herself with the nothingness inside silence.

After wrapping the grandmother rug around the remaining pieces of her doll, Sarah took the bundle outside and digging a hole, fed the tree.

At the pool's edge, Sarah watched her grandmother's face float up from the bottom of the clear water. Leaning closer, she could almost hear what the old woman whispered inside sparkles rippling just below the pool's liquid skin. Suddenly, darkness grabbed her and pulling her deep into its belly, burned her lungs with chlorine. She splashed, beat, turned the broken voice-lights of her grandmother's words into a strangling and silent, dead water sound. Sarah fought against death and dragged herself out.

"Pushed you in." Her cousin Edith danced.

"Got you good." The other cousin, Ida, sang.

Sarah coughed out the remaining seconds of childhood foolishness. Dead grandmothers didn't go for a swim in the neighborhood pool. She had a mother. That was it. Inside the brightness of sunlight glaring off concrete and water in a world of taunting, cousin laughter, Sarah held herself and shivering, knew when she got married her husband would bring her flowers and hold her close.

Her movie star father had promised…

"Sit, relax, Sarah. Bring Mr. Goldblatt some of that cake you just made. She's such a good cook and so clean around the house. My cousin and her daughters never have to lift a finger—and believe me, they don't. Serve our guest, Sarah. Doesn't the cake look wonderful, Mr. Goldblatt?"

"Yes. It does." He smiled at Sarah who blushed.

"Mr. Goldblatt has a good job in a factory."

"I'm the foreman. In two or three years, I'll have saved enough money to start my own business."

"Your own business. Did you hear that, Sarah? Don't look down. Someone might think you're trying to hide your face. Such a pretty girl. Don't you agree, Mr. Goldblatt?"

"Very," he said.

"Give Mr. Goldblatt some more cake."

While serving him, Sarah drifted into the attic room she shared with her mother and locked the door.

He ate and while smiling, measured her legs as he would a piece of cloth.

"I don't love him."

"Love, *shmuv*, he'll be a success, that's all that matters. For once in your life, get out of your dream world. You come from a poor family. You're not getting any younger. It's not like there's other boys beating down the door for you. He'll be a good provider and you'll live in a nice home. Make your old mother happy. Get married. Have some babies."

"Girls?"

"Of course."

Sarah saw daughters playing in sunlight with a dog.

Her mother nodded a hug.

He had promised a honeymoon at Niagara Falls. Instead, on the winter road north toward Cleveland, Myron Goldblatt pulled over and climbed into the back seat of his shiny new Buick.

"Sarah," he whispered, his eyes like red hot stones. "I can't wait."

Remembering what her father had said, that he would be the husband who loved her, she went to him and softly kissed his lips. Myron pushed her down. Sarah bled on the red rose he had planned to give her.

"Here. I always pay for sex. Exciting, isn't it?" He placed a dollar bill on her stomach. "Hey, what's this? Another buck."

In the center of his descending eyes, Sarah saw her daughter. Instead, nine months later, she felt her insides excrete a boy whose crying reminded her of everything lost.

"Again, then," she told herself on the hospital bed. She suckled her baby until the nurse left. After her twin daughters were born, Sarah locked her legs tight and wrapped her husband in words.

When meeting his blonde mistress, Myron Goldblatt never brought chocolates or flowers but instead, complained about his family. For him, that was foreplay.

"He took her away. She's a cold fish. Our honeymoon was

a nightmare. We spent it in Cleveland. Still, things might have been different if he hadn't been born. Stevie's eight now and all he still wants from her is *sitska*. He's a baby. Aggravates her. Gets her talking and the only way to stop it is to slap him a little. Not too hard, just enough so he'll grow some balls. The other two are okay. Nice girls. Chubby, but they don't bother anyone. That mother-in-law of mine was another story—a witch until the day she died. One of the biggest mistakes I ever made was letting her move in with us. She didn't like this. She didn't like that. She'd argue with my wife and start yapping at me as soon as I walked in the door. She hated men. It's no wonder my wife thinks I run around. There's no peace and quiet at home, that's for sure. Good thing I have you."

He rubbed against her, moaned, and when leaving left twenty dollars on the bed.

SHADOWLANDS

ALAN KESSLER